Who is Warren West?

Transcribed and Edited
with Illustrations and Additional Text
by
Chris Henderson

For those people
that know who they are...

CHAPTER 0
by Chris Henderson

This is actually the foreword, but I know that when most people see
"Foreword" in a book, they translate that as "the pages I can skip."
I've kept it short, so please don't skip this chapter.

Sometime around May, 2007, I was sitting around watching TV when a UPS guy knocked on my front door. He made me sign for a package that contained twenty-one mini-cassette tapes and the following hand-written letter (there was no return address):

Chris —

Hey, I'll bet you're wondering what happened to me. Right?

Well I'm not dead but that's all I'm going to say right now because I want you to listen to these tapes. That's how you'll find out what happened exactly.

See that's the thing. What I did was I basically recorded my whole life story on these tapes and I was thinking it would make a great book but I'm not exactly a writer so I'm sending it to you because I figured maybe you know someone who could get it published or whatever. Anyways I told it in a way that I think maybe you could just type out exactly what I said most of the way. But you know if you have to fix some things I guess then go ahead. Just don't change any of the facts or the order they come in.

I don't know where I'll be when you get finished so I'll just get a copy next time I see you.

Anyways I appreciate it.

— Warren West

P.S.: I think every book is better with pictures so if you want to add illustrations wherever.

Now if you've ever taken dictation, then you know how time-consuming it can be; and he wasn't asking just that. So I'll tell you the truth. I didn't even listen to the tapes for at least a couple of months. I didn't have that kind of free time to dedicate to his project. Eventually though I came across an old mini-cassette recorder in the back of my closet and since I wasn't doing anything else at the moment, I figured why not listen to the tapes.

I put in the first one, and I'll tell you what. I didn't hate it.

Actually, I kind of liked it.

It was a little discombobulated at first, maybe, but interesting. And then I got pretty wrapped up in it as I moved through the rest of the tapes. So I figured what the hell. Warren's right — this would make a great book.

I left it pretty much the way he told it, except I took out some of those pause words, like "er" and "ah" and "umm," and I changed the names of most of the people who didn't want their real names to appear in print. He did also manage to misquote me a number of times, so I adjusted that. And you'll find a few footnotes, which I added. Besides that, it's exactly how he said it. And also I may have cut out one or two things when I felt like he was rambling too much. But other than that...

As for the truthfulness of the story, I can't really say one way or the other, but the things I was there for are pretty accurate. And since no two people remember an incident exactly the same way, who's to say it isn't a perfect recollection?

Warren believes it and I guess that's what matters.

Who is WARREN WOO?

CHAPTER 1

MATINEE

Her friend was, in a word, bubbly. But not bubbly in the way that champagne is bubbly, or soda pop. She was bubbly like an entire bottle of shampoo spilled on the carpet, where you just keep scrubbing and scrubbing, but it just keeps lathering and lathering and expanding its bubbly girth.

And speaking of girth, she was a big girl.

But it wasn't the friend that I noticed. Well, I mean I noticed her. Of course I noticed her. Everyone noticed her. It wasn't possible to not notice her. What I mean is it wasn't the friend that I took a particular interest in.

And that's where the story begins, at least as well as I can remember it. I was sixteen the first time I saw her, which was almost a decade ago. And I think it was her, at least I'm pretty sure. It wasn't until the second time, though, that I realized it had been her the first time. Like I said, I was distracted by the bigger girl, the friend, the one with the bubbly disposition.

It was at a movie theater, the first time was, a matinee. There weren't very many people there, and I was there by myself because that's what I liked to do, go to movies alone, because then no one would lean over and talk to me or ask me to explain what just happened, which in truth has happened a few times in crowded theaters with complete strangers, which I think is just weird. And so typically I pretend I can't hear them, which sometimes works but sometimes they just ask louder which annoys everyone. I love the movies, and when you see as many of them as I do, you'll encounter just about every scenario possible, including hearing a cell phone ring, hearing a guy answer it, then seeing what is presumably that cell phone flying through the air in front of the illuminated movie screen and crashing into a hundred pieces against the wall of the theater. That was a stand-up-and-cheer kind of moment for me, and I would have given a medal to the guy who threw it if I'd known who he was and also if I'd had a medal to give him.

Anyways, the girl.

She was not alone. She was with that friend, whose name I didn't know, but whose exuberance I would never forget. But if not for that freaky, fat friend, I may not have put the proverbial two and two together to realize that the second time was not the first time but its sequel.

But it would be a lie if I told you that I really for sure remembered seeing her exactly, that time at the movies, and I'm not going to lie to you.

Let me say that again: I will not lie to you.

I don't like liars. I mean, I usually don't like liars, which is to say I don't like when people lie to me.

So am I positive that it was her? No.

But I can tell you with ninety-five point seven percent certainty that it was, and that she sat two rows behind and four seats to the left of me. And I say that it was her, because she was with the friend who would, over the years, prove to be a constant, caustic companion to the gorgeous girl of whom I would spend many nights — and many monotonous science, math, and English lectures — dreaming.

That encounter at the movie theater, while brief and seemingly insubstantial, was merely a prelude to the second meeting, the one where planets collided and stars fell from the sky and crashed in the ocean and time stopped and alien spaceships descended, laying entire cities to waste. That's how magnanimous that second time — that I'm pretty sure wasn't the first — was, really.

That friend of hers, though.

The first time, she talked through the whole movie.

See I noticed the pretty girl. I did. In fact, I was so enamored that the sight of her caused my brain to basically shut down. I couldn't think. I was enthralled by that inimitable work of human sculpture, but because of my overwhelming stupor plus what I am certain was a debilitating case of temporary OCD, I found it impossible to draw my eyes from the movie screen. You go to the movies to watch movies, and my brain wouldn't let me compute my presence at the movie theater in any other way. It didn't matter to my synaptic processes that Aphrodite herself was sitting two rows behind me; there was a movie in front of me.

Plus I was sixteen, completely inexperienced in any facet of womanly pursuit, which is to say the pursuit of women. What was I going to do anyway? And at the time, I guess I just didn't realize who this girl really was, and I figured when it was all over I'd just walk out of the movie theater and forget all about her.

But I didn't.

But besides, still, like I said, she was two rows behind me. Turning around a whole bunch would prob'ly have been pretty freaky anyway.

Maybe if she'd been, y'know, directly diagonal in front of me. You know, in that perfect position where you can casually glance over or even hold a lingering stare without being noticed, and she's enough to the side where you can see that perfect profile, maybe then I'd have paid her more attention.

But the fact that I couldn't see her, coupled with the fact that her stupid friend would not shut up. Some of us were trying to pay attention to the film. Some of us...

All of us...

None of us cared about the boy she had a crush on — I think his name was Grant. And even if we did care, we didn't need to hear about it during the movie. And we especially didn't need to hear about it in full voice. And of all people, I'm sure Grant (even though he wasn't there) didn't want to hear about it, because no one likes to say no, even if the person asking is repulsive. And I'm sure she did ask him out, and I'm sure he said yes out of pity, and I'm sure he had a miserable time. Because she is a miserable person to be with. And she probably tried to hold hands. In fact, she probably took him ice skating. And I feel bad for the poor guy, had to skate around the rink for an hour with his hands in his pockets like some kind of Asperger's victim.

And I so wanted to be able to hear this movie over that girl's voice.

And I so wanted to talk with the other girl, if it indeed was the girl I'm sure it was. But by the time the credits rolled I was so angry at the rotund friend that I knew I couldn't control myself. At least that was the excuse I told myself for why I was too gutless to talk to this raging beauty. Is raging the right word? Anyways, you know what I'm saying, right? Not so much that the girl was raging but that her beauty was, in a nonviolent way.

So I left the theater as quickly as I could, and I basically power-walked home because I didn't have a car.

And I swore...

...a few dozen times.

And I kicked someone's rose bush along the way, and then I had to run.

There was some song playing the second time.

Well, there were lots of songs playing, but at the beginning, when I first saw her for the second time, there was some particular song playing. It's not really too relevant which song that was, because I don't remember exactly, except I think it was that Eiffel 65 song, y'know, about the little blue guy; or whatever was popular. I'm pretty sure it was the blue man song though, except that I'm not sure that song had come out yet, but maybe it had.

I'm not lying, just trying to remember a song from a long time ago.

Anyways, it was at a birthday party sort of. That is to say that someone was celebrating a birthday, but I have no idea who and I'm sure that more than half the other people there also had no idea. But she was there, again with her bubbly friend, who to my amazement was even more obnoxious at the party than she had been at the movie theater a couple years before.

It was like the friend was a rose, only not a good rose, not a pretty rose or a sweet-smelling rose, but definitely like a repugnant one. Like back at the movie theater she'd just been a rose bud and she'd had that scent, that odor that offends all of the senses not just the olfactory one, but it was still in its prepubescent stage. Since then she'd blossomed, she'd spread herself into a full-bodied, pungent bouquet of annoying. And speaking of full-bodied, I think she'd even put on some weight.

But the other girl — of my dreams. The one I'd been dying to talk to after the movie. I wanted to talk to her now. I wanted to ask her name and whether or not she knew whose birthday was being celebrated. I wanted to ask her if she would like to leave with me, but as I had no car that didn't seem polite. And then for a second I wanted to ask her if she would drive, then we could slip off and leave her malodorous friend to find her own way home.

I stood there in my own goofish thought bubble, trying to mentally compose some brilliant sonnet to turn into a word bubble directed at this stunning, stunning...

Then she disappeared into the crowd, and my legs wouldn't let me follow. My word bubble came forward, but all it read now was, "Oil can."

Some kid turned and looked at me.

"What the hell does that mean?"

I looked at him with my eyes. I couldn't turn my head, like I'd been out all day in the rain and I'd rusted solid.

"You're a weirdo," he spat and walked away singing something like "Dah-bah-dee dah-bah-die" or whatever. And he was gone, and so what. I didn't care about this kid. Unless he was her boyfriend, then I cared. Then I wanted to punch him in the face. I wanted to get him to walk with me around to the back of the house, where I could hogtie him and throw him in the trunk of my car if I'd had one, then I'd drive him out to the middle of the Bonneville Salt Flats, the desert, and I'd leave him there with a small canteen and a map to Nevada, and I'd tell him that if he ever came back, well...

I felt something wet and warm in the palm of my hand. Blood. I'd been clenching my fist so tight, my fingernail had broken the skin. I think it was the middle fingernail.

Man, I hated that kid, if he was her boyfriend. If he wasn't then I didn't really care one way or the other about him. I'll bet she didn't even have a boyfriend, come to think of it. And even if she did have a boyfriend, and even if that kid was him, I'd never do anything about it, because when it comes right down to it, I don't have a violent bone in my body, and also I'm a little bit of a coward.

I shook myself back to sanity and watched. I watched her soft brown hair weaving through the mass of faces and backs of heads sporting not-nearly-as-attractive shades of blonde, red, and brown, until I couldn't see her anymore. And I wondered if I would see her again that night.

I didn't.

I just stood there like a big metal statue for over an hour, and that's when my knees buckled and I passed out.

I don't know if you've ever passed out before, but it's not like when you just fall asleep. There are two big differences.

The first difference is that waking up sucks. Your head feels like a watermelon in a giant vice. In fact, it's like a giant vice with big sharp tooth-like spikes poking in from either side of the compress. In fact, it's even like those spikes are soaked in alcohol or lemon juice. And also, it's like someone is thumping your melon-head with their forefinger to check its freshness.

The second difference is that you don't dream, which is my favorite part of sleeping. It's like the whole time you're out is only a fraction of a second. In one instant you're standing there frozen, thinking about the woman you plan to grow old and have lots and lots of babies with, because even if you don't want babies, you want her to have them with you; and the next instant you're on the ground with some scraggly-toothed gamer hovering over you and speaking in C++.

This is my experience with passing out anyways.

When I came to, I scanned all the faces for hers. I scanned the crowd for her brown hair — chestnut, I had decided, was the appropriate name for the color — but I couldn't find it.

It was all a big fog and I kind of remember my ride saying he had someplace to be and it was time for us to go. I'm not sure if that was true, or if he was embarrassed because I'd said "oil can," or if it was fate tearing me away from destiny.

In any case, I remember staggering out of the party, not because I was drunk, but because I was euphoric, but in that not good way. And I wondered if I would see her again ever.

And I wondered that every minute of every day until that one minute on that one day when I finally saw her again.

But that's the third time.

CHAPTER 2

A STAR IS BORN

See I was born in May of 1981, along the side of the interstate just outside Pocatello, Idaho. I was three weeks early.

They had supposed that heading to Salt Lake City — well, West Valley City, just outside Salt Lake — would pose no serious problems. My parents, that is, had so supposed, since I wasn't due for quite a while, three weeks to be exact, as I said before, actually 22 days. Of course they were wrong, and just thirty minutes south of Pocatello my father's Mustang took the next exit and turned back toward the city. And I use the term "city" loosely in referring to Pocatello.

But they didn't quite make it.

And so, there I was being delivered in the back seat of that old Mustang.

♀ ♀ ♀

I've always said that my superhero name, if I ever developed super powers, would be *The Exception* and I'd get a big "X" across my chest as part of my...

...I don't want to say outfit, because that sounds gay. And I don't want to say costume; because it's not something I'd wear to a party or trick-or-treating. But you know what I'm getting at anyway.

There's this question we ask to get to know somebody. This kind of psychological thing:

> If you could choose one super power, of these four, which would you choose?
> 1. Fly
> 2. Go Invisible at will
> 3. Laser Vision
> 4. Infinite Stretchiness

The thing is laser vision is just plain destructive. And don't try to tell me that you'd use it to toast an English muffin or perform corrective eye surgery, because you're not only lying to me, you're lying to yourself. And if you pick stretchiness, you're that guy in high school who thought he was the class clown and just didn't understand that people were laughing at you, not with you. That or you're insane.

So there are really only two options, and this is how you really tell about people. Because we all have the two sides, y'know, the dark side and the other not dark side.

But let's face it, there are times when we'd all like to go invisible to find out something we're not supposed to know, or watch some hot girl in the shower, or listen to a conversation we're not supposed to hear, or move something and really freak somebody out, or get into a place where we're not supposed to be, or hide from someone, or pretend to be an invisible guardian angel and give someone we don't like some really bad advice that we know they'll take because they're really religious and have been praying for days on end for a guardian angel to come down and tell them what to do so they don't have to take any responsibility and actually make their own decisions, or any number of other things that we probably shouldn't be doing. But there's just no respectable, honest reason to really want to be able to go invisible, when you think about it. There's nothing you can do invisibly that's really, y'know, legit. And if it's not too legit, what option do you really have but to, y'know...

...well...

...you know.

But flying.

Nothing wrong with flying.

Unless of course you use your powers of flight for evil. But seriously I've never known anyone to do that.

I'd totally want to fly if I could, because...

...well, it'd be awesome!

So...

Anyways...

I was seven pounds, nine ounces.

When I was born I mean. I popped out like a wac-a-mole and my father, I usually called him "dad," wrapped me in this towel from the trunk that he usually used to wipe off the dipstick when he pulled into the service station.

He always checked the oil every time he filled up. I guess it's that thing, at least he always used to say, "An ounce of prevention is worth a pound of cured ham." And he laughed every time, like this was the most brilliant bit of comedy ever come up with by any man in the history of the universe. But the thing of it was that no one else really laughed, except in that courteous way, you know. But I have such a problem with that, because all a courtesy laugh does is encourages people who aren't funny to keep telling jokes.

And so I would just stand there stonefaced, and even though I'd heard the line a hundred million billion times, and even though my father knew

I'd heard it a hundred million billion times, he'd look at me and say something like, "What's the matter, don't you get it?"

"No, I get it, dad, it's just…"

"Are you sure, 'cause you're not laughing?"

"I get it, dad," as I'd roll my eyes a little, enough that he'd notice, but not enough that he could call me on it.

"It's funny because the expression is a pound of cure, but I changed it…"

"I get it. Dad."

"What's the matter? Things all right at school? You having trouble making friends?"

"No. I just…never mind."

And I'd go into the gas station to buy a fountain drink or a slushy beverage.

"We're not done with this conversation," he'd call after me, but we always were, because neither one of us wanted to rehash the thing.

Then that night over dinner he'd make some comment about not counting your chickens before the hash browns, if we were having either one of those dishes, or maybe something about not putting all your eggs in one basketball, which…

What the hell does that even mean?!

And my mom would titter and give him a kind smile, but I'd just sit there staring, unamused. And my father would look at me, as if for approval. But I just did not approve of this kind of behavior.

Afterwards, in the kitchen, where mom washed and he dried, I'd hear him tell her that he was worried. I didn't seem to be my usual happy self, which, since this kind of thing happened all the time, I don't know exactly what "usual happy self" he was referring to. And mom would say something like, "Honey, he's a teenager. All kids go through this phase. Look at Brian."

"Yeah," my father would drop something, maybe a fork or a different piece of silverware, and stoop to pick it up, "but Brian's an idiot."

And he was, but that's not the point right now.

"I wish you wouldn't say that about your own son."

"I just… Warren's just such a brilliant kid, with so much potential. I don't like to see him this way."

"That's true," mom would say as she scoured the casserole dish. "He is technically a genius."

"You're not kidding. He's really one of the most exceptional minds of his generation, if not the century."

I'd already stopped listening long before this, but I'm pretty sure their dialogue moved in this general direction.

And there's that thing. That's why my superhero name would be *The Exception*; because in most things, that's the way I am.

Anyways…

I wasn't named after Warren Zevon, who I guess was some kind of musician. And I wasn't named after former President Harding, or any of the other former president's for that matter. I like to tell some people that I was named after a county in Ohio, but that's mostly because sometimes I like to lie to people I don't like, but I don't know you, so I have no reason to dislike you yet, and therefore no reason to lie to you.

If you want to know what I really think though, along I-15 on the way down from Idaho there's a city or community called West Warren, and I think since the last name was already West, my parents just flipped it. Though I never confirmed this.

My dad grew up in West Valley, Utah with his mother and no father that he ever claimed to know of. Though I could never understand how you don't at some point go on an involved quest to discover the identity of your father if you've never been told.

In any case, after graduating high school then working two years of manual labor to save for college, my father attended Boise State for his undergraduate degree and met my mother in the vicinity. It took him five years to complete the four-year degree, probably because he took a semester off to get married and another nine months later when Brian was born. I was conceived somewhere during his senior year.

After graduation my family made the move to Utah for two reasons. The first, my grandmother was very sick and needed someone to take care of her. Also, my father was going to the University of Utah for his master's degree in some kind of engineering. It's sad I guess that I have no idea what my dad majored in or what he ever did for a living really.

When my grandma died, we inherited my father's childhood home, and that's where I grew up.

That's pretty much how I ended up in the barren waste of Utah, and that's also pretty much how I got stuck there my entire life.

I don't want that to sound like my whole life was terrible, because if it was then this story wouldn't really be worth paying any attention to, would it?

I mean, like anyone's life, mine has had its ups and downs so to speak. My childhood was all right, nothing spectacular to tell you about, so you're not going to get much there. I couldn't for the life of me tell you what I spent my time doing exactly or really tell you about any specific events. I just remember that there always seemed like there was plenty of time for everything, and I don't remember worrying a whole lot.

Now, it's different. For instance, the other day I caught myself thinking about my own existence. Well that's a hell of a thing. I stood there trying to find like meaning and stuff. That's something that never comes up when you're a kid. And I was worried about what will happen to me when I die, which, if I have anything to say about it, won't happen for a long time, but still I just couldn't help worrying.

I don't know. I won't say whether there's a God or not, because I don't know. There's definitely some kind of force out there, one that I call destiny. But God? I don't know. Life after this? I hope so, but I have a hard time believing in it.

But it's stuff like this that makes me understand what people are saying when they say they wish they could be young again. I don't think they really want to go back and be a kid again or even do those things they enjoyed when they were kids. They just want that freedom and that, like they just want to be able to remember more vividly what it was like to be happy and never to worry. But then I think, y'know, if anyone really had a totally crystalline recollection of what it was like to be a little kid, none of us would ever really go back to that. Because I think we choose what to remember and most of the time most of us choose to remember only the good things. But in perfect memory, everything's eternal, including all the bad things we've done and the bad times we've had.

If you were to ask a bunch of people what I was like as a kid, most of them would probably say something like, "Who is Warren West?"

But if you were to ask a bunch of people who knew me as a kid what I was like, you'd probably get a bunch of different answers.

Like, for instance, let's go back a few years to when my family was still a cohesive unit and you could actually get a straight answer from any one of them. If at that time you'd asked my dad what I was like as a little kid, he'd prob'ly've said I was a stubborn, rebellious little punk. Which is weird because my parents were so liberal it didn't leave a lot to rebel against. But fine, dad, if you ever read this, and you want to think that way, just keep on thinking it, because...

Whatever!!!

But if you'd asked my mom, she'd prob'ly have said something like, "Oh, he was such a sweet young boy." And that's just because that's what mothers say, good ones anyways. Because even Jeffrey Dahmer's mother probably said he was such a sweet boy.

Ideally though, I'd've had you ask my older brother Brian, because he'd prob'ly've said something along the lines of "ingenious." First of all because that's the only big word in his vocabulary. And second of all because everything I did was ingenious to him, because Brian was kind of an idiot.

Well...

...not really kind of. Brian was a *complete* idiot.

And everyone knew it. Even Brian. This wasn't something we tried to keep from him or protect him from. I think my parents figured out early on that the best thing to do was to just come right out with it.

See, I think my parents saw being an idiot kind of the same as being gay. They just felt it was better not to keep this kind of thing in the closet. Confront the problem and, in that way, you can overcome the problem. However, I'm pretty sure that if I'd ever come out and told my father that I was gay, which I'm not, I'd have been dragged out behind the shed and shot like an arthritic old dog.

But being an idiot was something my father could cope with, I guess. I mean, to a point.

As children, even though Brian was three years older, we were always about on the same level. That was up until about second grade, I mean when I was in second grade and Brian was in fifth grade "Resource" classes. Then I started to pass him.

Now I think I'm starting to sound kind of harsh ripping on Brian like this, but the thing is I'm not ripping on him. I'm just telling you how it is. See, it's not like Brian was retarded in the clinical sense. So it's not like I'm making fun of handicapped people. What I mean is that Brian was just simply an idiot.

How can I explain this?

Okay, so it's like Brian just didn't care about anything and didn't put any effort into improving himself at all. And you might be saying to yourself, "Well, yeah, because your parents just gave up on him." And you might be right, but the cause is not the issue; Brian is the issue. And the only term I can think of for someone who's totally given up on himself and makes no effort to improve himself is "idiot."

Also, Brian had severe anger management issues.

As kids, we'd like play in the sandbox and like maybe we'd have some watermelon or something, right? And if he finished his watermelon first, which he always did, then he'd look at my watermelon and insist that I give it to him. And when I wouldn't he'd pick up a handful of sand and throw it in my face.

See, I'd scream and drop my watermelon in the sandbox and run inside, trying to scrape the grains off my eyeballs. Meanwhile, Brian would pick up my watermelon and go to town on it, without even brushing the sand off. When I'd tell my dad what happened the answer was always the same:

"Well, Brian is an idiot."

As if that made everything okay.

I still had scratched corneas.

I still had no watermelon.

And if I retaliated. If I, say, played fireman and turned my fire hose on Brian, because of course in this game he was the thing on fire, I'd be dragged up to my room and put in a "time out" where I was to think about what I'd done, but where I usually ended up playing with some Lincoln Logs or something, and I'd build a cabin that Brian would come in and destroy, because he was, after all, an idiot.

Look, I'm all about tolerance, y'know. And sometimes permissiveness is necessary in allowing a person to live his life. But my parents were ridiculous. When we're talking about parents, you can't just allow your kids to do whatever they want and say, "I'm just letting him find himself," or, "That's just the way he is." You're a parent; it's your job to do something about your children's behavior. Sometimes you have to control your kid, not just say, "he's an idiot," and that's that.

And so Brian lashed out, without reason. He just made a scene every chance he got, like a self-fulfilling prophecy kind of thing. People said he was an idiot so he became an idiot. It's that thing, like, I don't know where it comes from, but like you're like kicking against the pricks and all you're doing is hurting yourself, right?

It's also like quicksand. From what little I know about quicksand, anyways. The more you struggle, the quicker it pulls you under.

Of course, on our elementary school playground I never did see any quicksand. We did have a soccer field with a backstop and baseball diamond in the corner.

The school was old and most of the climbing toys were made out of wood, which meant that several times each school year you'd go home with some nasty slivers in your hands and sometimes in your face.

And we had the blacktop which, if you're not familiar, is what we called the asphalt portion of the playground where we'd play foursquare or kickball. There was a basketball court with two hoops, both with bent rims and no nets. The backboards were giant plywood rectangles with the odd corner broken off and swears spraypainted across them. We also had tetherball poles but no tetherballs, so it wasn't until I was older that I realized what those poles had been for. I just remember seeing girls spinning around on them.

I always liked the monkey bars though. Not climbing across them from below like a monkey might do if he had a set of monkey bars. I liked climbing up on top of them. I'm trying right now, very hard, to figure out what the appeal was of sitting atop the monkey bars. I do remember being small enough that I could kind of squish my buttocks down between the bars, my rear kind of hanging there, while I supported myself with my arms and legs, my knees bent over the side bar and my armpits slung over the crossbars.

Yes, the monkey bars. And the ball pit.

Of course we didn't have a ball pit on the school playground. But I loved the ball pit in places like Chuck-E-Cheese. I still love the ball pit.

Because check this out: One day when I'm rich I am going to build a room in my gigantic house. And this room will contain a giant, hundred feet in every direction, ball pit. Oh man, that'll be so great. Can you imagine?

I've thought about building an adult-size playground, y'know, like as a business venture. I think it would do very well. You'd have adult height, and breadth, monkey bars. There'd, of course, be a huge ball pit. Slides that are, like, fifty-sixty feet high. A big spiderweb net thing that goes to the top of a high, high tower where there's a long zipline that drops you into a swimming hole or a big thing of mud.

You'd have rope swings, and swing swings, and they'd all swing out over huge bodies of water. And there'd be this network of tunnels, and they'd all be adult-sized.

And there would be other great things too, like I don't know what, but awesome things that everyone would want to play on regardless of age or size, except maybe really fat people might not be all into the physical aspect of playing on the stuff, which means that girl wouldn't come.

Adults would come from all around to play in my adult-sized playground. I'd call it Warrenopolis, and the entrance fee would be reasonable, perhaps five or six dollars for an entire day.

And there would be an area for picnics, because people don't have picnics anymore, at least not like they used to.

I don't know what that means.

But also there would be a giant tree house, in a giant tree, like the Swiss Family Robinson, only cooler. And everyone would want to climb up into the tree house, but we'd have to limit the occupancy, because I'm sure there'd be some issues with fire code, but everyone would get a turn. And they could get down by jumping from a high dive into the giant ball pit or something.

What adult, besides Jim Potter — this really boring guy I know — wouldn't want to spend a day of fun and fantasy in *Warrenopolis*?

CHAPTER 3

MARTY

As some men get old, their noses broaden and flatten against their faces like a sort of starfish. With age, Marty had grown a beak — a long, impressive, curvy beak. It hooked down over his top lip, and I wondered how he drank his coffee without getting his nose all gross.

Probably with a straw, like in that one movie.

I guess you could say he was my friend, but it sounds a little weird when you do. But I don't know what else you should call him.

Yes, I suppose. Go ahead. Call him my friend, I guess, because I suppose when it comes right down to it, he was... is... was... I don't know, is, I guess. It's hard to say which tense you should put him in.

Last I saw him, Marty was over seventy years old, somewhere there, maybe over eighty. Actually, I have no idea exactly how old he was; he probably didn't either anymore. But he had to be over seventy anyways. And since I'm only twenty-five, that puts like fifty years or more between us. If I did the math I could probably figure it out or close to, but it doesn't really matter how old he was.

What does matter is that Marty and I played chess every week since I was fourteen.

Chess is probably like one of the top five games in the history of civilization. And I'll bet that even before civilization they didn't have many games better than chess. Don't get me wrong, I'm sure the cavemen had some pretty kick-ass games, because once they hunted down a brontosaurus or whatever, they had food for like a week for a whole tribe. I'm just assuming that brontosaurus meat didn't go bad very fast, or at least that the people didn't get sick from the rotten meat, because either their bodies were used to it or it stands to reason that if there weren't many species of mammals and only like eleven kinds of dinosaurs or whatever, then there probably wouldn't be many bugs, like maggots y'know, probably.

So one kill a week would leave all those cave dwellers with a lot of free time to play games. Because I'm sure they didn't spend their free time sitting around thinking up new and more advanced ways to snare the brontosauri, because I saw that movie about the DNA reproduction of all those dinosaurs into that theme park. Actually, I saw all three of them, and

I have to say I was pretty disappointed by the third one. But that's not the point. The point is I saw all those movies, and also the one where the people are trying to return the baby brontosaurus to its parents or homeland or whatever, and also a lot of other dinosaur movies, and I know that a brontosaurus is about the easiest animal in the world to kill. It's like a huge cow with a long neck. You get a group of like seven or eight cavemen and/or cavewomen, because I'm an equal opportunity fantasizer. They all attack the dinosaur with spears or sharp sticks or whatever and the deed's done.

So I wonder what games they had. And since it was before, you know, civilization, there aren't really any records of what they did with their free time. I've seen those cave paintings and tried to see if there were really any pictures of the caveman games, but those pictures are all so weird and it's impossible to say at all what they're all about. For all we know, they could be mug shots, or like police sketches. Some caveman kills some other caveman and there's a witness, and the witness describes the killer to a cave-sketch artist and the cave-police look at the sketch and say, "Oh, it was the guy with the upside-down triangle body and no face. I know him. He hangs around that abandoned cave down in cataract canyon." And then they go arrest him.

I don't really think this is what it was like, y'know, but sometimes I like to think about that kind of thing, and just like let my mind go.

Sometimes it comes back.

I remember seeing this thing on TV from like National Geographic or the History Channel or something about the Mayans or the Aztecs or one of those Ancient American Indian groups from south of what is now the United States. It was about this game they played with like rings sort of like our basketball hoops without nets, and also there was a ball that archaeologists or anthropologists, or whoever it is that studies that kind of thing, believe the tribesmen bounced off their hips to get it to go through the ring to score points.

Now this is all well and good, and I can accept, in fact I'm sure, that these people played games like this, and maybe they even bounced the balls off their hips, which is weird, but okay. Where I begin to doubt is when these whatever-ologists try to tell me that these games were actually rituals and the ball represented the sun and the rings represented whatever and the court or arena was a representation of...blah, blah, blah.

It's a game!

That's all it is. I mean golf isn't symbolic of anything. It's not like the cup represents this golden chalice or some like holy grail, and the ball is a symbol for sin. And you take the nine iron, which is the wrath of God, and you whack the hell out of sin until it's cleansed in the cup of Christ. Then you get a green jacket which is symbolic of heaven or something.

No, it's a game.

I do sometimes pretend that bowling pins represent people I don't like though.

But the thing I love about chess is that it's the only game where there is absolutely no luck involved whatsoever. It's all about skill, and brainpower, and even in Marty's condition he was an excellent chess player. But the thing about chess pieces is that they actually are representative of something, which is weird. But that's not the point.

The point is me and Marty used to play chess all the time, and he was very good, and so was I, and sometimes we had some real knockdown, dragout chess battles. But the real reason I went to see him was for the conversation, the stories. Because Marty led a good life, and over chess I got to hear all about it.

Now he was just a recreational player, but he was so good it was like he didn't even think about it when he made his moves. He'd just look at the board, kind of stare at it, and move his pieces like it was a reflex or something. Like after I'd made my move, whoosh, and it was my turn again. And I'd spend forever staring at the board, analyzing the pieces, going over the consequences of each possible move, then I'd make the one that looked the safest.

That was at the beginning.

As I learned, it wasn't the safest move I'd make, it was the one that captured me the most pieces. Then the next year, it was the most strategic move, then the one where I could best predict how Marty would respond. Then I'd make the move that let me see the furthest down the road, as far as all the subsequent moves on both sides of the board. And then my strategy became more calculated and practiced. Then, finally, the only way to beat him was to be erratic in my moves, unpredictable. Sacrificing pieces that I didn't need to. Just doing things he couldn't possibly expect. And it only worked because he had never seen this before, and his brain could not adapt. Like sometimes instead of opening with one of my center pawns, I'd bring out one of the pawns on the ends. Just a move like this could throw him off balance for half a game.

It was 1995 when we started playing together.

At the time he still had his own home just a couple blocks from my parents, and the Alzheimer's hadn't set in so bad, with the exception of a few very minor episodes.

His wife had just passed, and my dad thought it would be a good idea for me to spend some time with him, keep him company. I suppose he might have sent Brian, but Brian would never have been able to grasp the concept of chess.

I was reluctant at first, not just because it was a little weird, but actually mostly because the whole thing was my dad's idea, and so I had to convince myself that absolutely no good could possibly come from it, just so I could prove to my dad that he was as terrible a father as I knew he was, sending his own son to some creepy old guy's house every Tuesday without supervision. Yeah, this was before the whole Catholic priest altar boy scandal, but any number of things could have happened and it would have been all my dad's fault.

Nothing happened though.

Marty was a pretty cool old dude.

He had a huge chessboard in the middle of his living room, handcarved by him. The board alone was like three feet by three feet. And all the pieces, which he also carved himself, were like six inches tall.

It sat, precariously balanced, on a coffee table right in the middle of his orange shag carpet, between his couch from the 1970's and his big arm chair from the 1970's. And next to the chessboard was a stack of old National Geographic magazines on one side and a dish of hard candy, probably also from the 1970's, on the other. And of course Marty hadn't bought new clothes since the seventies either.

He had me sit down on the couch and he took the arm chair. "You know how to play chess?"

I nodded.

"This isn't like that computer chess. I'm asking you if you know how to play real chess."

"Yeah," I said. "I know how to play real chess."

He picked up a piece. "This is your king. This is the piece you want to protect."

"Yeah, I know how to play."

"This is your queen. She can move in any direction as far as you want as long as there are no pieces in her way." As he went on with his explanation of what each and every piece on the board does, I looked over his shoulder to the photos on the wall above the fireplace.

In the center was a large portrait of Marty and his wife Sarah. I recognized her from around the neighborhood before she died. There was a picture of Marty, younger, in some kind of military attire, and one of him in machine-shop coveralls. There was a picture of a younger man, as in middle-aged, with a woman and a girl, probably ten years old. Then another smaller picture of the same girl with a puppy. And around all this were plenty of other pictures, Marty and Sarah at all ages.

I think I was caught staring a little too long at a photo of Sarah, very young, probably eighteen. She was beautiful.

Marty cleared his throat. Apparently, he was done instructing me on the intricacies of this game of chess.

"Sorry. Umm, how..." I didn't know how to ask.

"How did she go?" Like he knew what I was thinking. "She was quite the looker, wasn't she? I was seventeen when we first met. She was sixteen. That's," he paused, "how old she is in that photograph. There wasn't a man I knew didn't want to marry that woman there. And she chose me."

"Why?" Then I realized what I'd said. "I'm sorry, I didn't mean..."

He chuckled that old man chuckle. "Indeed. Why?"

He held out two closed fists.

I just stared at him.

He shook his fists upward slightly and looked in my eyes. "Pick one."

I pointed at the left hand I think, I don't remember exactly, and he revealed a black token. The pawns were much too big to fit inside his age-spotted hands.

"White goes first," he said, but of course I knew that.

He replaced the pieces on the board and made the opening move. He nodded at me then turned to that picture of his sixteen-year-old bride, lost in his memories for just a moment to me, but I'm sure he was gone for a lot longer in his own mind.

CHAPTER 4

FAME

I said before that I like the movies, and that's true, because that would be a weird thing to lie about. But it's more than just liking movies; I've seen just about every movie ever made, I think. That's what happens when you spend as much time by yourself as I did when I was in high school. Because you spend a lot of time by yourself when you don't really have any friends.

Well, I shouldn't say that, because that makes it sound like I'm trying to make you feel sorry for me, which I'm not.

And so a couple of things:

First of all, most of the time I preferred to be by myself. I'm not one of those people who needs to be surrounded by friends to fill my bucket, by which I mean to be happy or even to have a good time.

And second of all, I don't mean I didn't have *any* friends. I just mean, like, I didn't have very many friends. Y'know. I mean I had a couple of friends, but...none that I keep in contact with now, so it's easy to forget them, y'know. And your memories reflect your present state in a lot of ways, and so since I spend so much time alone now and have for years, those are the memories I remember best are the other times that I spent alone, like in high school and at lunch in the cafeteria when I'd eat by myself or...whatever.

Anyways, so I went to movies by myself all the time. It's weird at night to go alone, with all the people on dates and couples making out, which is very distracting, and families out on family nights, so I usually went to matinees. And sometimes midnight movies, which was also a little weird, but if it was a premiere you could always jump in with a big group of people that was obviously a whole bunch of friends and friends of friends and friends of friends of friends and no one would notice that you had just tagged along, and that's how I met a lot of people who've probably forgotten that they've ever talked to me. It was always bad though if the person I'd jumped in with was chatty, because they'd want to get to know you during the movie, not before, and not even during the previews, although that would have been equally annoying because the previews are what gets me excited to go to the movies again in the future. Sometimes, a lot of times actually, the previews are even better than the movie, so you'd pay $6.25 to see three or four previews and if someone talked through them all it was just, it was so irritating. And $6.25 was the evening price; matinees were $3.25. I can't believe how much they expect you to pay at the theater now.

I want to make this clear though, before we move on: As many midnight premieres as I've seen, I have never, ever dressed up like a character from the movie. That's just weird! And as much as you might think I'm a loser for not having a lot of friends, I'm not a loser like the Wolverines, or the Harry Potters, or the Goloms that I've met in my life.

My favorite movie? I can't pick just one.

That's like asking my mom which child is her favorite. She'd be totally torn between me and the twins, which, I mean, how do you choose? I mean, there are some options which are clearly out, like my brother Brian, but you can't pick just one favorite out of the good ones.

I like a lot of foreign films, especially European films, because they just seem to have this different look on life that seems so... not made up at all. And on the same wavelength, I like based on a true story movies prob'ly most. I just don't so much like getting wrapped up in something, letting something draw me in and affect me, sometimes deeply, only to get to the end and, as the theater lights come back on, realize that the whole thing was a lie.

The truth is so gripping, why do we need to make stuff up? That's what I think anyways.

♀ ♀ ♀

We didn't own a video camera when I was younger, as in when I was a kid and when I was a teenager. But this other kid I knew had one, and we used to make movies, little things.

All you really need to make a movie is a camera, a person to turn it on and point it at the stuff you want to shoot, and a bunch of people to exist in front of the lens as "actors." Yeah, there's technique and all that crap, but you don't need millions of dollars to have all that, like these big-budget Hollywood things. Sometimes a flashlight is all you need to see what you're supposed to see, and who cares if the camera shakes? That's real then.

We made this one movie about a guy who's homeless, and it wasn't a real homeless man in the movie, but I talked to a real homeless man to ask him about being homeless and what it was like and why he was homeless, and I asked him about some stories about being homeless, and then we filmed some stuff that was just like all the stuff he said to me about being homeless, and so it wasn't actually a true real homeless guy in the movie but it was a true story and it was real. The only thing was I was fourteen when I made that one and the guy playing the homeless guy was also fourteen and the real homeless man was like sixty, so it wasn't all believable, but it was still earnest, which was also the homeless guy's name — Ernest.

Not really. But that would've been cool.

So I watched this one movie, one of those true story things, which is probably why I liked it so much, but anyways, it was about this guy who was in a camp, like a concentration camp, only it was in Cambodia I think. Anyway, there's this bit where he catches this lizard, I think to eat it or something but it never shows this, and he puts the lizard in his pocket.

And it really made me think, I wonder who invented pockets.

And it seemed pretty ancient, the whole setting of the movie, even though it took place in the sixties or seventies if I remember right, during or after Vietnam. So I started to wonder when pockets were invented in the first place and where. Because when you think about it, the pocket was a really good invention. It keeps your hands free to do other stuff besides carrying stuff, like shaking hands with someone you haven't seen in a while or have just met; or pushing D-9 to get the Peanut M&M's out of the vending machine; or hailing a cab which I suppose you could do even if you had something in your hand, especially a handkerchief; or scratching an itch on your nose or your ear or right above your left eyebrow; or any number of other things. Regardless of what you do with your free hands, the pocket was a brilliant invention and I don't think it will ever lose its popularity, like you know some things, like Daisy Dukes or Parachute Pants (which I still wear on occasion) or flat tops, go out of style because they're just trendy or because some famous person wears them and then that same famous person loses all his money gambling, declares bankruptcy, has a nervous breakdown on some latenight "news" program, and checks into rehab, and then they're not famous anymore and the thing they made famous, the shoes or the pants or the sunglasses or whatever, is also no longer famous or popular or trendy, and any kid who still wears or has or uses the thing is mercilessly harassed by the other kids and has to sneak home at lunchtime (luckily he lives just up the street) to change out of those Pump sneakers, not realizing that buckling under the peer pressure has now made him a punching bag if you will, or if you will not, it's hung a giant bull's eye on his Girbaud knock-off t-shirt.

But like I said, I loved the movies, and I had this, I guess premonition that one day I would make one that would maybe change the world. And when I look back even at the little things I did in junior high, I think they're every bit as good as anything Hollywood's putting out, just on a smaller scale.

I told my cousin one time that I wanted to make movies, and he suggested, I mean he said he'd heard about this seminar or workshop thing or something. Anyways, where you could go and learn from people who'd been working in the industry for years about how to do it all and how to work your way up and whatever. And he said I should think about going. And I did. Think about it that is. I did think about it for like two seconds. But this is the thing. I don't think this kind of artistic stuff is something that can be learnt in a classroom, y'know. It's like, either you've got it or you don't, right? And I don't put much faith in any higher power or anything, but I do put a lot of stock in destiny. And if you're destined to make it, you'll make it. If the fates have other plans, well then, I don't know. But I know what's in store for me, because let me tell you a little story, okay?

Ever since the time I was very young, like about eight or nine years old, I wanted to be famous. But... But it was like more than just a desire, right? I'd watch TV or movies and I could actually see myself there, being not only that actor on the screen, but that character in the film. It was like, and I truly felt this way, it was like being famous was what I was born to do. I mean, you know. And who's more famous than movie stars, besides maybe the President of the United States and Steven Spielberg?

So anyways, I knew I was destined to become famous one day. And this is the point, and this is why I know I'll make it as opposed to some other people who I know won't. Because I'm not just another one of those bubble-gum pop celebrities. Sure I'll use the Hollywood system if necessary, but that's just a step in getting where I really want to be, which is in a position of fame and power where I can really, y'know, show people the truth, create great works of film art that touch people, you know emotionally, and inspire.

I'm in it all for the greater good, and unselfishly really. And you know, that's what it's all about...

Making a difference.

And also destiny.

The whole idea sort of came from the idea that when two people fall in love it's like they're the only two people in the entire world, like no one else and nothing else matters. So to take that idea even one step further, I decided to only have two people in the whole movie, y'know just two actors and no extras.

But I wanted to be careful and not make it creepy like that one movie where the guy wakes up in a hospital and wanders around London, or some other city in the U.K., and he can't find anyone else, and then later it turns out that everyone else in the world, almost, has been turned into like a zombie and he has to be careful because even one drop of zombie blood in his system would turn him also into a zombie.

But my movie is a romance, so this kind of thing would be totally inappropriate.

So I decided that the two characters could communicate with other people, like on the phone, but you couldn't ever see anyone else on the screen.

This was the movie I decided to make. I mean the real movie, the full two-hour-long thing, that I was actually going to have real actors and stuff for. And it all came about because of this one thing that happened that I'll tell you about later.

The opening scene was obvious, based on how I came up with it. Or at least, mostly obvious, as in I knew where it would take place. I didn't know at first exactly what would happen, exactly. I knew they had to meet, because how else do you start a movie about two people falling in love, because that's what it's about.

The first thing I had to figure out was who these two characters were. But you don't want to hear about how I sat around in my room and daydreamed at work and came up with all the ins and outs of my movie, so I'm going to skip ahead.

There is one part of my creative process I want to tell you about though, because it's, y'know, part of the story. When I needed inspiration, a lot of times I'd drive up the canyons, all of them, different ones: Farmington, Big Cottonwood, Little Cottonwood, Millcreek, Mueller Park, Logan, and whatever other ones. I was both looking for a place to shoot and hoping that I'd find my muse.

Mostly though, I spent my time in American Fork Canyon. Because when you see someone somewhere, you hang around that area a lot hoping that you'll see them there again. Like when I spent months hanging around that mall.

The first scene would have to be in a canyon somewhere, because that's where I came up with the idea. Yeah, I could move it somewhere else, but that was what seemed like the best idea to me.

So how do these people meet? Right? That's the question. And I looked over, and I saw this cliff face, and I thought, "Perfect!"

The guy, let's call him Eric, would be all sitting on top of that cliff, how he got there I don't know, and why he's sitting there I don't know, but that's not important right now. That's the details and I'll fill them all in later.

So then, all of a sudden, this hand reaches up over the edge of the cliff, and the girl, let's call her Stacy, climbs up over the edge, because she's been climbing the cliff face, right? And they meet. And they talk. And they connect. Because that's what it's all about, connection, right? And I don't know what they talk about yet, because that's the details again, and those will all be worked out.

But this I knew. They didn't hook up right there, because I wanted to make this thing as real as possible. In fact, maybe, probably they don't even exchange phone numbers. They just go on their way.

But what happens is that they meet up again, by chance — or destiny — way later, like maybe as much as a year later or so or whatever, and that's when the relationship really takes off.

This is where I was when I first started thinking about this idea. And it really developed from there, into actually a real story. And this was going to be my movie, I knew it. This was my purpose.

I'd need money though, and while I had a pretty good job at this little photocopy place, there was another thing I was saving up for that maybe took precedence over the movie. And even though the other thing wasn't my purpose, it was also my destiny. And well, but the thing is, what you have to understand, is that I was nineteen when all this came about, and so if this was truly my whole life's purpose, I had plenty of time to get it done.

But also I couldn't do it alone. First of all, I'd need actors, maybe a crew, and also some kind of a writer because I knew I couldn't do that part by myself.

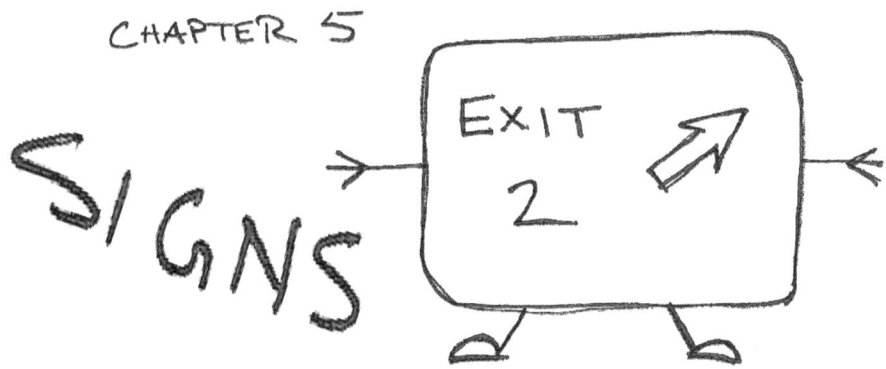

CHAPTER 5
SIGNS

EXIT 2

If you do the math, you'll realize that they didn't have *rent.com* when I was eighteen years old. At least it didn't exist that I knew of, because if it did, I'd never heard of it. But even if I'd heard of it, I wouldn't have known how to use it, because by the time I graduated from high school I'd sent maybe like three e-mails in my entire life, because Al Gore didn't even invent the internet until I was in like junior high I don't think.

So without a fancy internet site to find me a new place to live, I was out doing the old apartment search the old-fashioned way, and by that I mean driving around and looking at places from this little magazine-book-thing I'd picked up at the housing authority.

I'd just graduated high school about two or three weeks ago or something and I had to get out of my parents' house. But I wasn't going to college, because I don't believe in it. By that I don't mean I don't believe that college exists, because I know it does. I mean I don't believe in the idea of college, that you pay a whole bunch of money to people who are only teaching because they suck at whatever it is they're teaching so that they can teach you also to suck at that thing.

But I was getting frustrated because I couldn't really find anything in my price range which was small because I didn't exactly have a job.

Now I had a job, but not exactly. I worked as a projectionist at this little movie theater, but if you've ever worked as a projectionist at a little movie theater, you know two things, and those two things are that being a projectionist doesn't pay very much and also you can't really call being a projectionist a job. But you also know that as a projectionist you get to see a whole bunch of movies for free, and that's really the only thing that makes being a projectionist worth being a projectionist.

It's kind of like being a stewardess I bet. You don't make very much money and you have to deal with guys hitting on you all the time and pinching your bum, but you do get to fly all over the place all the time and see lots of cool places.

So, but the thing is, I wasn't only looking for an apartment, I was also looking for a job, but until I found a job I couldn't really afford an apartment, but I'd decided to look for the apartment first anyway, which turned out to be kismet or destiny or whatever, and this is for reasons that

I'll explain in a minute, but you're just going to have to hold your horses and be patient, because there's something else I need to say first.

There are times in your life when you make one decision that might seem totally against logic, like you might put your underwear on outside of your pants or something, but you do it anyway, and maybe you don't know why or maybe you do, but that doesn't matter. But that first decision, which was totally different than the one you maybe should have made or maybe shouldn't have made, but that doesn't matter, it's just the opposite of what maybe logic would probably dictate, and that first decision leads to another decision, and that leads to another decision, until you've found and followed and executed a whole string of decisions, and maybe you made the subsequent decisions logically or maybe you didn't, but that doesn't matter. The point is that maybe you put your underpants on outside your jeans, or maybe you wore them on your head like a hat, and then you went to school. And that very same day a new music video came out in which a very famous person also wore their underpants outside their regular pants or on their head like a hat, and suddenly people saw you as a sort-of trendsetter, and so now you're faced with the decision of whether or not to sit at the cool table in the cafeteria at lunch, because you've been invited, then you make that decision. And let's say for the sake of this analogy that you did decide to sit at the cool table. Then you got invited to a party that the cool people went to, and so on, and so on, and you had all these decisions.

Not that this ever happened to me like this, even when I did wear my underwear on my head like a hat, but this kind of chain of decisions based on one illogical one is the kind of thing that did happen to me and that I'm trying to tell you about.

And that illogical decision was to look for an apartment before looking for a job. Or maybe it wasn't illogical, but that doesn't matter.

Anyways, but I left the last apartment that I think was named after some nineteenth century author or something, and I headed down Redwood Road, and this is where I faced my first decision, or the second decision actually from the long chain, but the first of the subsequent decisions...

See, I noticed that my gas needle was approaching empty, so I was thinking, Should I stop at the Maverik and fill up?

Because the thing was I probably had at least enough gas to get home and then back out to a gas station. But I was tired a little and didn't really want to stop. So I debated with myself for a little bit, but not too long because the thing was that I was also very thirsty, so I figured if I stopped then I could also get a soda, so that's what I did, and as it turned out the soda was on sale, so that was a good thing.

But then, here's the real thing:

So after about five or ten minutes I left the Maverik and got on I-215 Southbound about five or ten minutes after I would have been there if I hadn't stopped. And I was heading back to West Valley, because that's where my parents lived, and their house was where my bedroom was, and my bedroom was where my TV, VCR and stack of rented videos was, so I had to get there.

So now I'm driving along, right? Prob'ly doing I don't know seventy, seventy-five maybe, in the sixty-five because I don't really believe in speed limits. And this little red Geo something or other roars on past me and cuts me off. So now I'm faced with decision number two, or three, depending on your frame of reference...

Do I flip off this driver or do I just let it go?

So after almost no debate with myself over this one, I rip it on up in the neighboring lane and pull even with that mechanical abomination. And I start to extend my arm out the window, like in that one movie where they do that. And I'm about to extend my middle finger when I get a good look at the other driver.

It's her.

It's she.

It's the one.

It's that beautiful girl whose name I don't know. That girl with the bubbly friend and the chestnut hair, and she's right there, and she's radiant as ever, and she's...

Crap!

No she's not crap. She's just...

She's about to look this way. I can see the skin of her neck creasing in just that slight way that a swath of satin might if it were wrapped around a cylindrical object, like a container of Quaker oats, and you were to twist that tube of oats. And also her head is turning.

And here I am with my arm extended and my middle finger in limbo, and I look like a fool and a jerk and whatever else, and there's really only one thing to do, and that's to slam on the brakes.

This could be called decision number three, or four, but it's not, because it wasn't really a decision at all. No amount of logic or illogic went into my foot slamming itself down on the brake pedal and my hand gripping the emergency brake and yanking it back full force, all while the car was traveling at a good seventy, seventy-five miles per hour because I don't believe in speed limits.

And there was no amount of logic or illogic involved in the stream of expletives that exploded from my mouth as through the windshield I saw the Geo, the median, oncoming traffic, the road barrier, and my soda — all at once.

When the car was done spinning I was facing east, still in the southbound lanes — two or three of them — and I was dizzy. Luckily this was I-215 in the middle of the day, in the middle of the summer, and the only person that witnessed what happened was some department store truck driver, whom I referred to earlier as oncoming traffic, and who was able to skillfully maneuver his truck around me while skillfully creating a new nickname for me using words I had never heard before.

But none of this mattered that much, because I was now faced with decision number...whatever. The next decision...

Do I follow the Geo?

And yes, of course I followed the Geo. Which did mean speeding up a lot and passing that angry trucker and hearing my new nickname again, but after not too long I caught up to that little red car, and she was still driving it.

And I wanted to pull even with her, y'know, and that so I could look over at her beautiful face that has not a blemish but is just perfect, like a thing that has absolutely nothing wrong with it. But I thought, as my front bumper was edging past her rear one, that maybe if I was driving alongside and staring at her the whole time, there were two bad things that could happen. Either I might not watch the road very carefully and get in a really bad accident that could maybe kill me or someone else or someone's pet, or just damage my car real bad, or make some other truck driver really mad at me. Or the girl would see me doing this and get really freaked out and maybe call the cops, but probably not call the cops until she'd gotten where she was going, because I doubted that she had a cell phone, because this was before cell phones were universal like they are today, and not too many people our age had one. But after she stopped, she might call the police. Or even if she didn't call the police, she'd think I was a weirdo and that would be worse even than being arrested.

So I tapped the brakes just a little to slow down, and I eased back into the lane behind her, which worked out well because I could see the reflection of her eyes in the rearview mirror, which was hypnotizing. I mean by that that seeing her eyes was hypnotizing, not her rearview mirror.

Though that might be cool to have a hypnotizing rearview mirror, or maybe not like a rearview mirror but probably like hypnotizing taillights, so that when someone is tailgating you and won't back off, you just activate your taillights and the aggressive driver behind you either like swerves off into the embankment on the side of the road or just becomes a courteous driver, or maybe he wets himself. I don't know, but I ought to patent that idea.

Anyways, so I followed her for a bit, not too long, until she indicated a right turn. But since there was no side street off the freeway, I knew she was just changing lanes rather than turning right, and I of course did the same. Then she flipped her turn signal on again, so I figured she must be exiting now. And I was right. Oh, I forgot to mention that we'd already before this reached the south end of the I-215 belt where it connects with I-15, and we'd merged onto this freeway, and the traffic had picked up, so it wasn't totally, totally obvious that I was following her, because there were a few cars in between us. The downside was I couldn't really see her eyes anymore.

But the exit we took was the 9000 South exit, which I think is Sandy City or something. I don't know if it was then, or just is now, or maybe it's something else altogether. In any case, it's near Sandy. And as I rolled onto the off-ramp, I heard this honking off to my left. And I looked, and this department store truck passed by and the driver taught me a little bit of sign language, but I didn't care, because I could see this girl's hypnotizing eyes again in her rearview mirror, and she was turning left.

I followed her up to State Street and then south a few blocks, where she turned into a big parking lot, which I realized, because of the big building with all these different store names all over it, was a shopping mall. So I turned into the parking lot too and sort of trailed her around until she parked. And I parked a few stalls back, where she wouldn't see me, and I waited.

And waited...

And waited...

And waited...

I swear it took her forever to finally get out of the car! What could she have been doing in there?!

But then she got out and walked over to the mall. And I figured it was probably safe to get out too and follow her. Even at a close distance, she probably wouldn't suspect anything, so it would all be okay. So this I did. And I had a plan, a classic plan, like from all the movies. I'd follow her into whatever store she was headed to and pretend that I was there too, looking for whatever. Then I'd work my way near her and strike up a conversation about whatever it was the store sold.

But a monkey was thrown into the works when I saw which entrance she was headed towards — the food court.

I hate the food court.

The food court is a room filled with every food smell known to man, all amalgamated into one noxious cloud of invisible ipecac.

See, when it comes right down to it, there is one super power that I know the Exception has, and this power is at once the source of his strength and his kryptonite. The Exception has a super sense of smell.

The following is a list of odors that make him nauseous:

- Perfume (cologne, aftershave, etc.)
- Broccoli
- Make-Up (read *cosmetics*)
- Urine, et al.
- Vomit (of any variety)
- Pine Cones
- Any Brand of Aerosol (Spray-Can) Air Freshener
- Static Electricity
- Rotten Fruits and Vegetables
- Fruity Lip Glosses (In Case You Don't Classify These as Cosmetics)
- A Ton of Other Things, and...
- Food Courts!

However, this super sense of smell does come with one really intense positive. I can smell rain as early as five days in advance and can predict, within ninety minutes, when the first drops will splatter on the ground. So really, I probably could be a super hero.

But so we reached the food court, and to my delight she was just passing through. But it truly took all my strength just to make it to the other end, and I had to hold my breath the whole time, which was like, I don't know, maybe two minutes, maybe.

Now it was a journey of stealth to find out which store she was headed for without making it obvious that I was trying to find out which store she was headed for. As it turns out, she was headed for a clothing store — all these years later, I don't remember which, maybe Mervyn's, maybe ZCMI, maybe JC Penney, I don't remember.

So I traipsed into the store prob'ly a hundred yards or so behind her, as if this is exactly where I wanted to be...

In the lingerie section.

"Can I help you with anything?"

"Umm...what?" I spun around to face the salesgirl. "No, I'm just, umm, looking for, umm, pants."

See now, the thing is, I've seen this very situation in all kinds of movies, where the guy finds himself in the women's underwear section for whatever reason and has to pretend that he means to be there, and this provides a setup for all kinds of devastatingly funny comedy, or at least the television laugh track tells us it's funny.

But in real life, you just say you're looking for pants and you get the hell out of there...

"Second floor," the salesgirl said with a condescending smile.

...to the second floor, where maybe you'll buy some pants or maybe you won't, but that doesn't matter. And then you'll go back downstairs and sit just outside the store and wait for the girl to finally reemerge, and in the meantime you'll concoct another devious plan for getting her to talk to you.

In my case, I did decide to buy some pants.

And I had to try them on, which I hate, because I wish someone could explain this to me...

Why can't the fitting room door go all the way to the floor? Especially when it's a unisex fitting room? And why is the door made of slats, even if they are tightly packed together? Why can't they make the fitting room door out of a solid piece of wood?

But I got myself a pair of pants, black ones that were kind of this fabric mixture, part cotton, part something else, and I asked about turtlenecks. Not because I wanted to wear one, but because I needed it for a thing. What I needed it for is a long story and has nothing to do with this one. But I couldn't find one, probably because it was the middle of summer. That's what the lady there said anyways. And then I went back downstairs and sat on a bench outside the Mervyn's, or whatever store I'd been in, and waited, thinking about what I might say to her. How could I get her to talk to me, flirt with me, fall in love with me, marry me, and spend the rest of her life with me?

And I had plenty of time to think about all this while I waited for her. Because see, at the time I had no idea how much time a girl really can spend in a store. And the most mindboggling thing about it all is that she can spend, y'know, like three-and-a-half days in a store and not buy a damn thing.

Anyways, now I know you're thinking that what's going to happen next is the girl is going to come out of the store and that obnoxious friend that's been with her both other times I've seen her will be with her, because they met in the lingerie section of the store after I'd run up to buy pants. Because that's what usually happens in these stories.

But the thing you need to remember is that this story is true, so it's not always going to follow all those plot conventions that fictional tales do.

However, in this case, it does. The fat girl was with her, and it almost makes me as queasy as the food court did to imagine what she was trying on in the lingerie department.

She was recounting what to her was an electrifying saga, about Grant I think, and telling it with such veracity that my dream girl was actually squinting and leaning away as though a mighty wind was blowing straight into her face, which I guess in a sense it was.

I couldn't go talk to her now though, not with that friend there, so I ducked behind a kiosk and watched her walk away, where I could not follow — into the food court. When she was gone my spirit collapsed inside of me, like my whole being imploded. I sort of sunk into this lump of mashed potatoes with clothes on the tiled gallery floor. But this is how a chain of decisions, doesn't matter whether they're logical or illogical, can lead to an erstwhile unforeseen conclusion. While I was down there on the floor, I found myself face-to-face with destiny in the form of two advertise-ments tacked to the side of the kiosk.

The first was from a jeweler's, advertising of all things wedding rings. It was a sign. Fate was speaking to me. No. Shouting. Is there another way to interpret it? Now if only I could afford this ginormous ring. But the second flier (this is how fate works, fella) was a *Help Wanted* ad with little tear-away nubs at the bottom with the phone number and address. It was for a little photocopy place not far from my parents' house, and I tore off one of those phone number nubs and shoved it in my pocket with the entire jeweler's ad.

It was then I knew what I had to do. If I wanted to win her, I had to sacrifice. I had to sacrifice big time. I had to stay in my room in my parents' basement and save my rent money for this ring.

And also I had to find out her name.

CHAPTER 6

IN DREAMS

The dream comes in four parts.

Wait.

Before we get to the actual dream, let me tell you about my mother because one of the parts is about her and so really you should have some idea sort of what she's about.

My mom got married at eighteen, right out of high school, to my dad. So you feel bad for her right away, right? You would for sure if you knew my dad.

Okay, so you gotta understand that I love my mother. What kind of person would I be if I didn't? My mother cared about me. She did. She cared about all of us, me, the twins, even Brian. And even right up until the end, I think she really cared for my father. But my mother is just...

I can't think of the best word for it. But, aloof, maybe? Flighty? She's just really out there, kind of disconnected from the rest of the world.

Both my parents were ridiculously permissive, but my mother was more permissive in the way that she couldn't have kept track of us even if she'd wanted to. She just wasn't the coddling, teaching, child-rearing type. So why she decided to have four children (granted, they only planned on three) I'll never understand.

See the thing about my mother is she lived in her own reality, one that ran mostly parallel to this one, except occasionally it would veer away for a few days. In my mom's reality things and time moved so fast that she was constantly trying to keep up, whether by remodeling the downstairs bathroom quarterly, or repainting the living room and the stairways three times a week, or trading in her current vehicle for a new one on the thirteenth of every month. I'm exaggerating a little, but it was seriously almost like my mom was on smack all the time and had to keep going, going, going. But one thing I can say for that is the house was always clean, and even if my mom was out doing who knows what, there was always dinner on the table.

Did you ever hear of *Amway*? My mom sold it. Did you ever hear of *Melaleuca*? My mom joined. Did you ever hear of *Team Builders*? My mom was a member. Any pyramid scheme you can think of, my mother was a part of it.

She had her own business ventures too, ways to make tons of money with hardly any work. And we all know how successful those plans always are. The thing of it was that she was always moving on to the next idea before even getting the first one off the ground. Y'know?

She had this idea for a restaurant that she wanted to open, and so she drew some sketches of the interior and made up a menu and scouted some locations and looked into the necessary permits, and then she steam-cleaned every carpet in the house. And this was all in one afternoon.

But the next morning she was bored of the whole restaurant idea and wanted to open up a pet salon, where she could do some dog grooming, because she loved dogs, even though we didn't have one because my dad was allergic. And she went to town on that idea, drawing up plans, analyzing costs and all that while basting a turkey. But by the time she went to bed, she had decided she was going to be a hairdresser.

This was how her life went day in and day out for years. Idea, idea, idea. One right after the other. And she kept them all in a folder. Or actually in a series of folders, in a series of filing cabinets. And I wonder where all those files are now, because there honestly were some pretty good ones in there that someone actually could turn into profitable businesses, and I don't remember what we did with the cabinets (if we even found them) when we cleaned out the house.

So we flew one time from St. Louis to New York City. We flew United, I think. Maybe Northwest. I don't remember exactly, but which airline it was isn't really relevant anyways. In any case, it was just a connection in St. Louis. We never left the airport. But that doesn't really matter either.

I was by the emergency exit. On the flight to New York, I mean. You have to be at least fifteen to sit there, and I was, just barely.

Once we were in the air, I fell asleep. A short sleep, but long enough to enter that REM stage, where you start to dream. And so I had a dream.

So the dream comes in four parts, like I said.

Here's the first...

Remember the girl? The one with the chestnut hair?

We were having a picnic.

Only it wasn't exactly that we were having a picnic together. It was like I was watching her have a picnic by herself. On this cliff over this swimming hole, like something out of Mark Twain.

I was there, watching, but she couldn't see me.

After a minute or so, she stood up and dove head first, still fully clothed off that cliff and down into the water. She just looked sleek and gorgeous when she resurfaced, and I hung above her in a tree, just watching.

And this was before I met her for the first time, you know. This was like a premonition or prophecy or whatever of things to come. I knew it meant something, this girl swimming around below me.

Then comes the second part, the part about my mom.

In this part of the dream I was like six or seven years old, even though I was fifteen having the dream, and it was late, like ten or eleven at night, which is really late for a six or seven year old. And I was out playing in the middle of the street, which we all know a six or seven year old should not do. What I was actually doing in the middle of the street or what the appeal of the middle of the street actually was is unclear, but it's not really relevant anyways.

So I went into the house and everything was dark, except for a light coming from the kitchen. And in our house you entered into the living room which was wide with a door straight ahead, but you went down the other end and it opened into the dining room, through which was the kitchen.

My mother was standing there at the sink, looking out the window.

You know that Donald Duck cartoon where he meets that girl duck and they fall in love and everything's great and they get married? Then right after they get married, he comes into the kitchen in the morning and the girl duck is there in this ratty pink bathrobe (at least that's the way I remember it), bags under her eyes, coffee in one hand and cigarette hanging out of her mouth, and her hair is in these nappy barrettes. And Donald Duck's like really freaked out.

Well, that's how my mom looked in the dream, only not a duck. Which was weird because my mom didn't smoke. And like Donald Duck, I was totally freaked out.

"You're late!" She shrieked in this unearthly voice.

"Sorry."

"Get to bed." She pointed to my bedroom.

Oh, yeah. And also she had this big metal colander on her head like a helmet, through which her barretted hair sprouted.

I slunk to my room and crawled into bed, and I was almost asleep when the whole room filled with this green light. I sat up, and as soon as I did this burlap potato sack was brought down over my head and I was swept off the bed by what I can only assume were aliens. I never did get to see them because I was swept into the third part of the dream.

In the third part of the dream I'm careening through downtown traffic. By downtown I'm talking about Salt Lake City's downtown, but this isn't Salt Lake City, not exactly. It's futuristic downtown Salt Lake. All the buildings are made of glass, but I don't think it's really glass but just looks like glass, but also it looks like metal. Actually when I look closer it's like it's all aluminum, but translucent aluminum, and there's some big kind of celebration going on that the whole city's getting ready for with lots of lights and signs and banners and whatever, but all that's neither here nor there.

But I say I'm *careening* through downtown traffic, because I have no brakes in my car. It's some futuristic kind of automobile that has no brakes and because I'm not from the future I don't know how to drive this thing. I do have a gas pedal though, so I'm trying to regulate speed with just that, but we're approaching a traffic jam.

By we I'm talking about me and this heavyset girl that's been chatting my ear off since I escaped from the aliens, who's sitting in the passenger seat. I've never met her and I don't know why she's driving with me.

You know who it was?

You know who it was.

So I've got to steer away from this traffic jam since I can't stop, but where am I going to go? And then I see it, this driveway hill thing, but I'm going to have to cross three lanes of oncoming traffic to get to it. But I have no choice.

And on the other side of this driveway hill is a huge mansion. And the driveway is like this hill like I said, where it goes up and then down on the other side into this kind of dip, then up slightly again straight into the mansion. So it's like that bowling ball game at the arcade or at Chuck E. Cheese's where I've got to apply exactly the right amount of pressure to the gas pedal to make it up over the hill so I don't roll back into oncoming traffic, but not so much that I smash right through the front of the mansion on the other side.

I'm sweating. I'm nervous. And the girl in the passenger seat won't shut up.

I gun the engine to clear the three lanes of traffic and hear the screeching of tires and honking of horns as I reach the edge of the driveway hill.

And now the test.

I apply pressure, a little at first and then a little more. I try to gauge whether I need a little more, and the girl keeps talking, and I put my hands together in front of my mouth, and I close my eyes, and I say something of a prayer to someone I don't believe in, and I press a little harder and release, and I hope and we roll. And we're going forward, forward, up and forward, up and forward, down and forward, down, and straight, and up, and up, and...

Backward. Whew!

I open my eyes.

An old woman runs out of the mansion. It's Sarah, Marty's Sarah, and she's cursing me.

I get out of the car and realize I'm standing in the middle of a giant chessboard. And I look again and Marty is coming out of the mansion, only he's young in his military clothes, and Sarah's young now too, like in her picture. And he puts his arm around her and kisses her on the cheek.

And the girl gets out of the passenger side of the car and pops the trunk. Inside, bound and gagged is that girl with the chestnut hair. The hefty girl slams the trunk shut and points at me.

Then I'm on a train, and it's raining, and this is the fourth part of the dream.

"Cut!" I shout, and I don't know why.

Then I realize that there's a camera next to me, and there are two actors in front of it.

"That's a wrap!" shouts some sunken-eyed fruitcake ten yards away. "That was amazing," he says as he walks toward me. "This is going to be awesome."

I'm still gathering my bearings, so I don't respond right away. I just look around and realize that this is not a real train. It's a set. I'm directing this film, and it ends on a train in the rain. And we've just wrapped.

"You were born to do this, Warren," says the guy. "This is your destiny."

I just stare at him.

Then I look around.

Every light on the set is pointed directly at me, and everyone is looking at me, and I'm looking into every pair of eyes at once. And the sunken-eyed one speaks again:

"When people ask you 'Who is Warren West?' what are you going to tell them?"

And the answer comes to me, and I'm about to speak when the sunken-eyed one pushes his glasses up on his face and smirks. Then he starts to speak again:

"Ladies and gentlemen, we are beginning our initial descent into JFK International Airport."

CHAPTER 7

Marty was born on the fourth of July in his parents' home above a small grocery store in Idaho. His father was a produce man on the ground floor. Actually not only there, he was a produce man for several little markets, but he operated mainly at this store and so they lived in a room above.

Marty's childhood is interesting enough, I suppose. They moved all over with whatever new career his father had. They lived above the grocery store. They lived near a machine shop and filling station, where his father pumped gas and, at age eight, Marty first got his hands under the hood of a car. They lived in a switch house, y'know for the trains, next to the railroad. They lived on a farm. No career lasted more than a couple of years.

When I first heard all this, I thought Marty's father sounded just like my mother, but he wasn't switching around jobs all the time because he was restless. It was because he was an alcoholic. Actually, it was because he was an alcoholic and an ornery old cuss who couldn't stand to work under anyone else. So he'd get fired and they'd all move somewhere new, and he'd start a new career.

I don't think Marty had a lot of respect for his father, not the way he talked about him anyways.

One time, right after he took my queen, I looked at that picture on the wall, the one in the whole military getup.

"You were in the army?" I asked him.

He chuckled. "No, I was never in the army."

"But that picture." I pointed.

"Merchant Marine."

Army, navy, air force, Merchant Marines, I didn't know the difference.

"'d'you fight in the war? In a war?"

"How old would you say I was in that picture?"

"I don't know. Eighteen, nineteen."

"I was fifteen," he said.

Young people in old pictures always look a lot older than people the same age today.

"It was World War Two," he went on, "but I never technically saw combat."

"They let you join the army at fifteen?"

"Merchant Marine. I told 'em I was eighteen. There was no way to check back then, or they didn't make an effort. Not like nowadays."

"Why?" I asked.

"Why what?"

"Why did you join the... What are the Merchant Marines exactly?"

"You've got to get the supplies to the soldiers somehow, haven't you?" he said. "We ran the cargo ships out across the Atlantic, takin' 'em food and weapons and whatnot."

"So you weren't technically military then." I think this offended him.

"As much military as anyone! We were in just as much danger. Our ship got hit by an air raid. I could've died several times. By the grace of God I wasn't on one of those ships sent to deliver supplies at Normandy. You know how many of us were killed in that war?"

I shook my head.

"A lot!" was all he said.

"Did you get any medals?" I asked after a healthy pause, trying to brighten him up a little bit.

"Hmph," he snorted. "I don't even get veterans' benefits. Nothing. Like the government's completely forgotten us. Not a damn bit of respect for any of us who risked our lives aiding in the defense of this country."

I tell you he said this, not to be political, but because he repeated this a lot, that Merchant Marines never got a thing for their service despite putting their lives at risk every day.

But I think Marty'd be pissed if I didn't stress also that he loved his country despite its problems. He was a true patriot, and he was very proud of the fact that he shared a birthday with the United States. He'd remind me of that all the time.

"So why'd you join?" I asked again.

"I didn't have anything better to do."

"You didn't have school?"

"I dropped out of school in the sixth grade. It was a different time. That was..." he trailed off. "I had a job making deliveries. Year and a half later we up and moved again back to Idaho, Rexburg. There I had this buddy Joe, was the same age as me. Said we'd join together, the Merchant Marine. So we go on down there, and they pull us into separate rooms for the physical examination. An hour later we come out and I'm an official member of the Merchant Marine, and come to find out Joe chickened out and told 'em he was only fifteen, but he didn't snitch on me, so I was stuck."

"No way," I said.

"Joe says he didn't pass his physical, but that's impossible, and later on he admits he chickened out."

I ask him what the Merchant Marines was all about, like what they did exactly for like training and everything, because I'd never heard of them. I don't remember the exact conversation, but he told me about what it was all like.

Apparently they lived on like a big ship in the ocean down at Catalina Island, and every morning at five a.m. they'd wake up and the first thing they did was jump over the side of the boat into the icy cold water. There was one guy, I forget his name, who was always scared to go over, and every morning he'd run to the edge of the boat and screech to a halt, looking down into the blue. And he'd just be there, like frozen. And this was how it was with him every day, until finally one morning Marty runs out behind him and tackles him over the edge down into the water while all the other guys are laughing and hollering.

Marty got KP duty or something, some kind of punishment anyways, for that, and I don't see why, because it was the other guy that wasn't following the rules.

"That's life," says Marty, even though I don't think it should be that way. "You can't expect it to be fair, 'cause it's not."

In the Merchant Marines, where Marty spent two years of his life, he met another soldier (or, I guess, Marine) from an area in Idaho not far from the city Marty lived in last he'd heard.

This guy's name was Hyrum Coldwell and his father owned a bakery.

And when they were together, Marty and Hyrum, doing whatever, like scrubbing the floor or brushing their teeth or whatever, Hyrum would tell Marty all about what it was like working in the bakery, and all the stuff they baked there. Like in that one movie where they're training for the army and the one guy just keeps talking about shrimp forever and ever.

Honestly, that's probably not at all what it was like and that's just how I see it because I'd seen that movie not long before Marty told me this story. But what prob'ly really happened was one time Hyrum told Marty about the bakery, and since Marty and Hyrum were such good friends and Marty had nothing really waiting for him at home, he thought it would be cool to go work at the bakery after he got out of the Merchant Marines.

I wonder if I could just start calling it the Marines, instead of the Merchant Marines, or if it's so specific that you have to say Merchant Marines every time. I don't know, but every time Marty said it he used the whole name, or actually he did what I guess is an old person thing where he left off the "s" and referred to the whole troop or corps or whatever as just the "Merchant Marine."

Anyways, what Hyrum neglected to mention to Marty was that his father, who owned the bakery, was not a very honest man and therefore not a very decent employer.

Abe Coldwell, that was his name, did hire Marty on the spot when he and Hyrum strolled into town, duffels slung over their shoulders. Marty ran the mixer, y'know for the dough, for something like eighty cents an hour.

"And it weren't easy work," he says. "And Old Abe, he was a terrible man to work for."

"So how come you stuck at it? Why didn't you just quit?"

When I ask that, Marty winks at me. "One day you'll understand. Checkmate."

I look down at the board. He's right. I have lost again, and one day I will understand.

"Well," I say, and I stand up from the couch, "I guess I'll see you next week."

"You practice between now and then, maybe with one of those fancy computer programs," he points at me with his curved, arthritic forefinger. "Let's see if you can't beat me for once."

As I reach the front door something catches my eye, something I've noticed before but never really seen. Marty's marriage license. It's old and yellowed, must be what, at least fifty years old now, but it's held up well under the glass.

I look at the names:

Martin Daniel Page and Sarah Coldwell.

CHAPTER 8

JUMPING THE OFF PLACE

I didn't really like the guy much at first. He was kind of arrogant, and he had an opinion on everything that he always had to share, whether you wanted to hear it or not. And see, also Chris is one of those sunken-eyed fruitcakes that speaks in hyperbole[1].

When I first met him he was taking me to look at an apartment. It was four years, give or take, after that failed attempt that took me to the mall and got me a job at the copy center. And I was finally getting out of my parents', well, my mom's house. I'd gotten tired of looking on my own, and I heard about this little rental company just down off the freeway, where they don't charge you anything to take you around to their apartments.

I walked in to the office and he was sitting at the main desk with a newspaper, typing something into the computer. Some other guy came in from the other room with a coffee mug in his hand talking eighty miles an hour: "Hey, how you doin', I'm Rick, are you looking to rent or buy, what was your name?"

"Warren."

"Hey Warren, I'm Rick, look, there's a paper we'd like to have you fill out, I can't find it right now, but it's just to get some basic information from, what are you looking for, a house, apartment, one-bedroom, two-bedroom, studio," while he went on and on he was shuffling through drawers and folders. "I can't find that, hey Chris, do you know where those forms are, this is Warren, Warren this is Chris, listen I'm gonna have him take care of you, you busy?"

Chris just stared at him with a kind of smirk on his face. He opened a drawer and handed Rick a form.

"Here it is, yeah, if you could fill this out, we'll get you going, hopefully we can get you into something today, is that gonna be good, like are you planning to move in today, next week, or what, oh, I forgot, I got another showing today, what time was that at?"

Chris pointed to a huge whiteboard with names and times and dates and whatever. Rick looked at his wrist for a watch that wasn't there. "One thirty, what time is it?"

"One thirty-five. I..." Chris looked like he'd had this conversation a million times.

---

[1] I am not a fruitcake.

"Why didn't you tell me, I gotta, sorry Aaron, was it?"

"Warren."

"Warren, sorry I gotta, I have a showing, so Chris'll take care of you, maybe show him the Lancaster properties or the, well what did you say a two-bedroom, right?"

Chris started chuckling.

"What, dude? Anyway, I gotta go, and hey we're outta coffee, can you get some more going before I get back?" And Rick was out the door, coffee in hand.

"Yeah, if you'll just fill that out, we'll see what we've got," Chris indicated the form I'd been given. "I reminded him about that meeting half an hour ago."

I sat down and took a pen from the cup on the desk and Chris went back to work on his computer. I'd gotten my last name down when the door flew open again.

"Forgot my keys, have you seen my keys?" Rick stormed back into the office.

"Your desk maybe." Chris didn't even look up from his work.

Rick rifled through the top desk drawer, pulled out the key ring, and shot towards the door.

"You might wanna take the apartment key," Chris shouted. "Just an idea."

Rick backtracked to a cabinet and stopped. "Which property was it?"

"Warner," I think is what he said, but that's not that important.

"I'm showing Dan Warner's place? That's like fifteen minutes away."

"Then you'd better hurry."

"Can you call the client and tell them I'm on my way, no you're busy with Warren, did he find you a good two-bedroom apartment? Where you gonna take him? Hey Kev, I need you to call this client I'm supposed to show and tell him I'm on my way but I'll be a little late."

"What?" From the other room swaggered a tall, clean-cut guy named Kevin in a very fashionable outfit. "What do you... Like I'm not busy enough. And you spilled coffee all over the file cabinet in there."

"Oh, clean that up too, thanks, you're awesome, and tell the client I'll be about ten, maybe fifteen minutes late."

"I'm not calling him," Kevin the metrosexual responded.

"Dude, call him, you're great, thanks, gotta run, don't forget to clean up the coffee, sweet, see ya, dude." And Rick was out the door again.

"I'm not calling him." And Kevin retreated to the other room.

"You want me to call him?" Chris shouted after him.

"I'm not calling him."

"I'll call him."

"No, I'll call him," shouted Kevin from this mysterious other room. "I just hate it when he does that to me."

Chris turned to me. "This place is awesome. This is like the best job in the world."

I handed him the form that I'd since filled out in full.

"Awesome," he said and looked it over. I don't see what was so awesome about it, but he used that word a lot. Everything was awesome, even if it wasn't.

He walked over to a closet and pulled out some files with apartments in them. "Here's some options if you wanna look through there, and we'll drive out and check some of them out."

I picked a couple and he got the keys out of the cabinet then disappeared into that secret side room. "Hey," I heard him say through the wall, "I'm gonna take this guy out. Probably be back in about forty, forty-five minutes, so..." Then as he was halfway through the door, "You're not really gonna clean up the coffee, are you?"

"No, I'm not gonna clean up the coffee. He spills half a pot of coffee all over the file cabinet and he wants me to clean it up? It's ridiculous. He can clean it up himself."

The car we drove around in was older than me, and older than Chris too, because we're the same age. Exactly, actually, because as it turns out we were born on the same day, only he was born in a hospital. It was an old, silver Toyota something or other, some car they don't make anymore. And I got yellow fuzz all over in my hair because the headliner was all eroded.

The first stoplight we pulled up to, I noticed him watching the rearview mirror, then all of a sudden he punched the radio preset, which I was kind of disappointed by because I liked the song that was on before. Then he flipped the station again, and again.

"Check this out," he said. And I looked, and he was still staring in the rearview mirror. "That girl behind us is singing along with the radio. I wanna see if we can find out what station she's listening to." And he punched another button. "Nope." And he punched another button.

"She might be listening to a CD," I offered.

"Could be, but let's not give up so easy." And he punched another button. "There it is." Then he started singing along. "You like this song?"

"I guess."

"You don't sing along with the radio?" he asked me.

"No, not really."

"No, or not really? Or not ever?"[2]

"No," I said, "I don't sing along with the radio."

"I don't believe that."

What does he mean he doesn't believe that? He said it so matter-of-factly. Why would I lie about something like that?

But I was lying. I don't know why.

Of course I sing along with the radio. Who doesn't? But that's what I'm talking about. That arrogance. That he just comes out and says, "I don't

---

[2] I don't remember this whole thing, which isn't to say it never happened, but definitely not the first day I met the guy. I'm not a crazy person.

believe that." And there are other things too, not just that. There are other things he does that are just the same type of thing that just drive me crazy.

But he did find me an apartment, and I did learn that he was studying film at the university. And even though I don't believe in education, as I've previously stated, I thought maybe he could help me out. I asked him if he'd be interested in writing my screenplay for me, and he asked what the story was. I gave him a brief synopsis and he seemed really intrigued. He even had a few ideas of his own that I wasn't necessarily crazy about, but the fact that he was excited about doing it and was willing to do it for free was enough for me. And he'd written things before, so that was a good sign.

He even came up with a great title for it:

The Jumping-Off Place

I love that title.

Finally, after three years of mulling this story around in my head, I felt like my movie was getting off the ground, y'know.

And for months after that I'd stop by the rental place all the time and talk over the screenplay with Chris, and that metrosexual had a lot of great ideas to contribute to the thing too.

CHAPTER 9

THE CAVE

At this point I'm nineteen, and this is the fourth encounter.

I'm talking about the beautiful girl with the chestnut hair and the bubbly friend. And I'm happy to say, and you will prob'ly be happy to hear, that the terrible, horrible, no good, very bad friend does not appear in this chapter. So I would like to excise the bubbly friend from my description of the girl, and from now on I will refer to her as only having chestnut hair.

Although this time she didn't have chestnut hair; she'd dyed it.

It was still beautiful, but now it was also just downright hella hot. It was a slightly lighter shade of brown (like she'd used Sun-In or something) and she had these dark red (not like orange-red, but red-red) streaks through it, which is just so...ahh!

Amazing!

She looked so good.

And this is the meeting you may have been anticipating, because I mentioned it briefly already, but in a different context. Actually, I kind of hope you're not anticipating it, because I'm afraid it might not live up to your expectations if they're really high. So I'll tell you now, kind of forget what I said about anticipation, because this chapter may or may not be very exciting.

Let me set the scene for you. Salt Lake City sits in the middle of what we call the Wasatch Front, which is kind of like bookended, y'know more or less, by Ogden to the north and Provo to the south. And the whole thing stretches across the west face of the mountains. Maybe this is the Wasatch Mountain Range, but it's funny, I lived there basically my whole life and I don't know what that range is for sure. Anyways, down near Provo, I think a little to the north if I'm remembering right, is a particular mountain, called Mt. Timpanogos in American Fork Canyon.

So during most of the year, except the winter months where it gets pretty damn cold there, you can hike the Mt. Timpanogos trail, and you can get a tour guide, but I'm not sure if you have to have a tour guide. Anyways, I had one when I went. Maybe you do have to have one; you probably do. And anyways, the tour takes like an hour. Oh, I should say that the tour's not just like this hiking trail. What it is is this tour of Timpanogos Cave.

Honestly though, I'm not sure why I went really, because hiking is really not my thing. Caves are cool, sure, but if I'm going to be in the dark, I'd rather be watching a movie. I mean, I went because my cousin was in town and wanted to go, and I agreed to go with him, but I don't remember why since I didn't really like that cousin. And I feel bad saying that since he was killed in Afghanistan, but I'm going for truth here, right? Maybe I went because he bought me a movie ticket afterwards or something. Or maybe it was destiny whispering into my brain, coaxing me onto that hiking trail.

But here's what happened:

On this tour, like on most tours, there's this part where two tour groups pass each other, and you can see where this is going, I'm sure. Well, our tour was almost over and we were approaching the cave entrance. I could see the light at the end of the tunnel. I don't mean to be poetic or symbolic or whatever. I just mean that that's where we were. And I looked outside the cave beyond all the stalactites and stalagmites, if there were even any of those, and I saw the next group coming toward us.

And in the middle of that next group, on the inside flank, so I could see her perfectly, was the girl. Her hair was pulled back into a pony tail behind her pinkish, radiant high cheekbones. She had on sunglasses but, approaching the cave, she pushed them up over her hairline, and I could see...

I could have drowned in those eyes.

She had on a tank top, ribbed so it clung perfectly to every curve of her body. And capris — strange for a hike, but on her...

She could have worn a clown suit and been a work of art. And I don't mean a Picasso.

But the scene melted into a Salvador Dali painting as I approached, and time trickled right off the cliff face. Everything slowed, and the world almost stopped turning.

Her guide reached the cave's entrance in almost the same instant as mine did. With great care, each tour guide's lead foot inched over the threshold from darkness into light or vice versa. And the crowds slowed even more, trudging along as crowds are wont to do but hardly faster than ketchup spilling onto the burgers of those who wait. I looked ahead at her shimmering hair, those new red streaks positively glowing in the sun that she was leaving behind to engage the darkness, that darkness that I was sacrificing for the light, but not by choice. If I could, I would stay there with her in that cave forever. Even if it meant staying in the dark with no movies. Even if it meant creating new games like the cavemen did; because those would be our games, mine and hers. Even if it meant resorting to cave painting for entertainment; I could cave-paint her portrait, but never with an upside-down triangle body.

I looked at her again.

Or had I been watching her the whole time?

The crowd was slowing still.

I looked into her eyes and I knew what had to be done.

Time stopped completely.

I stepped into the gap between our motionless tour groups and fixed my eyes on hers. Then she moved, raising her head to look at me and our eyes locked like the door to your hotel room just after you realize you left your keycard inside and you're in your bathrobe because you were just going down the hall to get some ice.

She stepped out of her group.

There we stood, face-to-face, just five feet apart. I took a step forward to narrow the gap, and she did the same. It was like our minds were one.

"Hi," I said. "I'm Warren."

"I know who you are," she said. "Warren West."

"Yes. I..."

"Shh." She put her finger to her lips and closed the gap between us. She put the back of her hand to my face and smiled at me, this beautiful smile, this...

Then she wrapped her hand around the back of my neck.

"How did you...know my name?" I asked.

"I've known you for as long as I can remember. You have always been in my dreams."

And I knew something wasn't right. She pulled my head down to kiss me, but I snapped out of it.

When I was back in reality, I was still looking at her and we were close now, about to pass each other at the cave's threshold. She saw me looking at her and eye contact was made.

"Hi." Was all that came out of me.

"Hey," she said with that same beautiful smile from the daydream. Then she scrunched up her face in that *Do we know each other?* kind of way, and we passed. I turned back to look at her and she was looking back at me, probably trying to figure out if we did know each other from somewhere. We made eye contact again, and I smiled. Then I ducked away embarrassed.

As she entered the cave, I emerged on the mountainside, in the daylight, nature surrounding me. I looked out at the canyon and the mountains and the cliffs and the valleys, and I got an idea. That one I already told you about. It was sort of like this, only completely different, but the idea was the same.

For a moment, chestnut hair girl and I were the only two people in the entire universe.

But I still didn't know her name!

I had a thought. I could hang around the gift shop and wait for her tour to end then introduce myself. But that would be like an hour, and how weird would that be to have a guy you've never met hanging around for an hour in a tiny gift shop waiting to introduce himself to you after you've already had a weird moment in passing up by the cave?

Also, I was with my cousin.

But here's the thing: Looking back now, I should have just told my cousin the whole story, about who she was and destiny and everything. Whether he believed in destiny or not doesn't matter. He probably would have helped me hook up with her, because as far as I know, he was pretty smooth with the ladies.

But he was a year older than me, and you know how that is. You always want to impress your older cousins and look like you can hold your own, because they make you think that they can.

So I kept quiet, and it maybe was the biggest mistake of my life, but that's what happened.

CHAPTER 10

TWINS

The trip to New York was the last vacation I think we ever took as a family, I mean all of us. Brian had just miraculously graduated from high school — I'm still not sure how — and New York was where he picked for his graduation trip or whatever.

For me high school was barely underway, and it was not a fun time. In most of my classes I'd sit in the back corner, unless the teacher had an assigned seating chart, which I hated, because I preferred to just kind of keep out of sight and quiet so no one would bother me.

I got good enough grades, and I probably could have gotten into almost any university I wanted, even with scholarships to some, but college was never something I aspired to. I hated, hated, hated formal education.

As soon as I turned sixteen, which was at the end of my sophomore year, I got a job at the local multiplex. I started as an usher and did that for about three months, then I worked concessions for a month or so, then I got my dream job as a projectionist. That meant getting paid to watch movies, even if you were seeing the same ones over and over again. It also meant that I got to take home the promotional posters once the movie went on to second-run theaters. Unless it was a big movie that everyone wanted the poster for, then we'd put our names in a hat and draw. Usually for those really big ones though, there was at least something for each of us to take. And for the really, really huge ones, we got special buttons, and sometimes hats and t-shirts.

Working at a theater though, the thing I hated was when a movie came out that I really wanted to see but it didn't come to our chain, and I actually had to pay for a movie ticket somewhere else. And so talking during movies is annoying, but if I had to pay for the ticket then I was ultra-pissed. At this time, thankfully, cell phones weren't all that common, so it was rare to hear one go off during your film. If one did, you always just assumed it was a doctor getting an emergency call, and so it was okay. It wasn't this feeling, like it is now, that you want to stab the person in the eye with a shish-kabob skewer.

But I did work at the theater during the whole laser pointer phase. I don't know why anyone ever thought that was funny.

Anyways, before I tell you about this next part I've gotta say that I'm not a racist. And I know that when someone says that, it usually means they are racist and are probably about to do or say something incredibly racist, but that's not the case here. Also, I'm not sure which is politically correct, because I once heard that African-American was right, but then because we don't say European-American we shouldn't say African-American, so I heard then that black was P.C. I don't really know, so I'm just going to say black.

And I honestly really wish that there was another black character that I could tell about somewhere else in this book. You know, some good guy that would balance out this bad character. That's what they do in movies. Like if there's a bad American Indian character, they'll put in a good American Indian character because they don't want to hurt anyone's feelings.

But whatever. This is just a little story about Derek and not about Derek's race. And let's call it fictional so I don't get sued, even though it's completely accurate, and let's also say that any resemblance to any real person, living or dead, is purely coincidental. And clearly Derek is a made-up name.

So anyways, I hadn't even been working at the theater for three months before I was called into the manager's office and told that someone had reported some discriminatory behavior on my part. The manager said he had no choice but to send written documentation about the incident to corporate headquarters. And he needed me to read and sign the write-up.

I couldn't believe what I was reading. Derek had gone to the manager complaining that I had been making racist remarks. I didn't know what he was talking about until I read on. Derek had heard me singing that song from the cartoon movie about the flying elephant. You know, the song about the housefly and the dragonfly and the needle that winks its eye. Well, I guess that because I sang the song in the same accent as the crows in the movie that I was being racist. I didn't even know how to respond to that. I wasn't being racist. I was singing a song.

My manager said that he didn't put much stock in this write-up himself, because Derek had filed a similar complaint about just about everyone working there. He stopped just after saying this and told me that this was all off the record and if I ever repeated it to anyone he'd deny it. Then he went on to tell me that he recognized that a guy like that was poison for the morale of the rest of the staff. But what could he do?

"If I were to even address the issue, he'd just file a complaint against me," he said. "Then, because I'm a manager, I'd probably be fired. And sued."

"That doesn't seem fair."

"That's life," my manager said, even though I don't think it should be that way. He was a decent enough guy though, my manager. He'd just had a baby, I think his second. He couldn't afford to lose this job.

The truth of the matter, as I learned, is that Derek just loved to get offended. He was that kind of person, and he walked around with this big Pringle on his shoulder and waited for something, anything, he could possibly construe as racist. Sometimes he'd even trap people, y'know, steer the conversation to a place where no matter what the other person said, Derek could twist it into a racist remark, then he could confront them.

I guess it's just a good thing he's not also a lesbian midget, because then he'd really have the minority market cornered.

Now, the thing is, Derek wasn't all bad. I don't want to paint him that way. He was just mostly a jerk, but sometimes he was actually very nice. But the whole write-up thing really caught me by surprise because I had thought, up to that point, that Derek and I were on really good terms. In fact, he'd never given me any indication that he didn't like me, and we sort of had some things in common. Like we both had seen just about every movie ever made and neither of us really liked our father. Also, Derek was an identical twin (his brother lived back east somewhere, I don't remember where), and I have twin sisters.

⁂

Ashleigh and Kara are about seven years younger than me, which means that I was almost seven years old when they were born, and I wasn't too excited to have them. They came into the world screaming and it seemed like they never stopped. They were so whiny and needy, always. And the real problem is that I was the one that always had to take care of them.

By the time the twins were born my dad was so burnt out on the whole parenting thing that he was just coasting through it, I think wishing that he could go to bed one night and wake up eighteen years later and we'd all be out of the house.

And my mom wasn't taking care of the girls for the same reason she never really raised Brian or me, because she wasn't capable. And also her myriad businesses had really taken off once the twins were weaned, at least in her mind. Not like she was bringing in any income at all, but she never saw things the way everyone else did.

And what was Brian going to do?

So that left it all up to me, didn't it?

Not so much that from age seven I was putting food on the table, or even preparing food for the table. My father was bringing in the money, but he was spending more and more time at work, including weekends. And my mother still never forgot to cook dinner. But it did leave me to provide emotionally, and when they got into kindergarten and first grade and so on, it meant that I was the one helping them with their homework and all that.

The worst, the absolute worst, was when Ashleigh got her period. She got it before Kara, which I don't know why, but I just assumed that since they were identical twins they'd get it at the same time, right? But I guess that's not the case.

I mean, just imagine to yourself being nineteen years old and having your little sister come up to you and tell you that she's been bleeding for three days.

And why didn't she know what was going on, is my question. I mean, yes, I guess she got it earlier than most girls, I guess, I don't know. But I remember when I was in elementary and we had the maturation program. And they were separate, boys in one room, girls in the other. So I don't know what they tell the girls in that thing, but they've got to tell them about ovulation and cycles and all that. But maybe she didn't go to that thing, or maybe she didn't even go to school very often for all I knew, because no one was really keeping track of all that.

And I wondered why my mom hadn't said anything, because she still did the laundry all the time, and you'd think she would have found something and talked to Ashleigh about it. But apparently Ashleigh was embarrassed and had thrown out her bloody underwear so no one would find out what was going on. And of course my mom didn't notice that Ashleigh's laundry loads were missing anything.

So one day I came home from the copy center and got on the internet to download music on Napster, back before all the lawsuits — but of course only songs I already owned on CD, because otherwise it would be stealing and therefore wrong. And it was taking forever on my 28.8 connection. And so while I waited and watched the little bar slowly fill to 100%, Ashleigh came into the room and sat down on my bed.

"Can I talk to you for a sec?" she asked.

"What, you need help with your homework? I'm busy right now, can we do it in like half an hour or so?"

"I need you to take me to the hospital."

"What?" I turned around. "What for? What's wrong?"

"I don't know." She looked like she was about to cry. "I must have sat on something. I'm bleeding a lot, and it won't stop."

"Bleeding where?" I asked.

She turned bright red and squished up her face. "From my..."

"Oh!" I shouted, and I thought, Well then I wish you wouldn't sit on my bed. "Oh, I see."

"What?"

"No, it's, umm, er, it's like... Okay, so... How old are you now?"

"Twelve."

"I thought..." I had no words. "Umm, it's, don't worry about it. Okay, this is... What we need to do is go to the store, not the hospital. Maybe mom can take you."

"Mom's not home," she said. "Why do we need to go to the store?"

"This is perfectly normal," I tried to explain. "When girls reach a certain age, I thought it was a lot older than twelve to be honest, they get what we call their period. And what that is... When's mom coming home? How do you not know about this?"

Ashleigh shrugged.

"Umm..." I tried to think how to do this. "Let's get in the car... Can you bring a towel or something to sit on? ...and I'll explain it all on the way to Albertson's."

I don't need to tell you what I told her because you probably know all about it, and if you don't, go ask your mother. But we more or less pretty much cleared the whole thing up in the car.

CHAPTER 11

LOVE STORY

Marty leads with his center pawn, the one in front of his king, and moves it two spaces forward. This is when I make that move, the one I told you about, where I take out my pawn from the edge of the board, queen-side, and move it forward two.

We've been playing for a couple of years now and I'm getting better. Today I'm going to win.

My move confuses him. He doesn't know what to do. He looks at the board, focuses on my pawn and then looks up at me. I raise my eyebrows. This is probably the longest it's ever taken him to make a move. He eyes the board again, and I can almost see the synapses firing inside his brain.

He rolls his fist under his chin, cracking all the knuckles, then extends his forefinger up in front of his lips.

He looks at me again.

I am going to ask him today. He's told me a lot of stories over the past couple of years, but he's been mysteriously silent on the subject.

He makes his move, what I thought he'd do. He brings out his king-side bishop to the edge of the board.

I had realized when I tried this open against myself that my second move had to bring out my knight or I'd be mated in like four or five moves. So I park the knight behind my pawn.

Marty still hasn't recovered from the open. He is searching for his move and trying to make sense of mine.

"Can I ask..." I tiptoe around the question, "...I never heard. What happened? I mean, how did..."

He looks up at me, that forefinger hooked over his lips again. His eyes are patient. He knows what I'm going to ask.

"Sarah," I say. "How did she die?"

He makes his move. King-side knight out to the edge, a mirror image of my move.

Perhaps I rush my next move, king's pawn forward, and I look him in the eyes again. He smiles at me.

"I don't remember," he says then looks down at the board.

"Do you miss her?"

"You're young," he says as he brings out his queen. "Do you like fairy tales?"

I know the story he's about to tell me. I've heard it before, but I'll indulge him.

"I like true stories," I say.

"This is both."

♀ ♀ ♀

Marty had been working for Abe Coldwell for almost a week before Sarah came into the shop. She had been away with some relatives and was just returning to town. He was the only one in the store when she dropped by. He wiped the flour from his hands and greeted her with a smile that she returned.

And he knew.

He knew.

She introduced herself and asked for her father. Marty said he'd heard all about her, even though he hadn't, and told her Abe had stepped out. He'd probably be back soon if she wanted to wait.

She respectfully declined the invitation, and as he watched her walk away from the bakery, seventeen-year-old Marty said to himself, "I'm going to marry that girl."

When Old Abe and Hyrum returned to the bakery that afternoon, Marty immediately pulled Hyrum into the back room.

"You never told me you had a sister."

"What, is she back?"

"She came in looking for your father."

"So?"

"So," said Marty, "invite me to dinner tonight."

"What? Why?"

Marty gave him that look. I'm sure you know the one.

"Oh, I see." Hyrum grabbed a bag of flour and carried it to the mixer. "Yeah, I don't know. I don't think you're the kind of guy I want with my sister."

"What?!"

"I'm kidding. Of course you can come to dinner."

So Marty went to dinner, and I guess he must have made an impression, because he and Sarah started seeing each other frequently. He spent a lot of time at the Coldwell residence and he felt like he was getting along great with everyone.

Marty was in love, there was no other way to say it and he knew he wanted to marry this girl, and he thought she felt the same way, but he had nothing to offer was the problem. He was running the mixer at her father's bakery making only like eighty cents an hour.

So Marty decided to ask for a raise.

He went into Abe's cramped little office one afternoon and stood in front of the desk.

"What is it?" Abe asked. "I'm very busy."

"I just, I'd like a raise."

"Why do you need a raise?"

Marty figured now was as good a time as any.

"Because I want to marry your daughter Sarah, sir," he said. "And I want to be able to provide for her."

"I see." Abe looked at Marty over the top of his spectacles. "And do you think you deserve a raise?"

"Yes, sir. I never come in late. In fact, I'm usually here early, and I usually stay late to make sure everything gets done." Marty was flustered, but he kept on. "And also, I've never missed a day for illness or any other reason."

"Yes, but you've also only been here for five months, Mr. Page."

"Yes, but if I'm not mistaken, we've improved efficiency almost threefold in that time, sir. And it's provided you with more time to spend at home with your family."

"And I'm supposed to thank you for that?" the boss asked. "With more money?"

"I would appreciate it, and I'm sure your daughter would too."

Old Abe stared him down for a moment. "All right, I'll put it on your check this week."

"Thank you, sir."

And Marty started to leave, when Abe stopped him.

"And you think you deserve my daughter?"

Marty turned back to the old man.

"No, sir."

That was all he said.

Abe nodded at him, and Marty left the office.

He spent the evening with the Coldwells again, and when he had the chance he pulled Sarah into the other room so they could be alone.

"Your father's going to give me a raise," he told her.

"Good." She looked confused.

"So I'll be making more money."

"I understand. That's what a raise means."

"So we can get married."

She gasped. "We haven't…"

"You want to marry me, don't you?"

She stood there in silence for a moment, and Marty's heart started to drop down into his colon.

"Of course I do," she said. "Yes, I do want to. I just hadn't thought, we hadn't ever talked about it."

"The first time you walked into that bakery I knew I was going to spend the rest of my life with you."

She smiled at him. "I love you." And she threw her arms around his neck and pulled him in for a pretty good kiss.

"Mmm," Marty said as they parted, "I love you too."

And he went back in to turn that pretty good kiss into a really great kiss. And as they stood there wrapped in each other's arms, making the most (and I do mean the *most*) of this moment, suddenly the light came on in the room.

"Ahem."

And they split to find Old Abe standing in the doorway.

"Dad, nothing was..."

"No, I'm sure." Abe scratched his chin. "Marty, maybe it's time you went home."

"Yes, probably," Marty said and looked at Sarah. He smiled at her then looked at Old Abe wondering what the etiquette was here exactly. Finally, he settled on a quick kiss on the cheek (Sarah's cheek, not Abe's) and darted from the room.

On Monday, when Marty got his check, there was no raise.

He went to Abe and asked about it, and the response was simply, "Oh, with all that went on that day, I guess I forgot to put it in. I'll make sure it's on next week's paycheck."

And the next Monday, still no raise.

So Marty went to Abe again.

"Oh, yeah," Abe explained. "It'll be on next week's check."

The next Monday, Marty looked at his check, and you're sensing the pattern now.

Marty went to confront Abe again, but the boss rushed past him into the restroom.

Marty crunched his check in his fist and leaned over the counter thinking about what to do. He scratched his head, face turning redder and redder, then finally he slammed his fist on the counter and stormed into the restroom.

He raised his foot and kicked in the door to the lone stall.

Old Abe looked up from his magazine in shock.

"Wipe your ass with this!" Marty shouted as he chucked the crumpled paycheck at his boss then stormed out of the room.

♀ ♀ ♀

I'm laughing so hard, I'm gonna fall over and die. "So what did he do?" I ask, even though I know the answer.

"What?" Marty looks at me across the chessboard. "What did who do?"

"Old Abe," I say, now confused.

"Old Abe?" He looks truly perplexed. "Old Abe died a long time ago."

"I'm sure."

"He was my boss at the bakery."

"Yeah, so what did he do," I ask, "when you threw your check at him?"

"When I did what?"

He looks down at the chessboard, makes his move. "Checkmate."

No! I lost again? I thought for sure I'd win this time. But by this time I don't care about the game. "So what happened next?"

"What do you mean?"

"In the story."

"What story?" he asks. "I win again, Hyrum."

"It's Warren."

"What's Warren?"

"I'm Warren."

"Yeah, since when?" He looks toward the kitchen. "I wonder if Sarah needs help getting lunch ready."

"Marty!"

"I should go see if she needs help with those sandwiches."

"There's no one in the kitchen," I say, getting nervous now and wondering if I should call an ambulance or something.

He starts to rise from his chair.

"Marty!" I shout at him.

He looks at me.

"Well," he says. "You practice again before next week."

I bite my tongue between my front teeth looking from side to side, almost wondering if this isn't some kind of joke.

"Take some candy if you want," he says. But I don't want to break my teeth so I don't.

Slowly I get up from the couch and make my way to the door.

He waves. "See you next week."

CHAPTER 12

THE CONVERSATION

It's sort of like a rap song only it's not about bitches and ho's. And also it's more melodic. And the beat isn't quite so prominent. The other thing is that it doesn't really rhyme most of the time. So I guess it's maybe more like jazz, only with a little bit of a spoken, y'know, rap kind of feel.

That's what the soundtrack to my life would be, if there was like an orchestra following me around all the time scoring everything I did.

See, because it's a syncopated four-four rhythm in a minor key with a blues progression. Of course there are different melodies and moods depending on what I'm doing and where I am and who I'm with and whatever else, so it's not always syncopated and it's not always four-four and it's not always bluesy, but the main theme is like a four-bar vamp with all that stuff I said. It starts off high and drops in a series of eighth-notes with a triplet at the bottom, then a half-note a step higher before it ramps into a swooping series of sixteenth-notes and a glissando back up to that top note to repeat again. And it's a blues progression like I said, so four times on the one, then two on the four, and so on.

And over that, any narration would be provided in rhythmic speech, though most of it's sotto voce. But in the most reverent of passages, there's a solo soprano singing in Latin.

♀♀♀

I walked into Rent-EZ[3], an upbeat cut from my soundtrack echoing off the mountains to the east, and it put me in a good mood.

"No, I'm sorry he told you that. He shouldn't have told you that. That's not how it works." I could see on Chris's face that he was about to explode. I don't know who was on the other end of the phone, but he wasn't happy with them. "Umm, the money has already been sent to the

---

[3] Not the actual name of the company.

landlord and you signed the contracts, so this is between you and the landlord now."

He looked up at me and held up a finger.

"No! I'm sorry. You're not listening to me. There's nothing we can do. I don't know who you talked to, but it wasn't me. I'm not even a licensed agent, I can't..." He paused for a second. "Yes, well thank you, same to you."

And he slammed the phone down. "Who's running this company?!"

"No one." Kevin spun around from the desk across the room.

"This is like the second worst day of my entire life." Chris said.

"What was the worst?" Kevin asked.

"I don't know, but I'm sure there was one. But this is pretty bad!"

"Yeah, check this out," said Kevin, carrying a flier or something I couldn't really see and handing it to Chris. "This is one screwed up advertisement, if I've ever seen a screwed up advertisement."

"Have you ever seen a screwed up advertisement?"

"I have not. But if I had, this would be it."

I just looked back and forth at the two of them, wondering if this was some kind of inside joke or if this was some kind of queer version of the Gilmore Girls.

"Anyway," Chris said, "I'm gonna take off for lunch."

"Where you going?" Kevin asked.

Chris looked at me. "Where we going? Melvyn's cool?" I nodded. "Melvyn's."

"Bring me back a cheese steak."

"Groovy." Chris grabbed his jacket. "Half or whole?"

"Half," said Kevin. "And a Coke, medium."

We left the office.

Melvyn's was right around the corner, actually in the same building but around to the other side. "Best cheese steak I've had outside of Philadelphia," Chris said. "You like cheese steak?"

I shrugged. "Never had it."

"You gotta try the cheese steak."

I got the cheese steak and had no idea it was a sandwich until they handed it to me. Turns out what it is, is like this thinly chopped steak with peppers and onions and mushrooms and cheese. And at this place, I don't know if they do this everywhere, they sprayed it down with salt water while it cooked.

We sat down at a corner table, and Chris just dove right in head first into the conversation.

"So I've been thinking about how to structure this thing and I was thinking about starting it in August, though we don't have to actually say this specifically, like we don't have to show a title that says 'August' or anything, but if we did maybe we could change the title to *August and Everything After* because that's the title of a Counting Crows album, but I don't know because there might be some issues with copyright, even though I know you can't copyright a title, but using the title of a CD for a movie, even though it's not like based on the album or anything, but maybe, anyway we'll probably not change the title, it was just a thought. But that's the idea. It's laid out like along a specific timetable, where each sequence takes place, see I was thinking originally that it would be every year, but that didn't work, and I thought maybe every six months then, but it couldn't be so regular each time because the events were too spaced. So I thought we want everything to be kind of summery weather, so we can shoot it all at once, right? So the first sequence is in August, the second in May, the third in August, then May, August, May, like that 'til the end. What do you think?"

"This is a good sandwich," I said.

"I told ya. So what about the movie idea?"

"I don't know. I don't see exactly..."

"Okay, so like the idea you had for them meeting on this cliff, right, it happens in August. And I mean we never really have to tell the audience this, time could just pass. This could just be for us as the filmmakers. I mean, I don't know. But then you said you didn't want them to meet again for a while, so I thought like nine months later they run into each other. And check this out, I was thinking the second meeting is at her apartment, because he's just moved into town."

I stopped him. "What do you mean he's just moved into town?"

"Oh, right," he said. "I forgot that was my idea. I was thinking this was part of what you told me about your whole outline. I get mixed up because you haven't given me anything like written down. So I was thinking he's a photographer, who's here in Utah, if we decide to set it here, but that's something we can discuss later, but he's wherever taking pictures for some magazine. And she lives here, and after they meet, he's so into her that he decides to transfer."

"What, his job just transfers him wherever he wants to go?"

"Well maybe he works freelance or something, right? So he can move wherever he wants."

"Okay, maybe."

"And so while they're up on this cliff he snaps a shot of her and gets her address so he can mail her a proof or something, right?"

"No," I finally said. "It's too contrived. The second time, it has to be coincidence."

He was talking so fast the whole time, I guess because he was so excited about the thing. Chris doesn't get excited very often, but when he does it's like he goes totally crazy, and it's hard to even catch half of what he's saying. Also because he slurs his speech a little, like he's got sort of a thick tongue.

But here he paused. I thought he was pissed that I didn't like his idea.

"Okay," he said, and then paused again. "Okay. But here's the thing. You can't just say coincidence and expect an audience to buy it. It doesn't make sense."

"But that's how it is in real life." I was becoming indignant. "That's how it has to be. What inspired me to make this thing happened just like that."

"You don't have to get defensive. I'm just saying..."

He sat there squinting for a while, and I half-expected him to stand up and overturn the table, throw his hands in the air, scream, "Then I'm done!" and storm out of the deli.

So I asked him, "You upset?"

"No." He shook his head. "Why would I be upset?"

"You look upset."

"I'm just thinking of how to make this work."

He sat there squinting for another minute. Then he looked at me and said, "Okay, so here's the thing. Just because something happens in real life doesn't mean an audience will buy it. You see what I'm saying? It has to make sense. It has to be logical."

"I don't agree," I said.

"You don't have to agree, but I'm telling you..."

"Listen, this is the way it has to be."

"Why?" He was so condescending with that question. "No, seriously. I'm being serious. Why does it *have* to be that way?"

"Because that's the point of the whole thing."

"I don't understand."

"That's because you don't want to understand!"

"No, I'm trying to understand," he said. "Maybe... Okay, you said this is based on real events. Maybe tell me what those events were, so I can better understand where you're coming from here."

"No, I don't want to tell you about that right now, but just trust me. This is how it has to be. It's like the point of the whole movie."

"So it's like the theme?"

"Yeah," I said. "I guess."

"Okay, so what is the theme?"

"It's about two people and how when they're in love it's like they're the only two people in the whole entire universe."

"That's not a theme," he said.

"Yes, it is. And it's about how when you're in a relationship each person has to sacrifice and compromise to make it work and if you're really in love you'll do anything to make it work."

"That's not a theme either." He stared at me waiting for a response, but I didn't give him one. So he went on. "A theme is like, say 'love' could be a theme. 'Sacrifice' could be a theme. 'Compromise.'"

"Okay, so destiny is the theme."

"Okay, so destiny," he said. "Okay, so then I can see why the coincidence is so important to you. Okay, so now we have to figure out how to make it work and be believable. What is it you're trying to say about destiny?"

"What do you mean?"

"You gotta take your theme a step further and turn it into a premise, like what are you saying about destiny exactly? What does destiny mean to your characters?"

"It brings them together," I said. "Look, this is just your school book learning talking, and I don't care about this stuff. You just figure that out for yourself and whatever. Just, the coincidence is vital. It has to be that way."

"Okay," he said, sipping his Coke, "then let's figure out how to make it work."

He sat there eating his sandwich, not saying a thing, for several minutes. Then I think I literally saw his eyes light up.

"I have it," he said.

He smiled this huge smile like he'd discovered the meaning of life.

"Okay, so let's say we stick with the thing about him being a freelance photographer."

I started to interject, but he stopped me with a "for now."

Then he went on. "And he does snap a picture of her, but he doesn't ask for a phone number or address. It'd be too obvious anyway I think. So they separate and don't see each other for nine months. In the meantime, and we don't see this, the guy, let's give him a name."

"Eric," I contributed.

"Eric. Okay. And the girl?"

"Stacy."

"Eric and Stacy. Works for me. So Eric does move to Utah, if we're setting it here, or wherever. Because he is taken with her, and he wants to find her, so it's like there is some effort being made, but what happens is this. One night Stacy is driving home from work, and let's say she's a workaholic, so she's on her cell phone the whole way home making deals or putting together proposals or something."

"What does she do for a living?" I asked.

"What do you want her to do?"

"I don't think it really matters."

"Okay, then she's a lawyer."

"I don't like lawyer."

"Okay," he shrugged and looked up at the ceiling annoyed. "She's in advertising. How's that?"

I nodded.

"So she's in advertising," he went on. "She's working on a proposal on her phone while driving home, and she gets stopped at a railroad crossing, which is good imagery, the arms coming down and all that, and the red lights flashing alternately. It'll look really good. So anyway, a car pulls up behind her, and she flips on the light inside her car so she can get some more work done while she's stopped, and Eric is in the car behind her, and he recognizes her when the light comes on, so he goes up to the car and they reconnect. So you've got your element of chance, destiny, coincidence, whatever you wanna call it, and also he's done some work to make it happen. How's that?"

Actually, it sounded pretty good. "Yeah, okay."

"And it's nice because we've already naturally got this interesting dynamic going with Stacy being a workaholic, a career gal, and Eric being the kind of free-flowing anyway the wind blows kind of guy."

"That's pretty common in these types of movies though, this opposites attract thing."

"Yeah, and there's a reason for that." He raised his eyebrows at me.

"I don't want this to be like every other movie."

"Well then," he said, "let's find some way to flip this whole thing on its head."

He crumpled his sandwich wrapper into a little ball and stood up from the table.

"Well good," he said. "I think we got a lot done here, came up with some good ideas and found a good compromise. I feel good about this."

I didn't feel so good about it. Yeah, we found a compromise, but what he'd forgotten is that this was my idea, this was my destiny, and I shouldn't have to compromise.

CHAPTER 13

THE RING

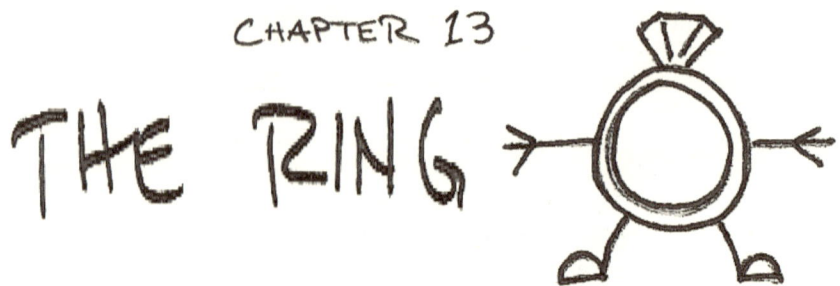

I'd been working at the copy center for almost two years now and I'd been saving every penny. I mean, I'd been saving every penny except the ones I spent to go see movies, and actually I'd just bought my first DVD player, which was like a hundred and fifty bucks, and of course a few DVDs and also a new television and surround-sound speakers for my new kick-ass bedroom setup. But I'd been saving most of my money for that ring, the one in the advertisement. And I probably had enough to buy it, I'd assumed, because the copy place paid pretty well, even if it wasn't the funnest job. I couldn't have spent that much on movies and stuff I figured, and I was still living with my mother, so I wasn't paying any rent. So I for sure had to've had enough money, but I wasn't positive so I had to go check at the bank.

Let me tell you something though, living at home with the twins was really starting to wear on me, because they had now both entered puberty. It was almost like at age twenty I was already the father of two teenage girls. So I was getting impatient with destiny and with the universe in general right now. Why couldn't I find this girl? Then it hit me.

Maybe I had to take the first step. Maybe I had to take a leap of faith. Maybe I needed to sacrifice instead of just waiting on the universe to do all the work. What I needed to do was buy the ring then destiny would lead me to the girl.

I wondered if she still had those red streaks in her hair. Or had she done something new now?

But I would buy that ring.

I mean it sort of made sense, right? And it wasn't like it was really a gamble, because if she arrived in my life today, I'd marry her tomorrow. I mean, I'd marry her tomorrow if that was alright with her, but she'd probably want this big, lavish wedding that she'd been dreaming about since she was like six or seven years old or maybe even before that. And she could have it. She could have anything she wanted.

I wondered if she felt the same way as I did, knowing that I was the one she was destined to be with but not knowing how to find me. I wondered if she was out looking for me or if she was sitting around waiting for me to reappear in her life.

But I was tired of sitting around, so I went to the bank. I'm not going to tell you the advertised price of the ring, but I will tell you that I had more than enough money to pay for it.

I took that folded-up advertisement that I'd been keeping in the back pocket of my jeans for the last two years and unfolded it. The jeweler was in Fort Union, so why the ad was posted in Sandy I don't know, but I drove up to Fort Union anyway, to the address listed on the sheet. I drove past, and I couldn't find it. So I turned back and tried again, still with no luck.

So what I did was I parked the car and walked down the street, looking for the number on my ad. Finally, I saw it, tiny above a mail slot, and I looked up at the business it was connected to, some insurance company. I double-checked the street name; it was the same. I cocked my jaw and stared at nothing.

"You gotta be kiddin' me," I said to myself.

I went into the insurance company anyway to see if maybe the jeweler had moved to another location or something. The receptionist was on the phone, so I waited. I looked around the office, and it was pretty boring. There was a fake tree in the corner, next to two uncomfortable-looking wireframe chairs and a little square table with a couple of *Reader's Digests* and a rack of insurance pamphlets. The receptionist's desk was the only one in the room.

I can't remember exactly what she was talking about with whoever was on the other end of the line, but I was pretty sure it had nothing to do with insurance. And I'm sure she wasn't in a hurry to wrap it up, because she glanced at me in my holey jeans and ratty t-shirt and knew that I wasn't here to purchase an insurance premium.

I refolded and unfolded and refolded again the ad, then passed it back and forth from hand to hand, staring at the floor. She was probably getting annoyed.

I noticed one of those 3-D art computer-generated things behind the desk and stepped closer to see what was hidden in it. It was kind of far away, so I leaned over the desk, squinting, trying to adjust my eyes.

"Hold on just a second," the receptionist said into the phone. "Can I help you?" She looked at me like I was not only responsible for the rising gas prices, but also for the entire national debt, and maybe also global warming.

"Yeah." I suddenly felt ashamed, and I fumbled with the ad, trying to unfold it. "Umm, I'm looking for…" I got it open, "…this jeweler."

"They went out of business eight months ago. Is there anything else?"

"Were there any other locations or was this the only one?" I asked.

"What do I look like, information? I don't know, I think this was the only one."

"Thank you," I said, but I don't think she heard, because she went immediately back to her phone call. I slunk out of there as quickly as I could.

I got back into my car and pounded my fist against my forehead in a rapid rhythmic movement. I'd waited too long. What was I going to do now?

Well maybe it didn't have to be this jeweler, just this ring. The mall was just up the street, so I decided to stop in there and see what could be done.

Going in, I deftly avoided the food court and went right into the center of the mall, where there were it seemed like three or four different jewelers facing each other. I went to the first and talked to the woman at the counter. I showed her the ad and asked if they had this ring.

"Umm," she said, "we don't have that exact ring, but we do have some like it."

"No, I don't want anything like it. It has to be this exact ring."

"Well, we can do a lot of custom rings."

"Great, then I want this one."

"We have to see. She pulled out this big book. That's going to be a very expensive ring."

"I know," I said. "The price is right here."

"Well, that price is for the band and a cubic zirconium in the center. You're going to want to set that with an actual diamond, and that looks like a three-carat, so that's going to be expensive, and to have it custom-made..."

"I don't care. It has to be this ring."

"Okay, look," she said, pointing at some pictures in her book. "We've got this band, which is really close to what you're looking for."

"No," I said. "You're not listening to me. I don't want close. It has to be exact. It has to be exactly this ring."

"I understand that, but what you want is going to be really expensive and we're going to have to basically create that design just for you, which I don't know if you can afford."

"Okay, fine. I'm just going to go somewhere else."

I walked straight over to the other jeweler across the way and had basically the same conversation with the guy there. And then I had the same conversation with the other jeweler and over the next few days with many, many other jewelers, and no one had my ring, and no one could custom-make my ring without creating a new design, which they all said would be expensive.

And also during those next few days I learned how much a good three-carat diamond costs.

And I thought that was a bunch of crap that they put out this ad with a price on it but that price doesn't include the diamond! I hate that kind of thing. Because seriously who's going to buy a ring like that without a real diamond anyway? It's total misrepresentation.

So I went from having more than enough money for the ring to not having nearly enough money for the ring without spending a dime.

But it had to be *that* ring. It had to be.

So I was just going to have to keep working and keep saving and stop spending, which meant I couldn't go to movies and I couldn't buy any more DVDs, and because that's what it took, that's what I did.

So there was like this twelve-month stretch at the end of 2001 through most of 2002 where I didn't go to the movies once. It practically killed me, because I was used to seeing four or five movies a week. And so the only things I saw were the ones my sisters rented and brought home, and I wanted to strangle Mary Kate and Ashley, but I have to admit that I did sort of like that one with Mary Poppins in it, where there's this girl who finds out she's a princess or something. But I'd never admit that to anyone else.

But after like another year or so I was finally able to buy the ring, and I had to have it specially ordered and it did cost a lot of money.

But the thing is, and you don't have to believe this if you don't want to, but the day I picked the ring up from the jeweler's I saw her again, and this time I learned her name.

CHAPTER 14

CLASS

I pulled up in front of my parents' house, to the curb, where I usually parked unless my dad was out of town on business, then I took his space in the garage. But on this day he was in town — well, at this moment anyways, he was in town — so I had to park along the curb.

I got out of the car and pulled that jeweler's ad from my pocket and unfolded it. I pulled the little nub with the copy center phone number on it out of the middle. I was going to call them immediately.

I walked through the front door and was promptly accosted by my father. "Where have you been?"

"What?" I said. "I can go wherever I want. I don't have to tell you everything I do."

"Where were you?"

"I was at the mall, Jeez."

"Spending what money? Mine?"

"No." I paused in disgust. "Mine. I just bought a pair of pants, and I found this," I held up the nub, "help wanted ad. I'm going to get a new job."

"About time you got a real job." He was really starting to piss me off. "Where's your mother?"

"I don't know. Getting a new business license maybe." I don't remember what her project was that day.

"It's Saturday. They're not... They don't do those on Saturday."

"They don't?"

"I don't think so, no. So where is she?"

"I don't know!" I shouted and went into the family room and flipped on the TV.

"Don't just walk away from me," he shouted as he followed me in.

"Leave me alone," is all I said before an empty cereal box flew in from the other room and nailed my dad in the face.

"Who ate all my pops?" came Brian's voice from the kitchen, which was weird because it wasn't even a Corn Pops box he'd thrown. It was like Smacks or Berry Berry Kix or something, I don't remember. I just remember that it wasn't Corn Pops.

Then Brian burst into the room in a fury, punching things with his fists and kicking things with his feet. "Gotta have my pops!" he shouted.

Things were breaking left and right at the hands of my idiot older brother.

"Can't you get control of him?" my father shouted at me.

"Oh, that's my job?!"

"It's not mine!" he screamed. "Not anymore. I'm done with this. I'm done with all of you." And he left the room.

"Brian, quit it," I said, and he stopped. "Where are Ashleigh and Kara?"

Brian shrugged.

"Whatever. Fine," I said and put in a VHS tape.

I heard things banging around in the master bedroom, but I was too mad to investigate. I just watched some Italian movie about a guy in a World War II concentration camp. It was a pretty good movie about this guy who loves his wife and kid so much he'll do anything for them, which I found terribly appropriate given the current climate of my household.

My father stormed through the room with two huge suitcases. He threw open the door to the garage, hefted his suitcases through it and turned back to me. "Have a good life," he all but shouted in his most sarcastic tone.

And he was gone.

Somehow I knew this was real, but I wasn't letting it sink in yet, and I definitely wasn't letting myself care. He was a jackass anyway. And the only thought I let into my head was, Well at least now I get to park in the garage.

⊊ ⊊ ⊊

I watched the rest of my movie in virtual numbness, and I may have cried at the end, but only because it was a sad movie, and for no other reason.

As the tape ran out and rewound itself, the screen went to static, and I just stared at it.

I fingered that nub from the copy center. I was rubbing it so much the phone number was starting to smudge. I would call them in the morning. No, tomorrow was Sunday. I'd call them first thing Monday morning.

I don't know, maybe five minutes, maybe five hours later, Ashleigh came home.

"Hey," I said. "Where've you been?"

"None of your business," she said.

"Okay."

"Why are you just watching fuzz?"

"I don't know."

"I wanna watch a movie."

"Okay."

"I'm gonna watch a girl movie."

"Okay," I said. And we watched a girl movie.

"Where's Kara?" I asked later.

"She's sleeping over at Kelsey's."

"Good," I said. "Do you know where mom is?"

"No."

"Okay."

"Hey listen," I said when the movie was over. "We might not ever see dad again."

"Why not?"

"He left." I paused, trying to see if she understood. "I mean..."

"I know what you mean. I'm eleven years old." And she stormed out of the room.

I was eighteen, and I didn't even know what I meant.

I didn't know where my mother was, and I didn't want to know, because that was a conversation that I really didn't want to have right now. I didn't see her that night, so I just went to bed.

♀ ♀ ♀

When I woke up, my mom was cooking breakfast like she did every Sunday morning. I stumbled into the kitchen wondering if she knew, if my dad had called her or if I was going to have to tell her.

She scooped a spatula-full of hash browns onto a plate in front of me.

"So did your dad have to work late again last night?"

She didn't know.

"No. Umm..."

How was I going to tell her?

Then I just blurted it out. "He left with two big suitcases, said 'have a nice life' and he was done with all of us, and I don't think he's coming back."

"Hnh," she said like I'd just told her that we were all out of skim and she was going to have to drink one-percent.

"Hnh?" I said, almost in a rage. "You can't just say 'hnh' and move on. Your husband left you and he didn't even tell you."

"It's not like I wasn't expecting this to happen."

"You can't just say that. You have to break down and cry or scream or something."

"What good would that do?" She put some sausages on my plate. "Oh, I have these swatches I want you to look at for the family room."

"I don't want to look at swatches."

"Then I'll just pick one myself."

"You don't want to talk about this?" I asked.

"There's really nothing to talk about. Your father's been seeing another woman for a long time. We haven't slept together in the biblical sense for years..."

"I don't need to know that," I interjected.

"And he's never been much of a father to you kids anyway. Speaking of which, does everyone know?"

"Brian and Ashleigh know, but Kara spent the night at Kelsey's."

"Oh, is that where she is?"

I just took my head in my hands.

"Well, will you make sure and tell her?"

"Me? You're her mother!"

But my mom just smiled and poured me a glass of orange juice.

Then she did something I don't think she'd ever done, ever. She tousled my hair, pulled me in, and kissed me on the top of the head.

When Kara came home I told her, and her reaction was about the same as Ashleigh's only she was much angrier and kicked a hole in my bedroom wall.

Surprisingly enough, our lives pretty much went on like they always had. My father did send checks to my mom, but there was no return address on anything, so we didn't really know where he was. We found out that he'd quit his job for Boeing and had been hired by some other company, we didn't know which. We also assumed he was now living with this other woman my mom had mentioned, though none of us children had known anything or seen any evidence of this relationship.

The truth was simple though...

My father left us a long time before he really left us.

CHAPTER 15

FREQUENCY

Over time, I'd gotten pretty used to Marty having episodes when I came to visit him. It didn't happen every time but it happened often enough. And as it happened, y'know, over and over again, you just kind of realized that it would pass.

What I was worried about was Marty being alone in that house all the time. I'd told my dad about that first incident and he'd called the police or a doctor or someone. The government wouldn't send anyone around, like a social worker, to check on him but they didn't hesitate to take away his driver's license. I guess they did have someone examine him once and they decided he was still fit to take care of himself, so a few people from the neighborhood agreed to take turns looking in on him, which I'm sure he just hated, but he never said anything to me about it.

What I wanted to know was why his kid wasn't taking care of him.

It had been a few months since that first episode and I'd heard probably most of his stories several times over, but I didn't mind hearing them over and over because they were good stories and I knew he really liked telling them. I don't remember if he really told me this next part on this occasion, but he might have and I might as well pretend that he did just to keep this thing as linear as possible.

So Marty held out his two fists and I tapped the left one maybe — black.

He led with his king's pawn out two spaces, just like always.

I decided to try my luck with my crazy move, queen's flank pawn out first.

Marty looked at the board like he'd never seen such a thing even though he had several times now, but it really seemed to shake him up. He hooked his forefinger over his lips and looked at me. He smiled. With his other hand he brought out his king's bishop all the way to the edge of the board.

"Obviously," his lips moved around his finger, "I couldn't work there anymore."

♟ ♟ ♟

Like Marty said, you don't kick in a bathroom stall when your boss is on the can, throw your check at him, and expect to still have a job.

Marty was always good with his hands and had a very technical mind, so he got hired on pretty quick as an apprentice mechanic at the auto shop, making more than he made at the bakery, quite a lot more. And over the next few weeks, he tried everything he could think of to get in touch with Sarah, but Old Abe prevented them having any contact at all.

One day Hyrum came into the auto shop. Marty looked up from under the hood of a Ford or something and waved.

Hyrum walked right up to Marty and decked him in the face.

"What the hell?" shouted Marty, grabbing his jaw.

"Stop calling."

"What?"

"Stop calling. Stop coming by. My dad told me what you did."

"So what exactly did Dishonest Abe tell you?" Marty asked.

"Dishonest Abe. Are you trying to be funny?"

Marty shrugged.

"He told me," Hyrum said, "that he caught you feeling up my sister in a dark room. That's... I have a problem with that. We don't do that."

"I did no such thing. And even if I had..."

"My father saw you."

"Your father is either lying or he was seeing things, because... Well either way, he's remembering it wrong and I did nothing inappropriate. I've always treated Sarah with the utmost respect."

"You understand," said Hyrum, "that we believe sexual relations should be reserved for marriage."

"I understand and respect that, and I'll wait forever if I have to."

"So why'd you do it then?"

"I didn't! Listen to what I'm tellin' you. We just kissed. That's all. Ask Sarah."

"That's not what my father says."

"I know." Marty was getting annoyed now. "You've said that."

"Swear to me."

"What, are we in the boy scouts?"

"Swear to me that you didn't touch her."

"I swear."

It was one of those moments then, where Hyrum stood there still fuming, but his blood pressure falling like Keith Richards from a coconut tree.

"I love her, you know," Marty said finally.

"I wish there was something I could do, but my father..."

That night Hyrum went home and talked with his sister. She told him that she'd begged and pleaded with her father to let her see Marty. He knew Marty's intentions and told her that it would be over his dead body that Marty and Sarah would be married, and in a fit of anger she told him she'd have it no other way. It was then that he told her she was not to leave the house.

After some long hours of deliberation, Hyrum realized that his father was wrong, and that his sister loved this man. This man that Hyrum himself had served with for two years and trusted with his life. And this man loved his sister, and even deserved her if any man did.

And Hyrum came up with the plan himself. It was a simple plan. Little risk for either of the lovers, but for Hyrum it was like throwing himself in front of the train that delivered the flour and supplies for the bakery. He'd just have to hope that that train, meaning Abe, didn't kill him.

The plan was as easy as telling his father that he was taking Sarah with him to see some new baking equipment at some bakery in Boise, because that was basically what the plan was. She'd been shut up in the house and wanted to get out for anything, even to look at the newest culinary technology. Abe didn't even question it; he trusted his only son implicitly.

Marty was waiting at the shop with his bags packed. He climbed into the car and shared the purest kiss with his true love. And they held hands in that most innocent way all the way to Boise.

When they reached the state capital, Hyrum handed Marty all the money he could spare. "Thank you," said Marty. And Sarah threw her arms around her older brother, tears streaming down her face.

"We'll let you know," she said, "where we end up."

Marty put his arm around the waist of his soon-to-be wife and smiled at Hyrum.

"You're both sure about this?" Hyrum asked.

They looked at each other, smiled and looked back at Hyrum.

"Yes."

"Thank you again," Marty added.

Hyrum tipped his hat and got back in the car. "Gotta go see this oven," he said. "Exciting stuff." And he drove away, knowing what he was going to face when he returned home. But these two would be happy, and that was more important than anything that would happen to him.

♀♀♀

Marty and Sarah were married in a chapel right there in Boise and then made their way down into Utah, where Marty got a job as a full-time mechanic. Seven or so years later, Sarah gave birth to a seven-and-a-half-pound baby boy. Telling me that story was the first time Marty ever said anything about his son.

They named him...

"Steven!" Marty looked at me over the chessboard. "Steven, it's your move."

"It's Warren. My name's Warren."

It was happening again, but I was more calm this time. I was used to it.

"Steven Hyrum Page, I don't need any of your lip."

Sometimes it was just best to play along.

"I'm sorry."

"I don't know why you don't respect me anymore, but I wish... If you only knew how much this hurts your mother, this anger between you and me."

I made my move, and he made his.

"Checkmate," he said.

"Checkmate," I repeated in surrender. I lost again!

"I'm doing everything I can to reach you, boy. But you just keep pushing me away."

"I'm sorry," was all I could think to say.

"If you'd just try a little harder."

"I'll try harder." I wished I knew what he was talking about. "I'm gonna go help mom with the dishes."

"Yes," he said. "You should do that."

And I got up and went into the kitchen and out the back door. Whenever I did things like this, I wondered how long it took him to recover and what exactly happened in his mind after I left. But hell, I didn't even understand what was happening in his mind while I was there.

CHAPTER 16
THE
BREAK-UP

He ended up working on the damn script for like three and a half months, which I thought was ridiculously excessive. I thought he should have been done in like three weeks maybe. But anyways, he finally finished it, and we were going to go get some dinner while we talked about pre-production. So Chris picked me up and when I got into the car he tossed the manuscript into my lap. I had not read it yet.

"Where you wanna go?" he said.

"I don't care. Someplace cheap."

My bank account was still recovering from the purchase of an extremely expensive, but extremely worth-it, diamond ring, even though I'd had it for over six months now. And since I was now paying rent, I was really working to balance a budget.

"Cheap it is," he said.

A minute later or so we were on a main road and I noticed a bank I'd never seen before. It must have been new; it looked new and it wasn't in the phone book.

"Hey, can we stop by that bank?" I asked.

"That's not even your bank."

"No, but I need to stop in there."

"What for?"

"Does it matter?"

"It's almost five."

"They're prob'ly open 'til like six or seven anyway," I said.

"Fine."

He pulled into the parking lot and we went inside and got in a pretty long line. I looked around at all the loan officers and tellers. Someone came out of the bathroom and I turned immediately to see who it was — just some old lady.

After about ten minutes, we got to the front. "Is there an Allison that works here?"

"Not at this branch," the teller said.

"Thank you." And we left.

Once we were outside Chris looked at me.

"What was that all about?"

"Nothing," I said, and we got back in the car.

We arrived at Denny's prob'ly like four or five minutes later and we were seated almost immediately. I skimmed the menu, quickly decided, then traded it for the manuscript.

I loved the first scene, probably because I could picture everything in it, because I'd figured out where I'd shoot it. And also, it said everything pretty much that I wanted the first scene to say, and I could just picture the beautiful chestnut-haired girl in the role. Hey, maybe she was also an actress and would show up to the auditions, and then it would be like my one destiny colliding with my other destiny into this like mushroom cloud of fate.

Anyways.

And the second scene, while I'd been skeptical when we discussed it before, actually worked. And he was right about the imagery. I could see it in my head while I read it and it actually looked really cool in there.

The whole thing was just over ninety pages, so it only took me about an hour to read. Chris just sat there opposite me, eating his food and getting refills on his soda and watching my reactions.

By the time I got to the end, I was really, really, really annoyed. It was like he didn't get it at all.

"This isn't what I wanted," I said.

"This is what we talked about."

"No, it's not! I told you I wanted this to be like an exploration of relationships, a journey into one couple's feelings for each other, with a focus on the fact that they're destined for each other." I was almost screaming.

"Okay, yes, and I thought I did that," he said. "But you have to also have a story. [You can't just have these two people sitting around talking about what it's like to be in a relationship.]"

"But this, what you've written, it isn't even like a real relationship. This is like kitschy, contrived crap."

"Have you ever even been in a relationship?" he asked, in this dry, condescending way that made me want to reach across the table and strangle him.

"Okay, no I haven't. But I've seen enough of them and I've talked to enough people to know that this is not what it's like. And the dialogue is ridiculous. It's kitschy and awful," I told him.

"Hmm, okay, I don't agree. And you keep saying kitschy," he said.

Then he just sat there, staring at me.

So I was like, "You just don't even understand the whole point of this thing."

"[Well, for the number of meetings we've had and the number of times we've discussed this, if you can't get me to understand, I don't see how you're going to get an audience of a couple hundred people to understand what it is you're trying to tell them.] I thought we were on the same page here." He picked up the screenplay. "I thought this was exactly what you wanted."

"Well, I guess you were wrong."

"I guess I was."

We just sat there for what felt like several minutes.

"Okay," Chris finally broke in, "so let's go back to the beginning here then. What is it you're trying to do with this?"

"It's an exploration into the nature of relationships."

"You keep saying that, but I don't understand what that means. I thought I did, but I guess I don't."

"I mean," I said, "that it's supposed to be like philosophical, where the characters learn what it is that brings them together."

"So you want them to actually talk about their feelings, like outright?"

"Yeah, like in that first scene you wrote, that's exactly what I'm going for throughout the whole thing."

"In the first scene they're just meeting. It's okay for them to talk like that, because they're each trying to impress the other and appear, y'know, intellectual."

"Exactly," I interjected. "Intellectual."

"You can't intellectualize feelings. That's why they're feelings. When they meet, they talk this way, but once they get deeper into the relation-ship, those feelings become internal and they're going to feel them and act on them, but what they're not going to do is talk about them."

"But that's the point of the whole thing."

"You've clearly never been in a relationship," he all but shouted.

"So what? I don't see how that has anything to do with anything."

"You want a script where two people sit around and talk about their feelings for each other and wax philosophical about the mysterious forces of the universe that have brought them together. Am I right?"

"Well not the way you say it—"

"That'll be the most boring movie ever made."

"Well that's the way it has to be. And let's talk about the ending. This isn't at all the ending I told you I wanted."

"Yeah," he said, "but when I got to the end in the writing, that just didn't work, what you wanted. Every romance movie in the world ends on a train or in the rain or on a rooftop or in the airport. Every single one."

He's such an exaggerator.

"But that's how this one has to end," I said. "So you need to rewrite this whole thing the way I told you and I want the ending the way I said, on a train in the rain, and the rhyme is just a coincidence."

Then he flipped out. "You can't tell me what I *need* to do. Look...

I will not end it on a train
I will not end it in the rain
I will not end it on a boat
I will not end it with a note

I will not end it in the park
I will not end it in the dark
I will not end it here or there
I will not end it anywhere

I will not write this script, Warren
I think the idea's boring
Now see? I've used an almost rhyme
This movie is a waste of time

Get someone else to write the script
Really, Warren get a grip
Another almost rhyme. You see?
Do this project without me.[4]

"This is my purpose," I responded. "It's the most important thing I'll ever do!"

"[You're not going to say anything that hasn't been said before.] And I don't understand why you keep saying this is what you were born to do. It's just a movie!"

That was what he said, right before he stormed away from the table. He left me there with no ride, so I walked home angry. That last thing he'd said really killed me. And I don't know why I cared so much about what he thought anyways.

♀♀♀

"Were you serious about finding someone else to write the script?" I asked when I called him up the next morning.

"You have it in your mind what you want but you're not communicating it to me. And you have no idea what the hell it is you're talking about," he said.

"And you do?"

"Whatever. You have no story. Whether I know how to write it or not is beside the point."

"Beside the point?"

"[You're so self-important with this thing. 'This is the way it has to be.' 'This is so important.' 'People need to hear this.'] Come on! You want my help, you have to realize that this is a movie, it's not anywhere near as important as you think it is."

He just didn't understand that this was my purpose in life. He just didn't get it, no matter how I tried to explain it to him. I couldn't make him see the vision.

"You just want to turn it into a Hollywood thing," I said, "an eye-candy piece of entertainment crap with no substance."

"With your budget, this is no 'Hollywood' thing." He paused, then added, "You're such an artiste."

"What is that supposed to mean?"

He didn't really have a good answer for that [...except, "You think everyone is interested in what you have to say, just because you're saying

---

[4] I never spoke in rhyming verse, but the point is there.

it. You live in your own little fantasy world vacuum occupied by yourself and probably some intellectual elitist friends who sit around dreaming about changing the world, instead of actually doing it. You don't care about giving people what they want, only about giving them what you want them to have. You might as well paint pictures to hang in your closet or write songs to sing to yourself in the shower for all anyone else is gonna want to see this."]

[...]

"Well just because you don't have a creative bone in your body..." I shouted.

And I slammed the phone down.

I didn't talk to him again for a long, long time.

CHAPTER 17

A SIMPLE PLAN

I didn't want anyone else in the house to know that I'd just spent thousands and thousands of dollars on a wedding ring for a girl that I hadn't even officially met yet. So when I pulled into the garage I went immediately down to my bedroom in the basement.

It was almost uncanny, I'm telling you, but I sat down on my bed, opened the ring box, and while I was staring at this staggeringly illogical leap of faith in the palm of my hand, I reached over and clicked on the TV.

So this was 2002, and at this time America found itself in the middle of something that would change the world forever.

No, I'm not talking about the pre-Iraq War "fact" gathering or the post-9/11 investigations. I'm talking about the first season of *American Idol* on the Fox Network.

Now actually the first season was over by this time, and I'm not trying to tell you that the chestnut-haired girl had been on the actual show. But what I am trying to tell you is that as a result of the unprecedented success of *American Idol*, every single local broadcasting entity tried to create an *American Idol*-type show of its own. There was an *"Idol"* for just about everything. There was an Idol for Utah, for the cities of Sandy, Kearns, Bountiful, and Salt Lake, among others. I mean I think there was one of all these, but I really could be lying or making stuff up or remembering it all wrong or whatever. But that's not even the point. The point is that there were all these different idolatrous contests. Radio stations held competitions, TV stations did, even furniture stores with taglines like "We're searching for Utah's next singing sensation, and you can search for sensational savings at Woods Cross Furniture," or whatever the company was.

I'm sure your area did the same kind of thing, probably.

But this, this is where I first learned the name Allison Shepard.

I almost didn't believe it myself. There I was in my room staring at a diamond ring I'd bought for this chestnut-haired girl I'd only seen a handful of times in passing, then I looked up at the TV screen and there she was with her name in bold print right there, half-covering her beautiful face like she was gnawing on the banner, "Allison Shepard, Bank Teller"

It didn't say what bank, but now I knew what she did for a living, and maybe I could find her. All I had to do was go to every bank on the Wasatch Front.

I also made a vow to myself that I would watch this show, whatever it was, every week so I could see her face and hear her angelic voice. But she performed and was kicked off immediately, so I didn't have to watch it anymore and I've forgotten what the show was even called. I thought it was unfair, though, that she was eliminated so quickly, because I thought she sounded great. I guess the judges didn't agree, which is okay, because if she'd actually become famous and sought after, it would have made my task of getting close to her just that much harder.

But now I had my mission: Track down that bank teller, Allison Shepard.

I dashed up to the kitchen for the Yellow Pages and practically collided with my little sister, one of them.

"Hey," said Ashleigh, "I need help with this math homework."

"I'm not good at math," I told her.

"Well this is easy math, and I can't do it myself." She was in eighth grade, so really I probably could help her with whatever it was, but I was on a mission.

"When did school start up again?" I asked as I rummaged through the cabinet under the microwave and pulled out the phone book.

"About two months ago."

"Uh," I clutched the phone book to my chest and headed back to the stairs. "Can we do it later?"

"I have other homework too."

"So then do that now, and we'll do the math when I'm not so busy."

"What are you so busy with?"

"It's none of your business," I snapped.

"Jeez, fine."

And she slammed the book down on the kitchen table.

"What's all that noise about?" my mom screamed from the other room.

She was home? She must be wallpapering or something.

"Warren won't help me with my homework," Ashleigh whined.

"Warren," my mother said, "help your sister with her homework."

"I'll help her later, I told her that, when I'm not busy," I shouted.

"What are you busy with?" my mother asked.

"Nothing. I'm just busy."

"Help your sister with her homework."

Ashleigh smirked at me.

"Give me an hour," I said.

"Mom said now."

"Please, Ash, give me an hour."

"If you tell me what you're so busy with."

"Nothing."

"Mom!"

"All right. Gosh, you're a brat," I said. "I have to... I'm looking up all the banks around."

"Why?"

"Just because."

"Because there's some girl that works at one of them?"

"Hgck," I coughed. Why would she even guess that? Had she been watching the singing show on the upstairs TV? "No. Because I need a new account, because of this... It doesn't matter, I need a new account, and I'm trying to find which is the best. Okay? One hour."

She looked at me skeptically and left the room.

I went back to my room, and what I did was I tore out the map from the front of the phone book and I got out a really fine-tipped ballpoint pen, and I sat down at my desk, which actually was small and a mess, so I had to clean it off first, which meant, because I was excited and kind of in a hurry, that I just kind of swept the stuff onto the floor, except some of it that I stacked up and just transferred onto my bed, then I was able to set down the city map and the phone book on the desk, so that's what I did and I sat down.

I opened to "banks" and the entry was over six pages long, which might not seem like a lot until you consider that the pages with big ads on them probably still had like fifty entries and the ones without ads, with just tiny print, contained several hundred. And there was also a little box with "Related Categories to consider..."

And this was just the Salt Lake book.

I looked at the ballpoint pen in my hand and then down at the little city map, the one I'd torn from the phone book, and realized that there was no way that I was going to be able to mark all the banks on this tiny thing, even if the point of my pen was very fine.

What I needed was a much bigger map, a pen with a finer tip, a lot of pins (the kind with the round colored heads), a Snickers and a Coke. But the thing is I knew how to tackle this problem, because I was an avid player of the board game Risk, if you know that game. And even if you don't, I was still an avid player.

I didn't need a jacket, because it was warm outside that evening, so I didn't take one. And I also didn't have to grab my keys, like people say "I grabbed my keys and headed out the door," because I had my keys in my pocket like I think most people who wear pants with pockets and have keys usually do, but maybe I'm wrong. So what I did was I headed out the door without grabbing anything, then I pulled my keys out of my pocket before I got into the car even though it was unlocked, because I don't like when I forget and kind of have to twist around in the seat and stretch out in a position awkward even, I'm sure, for a Yoga instructor, so that I can get the keys out of my pocket. Then I got in the car, started the ignition, and put the car in reverse before I realized that the garage door was still closed. But I didn't push on the gas before I realized that, so I didn't back through the garage door like that one guy in that movie where his girlfriend breaks up with him so he tries to kill himself in all these different ways. Anyways, to wrap things up here, because you don't need to hear every single little, tiny detail of every single little, tiny thing I did that evening, so let's just say that I went to the store and bought all the stuff I needed and I came home. I carried the bag down to the basement and kicked open, not in a violent way, the door to my room.

"It's been over an hour," Ashleigh said, sitting on my bed. "And what's this?"

She held up the diamond ring, in its box, but the box was open.

"Nothing." I froze.

"I'm gonna tell mom about this."

"Go ahead."

"Okay, I will." And she got up to leave the room.

"Okay, wait," I stopped her. "Please don't tell anybody."

"Why not? Why do you have this? Did you steal it? It's a real diamond, I can tell."

"How can you tell? And no, I didn't steal it. I bought it, and just please don't tell anybody, please."

"Why did you buy this? You don't have a girlfriend," she stated, then added in this almost laughing skeptical way, "Do you?"

"No."

"I didn't think so."

"Okay, listen..." I told her the whole story, like I've told you to this point about the girl and the dream and the ring and destiny and even the TV show. I looked at her face and there's really no way to describe it, but I'm going to anyway, and if you've ever seen this expression on a person's face you'll know exactly what I'm talking about, and if you haven't I don't know, but maybe you'll get what I'm saying. It was like she wanted to laugh, but it was too sad, so she was almost crying, and also like her eyes felt sorry for me, but at the same time they were afraid, because I might really be insane, and also her whole face was glowing in this sort of romantic way like she was impressed that I would take this huge leap on a feeling but kind of frozen in this way that said even at fourteen she wasn't so naïve to believe in this kind of cosmic destiny that I was basing my entire life on. And we were both very still there for a long, long time, and it was almost like someone had come in and sprayed their ice blaster over the entire room until it had frozen over completely and so had we along with it, and we both wanted to move and speak but we couldn't.

Finally, Ashleigh shattered the ice with:

"I'm telling mom."

"Please don't."

"Why not?"

"I..." I spun from side to side looking around like I was hoping someone would swing in and save me from this...this whatever it was. "I don't know. Just, because I asked you not to."

"You're ridiculous," she said.

"I know!"

"So why?"

"Because it feels right. It's the way it has to be, and I don't know why, and I just do it, and it doesn't have to make sense, because it usually doesn't, but in the end it kind of does, y'know?"

"No, I don't know."

"Well you don't have to understand, but just please don't tell anyone, because I know they won't understand and I don't want to have to go through this with anyone else. And if for no other reason, think about this. Because one day you'll have some kind of secret that you don't want anyone to know about, and I'm going to find out about it probably by accident like this, and you're going to beg me not to tell anybody, and you're..."

"Okay," she interrupted me. "I won't tell anyone."

"Thank you," I said. "I don't want people to think I'm crazy."

She laughed a little at that, but I didn't think it was very funny.

"So you need help with your math?" I asked.

"I'll do it on my own." And she left the room.

I sat there still petrified for several minutes, wondering if she'd lied and gone right upstairs and told my mom and Kara and Brian and then gotten on the phone and called all of her friends from school who would tell their older brothers and sisters, the ones I'd gone to school with and it would spread all over, and I'd go to work tomorrow and everyone there would know and it would just be a disaster.

But Ashleigh never told a soul.

When I was finally able to move again I hung the giant map of the Wasatch Front on my wall. I took out my Snickers and Coke just for a snack, and I opened the phone book, back to banks.

Between sips of Coke and bites of Snickers I marked every bank on the map with the *very* fine-tipped pen I'd bought and put two larger dots on my house and the copy center, the two places I spent most of my time. I also marked all the local movie theaters.

After about a half an hour, there was a knock at my door. I froze. I turned around slowly to find Ashleigh standing there with her math book in her hands.

"Okay," she said. "If you help me with my math, I'll help you with that." She pointed at my map.

"What are you going to do?"

She took my pen and drew a big dot on the map.

"That's my school," she said. "I can check into all the banks between here and there. And sometimes if we drive down the main roads, I can take the banks on the one side of the street and you can check the others."

"That would be good," I said. "And I was thinking we'll make our house the main center of operations and we'll work outward from there, kind of creating these concentric circles..." I sort of drew them with my finger. "...until we've hit every bank on this list. And if we don't find her, then we get a Davis County phone book, then a Summit County if necessary, then Utah County..."

We spent the next few hours planning our bank strategy and doing math homework. And I was shocked that I would actually find an ally inside my own family.

"What about credit unions?" she asked just before we went to bed.

"I didn't even think about credit unions! Do you think... I mean, it said bank teller. Do you think credit unions..."

"I think credit unions qualify."

"Well then," I said with authority, "let's meet here again at seventeen hundred hours, after I return from work and you from school and we will plot credit unions."

We spent the next several, well, I don't want to tell you exactly how long yet, because that would give things away. But we spent the next while, Ashleigh and I, dropping into every bank and credit union we could find, searching for Allison Shepard.

CHAPTER 18

FACE VALUE

Look.

All I know about life is that it's too confusing to be all that important.

What I'm getting at, I guess, is that with all this lack of clarity, I don't really know how important anything is. That is, I don't really see that life has any real significance at all. And maybe, I don't know, maybe after everything I've kind of forced myself to feel this way, but that doesn't matter. All that matters is that that's the way I feel about it.

So let me ask you this, and I know you can't answer me because this is a book, but think about your answer in your mind. How much is a life worth?

Well I just happen to know the answer.

A human life is worth forty-three dollars and seventy-five cents and a Subway Club Card with twenty-two points on it.

I know this from experience.

After my father left, we stopped seeing a lot of Brian. He was never around, and I'm still trying to figure out if there was a correlation or if it was just coincidence.

So where did Brian go?

For a long time, I didn't know. And really, I didn't care. I barely noticed that he wasn't around anymore, except that there wasn't as much broken stuff around the house, and there was no screaming when we ran out of cereal.

Brian came and went, y'know, like I saw him from time to time, but sometimes that meant he was home one day a month, or sometimes he'd stop by more often than that. There was really no method to his, y'know, stopping by.

It's not like we were worried, because he was twenty-one, and even if he was an idiot he could more or less take care of himself. And he did have a job picking fruit at this orchard not very far from our house, but the thing is I don't know if you've ever picked fruit before, and I mean for a job, not just pulling fruit off a tree or a vine, but it really doesn't pay very well. I'm talking like really low pay. It's my understanding anyways that some of these places pay by the hour, and I'm told that in agriculture minimum wage is lower than for other industries. I don't know if that's legitimate or if these people that own these businesses are just slimy. Anyways, so the hourly rate can be as low as four dollars an hour. But Brian was paid by the bushel, or the basket or whatever it was I don't know, and he made very, very little money, especially if he was drunk or hung over or whatever one day and wasn't exactly productive, which I would assume was the case more days than not. So what I'm saying is I don't know where Brian stayed when he wasn't home or how he paid for it.

This went on for a long time, several years, that Brian would show up when he wanted and not show up when he wanted and no one would ask any questions.

But I told you before, however briefly, that I got my own apartment late in 2002. Then one night the following January Brian showed up at my door. I don't know how he found my place, and I literally, to the best of my memory, had not seen him for almost four months.

Brian was always skinny. It probably came from a combination of super-high metabolism, a fairly active lifestyle, and a diet of pretty much cold cereal and peanut butter sandwiches. But that night he showed up at my apartment he looked downright emaciated. His eyes were bloodshot, almost glowing red, and he was even more spastic than usual.

He said he needed money.

I said yeah right.

He left.

I called Ashleigh, asked if she knew how he found out where I lived. She didn't tell him, asked Kara, she didn't either.

No one knew how he found my place.

The whole thing was weird.

A week later, or a few days or something, he showed up again, only I wasn't home, so he kicked the door in. I lost my deposit, and that made me pretty angry.

So when I came back from work he was sitting on my couch, watching my TV, and eating my cereal.

"How did you find out where I live?" I asked him.

"I'm not an idiot."

"Yes. Yes, you are," I said. "You are an idiot."

He just rolled his eyes and drank the milk from the bottom of his bowl. Then he walked back into the kitchen to pour himself some more.

"What are you doing here?" I asked.

"Eating your cereal."

"I see that. Why?"

"I'm hungry."

"It's my cereal."

"And you're sharing, and I appreciate that." He smiled at me.

"What do you want?"

"I know where dad is."

"So what?"

"So, don't you wanna know where he is?"

"Not really, no. I don't really care."

"Then what am I doing here?" he said.

I just shrugged and looked at him.

"He had another woman," Brian told me as he sat back down on my couch. "He lives with her now and has been living with her since he left."

"I know."

"Yeah, because I just told you."

"I knew already, I mean I assumed," I said. "Mom told me that he'd been sleeping with someone for a long time."

"You're a liar."

"You're an idiot, so we're even."

"I found him. I found out where he lives and where he works. I tracked him down."

"Why do you even care?" I asked.

"Because he shouldn'ta left."

"Okay."

"It was wrong of him to do that."

"I won't argue that, but... It's not like he was really any kind of a father when he was around anyway."

"Wrong!" he shouted, pointing at me.

"What do you mean wrong? What's wrong with you? What are you... What are you doing here? Why are you tracking dad down? Why does any of it matter? I don't understand at all what is going on here."

"What is going on here is I'm a tracker. That's what I do."

"What does that even mean?" I asked him.

"It means I tracked dad down, and I tracked you down, and that's what I do. I'm a tracker."

The thing about this was that it was crazy, yes. But it was also one of the more lucid conversations I'd had with my older brother, prob'ly ever. My brother, the tracker, and he was so excited about this.

"I need money," he said.

"You told me that last time you were here."

"I quit that job picking fruit."

"If you need money, you prob'ly shouldn't have done that."

"I'm not a fruit picker. I'm a tracker."

"Yes, I understand that, but I don't see what..."

"I can find things and I can find people." He pulled out his wallet and held it open to me, empty. He pulled out a plastic card. "I got twenty-two points on this card, and that's all I got, plus the three quarters in my front pocket. I need money, and I'm telling you I'll work for it."

"You'll work for it." I just stared at him.

"I'll sell you the information about where dad is."

"I don't care where dad is! For the eight-billionth time..."

"Then I'll do something else. Is there someone else you need to find? Or something?"

He sat there on my couch, eating my cereal, and looking so beaten down. The whole thing was ridiculous. He was a tracker? I don't think he even believed it. He was just so desperate.

"You're not on drugs, are you?" I asked, already knowing the answer, I think.

"I'm not on drugs!"

I don't think he was telling the truth, but I felt so sorry for him, and even if he was just going to go buy liquor or worse, I felt like I had to help him out.

"Okay, there is this girl," I said.

"What's her name?"

"Allison Shepard. She's probably about my age. Chestnut-colored hair. She either works at a bank, or she used to work at a bank. That's about all I know."

"My fee is two hundred dollars."

"If you find her, I'll pay you two hundred dollars."

"Half now, half later."

"I don't know."

"You don't think you can trust me. Is that what this is all about?"

"No, it's..." I started, but he interrupted me.

"I could have robbed you, taken your TV, your little DVD player, all your movies, and anything else..."

I immediately thought about the ring. I would never let that out of my sight again.

"...but I didn't," he continued. "Because I'm not a thief, I'm..."

"...a tracker," I finished his sentence.

"That's right. And I'm trying to help you out. So it's half now, half when I find this girl."

"I don't have a hundred dollars on me."

"I'll take whatever you've got, then the rest when I locate Allison Shepard, chestnut hair, maybe works at a bank."

I opened my wallet and handed him all the cash I had. I had to do it. He was my brother, even if he was an idiot...and a tracker.

"Here's forty-three dollars," I said. "It's all I have."

He stuffed the money into his wallet and dumped his cereal bowl in my kitchen sink.

"Do you need to stay here for the night or anything?" I think I at least offered.

"Nah, I got a place I'm staying," he said. And in a way I was relieved, but also sort of worried about him.

I stopped him as he was half-way through the front door, "Incidentally, where is dad?"

"I thought you didn't care."

"I don't," I said. "I'm just curious."

"He's been working for Mercedes for the past couple of years, in Berlin."

"Berlin, Germany?"

"Yes, Berlin, Germany," he said. "What, are you an idiot?"

And with that, he left.

At two in the morning I awoke to the police pounding on my door. There'd been a homicide two blocks over and someone had seen the victim leaving my apartment.

Did I know anything?

"He was my brother," I told them.

Could I come with them and make an identification was what they asked me, and I didn't really think I had a choice.

I asked what happened, and they said the victim's wallet was stolen and they suspected it was a robbery. They asked if Brian had any other family, and I told them no. Because what good would it do, really? No one would care, and that would kill me more than keeping it a secret would.

And, y'know, it's possible that they found out I was lying and contacted my mom, and she just decided not to tell any of us. I don't know. But if she knew, we never talked about it.

I told Ashleigh, and she cried, but she agreed with me that we should never tell. So, even to this day, as far as I know, the rest of my family believes that Brian is just out living somewhere and picking fruit.

They don't even know that he was a tracker.

CHAPTER 19

IDENTITY

I want to tell you about the single greatest invention of my lifetime. It's not the CD player; it's not mp3 technology; it's not even the internet. The single greatest invention of the last twenty-five years is [a trademarked product][5], and I'm not even being paid to say that.

I don't know when this product actually came out, but the first time I saw one was just last year, and I was amazed at the stains it could pick up. I wished I'd known about this thing, if it even existed, five years before.

Because see, after Marty started to really decline, we didn't just play chess. He needed help with a lot more than that. I had just started work at the copy center and my manager was a really good guy. He arranged it so I could get Tuesdays off all day, so I could, y'know, hang out with Marty, and we still played chess and all that, but he also needed help doing things like getting groceries and doing laundry and cleaning the house. I didn't like it, but I liked Marty, and he was my only real friend, so it wasn't like I had anything else to do. And really, what kind of a person would I be if I didn't help him out?

So it'd been this way for about five months now, and Marty was getting worse and worse and worse and worse.

And I wasn't just going over there on Tuesdays. I actually checked in on Marty almost daily, I don't know, maybe I was just checking to make sure he wasn't dead, but I had to see how he was, y'know. And I wasn't the only one going over; there were a few other neighbors that would look in on him too.

I was under the kitchen sink one afternoon fixing a pipe. I'd gotten pretty handy at this kind of thing, repairs and stuff. Anyways, I had the pipe elbow taken off cause it was leaking, so I was going to replace it.

"You know, you remind me a lot of my son Steven," Marty said from across the room, sipping on a glass of prune juice.

"Yeah? Well, you remind me nothing of my dad," I said. It had been almost nine months since my dad had taken off, and even though I didn't really care, I was still pretty pissed about the whole thing. But I didn't really care that much. So like I don't mean that I was pissed about his leaving or that I didn't have a father or any of that. I was just... I couldn't believe that a man like that existed.

---

[5] Stupid intellectual property law.

"I'll bet you still talk to your father though," Marty said.

"I told you already. He left us," I reiterated.

"I find that hard to believe. He'll be back. Listen, I know it's hard to see from where you stand right now. You're young. But I've known your father for a very long time, and he is a good man."

I scoffed.

"Maybe you'll see it one day."

"Yeah," I said. "Maybe."

"My son was a great baseball player when he was younger. You like baseball?"

"Sure," I said, even though it was a lie. I didn't like sports at all really.

"You good?"

"Sure." As long as I was lying...

"I'll bet you are." He got up and walked over to the sink above me and turned on the faucet to rinse his glass.

"Turn it off! Turn it off! Turn it off!" I screamed as I was sprayed in the face. "Marty, you can't turn the water on while I'm working on the pipes."

"You should have turned the water off before you started."

He was right. I grabbed that handle and twisted it to "off." Okay, so maybe I hadn't become as handy as I'd thought I had, but whatever.

I wiped the water out of my eyes and tried to see the pipe again.

"Did I ever tell you about my son?" he asked.

I shook my head then realized that he couldn't see me, so I shouted, "No," loud enough for him to hear. "Huh-uh."

"He was a good boy for the most part..."

Steven was born sometime around 1950, I don't know exactly when because Marty never gave me specific dates for anything. He probably didn't even remember.

Steven did well in school. He did well in sports. He was an all-around popular kid. He was even his high school's valedictorian.

Then he went away to college, a big university on the east coast. He came back home a year later for the summer, "head pumped full of all this liberal nonsense," as Marty put it. He stayed in his parents' house for those months, but something happened in that time that changed everything.

Marty had to work late one night in the middle of August at the shop, he was rebuilding the engine of a 1959 Chevy Impala. (Oddly enough, he still remembered the exact model of the car.) So it was close to ten when he got home, and the light was still on in the living room. He parked his car in the driveway, because they didn't have a garage, and approached the front door.

Steven was shouting, "You can't tell me that! You can't just say that! I can't accept that as a response! You can't just say something like that and I'm supposed to say, 'Oh, then everything's okay!'"

Marty paused, listening for a response and there was none. He crept around the front of the house and peered through the curtained window.

"You have to do something about this!" Steven was still shouting.

Marty saw his wife sitting on the couch, sobbing, pleading with her son, but so softly that he couldn't hear what she was saying.

"How can you be so stupid?!" Steven screamed.

Marty's adrenaline popped like the eyes of gerbil squeezed around its midsection. He literally kicked down the door, splinters of wood exploding across the tile of the front entry hall. Marty hurled himself into the living room and grabbed his son by the throat slamming him against the wall next to the fireplace.

"Let me go, you sonofabitch," Steven choked, grappling to pull his father's hand from his neck. But Marty was much stronger.

Marty grabbed the fire poker and held it to his son's eye, his rage thicker than a triple-thick chocolate-banana milkshake. "Don't you ever talk to your mother that way."

"You don't even know what the hell you're talking about," Steven said. With the weapon present, Marty had loosened his grip.

Sarah was pleading with him, "Honey, let him go. Please."

"You get out of my house," Marty said to his son in a voice too even to be comfortable. "And you will not come back. You never, NEVER speak to your mother like that!"

"Honey, please," Sarah continued to plead.

"You will leave this house this minute," Marty said. "And I will drop your things on the front lawn in the morning. You will pick them up and you will not come inside this house again."

He released the boy and lowered the fire poker.

As he ran across the front door, Steven shouted at the top of his lungs, "You stupid, selfish bastard!" And he looked back at his mother as he disappeared into the night.

♀ ♀ ♀

"She cried for days after that. We still loved each other. We still loved each other deeply. But our relationship was never the same."

I looked out from under the sink and could see that Marty had forgotten I was there. It was like he was talking to himself.

I cranked the wrench a last turn and pulled myself out of the cabinet. "All done," I said, wiping my hands.

"Who are you?" Marty asked.

And I looked up at him. Here we go again.

But this was different.

His eyes were different.

"Who are you and what are you doing in my house?"

"It's me. Warren. Marty..."

He stood up from the table and lunged at me. I rolled out of the way.

I'd never been in any kind of a fight at all, and I was reacting purely on instinct.

He grabbed his glass from the sink and threw it at me. It was heavy and cracked me in the head.

"Shit!" I screamed and put my hand to the wound.

Checked for blood.

None, but...

He'd grabbed a butcher knife now and was coming toward me.

I scrambled backward, still on the linoleum.

"What the hell, Marty? It's me! What are you doing?"

I didn't know what was behind me.

I couldn't think, but I was still moving backwards.

He poked the knife towards me, and stupidly I tried to bat it away.

It sliced my arm.

I screamed and pushed further back, over the first of a long case of stairs.

I toppled backwards, then sideways, out of control, down to the unfinished basement. I cracked my head on the concrete foundation.

I knew I'd broken something. I had to have.

My head hurt like hell and my arm was burning.

I grabbed it, my arm, I guess to stop the blood, or because it hurt, I don't know, but it was what I did.

I looked up the stairs at Marty, still standing at the top, still holding the knife.

I sat up and it took forever to do it.

"What are you doing here!" he screamed.

He reared his arm back, the one with the knife.

He was going to throw it at me.

I let go of my forearm, took my good hand and pushed against the wall as hard as I could. I slid away from the staircase just before the knife hit the floor.

I don't know if the blade hit or if the handle hit, but I was scared out of my mind and I wasn't going to look and find out.

And even though I was out of the way, I still hoped that it was the handle that hit, because just in case, I don't know.

I got to my feet.

I hadn't broken anything, but I was weak and bruised and sore and I couldn't move very well. But I heard him coming down the stairs now.

I spun around, or actually turned around as fast as I could, which was slowly, looking for a door or, at the very least, a window.

The windows were too small, but across the room was another room, and it was dark, but it looked like there might be a door there. I'd never been in this part of the house.

I hobbled to the other room, pulled the cobwebs from my face.

It was a door.

I fumbled with the lock. I don't know why. I'd never fumbled with a lock before. Locks are easy. I lock and unlock doors all the time.

I heard Marty pick up the knife behind me.

"Get out of my house!"

"I'm trying!" I screamed as finally I clicked open the lock.

I threw the door open and got outside.

Marty was running towards me.

I pulled the door shut and heard him slam into it. He locked it.

I made my way up the cement stairs into his backyard, praying to something I don't even believe in to let me get away from this house before this crazy old man came outside.

I got around to the front and there was no one there. I never saw him come out. I don't know if he did.

I ambled all the way home, y'know, just two blocks, with my bleeding arm and my pounding head.

My mom was painting when I walked through the door, preoccupied so she didn't notice anything was wrong.

I went straight into the kitchen and called the police.

What else could I do?

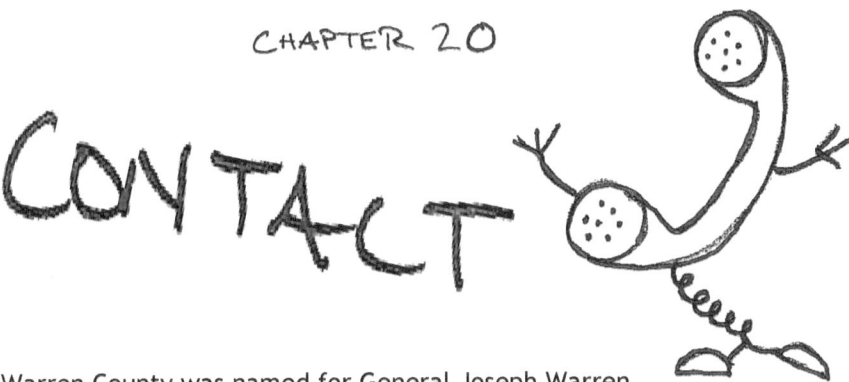

CHAPTER 20

CONTACT

Warren County was named for General Joseph Warren.

General Warren was both a physician and a Major General during the American Revolution. Also, he died at the Battle of Bunker Hill.

This isn't where I tell you about how I'm opposed to war, and I think the U.S. is in a big mess over in Iraq. But this is where I tell you that in 2005 I'd've joined the armed services if I wasn't so terrified of being shipped over there.

See my life had pretty much turned to crap, and reading about General Warren, who came up on the internet when I googled my name, I thought about trying to do something noble like joining the army. This, despite the fact that General Warren was killed in battle.

I don't know, a million things went through my head. I mean, reading all that, I even thought about becoming a doctor, because he'd been one. I didn't even know the man, and I'd also never been to his county.

Or maybe the Merchant Marines.

I don't know. I was just searching for something.

What I came back to, though, was destiny.

My destiny was to be famous, and who was I to deny that. And I kicked myself for being lazy and in effect fighting fate. What I needed to do was get it all back on track and get my damn movie made.

Plus I think my sister would've kicked my ass if I hadn't stepped up my game.

I had a few problems though:

1. I didn't have a lot of money.
2. I didn't really have any friends or associates or whatever who knew anything about making movies.
3. I didn't have a script or the ability to write one, and...
4. Rent-EZ had gone out of business and Chris had a new phone number that I didn't know and I didn't really want to call him after two and a half years and beg him to work with me again.

But as the French say, "That's life."

I'd thrown out the script Chris had given me, which was prob'ly a mistake because even if it wasn't exactly what I wanted it to be at least it was something to work with, though I'll bet he'd'a been pissed if I'd gone ahead and shot what he wrote anyway. So anyways, I'd tried to write something, I'd worked with an outline over and over and over again, trying to come up with something, trying to write something, but I couldn't do it.

I thought through everyone I knew. I thought through everyone I'd ever met. I thought through everyone I worked with. No one. There was no one I knew who could write that I knew of. And it didn't help that I didn't really know very many people.

I had no other choice. I had to call Chris.

I remembered he didn't only work at Rent-EZ. He also had another job at one of the local TV stations, but I couldn't remember which one, and I didn't even know if he still worked there. But I figured what could it hurt to call them all and see? There were only like four, because I knew it was one of the main network affiliates.

I called the first one and asked if he worked there, and they transferred me to human resources, where I asked the same thing, and they said they weren't allowed to give out that information unless I was a potential employer calling to check references.

So this is the thing about that: whoever that was in human resources that I talked to was not very bright, because what they were basically telling me was that I had to call back and pretend to be a potential employer. She might as well have just told me whether or not he worked there because that's exactly what I was going to do. However, because I didn't want to get the same person right away and have her remember that I'd just called and was now obviously pretending to be a potential employer just to get information that I was not allowed to have otherwise, I moved on to the second station first.

I pretended to be a potential employer when I called the second station and learned that Chris was not and had never been employed there. The third and fourth stations were the same, which meant that it was the first station and I was going to have to call that same HR lady back. I couldn't do it today, because I'd definitely get the same person, and just in case I did get the same person again I wanted to put some time between now and the time I called again so hopefully she would forget that I'd called before.

A week would be enough, I figured.

And you might be asking why I needed to call at all when I knew it was this station where he worked. It was actually that I needed to know if he still worked there. And you might also be saying, "Well, you could have posed as a loan officer, instead of a potential employer, verifying employment status. Why didn't the lady tell you that the first time?" And I know you might be thinking that, because when I told this story to someone one time, they got all hung up on that, and all I have to say on that one is she just didn't say that, that's all. And what the hell difference does it make anyway? That guy was missing the whole point of the story. And it's not like this is a totally thrilling little story that I'd make up to impress someone. That guy's just hung up on all the wrong things in life.

Whatever, anyways, finally I called up that first TV station and asked for the human resource department. When the HR woman answered the phone I wasn't sure if it was the same one or a different one. Either way, I had my plan.

"Hello, I'm calling from Warren West Media. I've got an application in front of me for Chris Henderson. He lists your company as a previous employer and I'm just calling to verify that."

"I recognize your voice," the woman on the other end of the line said. "You called last week asking for the same information."

"I'm sorry. You must be mistaken," I said, in my most professional tone. "I'm calling from Warren West Media." How in the world did she remember that? It's not like a little company with half a dozen employees.

"Hold on, please."

And I got to listen to their radio affiliate for a moment, some conservative pundit going on about how we need to put our trust in our leaders and not question those who know better than us what is really going on in the world.

Whatever. I don't pay much attention to politics.

"Sir?"

"Yes," I said.

"You were asking about Chris Henderson?"

"Yes."

"He is currently employed by our company," she said.

"And what department is he in?"

"What, he didn't indicate that on his resume?"

"No, he did. I just want to verify that he works in..." *Where did he work? Umm...* "...TV News."

"Production."

"Oh, is that different?"

"What media company did you say you were from?"

"Thank you." And I hung up the phone.

So I knew where he was. I dialed the main desk again and asked for the TV production department.

"Who would you like to speak to in production?" the receptionist asked.

"Umm, Chris Henderson."

"Hold on."

And I got another earful of the conservative radio show, the host sounding really irritated now.

"Sir?"

"Yes," I said.

"He doesn't have an extension. I can transfer you to the control room."

"That's fine."

And without another word, the phone was ringing again.

"News control," some man on the other end picked up.

"Hi, I'm looking for Chris Henderson."

"Is Chris here?" I heard him shout, not to me.

Then, "Right here," I heard.

"Why is someone calling you on this phone?" the first man asked.

"I don't know." I recognized Chris's voice. "Who is it?"

"Some guy," replied the first man.

"It's your gay boyfriend!" a third voice chimed in.

"Probably," said Chris, "but he should know better than to call me here."

The other two voices laughed.

"Hello," Chris said, presumably to me.

"Hey," I said and waited for a response.

"Who is this?"

"It's Warren West."

"How did you get this number?"

"I called the front desk," I explained. "They transferred me to you."

"This is the director's phone."

"Well I didn't know that. Are you the director?"

"No."

"So how ya doin'?" I asked.

"Fine."

"How's your wife?"

"Fine. What do you want?"

"Just... Haven't talked to you in a while."

"Yeah. What do you want?"

"I just wanted to see how you were doing and see if you were interested..."

"Look," he said. "I can't talk right now. Do you still have the same number?"

"I have a cell phone now." It was brand new.

"Good for you."

A long pause. I wasn't sure if I was supposed to say something or what.

"What's the number?" he asked.

I gave it to him, but I'm not going to tell you what it is, because I don't want to be flooded with calls eating up my minutes.

"I'll call you back later tonight," he said.

"All right."

"All right, see ya."

"All right."

"See ya, bye," he said and hung up on me.

Pretty much what I did was just laid there on my bed staring at the ceiling for the next few hours until the phone finally rang. And this wasn't so much that I was depressed or didn't have anything to do, as much as it was just because I didn't really want to do anything. But the phone did finally ring, y'know, like later, and it was Chris calling, which I was half-surprised by, because I wasn't sure that he would actually call, because if I'm being honest, I didn't think he really sounded that happy to hear from me.

"Hello," I said.

"Hey, it's Chris. So what did you want to talk to me about?"

"How's it going?"

"It's going fine. What did you call me for?"

"You remember that script you were writing for me?"

"The one you hated?" he said. "Yeah, I remember that. What, three years ago?"

"Two and a half," I said. "Umm, but anyways, do you still have it?"

"Yeah, probably on my computer somewhere."

"Great. Umm... hey, so I was wondering if I could get a copy of that from you."

"What happened to the copy I already gave you?"

"I don't know exactly. I lost it somewhere, I guess."

"Yeah, you gonna come pick it up, or..."

"Actually, I was wondering..." I paused. "Well here's the thing, could you bring it by my apartment?"

"You still in that same place?"

"Yeah, I am actually. That one you found for me. Thanks, by the way, for that. It's a really great place."

"So you want me to drive all the way out there, which is a lot of gas, to drop a screenplay that you hate off to you, because you lost your copy?"

"Look," I said. "Here's the thing. I want to actually, y'know, get this movie made, you know?"

"Oh, that hasn't worked out for you already? I'm really surprised by that. You seemed to know so well what you were doing."

"Yeah, you don't have to be rude about it," I said.

"Fine. So you want me to come by with the script so we can figure out how to get it actually produced. Is that right?"

"Yeah, pretty much, except I do want to do some work on the script, I mean together, we'll compromise this time. I don't mean I'm just going to change it all, but I think there are a few things that need to be changed. But it's not like... I mean, I really need to get this thing done, so whatever... I mean not whatever, but we'll figure something..."

"Yeah, okay," he cut in. "I'll bring it by and we'll talk."

"Great, awesome," I said. "When, tonight?"

"I'm at work tonight."

"Oh, I thought you were off, that's why you're calling."

"No, I'm on my dinner break."

"Oh, okay, so when, then, will you bring that by then?"

"I don't know," he said. "How about Saturday? Like ten?"

"I have to work."

"Friday?"

"I work until five," I told him.

"After that?"

"Yeah, sure."

"Okay then, I'll see you Friday," he said.

"See ya Friday."

"All right then."

"All right."

"See ya, bye," he said and hung up on me.

CHAPTER 21

BLACK
AND
WHITE

The copy center wasn't a bad place to work, but it wasn't a great place to work either. And some days were better than others, and this was mostly due to the fact that at the copy center, like at any store, you had to deal with customers on a daily basis. And the simple fact is that most customers are either morons or assholes or both.

I mean, come on. Any idiot can operate a copy machine. Brian, on his worst day, could make a photocopy.

At our place, we had out along the edge half a dozen copy machines that the customers could use themselves, all black-and-white only, and all they had to do was come up to the counter, take this little ticker cartridge, insert it in the machine of their choice, and it would track the number of copies they made. Then they'd bring that cartridge back up to the counter, I'd ring up the total, and they'd pay me.

And they could pay with a credit card, a debit card, check (until recently), or cash. It was as easy as paying for anything else.

And if you needed a color copy or something oversized or binding for your manuscript or whatever other one of the services we provided, all you had to do was come up to the counter, tell us what you wanted, and we had all these special machines in the back that we were trained to operate, and we'd take care of it for you. And then you'd pay, again by credit card, debit card, check (until recently), or cash.

The employee training took all of one afternoon, because even these complex machines, well the more complex machines in the back, were ridiculously easy to operate. So what I really didn't get was how many people came in and needed assistance in operating the simple black-and-whites.

If they didn't get the whole cartridge thing, and I don't know why they wouldn't since there were signs all over the damn place explaining how everything works, they'd ask and I'd say something like, "Okay, you take one of these cartridges," at which point I would hand them one of the cartridges, "and you insert it in the slot there on the copy machines..."

"What slot? I don't see a slot," the customers'd whine.

And I'd walk over to the copy machine where I'd point to a glowing fluorescent arrow pointing to a slot with accompanying text that read "Insert Cartridge Here."

"You insert the cartridge here," I would tell them and I'd put it in myself. "This will keep track of how many copies you make, then you just bring this back to the counter when you're done."

Sometimes people would try to insert the cartridge upside-down or sideways, and when it didn't fit, they'd just jam it down really hard and wonder why it wasn't working.

Sometimes I thought it was funny to watch people come in with this huge stack of papers and lay each one on the glass, copying them one by one, because they didn't know about the tray on the top of the machine where you can put a whole stack of paper and it feeds them in automatically. You know probably what tray I'm talking about.

Then there were the people who would, without knowing what they were doing, up the contrast way up or toggle the negative/positive setting or something like that and print out an inky black sheet of paper. And when that wasn't what they wanted, they wouldn't try to correct the problem, they'd just hit the "copy" button or the "go" button, depending on the machine, again and print another black sheet. Then again and again and again, before finally coming up to the counter and complaining that the copy machine was broken. And they'd hand me half a dozen still-wet black on white sheets of paper. "I'm not paying for these," they'd insist.

"Why didn't you come get me after the first one?"

They never had a very good answer for this.

And I'll tell you one more thing, and that's this: I worked with each and every one of those black-and-white machines many, many, many times. And I never, not once, had a paper jam. I don't know what these people were doing to our equipment, but we'd get at least half a dozen jams a day when our customers were running them.

And the customers were so rude, so often. If they asked us to bind something for them and it took longer than, say, ninety seconds, which it always did, they'd get all huffy and whine about why it was taking so long. It's not like they had nothing better to do with their time, they'd always tell us. And if the equipment jammed, probably because of something they did, they'd get all irritated and stomp around making "tsk" noises.

Especially the old people were impossible to keep happy.

I guess maybe the attitude was, *Why be nice to the copy center guy? He's probably not even college educated. And he's young, so presumably he's a drone on society, so he doesn't deserve to be treated with respect.*

And maybe I'm exaggerating a little bit, because the actual truth is that most of our customers, probably even 75% of them, were gracious or just went unnoticed because they didn't cause any problems. But that 25% that was just so disgruntled made my job just absolutely miserable sometimes.

But I want to tell you about this one customer I had this one time. She was both the best customer I ever had and the worst.

It had been more than two years since I'd seen that *American Idol*-type show on the television. Actually, I'd seen another one just the other day. But the one with Allison had aired more than two years before this.

Ashleigh and I had spent more hours than I can count traveling up and down the valley, going into bank after bank after bank and credit union after credit union, searching for this girl, not knowing what my next move was, but knowing that my first move was to find her.

I'd even resorted to going through the phone book and calling every household with the name Shepard and asking for Allison. There were a couple where there was a girl named Allison in the house. In one case, it was an older woman, in another a little girl, and I worried about someone checking the caller-id and coming after me for I don't know what. At that point, I decided I should probably stop, and so I didn't finish going down the whole list.

It wasn't just because of that though, it was also because a couple of the people really got really pretty mad at me and asked if I was just going through the phone book calling everyone named Shepard, and I admitted to it, and they said if this Allison girl didn't give me her phone number it probably meant that she didn't want me to have it, and they told me I was a creepy little pervert and they were going to call the police on me.

If they did call the police, I never heard anything about it, but after two of those conversations and then accidentally getting a little girl on the line, I decided that enough was probably enough.

Ashleigh and I had checked every single bank that we could find in Salt Lake County. If we heard about a new bank opening, we checked there just to see if maybe she'd been transferred from another branch.

We checked a lot of the banks in Davis County and even up into Weber if we were up that way. But this whole process was taking a long, long time, and after about a year we figured if we hadn't found her by now we probably weren't going to find her. I mean, I knew that a job as a bank teller was only like a step or two above fast food worker, movie theater projectionist, or copy center employee, and most people don't stay in those positions for very long. It was more than likely that she had worked at one of the banks we'd checked into but didn't work there anymore. So we'd pretty much given up on the whole bank job.

In defense of my keeping my job at the copy center for so long, I had been promoted to assistant manager, which meant a cushier shift and a pay raise, which was nice, but it still didn't mean that I really had any real money to speak of, but hey, whatever.

⚥ ⚥ ⚥

So it was on October 27th, 2004 that my life was officially ruined.

I was sitting behind the counter reading a paperback novel. I'd recently discovered the joy of reading, but prob'ly only because I wasn't allowed to watch movies at work. I learned that the hard way, as they say.

So I was sitting there reading when this woman came up to the counter. I immediately put down my book, because it's rude to make people wait even for a second, even if you are at the very end of the chapter.

I hate that, when I go into a store and the person at the counter is either on the phone or reading a book and they make you stand there forever while they finish up their personal business. And also what's annoying is when you go up to the counter in like a fast food restaurant and they don't greet you or ask if they can take your order; and even worse is when they don't even make eye contact and just wait until finally you decide you'll volunteer your order for them.

But anyways, what I was saying is I was sitting behind the counter when this woman approached.

"Hi there," I said. "What can I help you with?"

"Hi," this woman said, so sweetly. "I'm not sure how you do this, but I've got these…" She pulled some things out of her bag. She set what looked like a photo on the counter and laid a CD alongside it. "I've got this, and it's also on this CD-ROM. I don't know which way you'd prefer to have it, but what I need is six hundred copies."

"Okay," I said. "Let's see what you've got."

I picked up the photograph, which it wasn't. It was actually several pictures arranged in kind of a montage or something, with text over it:

"Robert and Marie Shepard are pleased to announce the marriage of their daughter Allison Nicole…"

I stopped reading.

I looked at the photos; I hadn't noticed them right away.

It was her. It was *that* Allison Nicole, I hadn't known her middle name, Shepard. She had that chestnut hair and those high cheekbones and she had something new.

On her left hand she had a diamond ring.

But that's not the right ring. That's not the ring she's supposed to have. The ring she's supposed to have is in my backpack in the back room.

And in one of the little pictures, Allison was kissing this other guy.

That's not the right guy. I'm the right guy. It's destiny.

She was ignoring destiny.

How could this be?

Even when I'd given up my bank search, I'd assumed, I'd believed, that destiny would bring her back into my life some way, but not this way. This was all wrong!

I slammed the invitation down on the counter and started breathing heavily. I'd never hyperventilated before, but maybe I was hyperventilating. This was probably what hyperventilating felt like.

"Are you all right?" the woman, presumably Marie Shepard, my destined mother-in-law, asked.

I shook my head, still maybe hyperventilating.

"Can I get you something? Can I get you some help?"

I shook my head again, then I felt something worse than the possibly-hyperventilating feeling. It was something rising up my esophagus.

I couldn't breathe and I couldn't swallow and I couldn't move.

Every muscle in my body was tense, or at least most of the muscles in my body, or at least enough of them to make me lose complete control, and I toppled onto the floor.

I didn't pass out. Because by now, if you remember, I knew what it was like to pass out, and also, because I never technically lost consciousness, I knew I hadn't passed out.

Marie rushed around the counter, despite the fact that it specifically said *Employees Only*. "What's wrong?" she asked, seeing that I was, in fact, still conscious.

I was still queasy but my mind was slowly coming back to me. "It's just," I mumbled, "low blood sugar."

"I have a candy bar in my purse," she said and pulled out a Snickers, which was my favorite candy bar. Still is.

She unwrapped it with amazing speed and literally shoved it into my mouth. It almost choked me to tell you the truth, but the gesture was appreciated. She helped me sit up while I munched down the candy bar.

"I'm really sorry," I told her.

"It's not your fault," she said. "Is there anything I can get for you?"

I shook my head. "Let me pay you for the Snickers."

"Nonsense."

"Well, thank you," I said. "About those wedding invitations..."

"That can wait. I've got plenty of time."

"Excuse me," a man said from across the counter. "I can't get this cartridge into that machine over there."

"It's not rocket science," Marie said to the man. And she got up and crossed the store with him to insert the damn cartridge.

At that moment this woman was my hero. And she was supposed to be my mother-in-law, but now she was going to be some other guy's mother-in-law, and I'm sure this guy would never grow to respect her the way I respected her already.

Once I'd regained my senses and gotten to my feet, we made an arrangement to print the wedding invitations. And even though it's maybe arguably unethical, I made an extra copy for myself, which I took home to show Ashleigh.

And then I tried to figure out how to stop this wedding from happening.

CHAPTER 22

Living on my own was nice for the most part, mostly because most of the time I didn't have to worry about anyone else but myself. But that's most of the time, because sometimes I did worry about other people, specifically my mother.

I didn't worry so much about Ashleigh, because I saw her enough to know she was doing all right. And Kara was pretty self-sufficient, like me, and if she specifically wanted nothing to do with me (and she said it!) then worrying about her was just a waste of my time. But my mom, as distant and flighty as she was, I couldn't help but worry about her.

I mean, she'd lost her husband and her oldest son — whether or not she knew the whole story, he'd disappeared from her life — and she wasn't showing any signs that either of these things affected her at all.

So I tried to stop by every once in a while and check on her, y'know, just at least say hi. But I didn't go too often, because it could be very frustrating.

For instance, one time I went over there and my mom was working in the garden, pulling weeds or something. And the reason I was going over wasn't just to see her, y'know; it was to talk to her, find out how she was doing, really. And so even though I hate yard work, I got down on my knees (and got grass stains on my jeans) and helped my mom in her flowerbeds.

"So how's it going?" I asked after a minute or so.

She might as well have completely ignored me as she said, "The grass is getting pretty long, don't you think?"

"I guess so."

"I need to do something about that." And she got up from the half-weeded flowerbed and went into the garage. She came back with the mower and started mowing the lawn.

I thought about yelling over the sound of the motor, but I just saw no point in it. So I finished weeding my mother's flowerbed for her, while she mowed the lawn, then I went inside the house to wait.

When my mother came inside I quickly clicked off the television and stood up. "Hey," I said, not wanting her to get away. "I wanted to come by and see how you are."

"I'm fine," she said and just walked on through the room.

"Well I wanted to talk to you."

"About what?"

"About whatever. I just...wanted to talk."

"Well I have to shower," she said, still on the move. And she disappeared into her bedroom.

I just left, and I was pretty upset.

It was several weeks before I went back again.

Visiting my mom was pretty much the same every time. Either she was busy in the yard, or busy painting something, or busy steam-cleaning the carpets, or she wasn't home and sometimes hadn't been for more than a day. Ashleigh said she just kept getting worse and worse and flightier by the hour.

If she'd say anything to me when I went over there it was just to tell me about this new idea she had for a business, or not even a business just this half-baked way to make some quick money. And her new ideas were even more hare-brained than the ones she used to have. At least before she had like an actual plan and at least seemed to understand all the intricacies of running a business. Her old plans were full of figures and costs and sketches and all those things you need to have to open up a new business. But now, her sketches looked like she'd just been doodling and this was what came out of her pen. She had no explanation of how the thing would generate income, and she had no viable plan for starting things up or drawing in clientele.

Not that it mattered really, because we all knew (I think even she knew) that none of these things were ever going to happen.

But it was almost scary to see her wound up like this, wound up so tight that she was about ready to explode, and she was keeping everything inside. She had to let it out, and this was why I was worried about her.

This was why I kept going over there, even though every single time felt like a complete waste of time.

Something was wrong, and it was something more serious than just my mom being crazy.

I guess I should kind of put this in perspective by way of, y'know, time. Because it might not be exactly clear when this was. Of course this is over a sort of long period of time, starting basically right after I moved out in 2002. And after what happened to Brian I started taking these visits more seriously. But what I'm getting to occurred in the summer of 2004.

I told you before that all my mom's erratic behavior and speed of light lifestyle resembled someone running around on smack. Well, I'm not going to tell you that this was really the case from the beginning, because I don't know that it was.

What I do know is that now she was on uppers something serious.

Ashleigh told me she went into my mom's room one morning before school because she needed a signature on some paper so she could do her driver's ed. or whatever. Kara had just forged hers. But Ashleigh saw my mom taking some pills when she went in there.

She got her paper signed and didn't really think anything of it.

But one time when she was staying over at my apartment a few months later, we were laughing at how crazy mom always was, and I told Ashleigh about some of her business ideas from when I was younger and how mom always ran around like she was on speed.

Ashleigh stopped laughing and told me about what had happened, about seeing my mom taking those pills. I thought about it then finally said, "No, she couldn't possibly be on drugs really. It was probably just like a Tylenol."

"That's what I thought," said Ashleigh.

But as I lay in bed that night, I couldn't get the idea out of my head that maybe my mother actually was a drug addict. That would certainly explain a lot. I tossed and turned, playing over and over in my head this scenario where I go into my mother's bathroom, open the medicine cabinet and inside I find...

In one scenario it is just a bottle of Extra-Strength Tylenol. In another, I find a prescription bottle of Ritalin. In another, it's amphetamines. In another, I open the medicine cabinet and find a half-dozen used syringes and latex tubing. In the worst, when I'm just falling asleep, I go into my mother's bathroom and find her in the tub, naked, covered in her own vomit, barely conscious, then she's gone.

If I slept at all that night, I don't remember it.

The next morning I took my sister home and hung around until my mom left the house, which wasn't long. I decided I did need to see if I couldn't find anything, and the first place to look was naturally the master bathroom.

It was just like those scenarios I'd run over and over in my mind. I walked into the room and opened the medicine cabinet and at first didn't see anything. Then I looked behind a bag of cotton balls and found a prescription bottle for some kind of amphetamines.

But the bottle was empty.

I looked at the date.

August, 1999.

The prescription was five years old.

But then I thought, That could just be where it started.

I pulled everything out of the medicine cabinet, but there was no trace of any drugs or any paraphernalia or anything. So I tried to put everything back exactly the way it had been.

I got on the internet in the family room. I googled the exact name of the drug from the prescription bottle to see just what it was. Turns out it was commonly prescribed by psychologists or psychiatrists, whichever one it is that can prescribe drugs, I can't remember, to treat depression. But it also turns out that it's not a very common prescription anymore.

I found the doctor that prescribed it in the phone book and called to find out why. I couldn't get a hold of the doctor personally but the lady that answered the phone told me that she wasn't allowed to give out that kind of information, even to immediate family.

Kara wasn't home, but I got Ashleigh to help me scour the whole house looking for anything we could find, and fast because you never knew when mom was going to show up again.

I didn't know anything about drugs, but I figured what we were looking for was probably either pills or powder.

We found both, and in the weirdest places.

Honestly, she had things stashed all over the house, which didn't really make a lot of sense. It was like she expected people to be looking for the stuff, so she invented all these crazy hiding places.

There was a lot of it, and a lot of different kinds.

If you want to know the truth, we found the first little baggy of powder stashed underneath the corner of her nightstand, next to her bed. It was kind of tucked up under the base. We found the first bunch of pills (about a dozen or so) stashed actually in her medicine cabinet, but in a bottle of Advil. But this was just what Ashleigh found within about twenty minutes.

I was searching the other rooms, and I just kept shaking my head when I'd come upon something. Like I found a stash wound up in the cable on the back of the stereo speaker. And I found another little bag of pills stuffed in the gearbox of our clock sitting on the mantle above the fireplace and in so many other weird places, there were too many to tell you about.

Have you ever seen someone on speed? (Amphetamines are basically the same thing if you're wondering.) If not, imagine feeding a five year old a pound of sugar or a fifteen year old three pots of coffee, and then multiply that by like ten or twenty. And you know how after that sugar rush or that caffeine rush, they'd crash really hard? Well multiply that crash by like fifty and that's what someone's like coming down from speed, unless it's helped along, which I don't know how to do.

This is what the internet says about it anyways.

And I can vouch for the manic part, because that's how my mother was pretty much all the time lately.

I want to say though that even though I said she was always like this, it was different now. If you want to know what I think, I think when my father left she got that prescription from a shrink or something that none us even knew she was seeing, and I think she liked it, and I think she abused it, and I think it ran away with her.

I think this was all my dad's fault is what I think.

Me and Ashleigh laid all those pills and all that powder out on the bed and just stared at it and each other for a long time not knowing exactly what we should do.

"Should we call someone?" I said.

"I don't know."

"Should we confront her?"

"I don't know."

"What should we do?"

"I don't know."

I hadn't thought this far ahead. Maybe I hadn't really believed that I'd find anything, or maybe I just hadn't wanted to. But I had to figure out something.

"If we call someone, they'll take her away," I said. "Don't you think?"

"I don't know," Ashleigh said. "Where would they take her?"

"I don't know. A hospital maybe. Maybe jail. How do you think she's been getting this?"

I don't care if I was twenty-three years old. I'd never dealt with anything like this and I had no idea what was going to happen or what could happen or what I should do.

"I don't know," Ashleigh said.

"I think we probably have to call someone," I said.

"Who?"

"The police, I guess."

"Okay."

We both just stood there.

We looked down at the evidence; there was probably some explanation besides the obvious.

I looked at Ashleigh.

"You wanna call?" I asked.

"No."

"I should probably call."

She nodded.

I just stared at my sister, wondering what would happen to her if I made this call. If I didn't at least I knew she'd have a home and food and all that. But if I called, who knows what would happen to her. She could be sent to live with my dad, in Germany, if that's really where he was.

But I knew what I had to do, so before I could talk myself out of it, I ripped out my cell phone and dialed 911.

I told them I suspected my mother was on drugs.

They asked if she was there right now; I told them no.

They asked why I suspected this and I told them what I'd found. They asked if she had been showing any signs of manic behavior; I told them she was absolutely the most manic person I had ever known. They asked if I felt unsafe in the house and I told them not at all.

There were more questions and more answers and finally they sent a car over with a couple of officers to take a look at what we had.

When they got there, they asked if I lived there and I told them no but Ashleigh did. They asked her how old she was, and just like we'd planned she told them she was eighteen, even though she was sixteen.

The one officer said that they'd like to search the house for more stashes, but they couldn't unless they had permission from someone living in the house. Ashleigh told them they could go ahead, and I told them that I doubted they'd find anything because I'd looked everywhere already.

Surprisingly enough, the one officer actually found some more stashes.

The other officer went into the master bedroom with us to see what we'd found.

"When will your mother be home?" he asked.

I shrugged.

"Sometimes she's gone for days," Ashleigh told him.

"Do you know, is she also a distributor?" he asked.

"A distributor?"

"Umm, does she..."

"Are you asking if she's a drug dealer?" I said.

"Basically."

"I doubt it," I said. But then I wondered. "I mean, I can't imagine..."

"What's going on in here?!" my mother screamed from the living room, and we heard the front door slam.

"Is that your mother?" the officer asked.

I nodded.

He put his hand on his holster.

My mother burst into the room. "What are you doing in my house?"

"Ma'am," the officer said calmly. "Please calm down."

"I want you out of my house. You have no right to be here. What are you doing in my bedroom?"

"Ma'am. Please lower your voice."

"This is my house. I will scream as loud as I want. And you will leave!" my mother really did scream.

"Ma'am." The officer stepped forward.

My mother swung her purse full force, catching the officer across the face.

He grabbed her, pinning her arms.

She screamed, thrashing.

What had I done?

Maybe I shouldn't have called the police. This was not going to end well. Maybe I could have handled this myself. I mean, confront my mother, show her the evidence and help her. These men weren't here to help her.

The officer shoved my mom down face-first on the bed. The other officer stepped into the room and pulled out his handcuffs, slapping them on her.

You know, you always see in movies where the cop says, "You have the right to remain silent," and all that. Well he didn't say that here, and I don't know if that's because that's just a movie thing, or if it wasn't the rule in this case that he had to say it, but I kept waiting to hear that come out of his mouth.

My mother kept thrashing.

The officer who'd cuffed her grabbed his radio. I don't remember what he said, but he still never got around to that right to remain silent stuff.

After a bit, they hauled her down to the street, and maybe they read her her rights then when I couldn't really hear very well, I don't know, but I could see anyways when they loaded her into the back of the police car. I don't know if it was an arrest or what it was, but once they got her in, one of the officers came over to talk to me.

"How long has this been going on?" he asked.

I shrugged.

They took my phone number and address and said they'd be in contact.

It was a sickening feeling watching that police car pull away with my mother in the back and knowing that I was the one that put her there. And I wondered if I'd ever forgive myself. Actually, I still kind of wonder that.

CHAPTER 23

FATHERS AND SONS

I felt really bad about calling the police, of course I felt bad, but I really didn't know what else to do.

And so after I'd called the dispatcher or whatever, of course the cops that showed up wanted to talk to me. I made sure to tell them that I didn't blame Marty for what he'd done, that I knew it was the disease in his brain. I didn't want them to think that I wanted to press charges or anything; I'd only called because I was scared for him and 911 is the number you dial in a situation like this.

They weren't planning on pressing charges, and mostly they just wanted to make sure that I was okay. Fine, I said, and an ambulance had come too. A paramedic, or whatever they send in those, was bandaging my arm.

Oh, by the way, we were back in front of Marty's house now. A social worker or hospice nurse or something was inside sitting with him. He didn't remember anything, and it seemed like he was back to his old self, by that I mean not violent. He still had no idea what was going on, and the lady that was in there with him said that he kept asking for Sarah and asking if she would be home from the salon soon.

One of the people, it seemed like there were so many of them, asked me if Marty had any family that I knew of.

"He has a son," I told them, "but I don't know where he is. I've never met him. They haven't spoken for like forty years."

"Do you know his name?"

"Steven," I said. "Steven Page."

"Steven Page, like the songwriter?"

I shrugged. I didn't know what he, or she, meant. I can't even remember whether I was talking to a man or a woman.

"How is your arm?"

"I'm all right," I said. Several people had asked me that already.

"That's a nice bump on your head."

I smiled at whoever was talking.

"Well, I'm glad you're okay," the person said. "Could've been a lot worse."

Like they needed to tell me that.

"Can I see him?" I asked.

"I don't know that that's a good idea, considering," someone said, I don't know who. "You probably ought to go home. We'll make sure he's taken care of."

"What are you going to do?" I asked. "Are you going to put him in a home or something? Because..."

"We'll probably take him to the hospital for the night, until we can contact his son, then it will be up to him what happens." I wished I knew whether I was talking to a doctor or a police officer or what.

Someone else shined a light in my eyes. "I don't think you've got a concussion."

"Someone already checked for that," I said.

Who were all these people? And why weren't they more organized?

"Are you a doctor?" I asked.

I didn't get a response.

"He keeps asking for Sarah," someone said.

Didn't someone already say that?

I was confused.

"Son," someone crouched down in front of me with a notepad. "Do you know if he has any family?"

"I told you he has a son."

This was getting annoying now.

"The cut isn't too deep, so just change these bandages twice a day. Here's some gauze, if you need more you can come up to the hospital."

Who was that now?

"Maybe I should go home," I said.

"That's a good idea. Where do you live?"

Did I walk back here myself? I didn't remember.

I pointed toward my house.

"We'll get someone to take you," someone said.

And someone did, but I don't really remember it. I just sort of remember falling on my face on the living room couch and waking up in the middle of the night.

I tried to piece together what had happened based on the bandage on my arm and the bump on my head. I just felt weird all around. I remembered the whole escape from Marty thing, but the thing with the paramedics or whoever was sort of a blur. Maybe they'd given me some drugs or something. I didn't know.

All I knew was that I really wanted ice cream and we didn't have any in the freezer. So I got in the car and drove to the 24-hour grocery store nearby and bought some, and I went home and ate it. Then I watched an infomercial or something on TV and fell back to sleep.

The next morning I woke up again and called in to work. I told them I'd been attacked with a knife the day before, and I don't think they really believed me. But I told them I couldn't come in for a couple of days and when I came back I'd show them the knife wound.

I showered and changed my bandage. I looked at my head wound and touched it and winced, and then I did it again. It was like I couldn't help it.

I looked around the house, no one was home, but that was no surprise. The twins were in school. Brian was home then and again, but not very often. My mom could be anywhere and I wondered if she even knew what had happened.

Then I thought about Marty. I wondered if he was all right. I wondered where they had taken him.

I needed to call somebody.

Vaguely I remembered something and looked into the pocket of the jeans I'd been wearing. I pulled out a card, from one of the police officers apparently. I figured I could probably call this number and get some information, so that's what I did.

He told me that they'd taken Marty to the University Hospital. I didn't know where that was, and he told me at the university.

Where, though? Just follow the signs.

I went to visit him, but they wouldn't let me in. Marty was sleeping. I asked what was happening to him, if he was going to be staying there for a while or what. They said his son had been contacted and was flying in from Denver that afternoon.

"Denver, Colorado?" I asked.

The lady shrugged.

"How long before I can see him?" I asked. "Can I wait?"

She told me to come back later that afternoon around two. And I did, after walking around a park or something for a couple of hours, just trying to figure out what in the hell was going on with the world.

Then they let me in to see him.

When I walked into the room...

"Warren West!" Marty exclaimed.

I don't know why exactly, but it was one of the nicest, best feelings in the entire world to know that he recognized me.

"What happened to your arm?" he asked.

"I cut it trying to climb a fence," I said.

"Trying to get somewhere you weren't supposed to be?"

I nodded.

"Listen," he said, "can you get me..." he paused for a long time, this confused look on his face. "...that thing for talking," he finally came up with.

"That thing for talking?" I asked.

"You know," he said, "that I talk into. On the side of the head."

What was he talking about?

"I need to tell Sarah to come get me," he said.

"I don't think you'll be able to do that."

"Me and you," he smiled at me, "we don't follow rules."

"Yeah," I said, "but this time maybe we should."

"How about a game of chess," he suggested.

"I don't see a board anywhere around."

"I don't want to see him, I just want to know the details," boomed a voice from the hallway.

Marty sat up.

"Is that Steven? Help me out of this bed."

"I can't do that."

"Go tell him, go tell my son that I want to see him."

"Okay. Okay, you just lie down," I said, "and I'll go talk to him."

I went into the hall to hear the lady saying, "I'm sorry, sir, but his doctor is not here right now. I can tell you he's had an episode..."

"An episode?" a middle-aged man interrupted. "What does that mean, an episode?" Actually this guy had to be close to sixty.

"Well, sir, we believe your father may have Alzheimer's disease. Of course we can't determine that for sure until after, well... In any case, your father has some form of dementia, and he had an episode in which he attacked a boy."

"Attacked a boy? How old?"

"It was me," I volunteered. "He attacked me."

I stepped forward and continued, "I go over every Tuesday and help him out with things around the house. He forgot who I was and thought I was an intruder. It was just an episode, like she said."

"What's your name?"

"Warren. Your father would like to see you."

"Well I don't want to see him," he said and turned to the nurse. "When can I talk to the doctor?"

"You can either come back or call this evening after five. He's working the evening shift."

"I'll just call," and he turned down the stairs.

"Wait," I chased after him. "Marty really wants to see you."

"Imagine that!" the man shouted.

"You're his son, right?"

"Biologically."

He just kept moving.

"So why won't you talk to him?"

"It's complicated."

"He told me what happened," I offered. "How he threw you out of the house."

"Yeah?" he wheeled on me. "Did he tell you why? And did he tell you how he forbade me from ever seeing my mother again, and so we would meet occasionally without his knowledge at a diner or a café, just so she could see me, because it broke her heart?"

"No."

"He forbade me from seeing my own mother."

"Well, the way I understand it, it was with good reason," I said.

"What did he tell you?"

"He told me he came home to find you screaming violently at her and the only way he could get you to stop was to grab you by the throat."

"You know why I was yelling?" he asked.

I shook my head.

"It doesn't matter," he said and started walking again. "I don't have to explain myself to you."

"I'm sure if he'd known," I chased after him, "how much it hurt both of you..."

"If he'd known? You don't even know what the hell you're talking about."

"He feels bad," I said, "about everything. I know he does. I can tell."

"Well, that's good. He should feel bad."

"What are you going to do about him? He can't stay here forever," I said. "And he can't live on his own."

"Well," he turned to me, "I understand there's a pretty nice home near here."

"You can't just put him in a home. You have a responsibility."

"I have a responsibility? To him?" He was getting angrier. "What, are you an idiot?"

"Marty's my friend," I said.

"Good for you," he said and walked out of the hospital.

The next morning I went by Marty's house to find a *For Sale* sign on the lawn. The front door was open, so I went inside.

Steven was there in the living room packing books and things into boxes. He'd thrown out the old candy from the dish on the coffee table, and even though no one was ever going to eat it I thought what a terrible waste. He chucked the old *National Geographics* in the trash and I fished them out.

"What are you doing?" I asked.

"Packing everything up," he said simply, as if it needed no further explanation, which I guess it didn't, but I wanted one anyway.

"What do you mean?"

"I thought you might want this," he handed me a brochure. "This is where he'll be living out his days, so if you want to visit him."

I looked at the brochure and wanted to spit on it, tear it into little, tiny pieces and throw it in his face.

"It's what has to be done," he said.

He went over to the large chessboard and started removing the pieces.

"He carved that himself," I told him.

"Good for him."

"You can't have it."

"What, you want it? Fine. Take it."

I glared at him. How could he be this way?

I set my *National Geographics* on the board and replaced the pieces he'd taken. Then I picked it up and walked to the front door.

The board was too wide to go through horizontally, so without thinking I tipped it to the side and all the pieces together with the magazines slid to the floor.

Something like this might have been funny in a sitcom or something, but here and now it just made me cry. Literally cry. And I broke down and collapsed on the floor.

"You want a bag for that?" Steven asked.

"You're a real son of a bitch, you know that?"

"I'll get you a bag."

He brought one and I stuffed the pieces into it as fast as I could.

"You deserved to be thrown out of here!"

"Yeah, of course you think that," he said. "You're just a dumb kid."

I glared at him, then I picked up the chessboard vertically, and just before I left I said, "Your mother would be so proud."

CHAPTER 24

MUCH ADO ABOUT NOTHING

What really brought us together I think was that Chris and I started working over the script again at the end of October, and some of the radio stations were already playing Christmas music.

"I hate that," I said.

"They shouldn't be allowed to do that 'til the day after Thanksgiving," Chris said.

"Exactly." And I think we had a mutual respect for each other from that moment on.

Also Chris was kind of different than before. Not necessarily better, just different. I mean, I don't believe that people really change, not fundamentally, but in little ways maybe. His hair was longer and his beard, and he wore I think a different hooded sweatshirt every day. And he was always talking about chakras and ancient grains, and he told me about how every part of your body is connected to your feet somehow and this stuff where you can like treat any ailment by massaging that part of the foot or something. I don't remember what it's called.

When we first met again, I asked him if he wanted to go grab a cola and he told me how he didn't drink caffeine anymore. Which was weird, because when I'd known him before it was like he had this cola iv pumping the stuff right into his arm. And he listed off like six things that caffeine does to destroy your body like he had to constantly remind himself why he didn't drink the stuff anymore. He said his mom was all about all this health stuff, and she'd given him this article about how bad caffeine is for you and he dropped the stuff right then, and he'd been off it completely for almost six months or something I think. But he said he would never read any articles about pizza because he loves pizza, and he stopped reading the article on high fructose corn syrup like halfway through, because he didn't want to give up soda pop altogether. So his new poison was ginger ale.

He brought the old script with him to my apartment then over ginger ale we went over it. Before we went over the content, I asked him about how much he thought it would cost. He gave me some rough numbers, and it was way more than I had to spend. He was talking about how much it would cost to hire a crew and pay actors and all that, even on an independent shoot.

"Why should we pay the actors?" I asked. "I met a guy once who told me he'd do it for free."

"Sure you'll find people who'll work for free," he said, "but if you don't pay them, there's no guarantee they'll show up on time, or at all, a lot of the days."

"But it's just two of them," I said.

"If that's a risk you want to take."

"Do you know anyone who'd do it for free?"

"I'd like to play the guy," he said, and I almost burst out laughing. I sputtered then sucked the ginger ale back from my lip before it sprayed all over him.

"You?" I exploded.

"My original major in college was musical theatre. I've done a few things already, like..." And he listed off several things, like he'd been preparing for this, but I wasn't really listening.

"Musical theatre?" I said. "What? Are you gay?"

He just looked at me like he'd heard that question before, probably so many times.

"Seriously, man," he said. "And you'd never have to worry about me showing up late or not showing up at all. And you wouldn't have to pay me."

"I don't know," I said. "Maybe." I didn't really want to tell him that I had no intention at all of casting him.

"Let's hold some auditions and see where we are," I told him. "Maybe we could do that like next week."

"Next week?!"

"What's wrong with that?"

"You can't audition people like eight months out."

"What eight months out?" I said. "I thought we were gonna start filming next month."

"We can't shoot until June at the earliest."

"Why not?"

"Well first of all we don't have a script..."

"Yeah, but you'll get that done," I said.

"Not right away. And secondly, I'm shooting this other thing in the spring, and I can't really focus on this until that's done. I mean, I can work on the script, but we can't start any production, not if you want me there."

"So when then?" I asked.

"I just told you June. Maybe the end of May."

"What are you working on?"

"Just one of my own projects. It's not important, unless you want to help me with it."

"Not really."

"Yeah, didn't think so."

"So when will you be done?" I asked.

He stared at me in that way like he was wondering if I was serious, but also getting irritated. Then I realized what I'd just asked and that he'd already told me twice the answer. Then I just sat there peeved and also annoyed. I tried to come up with a rational reason why we absolutely had to start right then. But there was none, and if I fought it too much, he might bring up something about how in exchange I should work on his thing, and even say something like if I did then possibly, but not likely, he could be done sooner.

"I guess we'll wait 'til June then," I said.

"Well that wasn't the response I was expecting. I was waiting for you to argue with me and tell me that this movie is your destiny and it's my calling in life to help you achieve it."

"Well," I said, "I've kind of got a new perspective on all that stuff."

"Hnh," he squinted at me.

He brought me a completed draft in January. I mean, we'd talked on the phone between then and then, but I hadn't read anything yet, and we hadn't really gotten together, y'know, face to face in that time. And our relationship wasn't the kind where you go to the same Christmas parties or even exchange Christmas presents.

This time I didn't read it there in front of him, but he recited a kind of outline of the whole story, scene by scene, so I had a pretty good idea of exactly what I was looking at.

"How are we going to afford that?" I asked. That was after he told me about this scene in there, where the guy goes to Europe to photograph Cathedrals.

"We'll just use some footage of the cathedrals from the outside, and we'll shoot the interiors here in town somewhere. No one'll know."

"Where are we going to get footage of the outsides?"

"I'll just fly out there and shoot it."

"You gonna pay for that?" I asked.

He'd lived in Poland for a while and wanted to go back, and he told me about how his wife (whom I have never met and whose existence I was beginning to question, given the musical theatre thing) worked for one of the airlines, I don't remember which, and he could fly out there for like twenty bucks.

"And you can't fly me out too?" I asked.

"I might be able to get you a buddy pass. That would cost around three or four hundred, and it's standby so you wouldn't be guaranteed to make the flight."

"I don't know. I prob'ly can't afford that."

"So anyway," he said, "read over the script and make some notes, so I can start working on the next draft."

"What next draft?"

"The second draft that I'm going to write," he said, like I was some kind of idiot.

"What, this isn't final?"

"No, it's not final."

"What's wrong with it?"

"It's a first draft."

"Well if you know there's things wrong with it, then why didn't you write it right the first time?" I asked.

He just stared at me for like a minute or something. Then he finally spoke without expression, and without his mouth even moving. "Are you serious?"

I just stared back at him.

"No one writes like that," he said.

"Yes, they do."

"No." He paused longer than necessary. "They don't."

"No," I said. "This is the final draft." And I held the script up. "If you keep on rewriting and rewriting, then you're just going to end up delaying production and it'll never get made."

"Are we really having this conversation?" he said.

"Because..." I didn't finish the sentence. I knew I was right.

"Because what?"

"How many drafts were you planning on writing?" I asked.

"I don't know, I usually end up with six or seven."

"Six or seven?! This one took you two and a half months!"

"The first one always takes the longest. I can write five or six more in a couple, three months. This is not even a rational conversation we're having."

I was adamant. "The other thing. I think everything should be published in its first-draft form. It's more real that way. I mean, seriously, in life if you mess up you don't get to go back and have a do-over. So if we're going—"

"No," he said. "That's ridiculous. You're ridiculous."

"I want it raw," I said.

"There will be a second draft."

Then we sat there just staring at each other for a while. Then he looked away and looked at the floor. I could tell that inside his head he was formulating an argument.

Finally, after a long pause:

"You still work in the copy center?" he asked.

I nodded.

"And when someone comes in with like an advertisement or something and wants copies made and the copier screws up and shoots these big ink-blots across the copy, do you say 'Well, the mistakes are all part of the experience,' and charge them for it anyway."

"That," I said, "is the worst analogy ever."

"It is, isn't it? But you don't see my point? It's like life..."

Great, another analogy.

"...if you're any kind of decent person at all. If you have a conscience of any kind, you don't just go through life in first draft mode. If you hurt someone, you don't just say 'well, that's life' and move on. You apologize, you revise, you fix whatever was wrong. That's what life is, is a series of excruciating revisions."

I just stared at him.

"Yeah, that sounded pretty cheesy. But you see what I'm saying?" he said.

"Was that on the fly?" I asked.

"Was what on the fly?"

"That little speech you just made."

"No, I stayed up all night thinking of it, because I knew you weren't going to want me to write a second draft. If I'd planned for it, I'd have come up with something much better than that."

The thing of it was that I suddenly realized that I was an idiot to say that we couldn't rewrite the script, that it was fine how it was. My argument made absolutely no sense whatsoever. It wasn't his argument that was so persuasive. I think it was just that I think I needed to argue with him about something, and that's what I'd picked. In any case, I realized that I was completely wrong, but I had a problem:

We'd just been having an argument, and I'd taken one stance, and he'd taken the other. And I'd never had nor had I ever witnessed an argument where someone actually switched to the other person's point of view. Every argument I'd ever seen was just each person shouting their view like they were only trying to convince themselves that they were right, and then both people would just either change the subject or leave in a huff.

So I didn't know what to do, because suddenly I agreed with his point of view. I couldn't tell him that. That's not what people do.

"Fine, just do whatever you want," I said.

"It's your movie," he said.

"Yeah, but, whatever, just do whatever."

CHAPTER 25

BETTER OFF DEAD

"I do," she said.

Whoever this woman next to me was, I thought I might have to go out and round up the animals two by two, she was crying so hard. A lot of people were crying, and I guess that happens at weddings, though I'd never been to one before this.

But the thing is, I didn't cry at all, at least not during the ceremony. And I think that's prob'ly because I was just more angry than anything else, just kind of angry at everything and at the world in general and at destiny and fate and all that crap that suddenly I wasn't sure I believed in any-more, and I was angry at this guy up there in the tuxedo lifting that veil and kissing that bride, and I was angry at the minister or the preacher or whoever that guy was saying "man and wife," and I was mad at Marie for not putting a stop to this and telling her daughter about the guy from the copy center, and I was mad at myself for not doing more to find this girl sooner, and I was mad at Ashleigh for not finding the right bank or credit union in time, and I was mad at my cousin for being so intimidating, and I was mad at that kid at that party that may or may not have been her boyfriend way back when, and I was mad at that department store truck driver and his sign language, and I was mad at the salesgirl in the lingerie department at that Mervyn's or whatever store that was, and I was mad at my father for leaving us, and I was mad at Brian for dying before he tracked Allison down, and I was mad at that hefty girl with the bubbly personality, and I was mad at my mom for never asking for help, and I was mad at Marty for having the true love that now I never would and also for stealing away my Tuesdays, and I was mad at Steven for hating his father, and I was mad at Chris for shooting down my dreams, and I was mad at Kara for...I guess I wasn't really mad at Kara, but I was mad at God and I didn't even believe in him, and I was mad at all those people who couldn't get the cartridges into the slots on the copy machines, and I was mad at General Joseph Warren for dying at the Battle of Bunker Hill, and I was mad at [trademarked character] for not inventing the [trademarked product] sooner, and I was mad at anything and everything else that I could think of to be mad at.

But I wasn't angry with Allison. I probably should have been, maybe I should have been, but for some reason I wasn't.

And I didn't know exactly what I was doing here, but I think maybe I just wanted to see. I mean I had no intention of actually breaking up the wedding or anything. Not now. Now maybe I was just hoping that destiny would intervene and stop this whole thing or maybe lightning would strike the groom down dead. I don't know. But I did know that things were pretty much out of my hands at this point, and I guess I was just here to watch.

I'd snuck in the back, pretending like I was supposed to be here. I'd rented a tux so I'd fit in, not realizing that regular people going to a wedding don't wear tuxedoes. And so I didn't fit in, but I tried to act like I was supposed to be there.

Let me take you back to the beginning though, before she said I do, before I showed up to that community center where the wedding was held, before I put on that tuxedo, after I took home that copy of that invitation.

I don't exactly remember the part where I drove home from work, it's kind of a big blur. But I did make it home, and I immediately handed the invitation over to Ashleigh.

"She can't get married!" she screamed.

"I know!"

"Not to this guy!"

"I know!"

"This isn't how it's supposed to be!"

"I know!"

"You were supposed to find her again, but not like this!"

"I know!"

"We have to do something!"

"I know!"

"But what are we going to do?"

"I don't know!" I screamed. You could almost see the exclamation points floating in the air.

"Well at least we know her parents' names now," Ashleigh offered.

"Yes, now we know her parents names," I said.

"So that's something then," she said.

"Yes, that's something."

"Well, so then we could look her up in the phone book."

"Yes, we could look her up in the phone book," I repeated.

"But I don't know that that would do us much good."

"Yes, that might not do us any good."

"Because she probably doesn't live there anymore."

"She probably lives somewhere else now."

I'm glad Ashleigh was able to keep a level head, because I couldn't even think at all. It was like my whole world had been picked up by this gigantic monster of fate and he was now spinning it on the end of his finger like he was a Harlem Globetrotter or something. Then he bounced it up and down on his head and dribbled it between his legs.

I forget exactly why it was like that, but it was.

"But at least it would give us something to go on," said Ashleigh, and she went into the kitchen to get the phone book.

I just stood there in the living room, annoyed and perplexed and in just a state of I don't know what but something bad that I didn't like. She came back with the phone book and looked up the name. "At least we can find out where they live."

There were three Robert Shepards listed, but one of them actually said Robert and Marie, so it was pretty likely that that was the one. Then I remembered she'd left the print order at the shop overnight and it had a phone number so I could call her when it was done or if there were any problems. In the confusion I'd forgotten all about that and also the fact that I'd written that number down and brought it home. I handed the scrap of paper to Ashleigh and she compared. The Robert and Marie number was the same one on the scrap of paper.

"So where do they live?" I asked.

Ashleigh just looked at me with that look that kind of, y'know, said it all. Her eyes were sad, but her mouth was like almost smiling. But also, she looked stunned.

"No way," she said.

As it turned out, Allison had grown up just a few blocks from my parents' house, but just across the boundaries so we never went to any of the same schools. But just to think that she had always been so close and I didn't even know it.

"Unbelievable!" I screamed. "So what are we going to do with this information?"

"I don't know," Ashleigh said. "We'll have to come up with something."

And we both started pacing, and we were pacing for a long time, just around and around the room, because we were just too distraught and confused and antsy and upset to sit still. It was like in the cartoons, and it reminded me especially of that one cartoon show with the rich duck where when he's thinking about something or trying to come up with a plan he paces around and around and around in circles, until he's walked out a full trench around his little statue thing.

And I started thinking maybe we'd pace so much that we'd create this huge ring-hole in the floor and we'd crash down into the apartment below, and I thought maybe that wouldn't be so bad to smash to a violent death right now, because really I didn't have much of anything else going for me. But we just kept pacing, and I'm sure I don't have to tell you that we didn't crash through the floor.

And as we paced, and as nothing came to us, no plan of any kind, I started to get angrier and angrier, until I was stomping around the apartment.

"This is unbelievable!" I yelled, and I stomped my foot down hard on the living room floor. "This was not supposed to happen!" And I actually jumped into the air, landing as hard as I could. I was just pissed. I stomped around in circles, shouting, even just noises like "Argh!"

"Quiet," Ashleigh said, "what about the..."

But she was interrupted by a loud pounding on the front door. I froze. I had forgotten all about the neighbors because I was too busy thinking about crashing down into their apartment. And I'm usually very considerate about all that, y'know, about sharing a building with lots of other people, even if I've never met most of them.

I really didn't want to answer the door and I just stood there frozen and silent, hoping that they'd just go away. But then the knock came again.

"Sorry," I shouted as I crossed to the door. I opened it to a tall guy about my age, well-built though I don't usually notice that kind of thing. "I'm really sorry."

"Yeah, I'm from downstairs," he said. "Umm..."

"Yeah, I'm really sorry," I repeated. "I just, I'm having a really bad day..."

"Sounds like it," he said with a smile. "Look, here's the thing. I don't want to be one of those neighbors. I really don't. But..."

"I'll keep it down," I promised. "And I'll stop stomping on the floor."

"Yeah, but what it is, dude," he said. "It's not that late, so I don't mind the noise so much. It's just that you've burned out every light bulb in my apartment with the stomping."

"Oh, I'm sorry. I'll pay for that."

"No no no," he said. "No. Don't worry about it. Just, I'm working on something and I don't have any spares, so can I borrow a couple of light bulbs from you until I can get out to the store?"

Was this guy for real?

"Borrow? You can have them," I said and left the doorway to go into the hall.

Ashleigh kind of made her way onto the living room couch and sat down, looking uncomfortable. The guy from downstairs stepped inside and waved at her.

"Hi there," he said.

Ashleigh just kind of gave him a half-wave and looked away, which was weird because usually Ashleigh was very friendly.

I opened up the hall closet and pulled out a four-pack of 60-watts missing one and came back to the living room.

"This is all I've got," I told him and handed them over. Then I pulled out my wallet. "Let me pay you for the rest."

"That's not necessary, man," he said. "Sounds like you're having a rough day as it is, so I don't need to make it worse."

"Really?" I asked.

"Seriously. Dude, if it's not too personal, what's the trouble?"

"No, it's just... I just found out today that this girl I really like is getting married."

"Dude, that sucks," he said.

"Yeah, well..."

"She's getting married or she is married?" he asked.

"Getting married. In three-and-a-half weeks."

"Well there's still time then."

"Yeah? What am I supposed to do?"

"You told her how you feel?" he asked.

I just shook my head.

"Well there's your first step." I didn't want to tell him I'd never actually even had a conversation with her. "Just go right up to her and lay it on the line. Then see how she takes it. What have you got to lose?"

Maybe he was right. Maybe this was destiny speaking to me through the neighbor from downstairs. Destiny burned out all his light bulbs, not me.

"Yeah," I said.

"Well, I hope everything works out for you," as he left the apartment.

"Yeah, thanks," I said. And I closed the door.

I turned around to see Ashleigh sitting there on the couch, pale-faced.

"Gee," I said, "what a nice guy."

Ashleigh kind of shook her head.

"What's wrong?" I asked.

Then she handed me something. The invitation. "It's him."

And I looked.

And she was right.

It was him.

That guy was going to marry the woman that I was supposed to marry.

And I thought that maybe I'd wait a few minutes until he put in all those light bulbs, then I'd stomp around some more and burn them all out again. But I didn't do that.

♀ ♀ ♀

A thought hit me in the middle of the night, while I was lying there, or actually not lying there, tossing and turning. I realized that if this guy was Allison's fiancé and he lived in the apartment below me, then Allison probably lived in the apartment below me.

I mean, I guessed she probably did since they were engaged and going to be married in a few weeks. I didn't know, y'know, what her religious beliefs or anything were and maybe they didn't live together. I knew she wasn't a Mormon, like a lot of people around here, or at least I assumed she wasn't because there was no temple or anything like that on the invitation. So she probably lived downstairs.

And if you've ever lived in an apartment, you probably know that you can live in a place for months or years even and never see the people living all around you. Or maybe you don't know that; maybe that's just me. But, y'know, I'd never seen her around.

And so I thought about all this in my head while I was lying there trying to get some sleep that I pretty much knew I wasn't going to get. But you probably know that if you're laying there trying to think about a plan or something and also trying to get to sleep, then you don't get very far into your plan. You pretty much get like one strand of whatever is in your head and it just keeps playing over and over and over with maybe some minor variations.

And that's pretty much how this went. All I kept seeing was myself sitting in my car in front of the building, watching that apartment door. And she would come out each time, sometimes wearing pants, sometimes wearing a skirt; sometimes in a t-shirt, sometimes in a tank-top; sometimes with sunglasses, sometimes with no eyewear at all; sometimes with tennis shoes, sometimes barefoot; sometimes with a purse, and sometimes with a handbag. And then I wondered what was in that handbag. What could she be carrying? And that's about as far from that original scenario as I ever got. But then of course I went back to it and it repeated over and over and over again until finally my alarm went off at seven-thirty and it was time to go to work, and I hadn't slept even for a second. Not even a wink, which is an expression I don't really understand, because who sleeps with one eye open?

♗ ♗ ♗

So of course the first thing I did, besides I mean going to work and all that, was to stake out that apartment. So I pulled into the parking lot, got a good view, and waited and waited.

It was getting dark pretty early, so it was almost black outside by the time I got home anyway, so no one really noticed that I was there. And I watched for a long time, maybe hours, I'm not sure, and I didn't see anyone come and go.

I thought probably she had gotten home from work before I did and that's why I didn't see her go in, and she didn't have anywhere else to go, so that's why I didn't see her come out. I mean, after all, I didn't see her fiancé come or go either.

And then their porch light went out, or whatever you call it since it was an apartment building and we didn't really have porches. The light outside their apartment door went out anyways.

So I figured there was only one sure way to see if she lived there and that was to wait until morning and watch her leave for work. And just in case, I would stay out there all night long, because she might work like a graveyard shift or get a craving for ice cream and not be able to find any in the freezer.

So I waited and I watched, and you'd think that I'd be tired, and you'd be right. I kind of was. But this was more important, and the thought that I might get to see the girl of my destiny was enough to keep me running for like another seventy-two hours probably I figured.

After what felt like nine years, six months, seven days, and a few hours, the sun finally came up. I was still watching that door, just below mine, which was on the second floor (the one I was watching I mean; mine was on the third floor).

It opened.

I sat up. And rubbed my eyes.

They were kind of blurry.

I looked.

It wasn't her. It was him. I hated him.

He was coming towards me, straight towards me.

He had obviously spotted me and put two and two together. And he got four because he was good at math; not that you really need to be good at math to add two and two. But he was coming out, and he was going to confront me, and he was probably going to beat me up.

I ducked down in my seat.

Being, y'know, fairly sleep-deprived, I couldn't think very well. So I couldn't really think of anything to do. So all that came to me was, *Lock the door.*

I reached my fingers up to the lock and tried to push it down, but they just slid off. I had like no coordination whatsoever.

I'd been up for like forty-eight hours now.

He was still coming towards me.

Then he changed course, just slightly, and I realized that he wasn't coming to beat me up. He was parked right next to me and probably he was leaving for work.

I sighed.

He spotted me and waved. Then he stopped and just stood there like he was waiting for me to get out of the car and explain myself.

So I did.

Get out of the car, I mean. I didn't really feel like I needed to explain myself.

"Sleep in the car, dude?" he asked.

His use of the word "dude" was really irritating.

I nodded kind of.

I staggered a little to the side, and it took all my concentration just to stay upright.

"Heavy night of drinking?" he asked.

I shrugged.

I didn't want to talk to this guy. I decided that maybe I could go knock on his door and see if Allison was home, now that I knew he wasn't going to be there. So I swung one of my legs toward the building trying to get some momentum going, but it didn't work so well and I almost fell over.

"You need some help getting inside?" he asked as he grabbed my arm and righted me.

I jerked my arm away and tried to sneer at him, but I think I probably just kind of looked like a doofus.

"Seriously, if you need anything," he said. "I'm just stopping by my fiancée's house for a couple hours, if you need me to pick anything up."

I could feel words trying to form in my mouth, almost like I was molding play-doh with my tongue. If he was on his way to his fiancée's house...

"She lives not here?" was all I came out with.

"Dude," he said. "You're in bad shape."

I had kind of leaned towards him and was now stumbling in that direction. He pushed me back on my feet.

"Let me help you inside," he said.

"No."

But he had his arm around my waist and was walking me to my door anyway.

I had to ask again.

"Your fiancée," I said. "She lives... Where does she live?"

"She still lives with her parents, until we get married next month," he said, "Then she's moving in here with me. So you'll meet her."

"Her name?" I asked, but I don't know why, because of course I already knew her name.

"Allison," he said.

If I'd had the strength I'd have punched him in the face.

Okay, so I probably wouldn't really have punched him in the face, but if I'd had the strength I'd have imagined myself punching him in the face.

He helped me inside my apartment, where Ashleigh helped me into bed, and I slept for a lot of hours.

♀♀♀

We spent pretty much that whole first week, Ashleigh and I, strategizing.

We knew where she lived, and that helped sort of.

We drew lots and lots of diagrams and things. I even bought a big white board with lots of dry-erase markers.

Some of the diagrams made sense, some of them didn't. Some of them were plotted with little "X"s and "O"s, like I'd seen in football movies, that represented like little armies or something, and these would be classified in the group that didn't exactly make sense, because seriously, where in the hell was I going to get an army? A lot of the diagrams included little stickmen, which represented the fiancé, being killed in fun and interesting ways. These were not feasible, but they were fun to make. One of the diagrams had a knight (me) slaying a dragon (a dragon) and carrying a maiden (Allison) off into the sunset. This was a metaphor or a parable or something, but not really a plan. Most of the diagrams however were just little maps of her house with different routes I could take in my car, and different places along the street where I could park, and different paths I could take walking to the doorstep, and also listing possible escape routes should something go terribly wrong.

The thing about all this was that I knew I was never going to go up to her door. I knew I was never going to use any of these. I knew I couldn't possibly just ring her bell and tell her how I felt about her. It wasn't going to happen. And not only because I was a wuss, but also because as isolated a person as I am and always have been, I still realize that it's a weird-ass thing to do to just walk up to someone you've never met and tell them that you're destined to be together, even if it is true. And the question I kept asking myself was why didn't Allison know it too?

"Maybe her mother teaches piano lessons," Ashleigh said, "and I could sign up. You could drive me over and sit there during the lesson, and maybe Allison would be there."

After seven days, this was the best she could come up with?

"Let's try it," I said.

Ashleigh picked up the phone and dialed the number.

"Hello," she said. "Is Marie there?"

After a pause she continued, "Hi, do you teach piano lessons? ... You don't? ... Okay, thank you."

And she hung up.

We both looked at each other.

"That was weird," I finally said.

"Well maybe she teaches voice lessons or flute lessons or something," my sister offered.

"If she did, she probably would have told you that."

"Yeah, you're probably right."

We sat in silence for another minute or so.

"Hey," I said. "You could go to their house selling girl scout cookies."

"I'm sixteen years old."

"So?"

"Have you ever bought girl scout cookies?" she asked.

"Yes."

"From a sixteen year old?"

"It's not like I asked for i.d.," I said.

"Well every time I've seen someone selling girl scout cookies..."

"Fine!" I interrupted. "But we've only got two weeks left. We need to come up with something."

She just looked at me, and I could see it in her face. She was giving up. I looked at her, and I was suddenly sadder probably than I'd ever been in my entire life, and I've had things to be sad about.

"I know," I said.

She started to cry.

Just like almost ridiculous crying, like sobbing, and kind of shrieking too. It was the most terrible noise.

"There's nothing we can do," I said.

And she buried her face in my shoulder. It was nice in a way, but I really wanted that awful noise to stop.

"It's okay," I said, even though it wasn't.

The noise kept coming at me, like so many acid raindrops if I were an ancient marble statue.

"Listen," I said and she quieted a little. "If it's destiny, something will happen to stop this. Something will have to happen."

But nothing happened, as you know already. And they were married at exactly three twenty-two in the afternoon (by my watch), and I stood there in my tuxedo at the back of the hall mesmerized by both her beauty and my own cowardice. The truth was I didn't deserve her.

As she and her new husband ran down the aisle, ducking under handfuls of some kind of fake rice (because I guess birds eat the real rice and it kills them), I pulled the ring out of my pocket and looked at it in its box.

I started to think, *What a waste*, but something stopped my brain before I got the whole thought out into wherever thoughts go so you can think them. Maybe it wasn't a waste, maybe...

And even though I was still pissed off, suddenly I wasn't I guess *so* pissed off.

When I left the community center... Yeah, it was held in a community center, which I thought was weird. I'd never heard of such a thing. Or it was like this little Community Arts building or something like that, not like a rec center. But it was weird.

Anyways, when I left the wedding, I wasn't feeling so great about life, and for obvious reasons. I just needed to go someplace to relax, to decompress, where I could just, I don't know, forget about everything.

So I unclipped my clip-on bow tie and slipped it into my pocket. I looked down the street in either direction, looking for what, I don't know. But eventually I found it. Not by looking down the street in either direction, but just by picking a direction and walking, I don't know, three or four blocks, turning and walking another two, and then just meandering in all directions or at least a few for a little while longer. Finally, I stumbled into a bar whose name I forget. Well, not so much a bar really as it was a sports bar, so more like a restaurant with a bar in it. But at the bar is where I ended up.

The thing of it is that I don't drink, I've never even had a drink, and I don't know if I drank that night. I can't imagine that I did, but I must have really. And you might be asking how I made it into my twenties without ever touching alcohol, and even though that's not important, I suppose I'll tell you anyways.

First of all, I grew up in Utah, and second of all, I didn't go to very many parties anyway. Also, I didn't have any friends who drank when I was a teenager, and after that I didn't really have any friends, you know, that I hung out with. So the thing is I never really had any occasion to drink.

But the real reason I never drank gives a whole new meaning to the word irony. It was because of my mother.

And it's not because she got hauled away for doing drugs and so I was scared of all that stuff and anything related to it. I had just found all that out a few months before this. I didn't drink because my mom had always told me not to.

See it comes from the fact that her father was an alcoholic and used to beat his kids. I don't care what you say about how lots of alcoholics have kids who drink responsibly. Maybe they do, I don't know. But my mother was vehement in her opposition to liquor, and she'd give what amounted to sermons about how every sip kills your brain and your body and your relationships with other people. And the new study out of UCLA or wherever says how a glass of red wine with dinner is good for your heart. And my mother gets all angry and screams, "How about some vegetables with dinner for your heart?" And you say, "Well I'm just a social drinker." And my mother says, "So was my father!" And I know my father liked to drink on occasion, and I know this was a huge source of tension in their marriage, when they had one.

Well at least my mom didn't turn into her father.

But oddly enough this was the one admonition that actually stuck, until I guess this night, but I don't remember drinking anything, but like I said I must've.

The point of this is not so much to explain why I don't drink as it is to explain that up to this point I had no idea what it felt like to be drunk, or wake up hung over, or to lose a large chunk of your memory.

I do remember sitting at the bar in my tuxedo, a glass in one hand, the other spinning the open ring box on the bar.

"Can I get anything else for you, buddy?" I remember the bartender asking.

I looked at him with what I'm sure were sad eyes and shook my head.

"You'd probably rather be left alone, huh?" he said more than asked. Then he went away.

I thought about fate for a moment. Then I thought about destiny. I wondered if maybe I'd been wrong about the whole thing. Maybe there was someone else out there for me.

There had to be, because the one woman that had ever meant anything to me, to whom I'd never even spoken, was now lost and gone forever.

There had to be someone else.

But the sign there in the mall with the wedding ring; it couldn't have been clearer. And I had that ring there in front of me.

Someone stepped up next to me. "Can I get a cranberry juice?" It was a woman's voice. I thought I recognized it but couldn't place it.

"Wow, is that real?" she asked.

The voice was louder in my ear and I assumed she was talking to me. Without looking up, I said, "Yep."

"You must be rich!" she said and sat down next to me.

I didn't say anything.

"Things didn't work out, huh?" she asked me.

How did she know?

Then I realized I was sitting there in a tuxedo with a wedding ring, and I knew what she must be thinking. And I wondered whether I should use that sympathy to my advantage here, but then she went on.

"My best friend just got married today," she said. "Not far from here."

I looked up at this woman. It was her.

No not her.

The other one.

The bubbly friend. She was sitting here at the bar next to me. What was destiny trying to do to me?

I'll give her this: She'd lost a lot of weight. I mean a lot, and she actually looked pretty good. Of course that could've just been the liquor, though I swear I don't remember drinking any. But that's alcohol for you, right?

Maybe. I don't really know.

And I started to rethink everything. I mean, I started to rethink all the signs and everything that had happened and I started to question destiny's true plan for me. Then she turned.

"Have we met?" she asked.

"No, I don't think so," I said.

"I'm Sherry."

"Brett," I lied.

"Brett, you wanna get outta here?" she asked. "We could go back to my place."

What time was it? How long had I been here? How drunk was I?

I looked at her up and down. I think she was still wearing a bridesmaid dress. At least I hope that was a bridesmaid dress because it wasn't very flattering. But she looked a lot better than I remembered and if this was what destiny wanted, then no sense in avoiding it.

"Okay, sure, I guess. Why not?"

CHAPTER 26

As far as I understand it, which isn't really very far, but anyways it seems they're pretty lenient when it comes to drugs unless you're distributing, which I don't think my mom was, but if she was they couldn't prove it. But my mom was what they called a housewife — even though she was no longer a wife and spent very little time around the house — supposedly this made her a part of the new target demographic for meth. So they weren't about to just plea bargain the thing down to simple possession with one night in jail, which the internet says can happen.

So they built up as many charges as they could, and if I remember right, there were four:

1. Possession of a Schedule II Narcotic
2. Child Endangerment
3. Assault on a Police Officer
4. Resisting Arrest

There was a fifth charge that I don't remember what it was because the judge threw it out immediately. And they'd tried to go after like intent to distribute or something, but they couldn't seriously prove that, even if she had been dealing, which I doubt but wouldn't be completely surprised to learn was the case.

Anyways, there's something else I need to tell you about first, so I'll get to the actual sentencing later — not that there's a lot to tell about it.

The first night they hadn't quite figured out that the twins were still minors, so Kara and Ashleigh moved into my apartment.

Now if you're at all confused or if you've forgotten or anything, this was in the summer of 2004, a few months before the wedding you just read about.

I did have a two-bedroom apartment but the spare room was packed to the ceiling with stuff, because I really have a hard time throwing anything away. We'd figure out what to do about that later, but in the living room I did have an old couch that I'd gotten from the D.I., which, for those of you who aren't familiar, is the Deseret Industries and it's pretty much like the Salvation Army or Savers, only the Mormon version. And the sofa did have a fold-out bed that was wide enough for two. Kara refused to sleep in the same bed as Ashleigh though, so we also got an air mattress out of my mom's garage and put it out on the living room floor.

I don't exactly remember who slept on which bed that first night, but since it's not really pertinent to the story you can just imagine whichever of the twins you want on whichever bed. But come to think of it, I think Kara probably slept on the sofa bed and Ashleigh took the air mattress. But anyways...

No actually, I think it was Ashleigh on the sofa bed and Kara on the air mattress, because...

Wait. No. We flipped a coin, because they both wanted the sofa bed, even though I told them it was kind of uncomfortable because the mattress was thin and there were bars going every which way, but neither of them wanted to sleep on the air mattress, probably because it had a slow leak and they'd wake up with their mid-section on the floor. But I don't remember who won the coin toss, so whoever that was they slept on the sofa bed, and I think it was Kara actually, but it might have been Ashleigh.

Anyways, that first night was really, really good. And I mean good in a genuine sort of way like a nice long walk on a cool day can be good, not like a chocolate chip cookie can be good, because in the end a cookie is full of fat and sugar and even though it's good at first, in the end it's really not so good.

But this first night, it was genuinely good. It was one of those times that I'll remember forever as one of those times where everything was right with the world even though there were so many things really wrong with the world. Because that first night there was no drama, no anger, no enmity, no contention of any kind. Well except the argument over who got to sleep on the sofa bed, but that wasn't even so bad because it was settled with a coin toss. And wouldn't it be nice if every problem in the world could be settled with a coin toss?

And even though it was sad that our mother had been hauled away in a police car, we sat around laughing and telling different stories about our parents and all the ridiculous things they'd done and all the ways they'd screwed us up. And I think for those moments we felt like a normal family, and it felt like we were all sitting around doing what any other family who'd been left by one parent and had the other parent arrested for drug use would be doing. But not even that, we'd seen other families bicker and fight and we'd seen other families have their problems, and that night we felt like we were one of them, and despite everything, we were still together.

I think if I think back, all the very best times in my life had nothing to do with things I might have planned or what I was doing. Every really good moment had everything to do with the people I was with and just kind of being — not doing.

In the morning, I made them pancakes. And I felt like a parent again, like I had when I'd lived with them only even more so now.

Since it was summer they didn't have school, so I asked what their plans were for the day.

"I don't know," Ashleigh said. "I think I'm just gonna hang out here."
"I'm going out with some friends," Kara said.
"Where you going?" I asked.

⚥ ⚥ ⚥

See, okay, if you haven't figured it out by now, I'll just tell you. When things are going good in my life, destiny has a way of sweeping in and just really screwing them up. And I don't know, maybe it's the same for you.

But that's what happened here.

And maybe there's a little bit of something I should explain to you about Kara, since she hasn't played much of a part in this book.

And it's not because I don't care about her that I haven't talked about her much at all. It's actually because I don't really know her very well.

And maybe you do, but maybe you don't have a sibling that you live with and you've known all his or her or your life, but you just really don't know anything about this person, and I mean really nothing except his or her name, y'know. That's how I was with Kara.

I mean I cared about her. Don't get me wrong. I just, I didn't know how to care about her, if that makes any sense. I didn't know what she liked or disliked, or how she felt really about anything, or even what she believed in since our parents never offered us any kind of religion. She could've been a Buddhist for all I knew. Or she could be an agnostic who believed in fate and destiny like me, or maybe she was an atheist. Hell, for all I knew she'd been baptized a Mormon, but probably not because I prob'ly would have heard about that one.

But let me tell you a little bit about what I do know about my oldest sister. See there's something, she came out a few minutes before Ashleigh did. I'm not sure exactly how many, or at what exact times, because I was only almost seven when they were born, but I do remember my parents saying on a few occasions that Kara was the older of the two.

Now for all I know, however, Kara and Ashleigh could have been switched at some point as infants, and my parents (especially my mom) may have not been able to tell them apart, and Kara was actually Ashleigh, and Ashleigh who is really Kara is actually the one that was really born first. When you have twin sisters you think about these things.

But Kara, supposedly, was a few minutes older, and she really seemed to think that gave her some kind of authority over Ashleigh, even though you'll remember that Ashleigh got her period first. Kara was the bossy one; she was the leader. When they played as kids, they always did what Kara wanted to do. They always played with Kara's friends, and they always went where Kara wanted to go.

As they got a little older, like teenagers, while Ashleigh became more reclusive, Kara became more social. On Friday and Saturday nights, Ashleigh would stay home to play Scrabble, while Kara would go out I don't know where and sometimes not come home until late, late Sunday night.

But here's the real thing about Kara. When she was about thirteen or fourteen, all of a sudden she started dressing in like almost all black. She started painting her fingernails black, and she even dyed her hair black. When I was in high school, we called people like that "Goths." But Kara insisted that she was not a Goth at all. She was just expressing herself.

And she got really involved in like art classes and things. And she took up painting. And actually some of her stuff is really good, though I don't see much point in painting, because you paint a thing on a big canvas, and probably you never sell it or see a dime for your work, but if you do sell it, even if you get lots of money, you never get to see it again, and I don't think I could take that.

The thing was most of her paintings were really either dark and scary-looking or they were really abstract and it was hard to tell what they were supposed to be pictures of.

She had this one that was done in all orange and red and black and purple. At first, y'know, it looked like a volcano sort of, but not really. And if you got closer, you could see that it wasn't a volcano, because it wasn't a mountain, but it was like this jagged cliff with lava or something running over it, but then if you looked even closer there was a woman in it there, and it's hard to explain here in words how it looked and how it made you feel to look at it, but not good, but not bad either, just kind of, I don't know, but the woman was crying sort of. And if you saw the woman then you stepped back, it was like the whole painting was changed and it was not a volcano or a cliff running over with lava, but it was like this woman's world being torn apart, as though she had like two lives or two lovers or two souls and they couldn't coexist. And you'd stand there and watch those lava tears running down her face, and you wanted to ask about the painting, why Kara'd painted it and what it meant, but you weren't going to, because that would ruin the whole thing, because in the painting maybe you just saw what you wanted to see, despite what it meant to anyone else or what it really was a picture of. And when you looked away and looked back, it was all gone, and it was just a mess of orange and red and black and purple on a three-dollar canvas.

Now that was a painting.

♀ ♀ ♀

"None of your business," she snapped. "I'll go where I want to go. You're not my mother."

Well that was a little extreme. I had just asked where she was planning on going with her friends. After all, she was only sixteen and I was responsible for taking care of her until everything was all worked out with the court. So I felt I had every right to know what she was doing, but all I said was, "Okay."

She finished her pancakes and left the table.

"Don't worry," Ashleigh said. "She pretty much takes care of herself. We both do."

"I have to go to work today," I said.

"Okay, I'll take care of the dishes and clean your apartment."

My apartment was already pretty clean, so there wasn't a lot for her to do really. But she got right to it, scooping up the dishes from the table and taking them to the sink.

I took a shower, got dressed, went to work and got frustrated with some old people who couldn't work the copy machines, and I went home. Ashleigh and I ate Hamburger Helper and played Scrabble, then we watched a movie, but I don't remember which. We went out and picked up some ice cream from the grocery store, and at about eleven o'clock we started to wonder where Kara was.

She didn't have a cell phone that I knew of, and Ashleigh didn't know any of her friends, so we really didn't have any way of getting hold of her. And I started to worry.

I started to worry like all those parents on TV and in the movies worry. I started to worry like I'd never seen my parents ever worry. I started to imagine all these horrible, terrible scenarios in my head. She'd been hit by a car and the driver had taken off and she was lying, bleeding in the street somewhere with no one to go for help and she was dying. She'd been walking somewhere and gotten robbed, or worse raped and murdered. She stopped by a 7-11 when it was being robbed and the police had come and she was being held hostage in a standoff. And the more I worried, the more ridiculous my imaginings became. She was hauled off by drunken Navy boys onto their submarine to be kept as a slave in the kitchen. She was eaten by a pack of hungry wolverines running rampant in the city. She was bitten by a vampire and was now roaming the earth preying on innocent people as one of the undead.

I was becoming frantic. But I never did imagine she would be abducted by aliens, because that's just absurd.

"Should we go out and look for her?" I asked Ashleigh.

"Where are you gonna look?"

"I don't know. Where would she go?"

Ashleigh shrugged.

"I think we should go out and look for her," I said.

"It's a big city. She could be anywhere."

"I know. But we can't just sit here. She could be hurt or in trouble or I don't know, but we need to find her."

"You watch too many movies," Ashleigh said. "She's fine. She's sixteen; she can take care of herself."

"No," I said, grabbing my keys, because this time they weren't in the pocket of my jeans, because this time it was late and I thought I'd probably be going to bed and so I'd left them on the kitchen counter. "We need to go look for her."

"Okay, fine," Ashleigh said, and she came with me.

I started to think over all the places she could possibly be, then almost right away it became way too obvious. So we drove over to my parents' house.

She was there.

And she wasn't like reliving old memories or searching for someplace familiar like they do in sappy movies. She was packing. She was packing everything.

Like everything.

Not just her stuff.

But she was also packing her stuff.

There were boxes everywhere.

"What are you doing?" I all but shouted.

"Packing," Kara said.

Ashleigh kind of hung back in the corner, trying not to be involved. Eventually she made her way to the couch where she sat down and watched.

"I can see that you're packing," I said. "Why are you packing? What are you packing?"

"Anything I can sell," she said.

"What are you talking about?"

"You don't want me living with you," she said. "You two have a relationship. You two have a thing. And I don't have that with either of you. And you know what? That's okay, because I've never had it with any of you. And this is my ticket out."

I hate that expression — ticket out.

"What do you mean?" I said.

"I mean mom's been arrested..."

"Not technically, I don't think."

"Whatever. She's been using forever. She's going to be jailed or committed or whatever they do to people like her. Should be locked up in an institution."

"I'll agree with you there. But I don't understand..."

"This is a perfect opportunity," she interrupted me. "When everything goes down, either dad's gonna come in and take everything or the government is."

"Why do you say that?"

"Well that's how it is. I don't know. And they're either gonna send me to live with dad or put me in a foster home or I'm going to have to live with you, which, no offense, but I don't want and neither do you, and you can't support three people working at the copy center."

"That's not true," I tried to convince both her and myself. "I do want you."

She scowled at me and gave out a forced laugh. "No, you don't. And so I'm taking care of myself."

"You're only sixteen years old!"

"And I've been taking care of myself for sixteen years! So I've gotten pretty good at it," she said. "I'm taking everything I can sell and I'm selling it. If you guys need any, speak up now."

"I'm good," I said.

"I'm good," said Ashleigh.

"Kara, listen," I started.

She stopped packing and looked at me.

I didn't know what I was going to say. Maybe I thought she was going to shout, "No, you listen..." like in the movies and explain her whole plan to me, but life's not like that. She was actually going to listen. That was until she realized that I had nothing to say.

"What?" she finally asked, after an uncomfortable silence.

"I don't know," I said.

She gave me some look that I can't describe, but it was basically saying to me, "Well, you had me for a second, but now you've lost me."

"What are you planning to do? Run off somewhere and be an artist?" I finally blurted.

She actually laughed in my face.

"Wouldn't that be poetic?" she said. "You live in this other world, don't you? Where everything's all about dreams and destinies and stuff. No. I'm just going to go. I haven't planned any further than that. Just getting out of here, that's what's important to me right now."

"And you think selling this stuff's going to get you enough money to live off of?"

"It'll give me enough for a while, then I'll figure something out."

"You should at least finish high school," I said.

"Why should I finish high school?"

That was a valid question, because I didn't really see much point to it. Maybe I was just grabbing at whatever I thought I could get a hold of and throwing it out there.

"Help me out, Ash. Why should she finish high school?"

"I don't know," Ashleigh said.

"Warren, I'm going," Kara said.

"What am I supposed to do? I tell the court that you just ran away? Is that what I do? Do I tell them we had this conversation?"

"You can if you want. I don't know what you should do."

"Do I call the police?" I asked.

"I'd prefer if you didn't."

"Where are you going to go?"

"I don't know."

And I looked at her, and she was determined. And I can't tell you what it was exactly, but suddenly I understood her, probably better than I understood anyone else I'd ever known. Probably better even than I understood myself. And it was like I knew her very well all of a sudden. It was like she was standing there packing everything away and leaving, just like I had wanted to do my entire life. But I was a coward, and she was doing it. And I knew why. And I was kind of jealous in a way.

And she looked at me, and she stopped packing again. And she knew she'd won.

She smiled and that was prob'ly the first real, genuine smile I'd seen from her maybe ever. And we had an understanding, where usually these kinds of connections exist between twins or a parent and a child, but here we had something different.

"You're letting me go," she said, like she wanted confirmation but didn't need it.

"I think so," I said.
"Okay."
"Do you need any help?"
She shook her head.
"What about your paintings?" I asked.
"I'm taking what I can."
"Can I have one?"

I looked back at her as I walked out the door with my painting — the orange and red and black and purple one.

CHAPTER 27

THE TERMINAL

For basically his whole first year in the home, Marty was pretty upset. I guess his son was so mad that he wouldn't even see him, and Marty never got to go back home at all. Steven, I guess, just paid for a hospital stay until arrangements were made, packed up all of Marty's things, and took them over to the home. Marty was delivered like a FedEx package a couple hours later.

I remember the first time I saw him there, and it wasn't an easy visit. He was furious at his son for putting him in here. I don't blame him. Marty was still pretty lucid at that point, at least most of the time, and so he was definitely aware enough to be aware of what was going on around him. He recognized me the minute I walked into the room.

"Warren!" he shouted. "Just the man I've been wanting to see. You've got to help me get out of here."

"I brought the chessboard," I said, shaking the pieces inside the collapsed travel board.

Marty was still able to play chess for the first long while. But the thing was as time went by he started not to be able to play it so well. And I knew something was wrong when I actually started winning every game.

But on that first day he beat me, despite being very distracted. The whole time he just kept saying that we needed to find a way for him to get out of this place so he could go on home. He didn't belong here. He was doing just fine.

I don't think he remembered stabbing me, and I didn't think I needed to remind him. Also, I didn't want to tell him that his home had been sold. And the way he kept talking about it and telling me he needed to get back there, I kept thinking about that one movie where that old lady is in the rest home and keeps telling stories about her diner where they sold fried green tomatoes.

"Checkmate," he said at the end of the game and without missing a beat, "These windows are all locked, actually painted shut I think. So we can't get out the windows, and there's security at the front door."

I just nodded through all this. I figured this would pass after a couple of weeks in this place. And I knew I wasn't going to break him out, even if it did make me sad to see him in here.

Then all of a sudden in the middle of his scheming he turned the conversation to his son.

"I don't know how he could do this to me," he shouted. "That ungrateful little…" And then he said some foul things. "Don't you ever do this to your father, Warren."

"My father left us, remember I told you?"

"That doesn't mean anything," he said.

"What do you mean that doesn't mean anything?" I shouted. I realized that he might not know what he was saying, but I was still getting mad.

"You don't know why he left."

"It doesn't matter why. Look, my relationship with my father is very different from your relationship with your son." I don't know if he was listening to me, but I couldn't stop. I had to get this all out of me. "My dad was an ass, and he never did anything to really help any one of us. And maybe his leaving was the best thing, but I'll never forgive him for it."

"I don't think you understand," he said.

"I don't understand what? What don't I understand?"

"You don't understand what it's like to be a father."

"I don't need to understand. What he did was wrong."

"Where is your father now?" Marty asked.

"I don't know. We don't have any contact with him."

"How long ago did he leave?"

"A few weeks or months or something, I don't remember." I was frazzled.

"Don't say you'll never forgive him."

"But I won't."

"Don't say that." He paused and hooked his finger up over his lips. He looked around at the few other people in the room. I'd forgotten that anyone was there, and suddenly I felt awkward for yelling and everything. Finally, he looked back at me and said, "One day he's going to regret what he did to you, to you and your whole family, and if he's a better man than me he's going to try to fix things."

I snorted in contempt.

"And he won't be able to," Marty continued. "But if you can't forgive him, you're going to live under his control for the rest of your life and that's no place to be. Maybe you need some time, but you could always find him and talk to him and start the process yourself. You'll feel better for it."

"No," I said emphatically. "No. No. No. I don't want to listen to this, because you're wrong."

I picked up my chessboard and tossed the pieces into it violently. I snapped it shut and stormed out of the rest home.

That was the first time Marty and I had gotten into a fight, and I couldn't figure out why it had made me so angry. The fact was I didn't care about my dad at all. Yeah, I thought he was an ass, and I was mad he'd just left, but it's not like it really made my life any worse. But it didn't really control me. It's not like I was just consumed with anger over what he'd done to me. I mean, I was angry sure, but not that kind of…whatever.

Marty was wrong!

My relationship with my dad was something totally different than whatever was going on with his son. It's not like Marty had left his family, and even though my dad did leave his it didn't really matter.

But the fact was that it didn't really affect me that much, so there was no reason for me to fight with Marty about it, and there was nothing else to say.

♀ ♀ ♀

I kept going to visit Marty every Tuesday, but now it was just for an hour or two. At first, I kept visiting because I wanted to see him; he was my friend. And he'd still tell me stories, little episodes from his life. Most of them I'd heard before, and as the weeks went by I started to hear the same few stories over and over. Sometimes he'd tell me the exact same story two or three times during the same visit. But we'd avoid talking about Steven or my dad.

Until one day, some three years later, when I had something to say, because maybe it had been on my mind. Actually probably because of what had just happened. Marty had been in the home for almost four years now, and he was still pretty coherent for the most part, but he had his good days and he had his bad days. Mostly, he'd just forget stuff or forget that he'd told you stuff, or he'd forget the words for things, or occasionally he'd forget who I was halfway through the visit or not recognize me and remember who I was halfway along.

Anyways, on this day I sat down and opened up the chessboard. I held out my hands and Marty chose the left. Black. As we put all the pieces on the board, I said what I think maybe I wanted to say, but I don't know why exactly.

"I heard my dad might be in Berlin."

"Berlin?" he asked.

"In Germany." I paused, then added, "In Europe."

"I know where Germany is," he said, half-smiling at me.

"Yeah, I guess he's working for Mercedes out there or something."

"Is that right?"

I wondered if he knew where I was going with this and he was being coy, or if this was just another one of his off days and he had no idea who my dad was or why I would bring any of this up.

Before Brian had shown up at my door claiming to be a tracker a few nights earlier, I'd almost put any thoughts of my dad completely out of my mind. But now suddenly I was wondering. I don't know what I was wondering about, exactly.

Then I started getting angry again. Angry that he could just take off. Angry that he could just leave, because you can't just do that. I could just leave, I could go wherever I wanted, because at this moment I didn't have any responsibilities to anyone, I don't think. Except maybe sort of to Marty, and to the copy center I guess. But anyways, my dad had responsibilities to a lot of people and he just abandoned them, and people don't do that. I mean people I guess do that every day, but those are asshole people. And that's not right.

And I looked at Marty over the chessboard as I made my opening move.

"I was just wondering," I said.

He looked up at me, his finger hooked over his lips.

"If you could sit down with Steven, what would you say to him?" I asked.

He brought out his pawn, just like I knew he would, then he looked up at me, and all he said was, "Maybe you should go see your dad."

Was that supposed to be helpful?

"I can't fly all the way out to Germany," I said.

"Hnh," Marty snorted waiting for me to make my move.

"I can't take that kind of time off work, and I can't afford a plane ticket to Europe, and I can't..." I don't know. "I just can't."

"Then you can't," he said.

I brought out a bishop.

He mirrored my move and said, "But maybe you should."

We finished the game pretty much in silence. I had expected something more than that.

♟ ♟ ♟

After a while, I think I was only visiting because I felt a responsibility to this man, and I was the only person he had. I asked, and I guess at first he'd had a couple of people from the neighborhood stop by once or twice, but I was the only one who still came around ever.

Don't get me wrong, it wasn't like I didn't want to see him. It was just almost like it wasn't him anymore after a while. I mean it was him, but he was different, and it was sort of uncomfortable. And the real thing of it was that it made me sad to see him like that.

Then one day he had a stroke. I'm not sure exactly what that means because I wasn't there when it happened and I didn't want to ask. I know there are lots of different strokes that a person can have, but I don't know what kind his was or how it affected him, except that I do know that after that he couldn't play chess anymore.

But I'd still set up the game every time I came over, and he'd sit in the chair on the other side of the board while I played both sides. Sometimes I'd win. Sometimes he'd win. I don't know why I did it and kept doing it. I guess it just made the visits that much less painful.

Y'know sometimes you see homes for the elderly and they've got this big visiting area and a game area and a TV area, and a lot of times on TV shows and in movies there are all these people in the home visiting their parents or grandparents or whatever, and the whole place is bustling.

But not really here.

I mean, they had a visiting area and it had a TV in it. And maybe there was another TV room and game room and puzzle room and all that, but I never saw it. In fact, Marty and I never spent any time even in the visiting area after the first couple of years or so.

He just reached a point where he no longer wanted to leave his room. And so I'd sit in there with him.

It was a small room, all white, with two beds. He had a couple of different roommates I guess you'd call them, but they died and were replaced and I never really knew any of their names.

There was a window that looked out onto a street, but not a busy one because this was a fairly secluded neighborhood, so there wasn't much to look at. The ceiling was pretty high, I would guess ten, maybe twelve, feet. And everything was concrete and cold.

And when I'd play both sides of the chessboard and he'd sit opposite me, he'd put his one fist up under his chin with his forefinger hooked over his lips. He had a cane now and his other hand was always propped up on that.

Sometimes he'd tell me stories that weren't quite right anymore. Sometimes he'd just sit there in silence. Sometimes he'd tell me about things that just clearly never happened, like how he'd gotten hold of some lawyer who was working on a plan to get him out of this place, so he could go back home to his wife and son.

Most of the time though, he did recognize me. He did know who I was, and seemed to understand why I was there. And that made me feel good. And maybe that's why I brought the chessboard, because maybe that did give me a reason to be there, even if his mind went completely and he had no idea who I was or what was going on.

A lot of times, when he was having a silent day, I'd just talk to him. I don't know if he heard or if he understood, but it was nice to have someone to talk to anyway. I told him about my mom being taken away and about Kara leaving. I told him about the wedding and everything after that. I even told him about Brian, because I figured he would never tell anyone.

When I went in one Tuesday early in 2005, they told me he'd had another stroke. This was roughly a year after the first, and they explained to me that this was relatively common in people with Alzheimer's and that I shouldn't expect for him to be around much longer. They said it was likely after episodes like this for him to forget large blocks of his memory and it may be a long time before he recovered those memories or he might never recover them at all. So they warned me that he might not recognize me. The one good indication they had was that his body hadn't started to deteriorate yet, as in he hadn't broken a hip or anything.

I wasn't sure how this was a good sign, because yes, this might mean he'd live a while longer, but pretty soon he wasn't even going to be a person anymore.

And that's how it suddenly felt, like there was just a body sitting across the chessboard from me. And he talked even less now, hardly at all. And most of what he said was just incoherent mumbling.

So I started talking to him more. But instead of telling him about what was going on in my life, I'd tell him all the stories that he'd told me. And I'd tell him these stories over and over again.

I don't know why I did this. Maybe I just couldn't let these memories die just because he didn't have them anymore. Maybe I felt like Marty was still Marty, like Marty still existed, if these stories still existed.

And so I told him about how he lied to get into the Merchant Marines at fifteen. And I told him about how he met his true love at a bakery in Idaho and how they ran off together. And I told him about that time when some guy came into the shop drunk out of his mind and Marty fought him off with jumper cables. And I told him all the other stories that I'd heard him tell.

And even though they didn't seem to resonate with him at all, I still kept telling them. Even when I'd talk about Sarah it seemed like nothing was getting through.

But I kept talking and I kept playing chess against myself, with Marty in the corner his forefinger hooked over his lips.

♟ ♟ ♟

And then I remember one day in the summer of 2005. It was Tuesday, so I went to see Marty like I always did.

When I approached his room I thought for a second that he might have another visitor, because I could hear him talking. But as I kept listening, I realized that no one was talking back.

I stepped up next to the open door and peered into the room. I could see Marty sitting in his chair looking at the chair where I usually sat and having a conversation with no one there.

"I think it would do him good to put a little more work into his swing," he said, and then he waited for a response.

"Well he might not now, but someday," he continued, then waited again.

"No. I know, I know. And you're right. I just want him to be happy."

I took a deep breath, I don't know why, and stepped into the room. Marty looked up at me and smiled. He tried to stand but really couldn't.

"Steven, your mother and I were just talking about you," he said to me.

I smiled.

"We were talking about the game. That's a hell of a pitch you've got, and I was telling your mother that it wouldn't hurt you to work on that swing a little bit if you want to make a career of it."

I didn't know what to say, so I just stood there.

I was a little uncomfortable.

No, I was very uncomfortable.

Have you ever been somewhere where there were like a lot of people and someone told a joke that was really funny and everyone was laughing but then all of a sudden you accidentally snorted in the middle of your laugh and everyone turned and looked at you and then started laughing again? It was like that, uncomfortable.

"I see you've got a chessboard," he said. "You think you can beat your old man? Have a seat."

I sat down and got out the chessboard.

"You know this is the real way to pass the time. Did you see the Palmers got one of those new color television sets?" he asked me/Steven.

I wondered if he was reliving something or creating a new memory with whatever was around him.

"Maybe your mother could make us some sandwiches. What do you say, my dear?"

Still, I didn't say a word. And he watched a person that wasn't there get up and walk out of the room.

"I'll tell you, son, your mother is the finest woman I have ever known. I love her more than anything in this whole wide world. And I'm lucky she puts up with me." With that, he laughed. More chortled.

I smiled at this senile old man sitting in this dismal little white-walled room with no company and no entertainment. And maybe I envied him just a little, being able to actually relive his happiest memories. And I honestly believe that for Marty, at this moment, there was nothing wrong with the world.

I wanted to be a part of this; I wanted to experience this, what he was living, right now with him. And I wanted it to be as pure and beautiful as it could be.

And so I turned to him. "Tell me more about Sarah," I said.

And it was like looking at the Mona Lisa and seeing someone punch a hole right through her face. Marty froze; he was no longer smiling.

I don't know, maybe I'd broken the illusion. Maybe I'd brought him back. I was trying to do just the opposite. Oh, this was stupid, so stupid of me. Why did I have to push it?

He looked at the chessboard and looked at me. He didn't know who I was, and I don't think he cared.

"Sarah died," he said as he turned away from me. "She had a heart condition."

And he sat back in his chair, tucked his fist up under his chin, and hooked his forefinger up over his lips.

CHAPTER 28

You'd think that if you're holding auditions for a major motion picture that you'd sit in a room for about a day watching great actor after great actor walk in and perform for you, then you'd have to pick the greatest of all the great actors to play the part in your movie.

That's what I thought.

But if you thought that, you'd be wrong in the same way that I was wrong when I thought that.

When we held auditions, man, there were some really awful ones, and also some really, really awful ones, and really if I'm being honest no good ones at all. At least for the first couple of hours.

We auditioned from nine in the morning until two in the afternoon, and I'll be damned if one straight guy walked into that room before noon.

And what was really aggravating is that a lot of these guys were people Chris knew and had called to audition. I suspect, though I can't confirm this, that he called these incredibly terrible, horrible actors so that when he did his read he'd look great by comparison.[6]

And we had mostly women audition. And these girls that came, though some of them were hot, were some of them so excruciating to watch.

There was the one girl Hillary. Listening to her read was like listening to someone trying to play a Bach concerto on a saw, but not on like one of those saws that you can bend and you might actually be able to play a Bach concerto on. It was like listening to someone trying to play a Bach concerto on like a buzz saw.

Listening to these people mutilating my script was like watching a kindergartener finger paint over *Starry Night*. Not that I'm saying that my movie is as y'know historical as a Van Gogh painting, but someday it might be and even if not the metaphor is still valid.

Then there was Kristin who just had one of those shrill voices, and I know it's not her fault that she sounded like a, I don't know, a shrieking bat or something, but every syllable swirled down my ear canal, shattered my Eustachian tubes and pierced the center of my brain. Seriously, I got dizzy just hearing her speak and I had to cut her off like three lines in because I couldn't take it, and I told her that. I said, "Look, you might be a great actress," trying to y'know at least make her feel good about herself a

---

[6] Yes. He's right. That's what I did.

little, "but your voice. It's just horrendous, and if I have to listen to it for one more line I just, I don't know, my head might explode."

She started to respond, but I quickly threw my hand up in the air. "No!" I screamed almost. "No, don't, not another word, please. I'm sorry, but you have to go now." And I put my hands on my head, like rubbing my temples, because my head seriously hurt.

And then there was Julie who was a fatty. And that just boggled my mind because in the audition notice I specifically said that the character of Stacy had to be in good physical shape. So why would this girl even show up?

And Barbra came in in prob'ly like the sluttiest outfit I've ever seen, where like the neck line came about down to her navel. I'm exaggerating of course, but not really. And she came up and leaned over the table, pushing her boobs together with her biceps and thrusting her cleavage right into my face, like this was supposed to make me think that she was a great actress. Because I could see all of her bra and most of her breasts?

And all these other people who came in to audition with resumes of all kinds, some with alleged real experience, though I remain skeptical. And they acted, after a fashion, to the best of their abilities, and I was distraught to say the least. I thought really for a second that there was no way this thing was actually going to happen.

And I told Chris he could audition, because he wanted to so much. And after he was done I thought, "Wow, maybe I will cast him," because after those first few hours he was great by comparison. But the fact was that I didn't really feel like we had two people who could really play the parts the way I needed them to be played.

But then this guy Jack showed up, and it was like the clouds parted as they say, even though I'm not sure really what that means exactly. I mean, I know that what they're talking about, those people who say this, is that after a storm the clouds part and the sun comes out, but the thing of it is that I've never really watched clouds part, y'know as much as they kind of all drift off or disappear or something, or whatever they do y'know, that I don't usually watch, because usually when there's a storm I try to go inside so I don't get all wet or whatever, so I'm probably still inside when the storm ends and the clouds part and the sun comes out, then I go back outside if I feel like it, unless y'know I've found something to do inside like a good movie that's not over yet or a 1,000-piece jigsaw puzzle that doesn't have a picture on the box to make it extra challenging, and once I start a puzzle I can be on it for like hours, just kind of in the zone as they say, which is something that I don't actually know either what it means or where it comes from or what they're talking about, these people that say these things. But the point is that I don't think clouds really part to let the sun shine down, because from what little I remember from science class, clouds all drift in one direction from the wind or whatever or the front — like a cold front or a warm front — if that's even the right word or I don't know. But I'm pretty fairly certain that you don't just have like two clouds right next to each other and one decides to head north while the other heads south and so they part and then the sun can shine through. Or maybe that can happen, because what do I really know? I'm just going off a high school science class, and not even that entirely as much as just what I remember from that class that I probably didn't really pay a lot of attention in.

But Jack did show up and that's the real point and he was really good, and he had like this whole list of projects on his resume, and I'd actually heard of some of these movies. And so like I knew I was going to cast him and I could see on Chris's face that not only did he know that I was going to cast this guy, but also he knew that this guy was better than him, which was good, because then I knew that Chris wouldn't fight me on it.

And I'll tell you now, even though this is jumping ahead a little bit, that we offered Jack the role and he was totally willing to make whatever accommodations necessary so that he could play the part even without pay, because he thought this was such a great script even though he hadn't read the whole thing yet and I'd just kind of synopsisized it for him. He also said it would be his first lead role in a feature-length film, so that was also a reason why he was so excited.

"Usually, I just do short films or get a line or two in some feature that comes to town," I remember him saying, "but this sounds like such a great opportunity." And it was a great opportunity, which is why I don't exactly understand precisely what happened later, but that's getting ahead of things.

What I need to tell you about now is casting our female.

Jack came around about one in the afternoon, and I already told you that we auditioned from nine 'til two, so he was getting on towards the end, and we still didn't have anyone to play Stacy. Well, that is, there was this one girl Rebecca who wasn't so bad, but she also wasn't so good, but I thought if worse came to worse then I'd cast her. It might not be ideal but it'd be, y'know, okay.

But the thing is Chris had told me about this girl Liz that he was friends with and he told me she was really good. The thing is that I was skeptical, very, because of the other people that I'd seen already that morning that Chris had invited. If she was anything like them, then well, Rebecca'd be our Stacy.

"I thought you said your friend was coming," I said to Chris around one forty-five.

"She said she'd be here later. She had some modeling shoot in Sugarhouse today."

"Well, I gotta be honest," I said, "if she can't even make it on time to the audition, I don't know if I can trust that she'll ever be on time for our shoots."

"First of all…" Chris started.

And I thought, *Oh great, here he's gonna go off on me again.*

"First of all," he repeated, I don't know why, "she didn't have an appointment to be late for…"

"But it's getting on near two and I don't see her and she knows we're wrapping this up at two, does she not?"

"And secondly," he just ignored my interjection. "Secondly, she's at a modeling shoot in Sugarhouse. She can't just bail on that. How would you like it if you cast her and she bailed on your shoot to make another audition?"

"Well, whatever," I said. "If she doesn't get here soon, we'll just have to go in another direction."

"If she's not here in the next few minutes, I'll call her cell and see how far out she is."

"So what about that guy Jack?" I said.

"I don't know," Chris shrugged. "What about him?"

"He was really good."

"Yeah. He was alright."

"He was the best we saw."

"I don't know about that. Jeff wasn't bad."

"Jeff?!" I just about exploded. "Jeff? That was that one dude you invited with the faux hawk, yeah? He was terrible."

"Not so terrible."

"I think we should cast Jack," I said.

Chris leaned back in his chair, and I could see that he knew he was going to lose this battle. But I was impressed with his resilience. He was not just going to let this go without a fight, and I could see all kinds of things broiling inside his brain.

"Yeah, but I don't know if he would really look good with any of the girls," was what he came up with. "Except that girl Kristin. He'd look great with her, but you couldn't stand her voice and made her cry."

"You know which one you'd look great with?" I said.

"Who's that?"

"Julie the fatty."

"Oh," he said and paused and smirked and laughed a little. "Thank you." Then he paused again for a long time like he was concocting some new argument.

"I just don't know if you'll really get the chemistry you need between Jack and any of those girls," he finally spat out.

"And you think you'd be better."

He just smirked. Then kind of half-shrugged in a way that said he didn't think he'd be better but still really, really wanted this.

"You told me," I told him, "that you'd step aside if there was someone clearly better…"

"But he's not clearly better."

"Yeah," I said, kind of wincing because the truth makes you wince, "he is."

"It's your call," he said, finally surrendering. And he sat there staring at the opposite wall for a while, and I was sincerely afraid that he might cry. Then he said, without looking at me, "I'm just afraid you might have some ego problems with him."

"Ego problems?"

"He might want to do things one way that's different from your way and you might really have some problems. That's just the impression I get."

"And I wouldn't have any ego problems with you?" I asked him.

He just raised his eyebrows and smiled. Looked at me then back at the opposite wall without saying a word, because denying that you're prideful is like the very definition of being prideful, and he knew he was.

"I'm gonna call Liz," he said and pulled out his cell phone.

While he listened, while the phone rang I assume, I looked over all the head shots and resumes we'd gotten that morning. I mostly looked at the head shots of the girls, and mostly the hot girls that I knew I wasn't going to cast anyways.

"Hey there," I heard Chris say. "You on your way?"

I don't really remember all the exact words, because it was a typical modern cell conversation with snippets of phrases and small talk and the gist of it all was that she was close.

I looked at the picture of Kristin and here's the thing. She was really pretty. It was such a shame that she had such an awful voice because... Well, whatever. And I threw the picture of Julie right into the trash, and you can think I'm shallow or whatever and maybe I am, but also she reminded me of someone I wanted to forget. And for some reason I really got hung up on Barbra's head shot, which was actually a couple of pages and the second one had several photos that looked like maybe some modeling shots or something and in any case she was on the beach in a bikini in one, and in another she was wearing some tight jeans and also she was topless, but you could only see her back because she hid her breasts with one arm and she was kind of leaning frontways against a palm tree.

"So you'll be here..." Chris said.

"...in about two seconds," I heard a female voice say from just outside the door before Liz stepped in and clapped her cell phone shut.

"Hi," she said.

"Hey there," Chris said and stood up to hug her hello, then nodded at me. "This is Warren."

"Nice to meet you," she said and extended her hand.

She was hot. I'll just say it, because that's what I did. "You're hot," I said, as I shook her hand. It was a good hand.

"Thank you," she said, like she heard that all the time, which she did.

"Never heard that before, have you?" Chris asked her.

"No, never," she laughed.

"So..." I said, but I kind of stumbled all over myself. "You look familiar."

"No, she doesn't," Chris said. "You don't know her. And she has a boyfriend."

I didn't really want her. She was just hot. That's all it was. And sweet. But my heart belonged to someone else, and you can't just...

That's just the thing I guess. With men. With people in general. You want it because it's there. You sometimes forget what you really want when something enticing is in front of you. So there I sat slobbering like an idiot all over myself. "So we'll..." I started then forgot what I was saying. "I can tell you're really good, and Chris said you're really good, so this audition is just a formality."

Chris looked over at me, smirking and scratching his eyebrow.

"What?" I said to him.

"Just a formality. You didn't even..." Then he trailed off. After a second he said, "Whatever, fine. You wanna read?"

"Yeah, sure," Liz said. "Which scene?"

I don't remember which scene she read, but she was good and I didn't regret preemptively giving her the role. When she was done I simply said congratulations. She was very gracious and even excited, asked about the schedule and things and I tried to answer her questions, but I couldn't really think, so Chris pulled out a production calendar that I didn't even know he'd made and handed it to her.

"I'll walk out with you," he said and got up.

They left the room, and I took a moment to pull myself together and think about what I'd just done, and I replayed everything over again in my mind and was just embarrassed for myself. That wasn't even me.

I couldn't decide whether it was a good thing that Chris was there or not. I mean, he was there to keep me from making a complete and total ass of myself, but he was also there to see and remember the thing forever.

"Shameless," was all he said when he walked back into the room.

"What do you mean?"

"Absolutely shameless. Without shame."

"What's shameless?"

"You. You are shameless."

"I didn't even do anything," I protested, because really I hadn't done anything, right? That's the way I remembered it.

"You started to, and I stopped you. And you're an idiot."

I shrugged like I didn't know what he was talking about and pulled a cola out of my bag. Chris pulled out his signature ginger ale and a slice of 14-grain bread that looked like something... I don't know, like something that a person shouldn't eat, like one of those things covered in seed that you hang in a birdcage for parakeets to peck at.

"So Jack and Liz, then," he said.

"I feel good about it." I took a swig of soda. "How long have you known her?"

"Since my freshman year of college. We were in the theatre program together." He sighed and folded his arms. He leaned back in his chair like he knew what I was going to ask next.

"Did you two..."

"No," he cut me off before I finished the question.

"You don't even know what I was going to ask."

"I'm sorry," he said. "What were you going to ask?"

"I was going to ask if you two were ever in any plays together in college," I said.

"Yeah, I'm sure that's what you were going to ask," he said, "yeah, we were in one show together. And also there was never anything going on between us, since that's what you were really going to ask."

"I wasn't going to ask that."

"Yeah, you were."

"So maybe I was, but you're telling me that you and her have been friends for what, seven years, and you never even like made out or anything?"

"No," he said emphatically.

Now I knew for sure that this guy was gay — not that there's anything wrong with that.

"Why not?" I asked.

"Why have you lived in Utah your whole life and never been skiing?"

I shrugged. "I'm not into skiing."

"Okay, then."

"But that's not like skiing."

"I'm married," he almost shouted.

"I'm talking about before you were married," I said.

"No. Nothing ever happened."

"You seem awfully defensive."

"Not defensive. Irritated," he said.

"Why? Because you tried to get with her and you were denied?"

"Never even tried," he said.

Definitely gay!

"Why not?"

"Because I didn't want to be like you or every other guy she's ever met in her life."

"What does that mean?"

"Slobbering all over yourself, speaking incoherently, treating her like a piece of meat."

"That's a little clichéd, isn't it?" I said.

"Well, I'd say it's pretty accurate."

"You never even wanted..." I started, but he cut me off like he felt compelled to keep on explaining himself.

"I like her a lot. As a friend. And even though she plays along when guys act like that, she doesn't like it. Not really. She's told me as much. And I don't want to be that guy. Which isn't to say that I've never been that guy. Just not with her. Also, when I was growing up, my dad always told me that if you're looking at a woman for any length of time and you can't tell me what color her eyes are, then you're probably looking at her the wrong way."

"I don't see what that has to do with anything," I said.

"How did we even get onto this topic? I'm not comfortable talking about this with you. That's all I'm going to say about this."

Like he was hiding something, I don't know.

If you want to know what I really think [...][7]

---

[7] No one cares what Warren really thinks.

And I don't know why, but then I steered the conversation in this direction. "You and your dad have a good relationship?"

"Yeah, we get along pretty well."

"Like you respect him?" I asked.

"Yeah."

"Really?"

"Yes, really. Why?"

"Hmph," I snorted. Maybe Chris was *The Exception*, because I didn't know anyone who liked their father.

"I hate my dad," I said.

CHAPTER 29

THE RING TWO

Really though, all I remember is waking up on a couch in a strange apartment with a really bad headache. And also, the thing you need to remember in this chapter is that at this time I didn't have a cell phone.

I sat up and rubbed my temples. I was still wearing my tux, which I thought was probably a good sign, though I didn't know what it was a good sign of exactly. And I wondered briefly whether I could get the deposit back if I'd slept in it, but then I realized that first of all there was no way the people at the tux place would know that I'd slept in it and also that place didn't require a deposit so it was a moot point anyway.

"Good morning, sleepyhead," some female voice that seemed eerily familiar carried shapeless and unpleasant images from somewhere behind me.

Who was that?

How did I know that voice?

Who calls someone "Sleepyhead"?

I started to turn around, but stopped halfway because I suddenly remembered...

I'd been at the wedding.

That terrible wedding.

The birds weren't all going to die, because they'd thrown fake rice.

I left the community building and went...

I couldn't remember exactly.

A bar?

But I didn't drink.

Did I drink?

I had a headache for sure. I had trouble piecing together all the events of last night and this morning. And I'd just woken up on the couch in a strange apartment.

These were all things I'd heard happen after a night of heavy drinking.

I must have been drinking.

I remembered the bar.

And I was there for hours.

And this girl came, that I knew from somewhere, and I had the ring.

The ring!

Did I still have it?

I checked my coat pockets.

No.

My pants pockets.

No.

I stuck my hands down between the cushions of the couch.

Nothing.

I got down on the floor. Looked everywhere. Couldn't find it.

I tore the cushions from the couch.

"What are you looking for?"

Who was that?

I needed to find that ring.

"I made you some breakfast."

I was looking under the coffee table when I heard the plate clap against the tabletop. I raised my head just a little and saw the ring on a finger attached to a hand that extended from an arm that went up to a shoulder bone connected to a neck bone that propped up a head. Her head. That girl! The fat friend. Skinny now, but she'd always be the fat friend to me.

Why was she wearing that ring?

"I hope you like pancakes," she said, like that was supposed to mean anything, because, seriously, who doesn't like pancakes?

"We didn't..." was all I got out, and I sat back on the couch, because there was no need to look for the ring anymore because I'd found it, on some girl's finger.

"Didn't what?" she asked.

I just stared at her.

If this was a movie what would happen is that I'd discover that after getting sloppy drunk the night before, and running into Sherry, that we drove to Vegas and got married and I probably passed out right after the ceremony and so she drove us back to her apartment while I slept in the passenger seat, and now I've woken up on the couch to the sound of a very sober woman, who was now my wife, cooking pancakes.

And you could easily hit Vegas in five and a half hours if you drove eighty the whole way and Wendover was only about two and a half hours straight west, but I didn't know if they did those quickie weddings in all of Nevada or just Las Vegas. Given the logistics, sitting there in my probably hung over stupor I started to worry that maybe the movie version of the events might actually be the real version of the events.

But the fact is that this is not a movie, it's just my life. And we didn't drive to Las Vegas and get married the night before when I may or may not have been crazy-ass drunk.

This is what happened, as I discovered from the formerly fat friend, and I'll just recap in my own words, because the way she told it to me took about forty-five minutes. Apparently she drove us back to her place where we went up the stairs to the apartment and sat in the living room. We talked for a long time, and I guess I told her about the ring and that I'd bought it for someone I hadn't even met, who'd just gotten married. But I hadn't told her who it was, and I hadn't told her that I'd seen her before, and fortunately I'd at least had the good sense to tell her that my name was Brett, and so she didn't know who I really was. She didn't seem to think that buying a ring for someone you hadn't met but were obsessed with was weird at all, and I know now that this should have set off all kinds of alarms in my head, but I was so tired and in such a daze that she just seemed like a nice girl. And apparently after I'd told her all that, I'd fallen asleep, and she'd left me there.

I was too hung over or whatever to really be irritated by any of this. But I was a little annoyed that she hadn't even given me a blanket before she left for bed.

"I hope you don't mind," she said, after re-explaining all this to me, "but you left this out on the table." She held out the ring, still adorning her left ring finger, where it was not supposed to be. "I just couldn't resist. After the wedding yesterday I just wanted to pretend a little. And who knows? Maybe I'm your destiny."

Yeah, I know this should have set off a siren inside my brain, but I just smiled and sipped whatever this beverage was, not coffee, but bitter and black like it.

"So, my husband," she laughed. "That's weird, isn't it? It's just pretends. So, darling," and she laughed again. "What should we do today?"

I just smiled and kept sipping my whatever. Slowly I started to realize what kind of a situation I was really in, and it wasn't good.

I looked at her over the rim of my coffee mug as I sipped. Her arm was fully extended in front of her with her fingers splayed in all directions, and she was admiring the diamond and grinning like that pink-and-purple striped cartoon cat.

This chick was out of her mind.

And so was I.

Could you blame me though? After the day I'd had?

And then I started to wonder...

And I know what you're thinking.

...but I started to wonder if maybe she wasn't right. Maybe she was my destiny.

She'd been there at the movies.

She'd been there at the party.

She'd been there in the mall when I found the flier for the copy center and the one for the ring.

She'd been there after the wedding.

AFTER the wedding.

Was this all just coincidence? Or was this fate?

She really might be...

She clapped her hands together. "I know," she exclaimed. "We could go for a picnic."

...my destiny?

Yesterday I'd all but given up on destiny. I'd even questioned whether it was real. But now I wondered again, was this destiny? Was I wrong about

Allison? Was I misinterpreting all the signs? Was it possible that I was meant to be with Sherry?

I started to wonder, y'know.

I don't know exactly what I was thinking except that I was thinking about all this stuff.

Sherry kept talking, but I wasn't really listening. I just kind of stared down into the bottom of my cup of...

What was this stuff?

Was it that drink that old people drink? I couldn't remember what it was called, but it came in that plastic container and had like grains on the label.

Postum!

That's what it was called.

But I don't think that's what this was, because Postum was lighter I think. I'd only seen it a time or two at Marty's place. But somehow I seem to remember that it was lighter than coffee, and even though this wasn't coffee, it was definitely dark like coffee and darker than I remembered Postum being.

So it probably wasn't Postum.

You know what it was. It was probably that other beverage that my dad used to drink, I forget the name. I think it was European or something, but it came in this big cardboard canister like Quaker Oats and I think it had an orange lid.

That's probably what it was.

I took another sip.

It needed sugar or something.

"What do you think?" she said.

"Hmm," I looked up. "I'm sorry, what?"

"What do you think?"

"About what?" I said. "What do I think about what?"

"Weren't you listening to a word I said? That's so like you. You never listen to me. It's like I can tell you a thing a hundred times and it never gets through."

I buried my gaze in my mug.

"And another thing," she continued, "you left the toilet seat up again. I swear, if I've told you once..."

"What are you talking about?"

"I'm sorry. I was just playing marriage again."

My jaw literally dropped and I kind of ran my tongue around inside my cheek. I didn't know what to say. There was nothing I could say. I was speechless.

This girl was...

There was no way this girl was my destiny.

"But what do you think about a picnic?" she asked.

"You want to go for a picnic in November?" I squinted at her, trying to figure out if I wasn't being Punk'd or something, but then I remembered that you have to be famous to get Punk'd, so maybe like a YouTube candid camera thing, but I think this was before YouTube so some other internet site is probably what I was thinking, like the *Star Wars* kid.

"Sure, what's wrong with that?" she asked.

"It's a little cold outside."

"You don't have to have picnics only in the summertime," she blubbered. "You can have picnics all year round. It's not like there's a law against having picnics in the fall."

"Yeah, but it's almost like Winter. There's snow on the ground."

"It's fall!" she said emphatically, and I thought she might actually stand up and slap me.

"Why don't we ever go out anymore?" she asked.

"What? Wha— Are we playing marriage again?"

She didn't respond.

"Umm…"

She started laughing, hysterically, like a hyena. I mean I've never heard a hyena laugh, but you know like in the metaphorical sense.

"I'm totally messing with you," she said.

I started to laugh, but didn't, y'know, because I was kind of scared. It was almost like if you looked deep enough into this girl's eyes you could actually see the psychosis.

"But seriously, a fall picnic is not such a bad idea. I mean if you want. You don't have to."

"Okay," I said. "Where should we go?"

"Sugarhouse is nice. I love Sugarhouse Park. Oh, and maybe we could get a kite."

"Okay."

"What do you like?"

I shook my head. "What do I like?"

"Like sandwiches. What kind of sandwiches do you like?"

"I don't know. Whatever."

"Like egg salad?"

"Egg salad's fine."

"And the deli down the street has a really good mustard potato salad. Do you like potato salad?" she asked.

"Sure."

"And we could feed the ducks."

"I'll bet there won't be any ducks there," I said.

"Why not?" She sounded almost mad.

"No reason. No, you're probably right. We can feed the ducks." Then I took a deep breath. "Here's the thing though, I need to return this tux, and I should really change if we're going to have a picnic."

"What? So you need to go back to your house?"

"My apartment? Yeah."

"Oh, you just have an apartment?"

"Yeah. Why?"

"No, nothing," she said. "I just thought you were rich."

"So I'll meet you at the park," I said.

"Well I should probably give you a ride home."

"That's not necessary. I can walk. I don't…"

I was about to say I don't live far from here when I realized that I had no idea where here was. I could be walking a long ways. Or there were always the UTA buses, but no one rode those, and I had no idea even which ones ran near my building.

"Sure," I said. "You can give me a ride. But we should get going."

"I'll get my keys," she said, and she tousled my hair as she walked by.

⚲ ⚲ ⚲

"So I'll go pick up the food and you'll meet me at the park?" she asked as we pulled up in front of a building two blocks from mine.

"Yeah, twelve-thirty," I said.

"Can I come up and see your apartment?" she asked.

"Yeah, umm, I don't know if that's a good idea. My sister's kind of sick and I don't want you to catch anything."

"You live with your sister?" she asked. "That's kind of weird."

"Why is that weird?"

"I don't know. Well, which one is yours?"

I pointed. "Third floor, second from the left."

"Oh. Do you want me to walk you up to your door?"

"No," I said with restraint, though I felt like shouting it. "I'll… No that's okay. You can just go as soon as I get out of the car."

"Oh no, I'll make sure you get inside okay."

This was going to be interesting.

I walked up to the building trying to formulate some kind of plan.

I could run.

I didn't plan on meeting her at the park anyway, and I wasn't planning on ever seeing her again. I could make a run for it.

But she'd probably chase me, and who knows what she'd do then?

I started up the staircase.

And she was going to wait until I got inside?

I got to the third floor.

I could pitch myself right over this railing here. That might be the best plan.

But what if I survived?

I'd be in the hospital for weeks and no doubt she'd be by my side every waking moment.

I had to fake it.

I got to the apartment I'd told her was mine.

Now what?

I pretended to search my pockets for the key. Not finding it I turned around to her and shrugged, mostly to see if she was still watching.

She was and she rolled down her window.

"Are you okay?" she shouted up at me.

I waved.

I could knock, and whoever answered, I could explain the situation to them and I'm sure they'd let me in. Especially if it was a dude. A chick might think I was being heartless.

Well fifty-fifty, I thought. So I knocked.

I waited like an excruciating thirty seconds. No answer.

"Can't you get inside?" Sherry shouted from the car.

"I'm fine."

I knocked one more time.

Still no answer.

A spare key.

Under the mat, I desperately hoped.

But was I really going to go inside this person's apartment if I found one?

"Do you want me to come up?"

Yes, I was.

I bent down to the mat and lifted it...

A dried leaf, some dirt and debris, and a couple of dead bugs.

No key.

I pinched the bridge of my nose.

"I'll come up," I heard Sherry shout. And a couple seconds later I heard the car door slam.

Then I noticed it.

The left door jamb was separated from the wall of the building just a little bit. I looked.

Yes.

Jammed inside the space was a key. Not a very good hiding place.

But you could barely see it, hooked to a little wire that I pulled on and out it came.

I stood up and held it out for Sherry to see.

"I'm all right. I've got a spare," I shouted.

She shaded her eyes with one hand and looked up at me.

"Okay," she said and headed back to the car.

Maybe she'd leave now, I thought. Maybe I wouldn't have to actually go inside.

But she wasn't going anywhere, just sitting in the driver's seat smiling up at me. What was she waiting for? I had the key. I'd shown her. I was going to be fine.

But she just sat there.

I inserted the key into the lock, turned it and pushed the door open. I turned back and waved at her before stepping inside and closing the door behind me.

One minute, I figured, would be enough. I just prayed that the tenant wouldn't come home in that time.

And the thing is if this had been a movie, either I'd've walked in on a couple having sex, or I'd have accidentally let the cat out (which I don't think I did), or the owner would come home just as I was about to leave, and I'd have to use some quick thinking to invent an excuse for being in the apartment, and mayhem would ensue.

But really, I just waited about a minute in a very average apartment that belonged to what was apparently a newly married couple and their newborn. That's what I gathered from the pictures and the mess in the kitchen anyways. Then I left.

♀ ♀ ♀

It wasn't until I got home that I realized I'd parked my car near the community center the day before and I was going to have to go get it.

It was then that I realized something else.

I was taking a shower when I noticed that the tub was leaking. I mean not a lot but a little, and it wasn't the tub exactly. It was like you know when you shower in a bathtub but you can't exactly get the shower curtain all the way up against both ends of the tub and you try to get it a little wet at first so you can kind of use the moisture to stick it to the tile wall, but inevitably some of the spray is going to get by it and get on the floor. And that's what I'm talking about, except that I also noticed this time, and actually it was just after I'd gotten out of the shower, that the sealing at the base of the tub was leaking a little bit.

I thought about calling the people in the office, but I didn't think it was enough water to really cause a problem, and if it was then the people downstairs would call.

See that's what I realized though I'd known it before because he'd told me. I realized who the people downstairs were. And it wasn't just going to be him anymore. It was going to be him and her. They were on their honeymoon now, but any day now they'd come back and it would be them living down there.

I'd have to move. But I couldn't wait to move; I had to leave now.

I didn't know when they'd be back. Either of them could be students, so they might have to have a short honeymoon and for all I knew could be back tomorrow. So I had to get out of there as soon as possible.

I didn't know what I was going to do. I didn't have any friends, and I couldn't afford a hotel, but I'd figure something out. And as soon as I found a new place to live I'd hire someone to go get my stuff and move it for me, if I could afford it or I'd figure something else out.

I pulled out an old gym bag and threw a bunch of clothes in there, enough for seven days at least, and I figured if it turned out to be longer than that, then I could always find a place to do laundry, or I could come back here in the middle of the night for like fifteen minutes and hope I didn't run into them or hear them or anything, and get some more stuff. Or maybe I could get Ashleigh to do my laundry.

I looked in the phone book to find when a bus ran near my house and what number I needed to catch and how much I needed to pay and how to get to the community building. I think it was only like the second or third time I'd ridden on a public bus. I mean, I'd taken TRAX[8] a couple of times, but I'm talking about a bus specifically.

---

[8] TRAX is the public light rail train system in Salt Lake City.

I was like Mark Knopfler during the 1980's and I didn't see a way out. And while I sat on the bus, clutching my gym bag and feeling like a homeless guy, which I kind of was right now, I thought about everything that had happened to bring me to this place in my life.

I replayed all the encounters with Allison. And I replayed the whole wedding, even the part where she said, "I do." And I tried to piece together the night before, when I'd inexplicably gone home with crazy Sherry, the formerly fat friend. And I re-experienced the waking up on her couch and her bringing me pancakes and wearing my ring and playing marriage. And then I re-pictured her from my fake apartment. I could see her getting out of her car to come help me find my fake spare key and looking up at me with the sun shining in her eyes and lifting her left hand to her brow to shield them, and I could still picture...

Holy crap!

I could still picture my ring on her finger, there below, shielding her eyes from the sun. She was still wearing my ring. She hadn't taken it off.

If I wanted my ring back, I was going to have to see her again.

Was it worth it?

On the one hand, the ring was worth thousands of dollars. On the other hand, there was no guarantee that crazy Sherry would give it back anyways.

But on the first hand, that ring was a symbol of my destiny. But on the second hand, I wasn't even sure I believed in destiny anymore.

But back on the original hand, that ring didn't belong to me, it was for Allison. But on the unoriginal hand, Allison was already married to someone else.

But if we were to say that the left hand is the one hand and the right hand is the other hand, then on the left hand, I was broke and selling that ring could make it so I could afford to move, or even give me a little money to produce my movie. But on the right hand, Sherry was psychotic.

But back on the hand that I didn't use to write, it would just be stupid to leave a ring worth thousands of dollars with a crazy lady just because I was afraid of her.

So I sat there on the bus looking at all the fingers spread out on both hands. And the extended thumb on the one hand made all the difference and I realized that I was going to have to meet Sherry at the park and do my best to get that ring back.

Sugarhouse Park is a very big park. It's not like Central Park big, but it's a big park. It's not like you just drive up and park and you can see everything. There's actually a road that goes around the whole thing, and even if you were to drive that entire road you can't exactly see everything in the park. And as I pulled onto that road I realized that it had been a big mistake for us not to decide on an exact place to meet.

But I remembered her saying that she wanted to feed the ducks, which was absurd but I figured the duck pond was probably the best place to look.

And really, it wasn't very hard to spot her.

See, she had this gigantic kite that she'd bought. It was orange and blue and had to be five or six feet across. And she had unraveled about thirty feet of line or so and was running dragging the kite across the ground, where it would stick and hop occasionally but never lift off.

But I'll give her this: she was determined.

I parked and since she didn't know my car, she didn't know it was me. So I just sat there and watched her for a few minutes as she ran back and forth across the grass pulling that kite back and forth behind her. I knew it was only a matter of time before it caught on a sprinkler head or something and the line snapped.

Finally I got out of the car.

"There's no wind," I shouted as I approached her.

"You came!" she screamed. "I didn't think you'd show up."

"Why wouldn't I show up?" I asked.

"I just thought you were trying to ditch me. To tell you the truth, I didn't really believe that that was your apartment at first."

"There's no wind," I repeated.

"What does that matter?"

"You're not going to get that thing up in the air without any wind."

"What are you talking about?" she asked.

"Your kite. You're not going to get it to fly without wind."

"You obviously don't know anything about kite flying," she told me, then added, "I'm bored of this anyway."

She started winding the kite in, her right hand holding the spool and her left guiding the string. And yes, there was my ring. I was about to ask for it back when I had this vision of her freaking out, saying that was the only reason I came (which it was), and hurling it into the pond. So I tried to play it cool, which wasn't hard in a park in November.

"Are you sure you want to have a picnic?" I asked.

"Why?" she said.

"Because it's kind of cold out here."

"Well, I already bought all the food. See?" And she pointed to a ratty old blanket about twenty yards away with a basket on it. "I even bought a picnic basket."

"Okay. Well maybe we could go back to your place and eat," I suggested.

"You men are all the same. You just want to go back to my apartment because you're hoping that after we eat I'll just throw myself at you and we'll make out."

"No, I don't," I said and I really meant it. "No, it's just that it's cold. Look, we could even spread the blanket out on your living room floor and pretend we're having a picnic."

She just stared at me.

"And I won't try anything, I swear," I said. "I won't even try to kiss you."

"Well, don't say that. What? You don't want to make out with me?"

No, I don't. I absolutely do not.

But that's not what I said.

What I said was...

"That's not what I said."

"So you do want to make out with me," she stated more than asked.

"No."

"Is it because I'm not pretty enough?"

Y'know, before this I guess I never *really* understood those movies where women have these kinds of conversations with men, where they trap them and twist their words and misinterpret, in the most ridiculous ways, everything they say. But suddenly all those movies made sense.

"I just want to have a picnic," I cried helplessly, "but also I don't want to catch pneumonia."

"But you do want to have a picnic," she said.

"Absolutely. More than anything."

"Okay. But let's have it at your place."

"I told you my sister's sick."

"That's right. K, fine. Do you want to ride with me, or do you remember where my building is?"

"I'll just follow you," I said and headed to my car.

I didn't even think about helping her with the giant kite or the ratty blanket or the basket, but I'll admit it was kind of funny to watch her struggling with all that stuff in one armload back to her car.

We had our picnic on her living room floor, on the ratty old blanket, which I'm sure was covered in lice or some other bacteria, and I couldn't stop scratching for the rest of the day. I may have even developed a rash.

After we ate, she made me watch that one movie with her, about the nanny and where they sing about flying kites. I think it was an obsession.

And I'm pretty sure that movie was intended for little kids, not for people in their twenties on dates, but she was crazy. And through the whole thing I tried to figure out how to ask her for the ring without setting her off.

When it was over she took all the dishes into the kitchen.

"I'll wash, you dry," she said.

I hadn't planned to help her, just to get my ring and get the hell out of there. And also there were a lot more dishes in there than just the lunch ones.

"Okay," I said. And she handed me a towel.

I hoped she'd take the ring off to do the dishes, then I could grab it and make a dash for the door, but I wasn't so lucky. And it kind of irked me that she was getting dish soap all over my very expensive diamond.

I wanted to ask about it, but I was struck with another vision of her screaming, "You never really loved me!" then chucking the ring down the garbage disposal and grinding it to a powder, then pulling a kitchen knife from the block and stabbing me through the throat.

And since I liked my throat I didn't say a word about it. Also, I couldn't say a word about it, because the whole thing had been so vivid I actually felt choked a little, like I really had been stabbed through the throat.

As she scrubbed the dishes, she hummed some song I didn't recognize. As I dried the dishes, I started counting my fingers again on the one hand then the other. When I got to the thumb on my left hand I forgot what I was doing and the plate I'd been drying fell to the floor.

It was one of those everything goes slow motion things as I watched it tumble through the air. When it hit I remember thinking, "Wow, putting carpet on the kitchen floor was a really good idea." I didn't know that I'd seen too many kitchens with carpeted floors.

I picked up the plate and handed it back to Sherry so she could wash it off again.

The logic of the one hand still outweighed the other and I knew I had to get that ring back. I didn't know how, but I had to get it back.

"Will you take me to dinner tomorrow night?" she asked as I dried off the last fork.

"Umm..." I had to keep her happy. "Sure. Where do you want to go?"

"No place expensive," she said, "just like not fast food. Someplace we can sit and talk and have a nice romantic evening out."

"Okay."

"You choose."

"Okay."

We walked back into the living room and she handed me my jacket, which I needed because it was cold outside.

"Listen," I said, "can I have my ring back?"

And briefly I saw her left fist coming toward me, diamond first, the stone square on my eye, piercing my cornea and plunging deep inside the eyeball, eye juice spraying everywhere. And just for a second I wondered what eye juice looked like, or if it was just blood.

But it was just another of my visions.

What really happened was something I hadn't expected at all but probably should have.

She burst into tears.

I tried to be sensitive, so in my most sensitive tone I said, "It is my ring."

"I know," she said. "But today was like the very best day of my entire life. I just like being married to you, Brett, even if it is just pretends. I don't know. I've just..."

And she blubbered and sobbed, then went on.

"...You're the first real boyfriend I've ever had."

First what?

But I wasn't going to say that. I just nodded compassionately. And though you may not believe it, you're about to learn that I really am, or at least I can be, a pretty nice guy.

"My best friend just got married, and though I always knew she'd get married before I did, it's just really hit me, you know?"

She stepped a little closer to me, and I knew what she wanted, but I just couldn't do it.

"I'm just lonely. And I just want to have somebody, so badly. I know I might seem a little crazy, and maybe I've acted a little crazy but I'm just reaching out I guess."

I succumbed. I put my arm around her and she cried into my shirt, which was a very moist and very uncomfortable feeling.

"I was afraid that the only reason you came today was to get the ring back and I'm afraid that if I give it to you, you won't come back tomorrow like you said you would."

She was absolutely right, but I couldn't tell her that. But the thing was that for some reason, I don't know why, right now I also couldn't lie to her. So what I said was this: "Why don't you hang on to it for the night. You can pretend we're still married or engaged or whatever, and I'll get it back from you after dinner tomorrow."

She smiled, though tears were still streaming down her face and her make-up was running all over the place. I looked down at my shirt and held back an exasperated sigh over the huge mascara stains. I smiled at her in that trying to be sincere way while holding back sheer frustration.

Then she surprised me yet again.

She raised up on her toes and pushed her face towards mine. It was a half-second before I realized what she was trying to do to me, and another half-second before I could react. But I did react, and I did react just in time.

I jerked my head to the side and in the same motion bent down and gave her a big hug.

"I'll pick you up at six," I said as I pulled away.

I opened the door as quickly as I could and stepped out into the hall. I waved and began my departure.

"Brett," she said, and I almost forgot that I was Brett and kept walking, but then I turned around.

"I love you," she said.

I was glad it was dark in the hall, because my smile might have looked sincere in the dim light. I'll tell you though, my smile was not sincere at all. It was a mix of annoyance, discomfort and also terror. I couldn't say anything, so what I did was I blew her a kiss and turned and walked away.

I got into my car and needed to think, to plan, to figure things out. I thought that maybe I'd drive around for a couple of hours, but gas prices were getting ridiculous (around $1.50/gallon) so I decided that wasn't the best option. So what I did was I went to the Dairy Queen and bought a sundae or something and sat down in the corner booth to ponder.

I'd done enough pondering about Sherry so I was done with that subject. The best thing was just to get her out of my head altogether.

What I was really thinking about was Allison.

How could she be married?

Really?

Was this all just a dream?

She was going to be my downstairs neighbor.

She couldn't be though, because I wasn't going to live there anymore, even though I did really like the building and the managers were good, and the rent was good, and the location was perfect for me. But I couldn't stay there, not with Allison and her husband downstairs doing whatever they might be doing downstairs.

It was kind of getting into evening, so I didn't have a lot of time to figure out a place to go. I thought about going back to my apartment just for the night, because it was likely that they wouldn't be back yet, but the truth was that I didn't really know for sure that they were having a honeymoon right now; they might be planning that for later because they just didn't have the time right now.

I scraped the rest of the ice cream out of the cup or bowl or whatever and I was suddenly struck with a solution.

Well, sort of a solution.

Let's call it a band-aid.

But for the time being...

And I don't know why exactly it struck me just then.

Like in a movie, what would have happened is that I'd finish my ice cream from the clear plastic bowl and I'd see there on the table, through the now see-through plastic, a newspaper, and the bottom of the bowl would form a perfect circle around the solution.

But that's not what happened. What happened was I just thought of it.

♀ ♀ ♀

They wouldn't let me in, and I was kind of relieved to tell you the truth.

I drove back and forth past the homeless shelter several times, watching the crazies and drunks and drug addicts in their little congregations outside. I wasn't going to park right there, obviously, but I wanted to kind of scope it out. And I was very nervous.

And really, I should have thought of this, because I'd driven by Pioneer Park countless times, and you always saw these people there, dirty and getting into fights, and also you knew there were all kinds of diseases. Because, in fact, I heard this story one time from a guy I worked with at the theater about a guy who was just walking through Pioneer Park one day and he got stuck in the ankle by a discarded syringe that had kind of flipped up from the ground. And that guy got AIDS, he said. And I don't know if that's a true story or not, but it's enough to make you scared of homeless people and druggies and Pioneer Park.

But I did park over by the Mexican restaurant in the two-hour parking, but it was only two-hour parking from eight a.m. to six p.m. I think or something like that but not in the middle of the night, so I'd be okay because I figured I'd be out of there before eight.

And so I walked the few blocks to the shelter with just a change of clothes in a plastic grocery bag and tried to get into the shelter.

I told them I was homeless and needed a place to stay.

The man there looked me up and down and told me I looked like a kid who was tired of living with his parents and didn't have any money for a hotel.

I assured him that that was definitely not the case, and I told him that I didn't have a place to stay.

He said that I looked too clean and tidy to be homeless and that was nice to hear, but I still needed a room. Then he said that they didn't have rooms, just beds. And I told him that that wouldn't do because I would need my own room, and I asked him if there was another shelter anywhere that had private rooms, and he just stared at me like I was an idiot. Then he said that they were full anyways, and I asked him why he didn't just tell me that to begin with, and he shrugged, and I called him a rude name and left.

"I know this is a little fast," I said, "but since we are married would it be all right if I stayed here for a few nights?"

I couldn't believe that it had all come to this. And I know you think I'm crazy for coming back here, but you maybe already thought I was crazy for letting her keep the ring for another day. And in truth I probably was a little crazy.

But you gotta understand. The love of my life, my destiny, had just gotten married. My life had shattered, for all intents and purposes, and you can't understand this until you go through it yourself. And I sincerely hope, unless you're a real jerk, that you never have to go through what I went through.

"Why?" she asked.

"Because we're married," I said and laughed, because this was so uncomfortable.

"That's just pretends," she said.

Why was she being sane now?

Now, when I needed her to be a little nuts.

"I got home and a pipe had burst in the bathroom. It was leaking into the apartment below. I called the apartment office and they sent over the repair guy and he had to call a plumber and the plumber came and he said it would take a few days and I wouldn't have any running water and also they'd have to shut off the electricity, but I could stay if I wanted, but it would probably be better if I found another place to stay so..."

"They didn't give you another apartment?" she asked.

"Our whole complex is full up," I lied again.

"And they wouldn't put you in a hotel?"

"I guess maybe, if I absolutely couldn't stay in the apartment, but they said I could if I wanted, so they weren't going to pay for anything."

"And where's your sister?"

"She's staying with the neighbor's upstairs. They have a daughter her age and so for her it's like a long sleepover. She's really excited."

"I'd love to have you stay with me, but..."

"But what?" I asked.

"You'll have to sleep on the couch."

I wouldn't have it any other way.

"And you should know," she said with a very stern, almost scolding look, "I'm not going to sleep with you if that's what you're trying, even if we are pretends married. I'm saving myself for real marriage."

"Oh, thank goodness," I said.

"What do you mean?"

"I mean I'm so glad that we share the same values. For I too am saving myself for marriage." I paused. "Real marriage."

"Are you just saying that?"

"No. I'm all about charity."

"Chastity."

"I'm all about chastity," I said. "And seriously, if it makes you at all uncomfortable, we don't even need to see each other while I'm staying here."

"Well I want to spend time with you, and we have that date tomorrow night," she reminded me.

"Well we definitely shouldn't like kiss or anything."

"I don't know that I'd take it that far."

"It's just that, y'know kissing leads to making out which leads to...other things and...well, y'know, we should be as careful as possible. Frankly, I don't know if we should even ever hold hands or anything, because that kind of thing, y'know, well I might have a hard time controlling myself. So, I mean, at least while I'm here staying in your apartment."

"Well," she said, "we'll just see what happens then."

I nodded.

She let me in and got me the ratty old blanket and an equally ratty pillow.

"I love you," she said as she left for the bedroom, and she hung in the doorway waiting for a response.

Really, I had no choice.

"I love you too," I mumbled half-intelligibly, and I think I could actually hear her smile as her lips curled up and she sucked in air between her teeth. Then she went to bed, and I tried to sleep, wondering what I'd gotten myself into.

♀ ♀ ♀

Did you ever do something at night when you were maybe really tired or not exactly thinking clearly and then wake up in the morning and the full impact of what you'd done suddenly hit you like a ton of bricks?

That's how this felt, only it was more like five or six tons of bricks.

See, I knew I'd been totally out of my mind, but that didn't change the fact that I'd done what I'd done. And it didn't change the fact that I was here. And it didn't change the fact that she was in the kitchen making breakfast again.

After we ate she said I could feel free to wash the dishes if I wanted to contribute, which was annoying. Y'know, because she could have just asked me to please do the dishes, or even if she hadn't I'd have done them anyways.

She said she was going to take a shower. And I forgot to tell you that she was wearing a bathrobe, not that that really matters, because either way, whether she was wearing a bathrobe or not, she was still going to take a shower and she told me so.

And as she walked down the hallway to the bathroom, I saw her take my ring, and the one she wore on her right hand, off her fingers and clutch them in the palm of her hand. Then she disappeared into the bathroom.

And I'm sure you know that what I'm setting up by mentioning that is that when it comes time for me to get the ring back that I'm going to do it while she's in the shower, and this could be a little awkward and require some stealth and strategy. And you're mostly right, but that comes later and we're not there yet.

Now I could tell you about every little detail, like how several minutes later Sherry came out of the bathroom in her bathrobe with a towel wrapped around her hair and asked what I wanted to do that day, and then I thought, "What, doesn't she have a job?" Then I remembered that I had a job that I was supposed to be at the day before, when I'd been at a picnic and that I was also supposed to be at today, but there was no way I was going to drag myself into work now, and I'd have to come up with a good story to keep myself from getting fired, but I'd figure out what that story would be later. And then how she got dressed while I was in the shower, and while I was brushing my teeth she came into the bathroom and wanted to brush her teeth alongside me, because she said there was something slightly romantic about that, and I thought that was weird, but it was her apartment and she was letting me stay here so I let her brush her teeth next to me.

And so I did tell you all those details, but there are lots of other little details that I also could tell you about, but I'm not going to, because they're not pertinent to the whole story that I'm trying to tell, and also I don't remember a lot of them.

What is important is that after we were both dressed and ready for the day, she asked me again what I wanted to do, and I shrugged because I didn't know and didn't really care. She suggested a bunch of things like going to the mall or the park (again!) or the batting cages, and I didn't want to do any of these.

Then she asked if I wanted to drive up to Logan and go to the cheese factory. This was an interesting idea to me for some reason that I don't know. I was intrigued. I'd never heard of this cheese factory, and I asked her about it. She said it was just a cheese factory up in Logan.

"Do we like go on a tour or something?" I asked.

"No. You can just buy different cheeses or they have all these different kinds of flavored milk, like vanilla or strawberry or root beer."

"Root beer milk," I said. "I haven't had that since elementary school."

"They also have squeaky cheese."

"Squeaky cheese?"

"Cheese curd, but it like squeaks when you bite it, so we've always called it squeaky cheese," she said.

"Who's we?"

She shrugged.

The cheese factory sounded like a decent enough idea, even if it meant sitting in a car with her for three hours round-trip. I'd like to see this cheese factory and try these flavored milks. So I agreed to go.

⚇ ⚇ ⚇

Even though it meant that I had to pay for the gas, I drove, because I'd ridden with her enough to know that I didn't want to do it anymore. Just that little stint from her place to my fake apartment was like putting my life on the line.

The fact that I drove turned out to be a major positive for reasons that I hadn't foreseen. See, I drove a stick-shift, not an automatic, which meant that I pretty much had to keep one hand on the stick at all times and the other on the steering wheel, so that no matter how much she tried, Sherry could not hold my hand.

And it was a long drive and she talked most of the way, about her life, and how beautiful the canyon was, and about this new outfit she'd bought just the other day, and about this other new outfit she'd bought a couple of days before that, and about her mother and how they didn't get along very well and she didn't think that her mother treated her father very well and she didn't understand why he put up with it and why they were still together, and about how her parents were pretty well off and even though she did have a part-time job she kind of made her own hours and didn't work very much because if she ever needed money, as long as it wasn't like a ton of money, she could always call her dad and he'd help her out, especially with like rent and utilities and stuff like that. And also she talked about many other things that I don't remember, either because they weren't important or because I zoned out.

The cheese factory was cool enough I guess. I mean it was basically just one room really, like a store kind of, but a small store that only sells cheese and also flavored milks. And so I bought a case of flavored milks with several different flavors. Which flavors exactly I don't remember, but it's not important anyways.

Also, I bought some cheeses, and Sherry bought a bag of smoked curd, and she was right that when you bit into those things they squeaked. And I remember this precisely, because the whole drive home she was squeaking in the passenger seat, and she kept chewing with her mouth open because she liked the sound of the cheese squeaking, and it was annoying as hell, and she never got tired of it, which I would think she would have, but she didn't.

There's one more thing I want to say about this trip before I move on to the next part of the story, and that's this: it wasn't as annoying as it could have been, the whole trip. And it wasn't as annoying as I had expected, because I expected annoyingness beyond all possible measure, like colossal annoyance, but she seemed to be like slowly drifting back down to earth and becoming a little, not a lot, but a little more normal.

Now here's the part that surprised even me.

We spent a very pleasant evening together when we got back to her apartment.

We decided not to go out, and so we ordered Chinese food, and we watched a movie, and she let me pick, and I chose that one where the Joker goes on that trip with the waitress and the gay guy. And even though she sat right next to me and laid her head on my shoulder, I still enjoyed the movie, and I actually kind of felt a little bit closer to her, even though I didn't necessarily want to be any closer to her.

Then after the movie we played that game with the DVD and you answer all the questions about the movies. I'd never played it before, and I don't remember what it's called, but I slaughtered her. And so we played again, and I killed her again, because like I've told you, I've seen pretty much like every movie ever made, so...

And when it was time to go to bed, I was almost disappointed, but also I was really tired. And we brushed our teeth side-by-side again, because she wanted to and before she went into her bedroom she stood in front of me and smiled.

And you know what's coming...

Yes, she did stand there and wait, staring at me, which made me a little uncomfortable.

Then she did sort of lean into me.

Then she did close her eyes.

And she did pucker up.

And she did continue to move closer and closer.

And I did know that she really wanted me to kiss her.

And here's what I did...

I kissed her.

I did.

It was short and simple.

And it was just a peck really is what it was.

It didn't mean anything.

And I'm not sure whether I wanted to do it, or if I was afraid she'd throw me out if I didn't, or if I just didn't want to embarrass her by deny-ing her again, or what I was thinking exactly.

But I did kiss her.

And it was the first time she'd ever been kissed. She told me that the next morning.

And after, she threw her arms around me and hugged me tight. And she was very happy, I think. And the fact that she was so happy made me feel bad, because I had no intention of keeping this up longer than necessary, and also I felt kind of like I was using her, which I guess I was. But she did have my ring, so...

Oh, and also I should tell you that that was my first kiss too.

♀♀♀

The next day was possibly both the oddest day of my life and also the happiest. Because what happened was totally unexpected and in a lot of ways completely nonsensical, but I can't say it didn't elevate my spirits higher than, I don't know, the highest thing ever.

See, I woke up to Sherry's voice. She was on the phone with someone, and all I heard her say was, "Sure. If you need anything, don't hesitate to ask." Then, "Byebye, sweetie."

I didn't really think about it, because that's not really what's important. What's important here is that I'd missed two days of work, and really for no good reason.

I looked at the clock. Seven. I could probably catch Ashleigh before she left for school or work or whatever it was that day. I don't remember.

So I called.

"Hello," she said.

"Hey, Ash..."

Before I could say anything else, she screamed, "Where are you? I thought maybe you went off and killed yourself because of the wedding."

"Would I ever do that?"

"Honestly? I don't know. Where are you?"

"I couldn't come back there, because of, well, you know, with them living downstairs, and..."

"They're not."

"What do you mean?" I asked.

"I had no way of getting a hold of you," she blurted. "You've got to get a cell phone. By the way, I covered for you at work. I told them you had Strep, so you'd better stay away for another couple of days. But I didn't really know if you'd ever be back."

"So what's going on?" I said.

"They didn't get married!"

"Yes, they did. I was there."

"Yeah, but not... No. Okay, so I ran into the guy from downstairs yesterday, which I thought was weird because they should be on their honeymoon, right?"

I shuddered at the thought. "Right."

"Yeah, but," she continued. "But they're not. I asked him what was up, said didn't you get married. He said no. I asked what happened, did he get stood up at the altar or what? He said they got through the wedding and all that, and technically they were married, but they started driving out of town for the honeymoon, he said they were going to Disneyland but were going to stay in St. George for the first night. So anyways, they're driving out of Salt Lake, they get to just like barely south of like Alpine or American Fork or wherever…"

Ashleigh had my ability to ramble, especially when you really wanted her to just get to the point.

"…and all of a sudden Allison says they need to go back. 'Did you forget something?' he says. And she goes, 'No, we just need to go back.' He gets a little concerned, because that's weird, right? And so they turn around and she tells him to pull over to the side of the road where she tells him that this whole thing just doesn't feel right. She doesn't know what it is exactly, but there's just something. And he's all sad, but what can he do, he can't force her. So she suggests that they go to the county offices and file for an annulment, which they do right then, that day. And so he comes back here, and Warren, even though this is great news for you, I have to tell you I kind of feel bad for the guy. He's so sad."

"Screw that guy," I actually said out loud, which I now realize was pretty heartless, "she's *my* destiny."

"Exactly!" shouted Ashleigh.

I believed in destiny again, with more conviction than ever before. The universe was on my side after all.

I got off the phone and ran into the living room to pack my stuff. I knew things would all work themselves out. I mean, I didn't exactly know it, because I had doubted, but deep down inside I think I did know it, y'know.

Sherry came into the room.

"Are you leaving?"

"Umm," I said. "I just talked to my sister. She said they're done with the plumbing already."

"I thought it was going to be at least a week."

"That's what they told me, but it looks like they're done early. So I can get back home."

"And you have to leave right now? You're not even going to have breakfast?"

I supposed it would be impolite to leave before breakfast, so I sat down with her, antsy as ever to get out of there, and we ate whatever it was that she cooked that I scarfed down without tasting it.

"Last night was really special," she said across the table and reached out and took my hand.

Then I remembered last night, and suddenly I felt really, really bad.

I was totally going to ditch her. She didn't even know my real name. And I was never going to talk to her again, and she'd never know why. I tried to come up with an alternative, but there was none that I could see, and so I felt really bad and also really nervous, like sick to my stomach.

"So, can I have the ring back now?"

And suddenly her eyes welled with tears.

"I do need it back," I said. "I'm sorry."

Then she was full on crying.

"I don't want to give it back. I love it. I love you. I..."

And she was just sobbing so hard she couldn't speak. And I felt so bad, but this was kind of crazy behavior again, a little bit.

"I know, but I'm going to..."

"No!" she screamed.

"No?"

"I'm sorry," she said. "I'm just, I'm not ready yet, to give it back. Just... One more day."

What was I supposed to do?

"One more day," I said.

"I know you're anxious to get back to your apartment," she said through the tears, "but could we maybe, I mean, I could drive you back there..."

"I have my car," I said.

"But I could go over there with you and we could spend the day together," she offered. "And maybe I could meet your sister."

I half-smiled, not in a happy way. And then I nodded a little, against my better judgment.

"I'll get these dishes," I said. "Why don't you go get showered."

She did.

And you already know what happens here.

And you prob'ly think I'm the world's biggest asshole, but really I'm not. I had no choice.

She went into the bathroom and locked the door behind her.

But it was one of those locks where it just has that little hole on the other side and you just use that tiny key that looks like a little screwdriver to pop the lock open. And like so many other people, she kept that little key over the door, which completely defeats the purpose, but whatever.

And I unlocked the door quietly and I slipped in and found my ring on the counter next to the sink, and I took it. And that was all.

I didn't see her naked. I didn't have to make up any reasons for being in the bathroom, because she didn't even know I was in there.

And I grabbed my bag and my cheeses and my flavored milks from the fridge, and I snuck out of the apartment leaving her with a sink full of dirty breakfast dishes.

Which I also felt bad about.

CHAPTER 30

LEFT BEHIND

Ashleigh cried pretty much the whole way back to my apartment, which I thought was a little weird, because Kara running off wasn't really going to change our lives that much. Even if we never saw her again, which we probably wouldn't, we'd seen her like maybe a cumulative hour and twenty-two minutes in the last five years anyways.

When she was still crying like three hours later, I decided I'd better do the brotherly thing and ask if she wanted to talk about it. She said no, and so I let it drop, because at this point in time, I didn't have that much experience with other people, and I didn't realize that even though she said she didn't want to talk about it that she really did want to talk about it. And I learned this from the fact that after she said no and I left the room, she started crying much, much louder.

And so I'm not totally retarded, and I realized that she was doing this because she wanted my attention. So I waited just a minute and went back into the living room and sat down next to her.

See, what she was upset about wasn't so much that Kara was gone, but she realized that Kara running off while under my supervision pretty much ensured that there was no way that I was going to get custody of Ashleigh. And even though nothing official had happened with my mom yet, we both knew that there was no way she was going to be released back on her own and also get her kids back.

So the only logical thing was that Ashleigh was going to be put in foster care, which sucked for so many reasons. That's why she was so upset, and once I understood it, it made me upset too. But I didn't really see a solution, except that I could make a case and I could fight it.

Despite everything, I figured they'd still probably let her stay with me until my mom had undergone the whole trial process and whatever had to be done, but at this point they, to my knowledge, still hadn't figured out that Ashleigh was a minor.

It was pretty much the next day though that they did.

And here's the thing about that.

They sent a social worker over to decide what to do about things. I don't remember the woman's name but she was short and I think half-Latino, but that doesn't really have anything to do with anything. She asked about Kara, and I told her more or less what happened, except without all the details like that I was there and basically let her go. She seemed to understand the whole running away bit and said with teenagers it happened often enough. What she didn't understand however was why I didn't call the police and file a report immediately. She said that clearly demonstrated poor judgment and a poor sense of responsibility or some- thing like that. And I just said that I figured she'd run off to a friend's house and would probably be back any day or any time.

But she also interviewed Ashleigh and concluded that for the time being, since I was immediate family and over twenty-one, she could stay with me. But the lady made it very clear that when everything was all said and done and my mom had gone to trial, it was very unlikely that the courts would grant me custody, and if they couldn't get a hold of my father Ashleigh would be placed in foster care.

Now if you remember that this whole thing that I'm trying to tell you about is all a true story, then you know at least one thing this chapter isn't about. Actually, you should know several things this chapter isn't about, like it's obviously not about an alien invasion or a Big Foot sighting or anything ridiculous like that, and it's not about like a 9.9 earthquake, because that definitely would have been reported on the news and since that's never happened, and also it's not about me being eaten by a shark or a bear or a python or a swarm of angry gnats, because then I wouldn't be around to tell you this story, would I? And Elvis does not have a cameo in this part of the story either.

But the one thing in particular that you know this chapter is not about is the one thing that you might think it's about if you forget that this is a true story. And that's that I decided to make a case to get custody of my sister and I was going to act as my own attorney and battle the courts and finally after months of blood, sweat and tears and heartache and brother- to-sister bonding and all kinds of stuff like that, then the courts would finally assign me custody of my sister and we'd live happily ever after and both get married (not to each other, because this isn't a weird French film) and have kids who would play together and we'd move into neighboring condos.

But that's just the movie version. What really happened was that I just planned to go to the court and argue to the best of my ability, but also I planned to lose, because as the social worker had said, I was probably going to.

But there is more to the story that actually turns the whole thing into a completely different story altogether.

See, I'd seen lots of courtroom movies and so I knew that trials were no speedy things, and me and Ashleigh hoped that this one would just drag on and on until she finally turned eighteen and we wouldn't even have to worry about custody. But we were not so lucky. This thing was all over in a matter of days, because my mom's public defender convinced her to plead guilty, because she was.

And she did.

But the thing about that was that her public defender was no idiot.

Though I'm not sure how the whole court system works exactly, I do know that by pleading guilty to possession, my mom's lawyer got them to drop the other three charges. And see that's one of those court things I don't understand, because I would think it would be pretty easy to prove possession, so why drop those other charges just because she pleads guilty. Wouldn't you have gotten a conviction anyways?

In any case, for my mom's sake, I was glad that it happened the way it happened, regardless of whether or not I understand why.

This was a few years ago, so I don't remember what the exact sentence was exactly, because what actually happened was this: instead of actually like doing time in prison or whatever my mother could complete what amounts to rehab at an inpatient drug treatment facility.

I don't know that it really made that much difference because the facility she was sent to wasn't much better than a prison, at least that was the impression I got the one time I visited her.

And before you judge me and think I'm this terrible person who only goes and visits his mother one time while she's locked up, I'll tell you why I only visited her once, and that's because that one time I did go she told me that it was my fault she was in there and that she hated me and never wanted to see me again.

I guess she hadn't gotten to step number nine, or whichever one, yet.

But here's another thing I didn't know still happened. I mean, I knew it happened way back when, like in the 1920's or something. But I didn't know that still today, people could be committed if a doctor, I mean a psychiatrist or whatever, diagnoses them as I guess insane.

Anyways, that can still happen.

Only if they feel she poses a threat, as in a violent threat, to other people, which I guess they decided she did. Maybe because she attacked the police officer, I don't know, even though that charge was dropped. Or maybe something happened inside the rehab place. I don't know.

Of course my mom was already locked up, so when they declared her clinically insane and a threat they just moved her to another facility. I guess they could keep her for up to one year or something like that. I don't know if that was like the limit, but that's how long they were committing her for in any case.

And in any case, since it's been a couple of years now, I know that she's since been released, but I haven't heard from her and neither has anyone else I know. To this day, I have no idea where my mother is.

I have to say that I still love my mother in spite of everything and I don't blame her for any of what happened. She was married to my father and that would make anyone go crazy.

But anyways. Through the whole court proceedings and everything, the question of custody was never raised, which I thought was interesting, but I wasn't going to complain, until I found out that they'd gotten a hold of my dad and he was flying over here — from Berlin, just like Brian had said — to take her back with him.

This infuriated me, because we all knew that he didn't really want her. He'd made that pretty clear when he walked out on all of us. He was only doing this because he had no choice. I tried to get this across to whomever, but no one would listen and because I'd just heard about this from a phone call, I didn't know whose attention I needed to stop this.

When the phone rang again a few minutes later and it was a long distance number I didn't recognize I passed it to Ashleigh, assuming the courts or whoever had given my dad my number and he was calling to make arrangements.

I was right.

I didn't want to even hear his voice.

After she hung up she told me that he was flying in the next day and that he had to show up in person to the courthouse to sign some papers and she could meet him there.

As she packed all of her things, the ones she had at my apartment anyways, I asked her, "Do you want to go with him?"

She shrugged.

"Seriously," I said.

"I've never been to Europe. They probably wouldn't make me finish high school," she said.

"You've got a point there."

"I don't know. There are worse things," she said. "And I'll be eighteen in not too long, and I'll be able to do whatever I want. Come back if I want then."

"Yeah," I was kind of sorry to hear this, because even though I liked living alone I'd gotten used to her here after only a few days. And also, I knew I'd be better for her than my dad.

"I mean, you don't really make enough money for the two of us," she said.

"But what if I did? I mean, what if I got another job or something?"

"Another job doing what?"

"I don't know," I said. "But what if, just what if, if you could choose would you rather stay with me or with dad?"

"With you for sure," she said.

"So maybe ask him," I suggested.

"Wouldn't that be illegal?"

"I don't see why it would be, but definitely not if no one knows about it. And it's in everyone's best interest, is it not?"

"I don't know."

"You could just ask him," I said. "It can't hurt anything to ask."

"You don't make enough," she zipped up her suitcase.

"I pay the rent already. What do you need, food and clothes? We could figure something out."

"Warren, I want to stay here," she turned to me, "but it's not practical."

"Isn't it?" I asked.

She shook her head and the tears started flowing.

"I guess it's not really," I said.

That night, knowing that she was leaving the country the next day, we went out for dinner and then went and saw a movie.

"Do you want me to go over to the house and pack the rest of your stuff for you?" I asked before we went to bed.

"No, I'll just have dad take me over there after."

"Good night," I said, and I almost felt like a parent losing a child, and I almost felt like I should tuck her in which was a weird feeling. I'd never tucked anyone in. I didn't even know what a tuck-in entailed, especially since she was in a sleeping bag and there was nothing to tuck.

The next morning I dropped Ashleigh at the courthouse at the appointed time with her one suitcase and watched her walk inside.

Maybe I should have gone in with her, I guess maybe just to make sure she was okay and everything went all right, but I couldn't face him. I did not want to see my dad.

I drove off angry and just drove and drove around, wherever I decided to turn or not to turn. I don't remember where I went or what I was thinking exactly. But what I do remember is arriving at both a decision and a destination at almost exactly the same time. See I finally decided that I was going to face my father and confront him about everything he'd done to us, to me, to my family, to my mother, and I was going to call him to the carpet, or the front walkway, and tell him that Ashleigh was staying with me. And so I arrived at my mother's house, hoping they were still there packing. But there was no car out front. I didn't see how they could have finished so fast, so I thought that maybe they hadn't gotten here yet, and I decided to go inside and wait.

I unlocked the front door and stepped into the living room. The kitchen light was on. I walked back to check it out, but there was no one in there. I could hear, however, some noise coming from one of the rooms upstairs.

"Hello?" I called.

A moment later, someone emerged.

"You came back?" I asked.

"What?" she said.

"You looking for more stuff to sell?"

"What are you talking about?"

See, normally, almost always in fact, I had no trouble telling my sisters apart. But for some reason now I didn't know who was standing in front of me. And I couldn't for the life of me remember what Ashleigh had been wearing that morning. And I certainly don't know what it was that made me assume that this was Kara. Then suddenly I could tell.

"Ashleigh?"

"Yeah."

"Where's dad?"

"Look," my dad said to Ashleigh as they pulled into the driveway of my mother's house. "I don't know how else to say this, but I don't really want you."

I was floored by his bluntness, but at least he was honest.

"I mean, you're my daughter and I love you and I always will, but I don't want you to come live with me. I have a new life now. I'm living with a woman. She's not really into children."

"I'm not a child," Ashleigh interjected.

He just smirked then said, "Wouldn't you rather stay here anyway? Couldn't Warren take you? Wouldn't you rather stay with him?"

She stared at him for a moment.

"I'd provide for you," he said finally, "financially."

"Can we live in the house?" she asked.

"That's another matter," he said. "The bank contacted me and this place is basically in foreclosure. Your mother took out a mortgage and a second and wasn't exactly responsible with the payments. But you can take everything in it. In fact I'd recommend it, and get it all out of here as soon as you can."

He pulled out his checkbook and scrawled an amount.

"Here," he handed her the check, "get a moving truck and whatever else you need. And what, I'll send you two thousand a month. That should take care of all your expenses right? Rent and stuff?"

"You can afford that?"

"You know what they say," he said, "if it ain't broke, it's really rich." I have to admit, that one was better than the ones he used to say. "It's less than I was sending your mother, and it's not like she'll be needing it now."

He paused for a second with no one speaking, then...

"I'm sorry, honey," he said, like the "honey" part was something he was reading out of a script and he was one of those auditioners that came to my casting call. "I really am, but neither of us would be happy if you came to Europe with me."

"That's okay," she said and opened the car door. He put his hand on hers and it was awkward for both of them, so he quickly removed it.

"Oh," he stopped her, "and this is, uh, very kind of, I don't know how legal this is, since I just technically signed for custody of you, so let's don't tell anyone about our arrangement, okay?"

☿ ☿ ☿

"So what are you still doing here?" I almost shouted after she finished the story.

"I'm packing," she said. "We have to get everything all moved out as soon as possible."

"Why didn't you call me?"

"I did, but you weren't home, and you don't have a cell phone."

This was true. At this time I also did not have a cell phone.

☿ ☿ ☿

We spent the next couple of days packing up the house, getting everything out that we could. It was also nice that that second day was a Saturday, so we could do a little yard sale, and that's how we got rid of most of all the old furniture. What we couldn't sell in the yard sale we pretty much either pawned or sold over the internet or we put in storage.

So we spent that Saturday afternoon, after the yard sale, cleaning out that second bedroom in my apartment so that we could move like Ashleigh's bed and dresser and stuff into it.

My stuff that had been in there we pretty much put into a storage shed with the other crap from the house. We agreed that I would continue to cover the rent for the apartment, but Ashleigh would pay the monthly on the storage unit. And we paid for the moving truck and all that with the money from my dad, which surprisingly was like a bonus check on top of that first month's "child support" payment.

After we'd gotten all our stuff out of the house we came back and took every single light bulb, including the fluorescents even though I didn't really know what we'd do with those since I didn't have any of that kind of fixture in my apartment. And we also took the 9-volts out of the smoke detectors, and I unscrewed all the little springy doorstops from the walls and took them. And I collected the mousetraps from the kitchen and bathrooms and the roach and wasp sprays from the garage, and also the light bulb from the garage door opener. And I took the shower heads that we'd installed several years ago, and shower curtain rod and shower curtain, and the old antenna and mini-satellite dish from the roof. And I took the washer and dryer to my apartment, which was nice because I had hook-ups but not the appliances. And I put the refrigerator with the ice cube trays in the storage shed along with the water softener. But I also took the potable water expansion tank off the water heater and took that too. And I dug up a lot of the flowers from the yard, until I was tired, and I gave those away to the neighbors, and also the vegetable plants. And I took the garden hoses and many of the garden tiles. And the lawn hadn't been mown in weeks and I left it that way. And I dug up the mailbox from the curb and I took it. And I also took a doorknob from one of the bedroom doors, but only one, because I didn't want anyone calling me asking questions. But I took everything I could think to take, because if these sons of bitches from the bank were going to take away my mother's house, I was only going to surrender the bare minimum.

I was going to just leave the key under the mat for these people, but I'd taken the mat, so I just left it there on the porch.

I'd also taken the hide-a-key rock.

The following Monday, after school and work, Ashleigh and I went to the post office to fill out some change-of-address forms — for everyone in my family — to be sent to my place.

And that was good, because a few days later I got this letter in the mail, addressed to my dad, saying that my mom's car (the one Kara had taken) had been found abandoned on the side of the road just outside Sparks, Nevada. And it said also that if I wanted to get it back I needed to show up in person and pay the impound fee and some other fees. Or else they could have it towed to Salt Lake, but the fee for that was something ridiculous.

Now this was both good and bad news.

It was bad news because it made me worry about Kara, and it made me wonder if she was alright. And it made me think about why she would just leave the car abandoned along the side of the road. The thing about this was that I knew that Kara was pretty self-sufficient and also that she could take care of herself. I didn't worry that she'd been kidnapped or murdered or whatever for too long, although some pretty gruesome thoughts did cross my mind. But what I also knew about Kara was that she was smart. I'm sure she figured that after she left in the car that sooner or later we'd have no choice but to report the incident and that we'd also tell the police or whomever what car she was in and that she'd be tracked down and brought back, so she had to get rid of the car. But the thing I know about Ashleigh and myself is that we're also pretty smart and when we did have to tell people about what had happened we left out the detail about the car. And what I know now about all those people, the police and whatnot, is that they're not too smart, because they didn't even ask about the car or look into it or anything.

And so I figured that since Kara was all into art and all that, and that Sparks is just outside Reno, which is right along I-80, which is a direct route from Salt Lake City to San Francisco, I figured that Kara was probably on her way there, since I think from what I know of the place San Francisco is a pretty big place for struggling artists.

So she'd probably ditched the car and hopped on a bus or something.

But the good news about the impound notice was that Ashleigh needed a car, and we didn't really have the money right then to buy her one. And we figured no one would come looking to seize the car, especially if they didn't know about it, also because it was paid off. And the title was under my dad's name, and we had that in our possession.

So what me and Ashleigh decided was that I'd take another couple of days off work and we'd make a kind of vacation out of it, and we'd drive out to Sparks, Nevada to pick up the car.

♀ ♀ ♀

If you've never driven I-80 between Salt Lake City and Reno, let me explain something to you. It is one of the worst drives ever, ever, ever in the world. I've never driven through Kansas and I hear that's worse, but still this drive is pretty bad.

This is what you see:

You head out of Salt Lake City and pass the airport, so it's just pretty bland so far. You keep going and eventually you wind around the Great Salt Lake and this part isn't so bad because as you look around this is a pretty big lake, and also it looks like the road kind of runs right over it and there's lake on both sides, but y'know pretty shallow on the south side and a huge expanse of water to the north.

While rounding the lake you come upon this like Arabian-looking palace thing along the side of the freeway. I don't know what it is, but it's kind of like something out of a Mario Bros. game. It's really weird.

You keep going and you pass a few little towns that are big enough to have McDonald's but not, I don't think, big enough to have Walmarts. Then you come to this exit that says "Iosepa," which I guess is the name of a town maybe, but all that's there is this busted down old auto repair shop or like an old storage shed and gas station or something, which actually kind of looks like an old abandoned drive-in movie theater. Being there, the one time I pulled off there to check it out, reminded me of that one movie where teen wolf goes back to the future and he's at that drive-in out in the desert before he goes off in the time machine to the old west.

As you head farther west you pass a lot of weeds and shrubs and there's mountains for a little while, but then they disappear way off to the north.

It becomes pretty flat and not pretty at all, but just before you leave the mountains you pass the turnoff for the military testing grounds, where I'm convinced they test out nuclear and chemical weapons without the knowledge of the local population. I tried to drive out there one time to see what's going on, but it's way the hell up there, because you get off I-80 and wind around this crappy road for a while, then it's this poorly paved road heading straight north, but even after like forty-five minutes you haven't gotten anywhere. So I turned around and came back.

But once you've passed the military testing grounds you're just in the desert. It's dry, it's dull, and it's ugly.

You'll see, if you're watching, these trains way off to your left, which is south, and they look like they're skimming across water, but that's just what they call a mirage I think, unless it's spring when it does get kind of wet out there in parts, and it's like it comes up from the ground, but I don't know for sure if that's the case, or if it's from the lake or whatever, even though the lake's pretty far from this place now. But they say this whole basin used to be a big lake, Lake Bonneville, but I don't know if that has anything to do with the water across the ground or not.

After a while you come to the Bonneville Salt Flats, which are actually kind of cool, because it's just white, like white white, and nothing grows there, because it's covered in salt. And it just goes as far as you can see.

Out there there's this weird like tree sculpture thing, which I think they say is the Utah Tree or something like that, but it basically looks like a big, y'know, standing coat hanger with big painted Styrofoam balls on each of the branches.

And then as you approach the Nevada border, you also approach the Bonneville Speedway, which is where they break land speed records and stuff and also shoot a lot of TV commercials and movies, especially commercials for cars and things like that.

But at the Bonneville Speedway you can get off the freeway and drive out on this road, which is basically like, once you get out there, being in the middle of this vast white waste.

Then you hit Wendover on the Utah/Nevada border and you've still got about six or seven hours to Reno. And this is the part that sucks so bad. It's nothing. It's not even the pretty white salt flats. It's just nothing, just dreary desert.

If you go past Reno, you get to a really beautiful mountain drive up into California to Sacramento, but we were only going to Sparks, and so all we got was the Nevada wasteland, and it is a wasteland, with the occasional sleazy casino town with slots in the grocery stores.

⚥ ⚥ ⚥

Well we got to the Sparks exit, there in Nevada, pretty late at night because we'd driven all day, and so we figured since we were staying over-night anyway, we'd just get the car out of the impound the next morning. We'd gotten on the internet to book a hotel in Reno anyways.

Also, when I'd arranged with my manager to take the time off work to go get the car, he gave me a dollar in quarters to play the slots. Ashleigh gave me a dollar too, since she wasn't twenty-one yet and couldn't go down on the floor.

So I put the coins from my manager in my change pocket there on my right hip, and I put Ashleigh's money in my left front pocket. And after we checked in I went down into the casino to play. I wasn't going to use any of my own money though, because I know the odds of winning and I don't like just throwing money away.

So first I turned Ashleigh's dollar into quarters and took it to the machine. I dropped the first coin into the machine and pulled the handle. I don't remember what exactly spun up on the dial, but I lost the quarter. I dropped the second coin in and lost that one too, just like the third and fourth. So much for Ashleigh's money. I told her it was a dumb idea and a waste, but she insisted that it's only a dollar.

Now it was time to play with my manager's quarters.

"Oh, I see where this is going," you're saying to yourself. "You're going to win big on one of your manager's coins and you're going to have this moral dilemma over whether you should actually surrender the winnings over to your manager or whether you'll keep them for yourself. And you'll battle your memory over whether your manager's money really was in your change pocket or if that was really Ashleigh's money and your manager's was in your left pocket."

Well, I'm sorry to say that that's not what happened. What happened was I played all four of his quarters and lost every one, and that was that and we left the casino.

We had decided we were going to go out and see what Reno had to offer as long as we were here and still had a little bit of money left over from my dad's check and the yard sale, I mean after the moving expenses and gas money to get here and back and the impound fee and all that.

They call Reno, or at least they used to call it, "The Biggest Little City in the World." I don't know what this means exactly, because the whole thing doesn't make a lot of sense. What I think is that they need to replace the "bigg" in that statement with "worst," which I guess then would make it "The Worstest Little City in the World," which I realize is bad grammar but still pretty well suits the way I feel about Reno. And if you've been there then you know what I'm talking about. It's just awful. I mean, maybe Fargo, North Dakota is worse. I've heard. But really, Reno's pretty bad.

If you're a gambler then I guess there's stuff to do, because gambling is all there is to do. There's really no good shows, there's no entertainment. There's lots of hookers, so I guess that's another thing there was to do, but even if I hadn't been with my little sister I wouldn't have been into that.

Which reminds me of another trip Ashleigh and I took the next year down to Southern California. We also decided to cross the border down into Tijuana, Mexico. And if you've ever been there then you know what I'm talking about when I say that we were walking down the street and right in front of my little sister some guy hands me a flyer to come see his "sister" upstairs. And then he says I can have a free joint with my entrance fee, and I assume he means marijuana. I tell the guy I'm with my little sister and he says, "Give her the joint, and you come see the show."

This kind of thing does not happen in Utah.

CHAPTER 31
THE LONG GOODBYE

Marty dies.

I'm just going to put that out there right now, like you didn't already know.

And there's no other story, you know.

I mean there's lots of other stories that he told me that I haven't told you. I could fill a whole book with Marty's stories, all kinds of things, like his ship being attacked while he was in the Merchant Marine. Or stories like him trying to open up his own shop, which might not sound interesting, but the way he tells it and with all the details and everything. And there's lots of other stories.

But what I mean is that there's no other story, no special last story, that he told me. We didn't have this final visit where he related some deep allegory that opened my eyes to the meaning of life.

Though I wish we had.

In fact, I'd been visiting him for prob'ly a couple of years since he'd stopped telling me stories, and a couple months since he'd stopped speaking in complete sentences. Most of the things he said now weren't even coherent.

And he didn't really have episodes so much now.

It was more like everything was just one big episode.

Where there'd been parts before — the dementia, the physical ailments, the broken speech, the memory loss — now there was only one all-encompassing condition. All four parts were coming together, had come together, into one whole. And this whole was deep and bottomless and heart-breaking.

And it about knocked me over seeing Marty, my good friend, in this barely functional state, and even that not really. Which is probably why I stopped visiting him so often.

I didn't stop altogether, going to the home to see him. And I kept going because even though he didn't know me, I mean I think he didn't know me, or I don't think he did, but even so I think it did him some good to have a visitor, y'know, every then and again. But I didn't go every week, because I figured it didn't matter much, since he didn't seem to comprehend time anymore. Chronology was just a haphazard mosaic at this point.

And when I thought about that, I wondered if he even had days anymore. Because, I thought, without days I think I'd go crazy, because when I have a bad day or whatever, the best thing I can say is that it will all be better tomorrow, you know. But without time, how can you have days? And without that, how are things even endurable?

And I still visited Marty every two or three weeks, or once a month, or as often as I felt like I could take it. Only now there was no chessboard in between us, just the disease and three feet of atmosphere.

But the point is even though he was mostly a vegetable, when he died it affected me like nothing else ever had. More than the things I've told you about already, and more than some of the things I haven't told you about yet, and more than what happened to Brian, which to this point was the only real loss of a life I'd experienced. And I think it affected me so deeply because it signified something, but the thing is I don't really know what that something was.

See I was in this church. Not when Marty died, and not when I found out that Marty died, but before that. I was there with Chris and we were shooting the interiors for our movie like he'd said we'd do.

And this was a big church, like a cathedral, with the pews and the stained glass and the big crucifix and everything. And I had the camera, and I was shooting all this stuff for coverage, which is what you call the extra footage in case you need something to show because you didn't plan well or something, is what I'm told anyways. But I was shooting this stuff anyways, and you know I'm not a religious person because I've told you that already. And you know I don't necessarily believe in God, so I didn't really have any qualms about shooting in this church, even though Chris did, which I thought was weird because he wasn't even Catholic, which I think this was a Catholic cathedral. I think his problem mostly was that we hadn't gotten permission from anyone to shoot in here.

But that's besides the point, because the point is with my eye to the lens I noticed this stuff in detail. Everything in perspective, and you can take that to mean whatever you want. But I'm not saying that I had this spiritual awakening or anything like that. And you're misunderstanding me if that's what you thought I was saying, because I wasn't.

All I'm saying is there I was standing in this church and observing this stuff, and I looked at this hand-carved Jesus and this stained-glass Mary, and I wondered if maybe there isn't something out there, some continuance, some sort of existence after we all die.

Some people seem to think so. I mean look how much time and persistence someone dedicated to constructing this building to worship in and all this stuff in it, with just this invisible sliver of hope that maybe, just maybe, there's something else out there.

Now I've got to clarify, because I'm still not saying that necessarily there is or isn't a God. What I'm saying is maybe there's something, not necessarily directed or designed by any being or essence or force, but just something. I mean I hope there's something, something to give it all meaning. Because it just sure seems like such a waste if none of this matters at all. It'd be like watching a crappy movie with no theme, just fluff. And I don't want life to be just fluff.

Or maybe there is a God, because what do I know?

But I stood in that church and thought about Marty, because I think he was a Catholic or even if he wasn't he was definitely closer to death than anyone else I knew, and I wondered if this was the real and ultimate end to Marty's whole existence. And I thought if it was, why couldn't it have all come to an end months ago when he still knew he existed and knew who he was and could feed himself?

What kind of cruel joke was this that destiny or existence or God or the universe was playing on him?

And before that guy with the white collar came out and told us we couldn't film in there and asked us to leave, I decided I needed to go see Marty again and at least try to make sense of all or some of this.

⚗ ⚗ ⚗

They knew me there, and I knew the rules and the hours and all that, so I just walked by, waved to the nurse, she smiled at me, and I made my way straight back to Marty's room.

It must have been a good day for him, because he wasn't in his bed. They'd gotten him into a wheelchair and he was sitting in the corner, his head kind of drooping because that's pretty much all it did anymore, and he had his right fist under his chin, not really lending much support, with his forefinger hooked over his lips.

I pulled a white metal chair, the kind made for stacking, across the floor in front of him. I sat down and lowered my head to achieve eye contact and he raised his head slightly acknowledging my presence, and I thought I saw the beginnings of what could have been a smile, but I may just be remembering something that I've invented myself. In either case, or both cases, I smiled back.

In the version I like to remember, Marty's eyes flicker with life and he speaks coherently. "How about one last game?" he asks. And because I carry a travel board in my backpack everywhere I go, I agree and set up the pieces. He doesn't move the pieces himself, because he's obviously too weak. So he orates his moves and I physically move the tokens. It's close, but I see my opportunity for checkmate soon enough, but I let it pass and I let him win. As I put the board away, he tells me he knows what's bothering me. And he tells me not to worry. It's not the end. He tells me he knows this because he's been there. "That's what this disease is," he says. "I can come and go freely between this world and the next, only I can't tell anyone about it. That's where I am most of the time," he says. "There with my beloved Sarah." And I ask him why he comes back at all, and he tells me that his body just isn't ready yet. But there's something out there, he assures me. That's all he can say, but what I need to know is that it all means something, that there is a point.

In the real version, Marty's head droops back down and I look at him with what is suddenly an unbelievable and overwhelming sadness. And because this is what really happened, I suddenly believe in the impossible. I believe that Marty can speak as long as what he says is profound. Does this make any sense? Of course not, but somehow it did then. And I ask him, "Is it all just a meaningless mess?" He doesn't move because he can't, or won't. He doesn't speak because he doesn't. And I don't even know if he can hear me. But I keep going, "Is there anything out there? Or is this it? If anyone knows, it's you, and I don't know why, but it is, and you've got to tell me." A nurse walks by the room, but doesn't stop, but I do, seeing her. I don't want to look crazy to anyone but Marty. After a safe few seconds, I grab his hand and he clutches, firm but weak, like a baby, you know. It's almost frightening but not exactly, and I almost yank my hand back but then I don't. I lower my head to make eye contact again. "What's the point?" is what I say, and it makes sense to me in the moment, but why I thought he'd be anyone to talk to about this I don't even know now except that he was Marty, or is, I don't know. But it's like he doesn't even hear me. He stops clutching. I pull my hand away.

Now this is the part, because his eyes close.

He's asleep.

Not instantly, but gradually.

I've seen him do this a hundred times, sitting here in a chair, his head droops down, and don't worry because he's strapped in; and he drifts off to sleep.

When this happens I usually leave and tell the nurse on the way out that I'll be back in a week or so. But this time what I do is I just sit there and watch him, thinking and wondering.

I'm pissed and sad and bewildered all at once.

I watch his emaciated chest rise and fall with each breath. It barely moves, he's so weak.

Why doesn't he just die?

I think this and immediately feel terrible for thinking it.

His frame rises and falls so slightly, hardly any air entering or exiting his lungs.

But if there is something out there, he'd be happier wouldn't he? If he died?

Rise and fall.

But if there's nothing...

Rise and fall.

Well, he wouldn't know, would he?

Rise and fall.

And he doesn't really even know he exists now, so how would it be any different?

Rise...

But how can there be nothing, really?

Fall...

That would mean everything is meaningless, and how can it all be meaningless?

Rise...

Is this whole life just a scatterplotted mess of nonsense that no one can interpret?

Fall...

There is no point. How can there be? Look at this man.

Nothing.

It's meaningless. Nothing matters.

Nothing.

Marty wasn't even breathing anymore.

Marty slipped away right in front of me, and I was too preoccupied with myself and my own unanswerable questions to even notice.

Marty was dead, and I didn't even know it.

See because even though I was watching him breathe, I didn't notice when he stopped.

And I left him sitting there lifeless, his empty shell drooped over in that chair, and I left the room. And I passed the nurse's station. And I told the nurse that he'd fallen asleep and that maybe he should probably be moved to his bed. And she smiled at my concern. And I left.

And a couple hours later I got a phone call that Marty had passed.

And I remembered watching him stop breathing and I remembered that he died right before my eyes. And I remembered watching the man die and I remembered. And I remembered.

And I could hear and see and feel that last breath.

And I remembered.

And I spent the entire night awake, remembering.

CHAPTER 32
THE JERK

"Sometimes life just works out in your favor," he paused, I guess for effect, then, "and sometimes it just sucks."

Scott did a nice, slow push in.

"And... Cut," I said and turned to Chris. "I need to talk to you."

"What's up?" he said as he approached me from the corner. He'd been holding up a light or something, I don't remember, or hooking up a gel.

"This still isn't working for me," I said.

"What do you mean?"

"This whole thing."

"I thought it was fine."

"Are you serious?"

"I think they're doing a great job."

"Yeah, but it's that, I don't know," I said, "that, whatever, like, I don't know, take another look at the whole scene."

"What are you talking about?" he said.

"Look, the thing is I think we need to take a look at the whole scene, we need to start maybe, uh, like from scratch. Just go back to square... rewrite the whole thing, start fresh, start from a blank page."

"No," he said. "No, we don't need to."

"Well," I sputtered. "Yeah, we do. We need to get it as... This is a pivotal scene. We need to get it as polished as possible."

"Is there a problem?" Jack said from on-set, and when I say on-set I mean from the couch area in the apartment we were shooting in, which was my apartment because it's not like we actually had like a place to go that was, well you know what I mean, but anyways.

"No, there's no problem," I said, and I swear I saw him and Chris exchange some kind of snotty little smirk. I was getting really tired of this. "Uh, go ahead and take five everyone," I said. And everyone, y'know, was only like five people. It was me and Chris and Jack and Liz and Scott, who was the cameraman I'd hired on Chris's recommendation, and he was an alright guy.

So Scott put his glasses back on and pulled out his cell phone, and I think called his wife, I don't know. He was always on the phone with his wife, or she was calling him or they were text-messaging or whatever. Always. It was kind of getting on my nerves.

Anyways.

Jack came over. "Is there a problem?"

"No, there's no problem, it's just, we need to work on this."

"Work on what?"

"Umm, the...scene, it's just..."

"Is there something I need to do better?" he asked.

"No," I said. "No. It's just... Yes. Yes. Actually, yes, but it's not just... Well, what we need to do is we need to rewrite..."

"Again?" he exploded. "You want to rewrite again? This is like, I swear like the eightieth version of the script you've given us."

Chris just shook his head.

"I'm sure he's tired of writin' 'em." Jack looked over at Chris who nodded.

"Well I don't care," I said. "I don't care how many times we have to write this thing. We have to get it right."

"I don't understand. I thought it was fine."

"So did I," said Chris.

"You don't know anything," I said. "And that line, that line..."

"Which line?" Jack asked.

"The last one you read, the 'sometimes life just works out in your favor and sometimes it sucks.' I don't buy it. First of all, life just sucks, so there's no truth to the statement you're making. The whole premise is false. And second of all..."

And I kind of lost track of what I was saying.

"Second of all," I finally went on, "I'm not feeling it. It's like you don't understand what's going on in the scene."

"What do you mean I don't understand what's going on in the scene?" Jack shouted, like the prima donna he was.

By this time Chris had retreated to the couch, but he felt he had to add an "It was fine, I thought."

"No, it wasn't fine. Look, we need to start, we need to go back and rewrite the scene and start fresh."

At that point I guess Scott overheard from the kitchen. "Are you kidding me? Are we reshooting the scene again?"

"Well, we have to get it right," I retorted. "It's a pivotal scene."

"I..." and he sighed, then went back to his phone call, shaking his head and giving me this kind of evil eye. It was like there was some kind of coup going on here, and everyone was in on it except Liz who just sat over on the couch going over her lines like a true professional, and except for her I felt like I was working with a bunch of amateurs.

"I'm not rewriting this thing again," said Chris. "And I seriously hope you're not going to be this way with all the other scenes, and make me rewrite the whole thing again and again, over and over and over. Because I'm not gonna do that. That's ridiculous. Seriously."

"You can't expect us to sit here and memorize a new script every single day," Jack ranted. "Sometimes two in a day. Sometimes we go to lunch and we come back, we've got a new script to memorize, and it's the script for the scene we just spent all morning shooting and you want to shoot it again, with the new lines that are hardly different from the originals."

"Well don't you want this thing to be the best it can be? I need it to be perfect. It's too important. Are you not dedicated to the project?"

"Well sure I am. But this is nonsense! I can't work like this. You gave us the schedule. Well, Chris gave us the schedule; you didn't even have a schedule..."

"Yeah, I wish he hadn't done that," I said, "because I can't be tied down like that."

"You have to have a schedule!"

"Thank you," Chris interjected.

"Chris gave us the schedule that said we were going to shoot this scene and three more on the first day. It's the fifth day of shooting and we're only on the third scene. We're supposed to be done with eighteen scenes by now, and we've wrapped on two. And you've rewritten it so many times, I can't keep it straight. We start shooting version number, uh, forty-B and I get a line in there from version three-C."

"Well that's your fault. You should be a better actor," I said. "It's your job to memorize the new version of the script, and not confuse..."

"No!" Jack screamed. "It's your job to run an organized set. You've got you being picky and irrational. You've got Chris rigging lights and rewriting scenes at every turn. And you've got Scott over there running camera and doing whatever else he can. If you want to be that picky you've gotta hire a crew and staff and start paying everyone. We're already four and a half days over the production schedule, and you said this was going to be a simple three-week shoot, twenty-one days..."

"I know how long three weeks is," I said.

"And I got that much time off my day job. I've missed several other auditions to be here through rehearsals which all turned out to be un-necessary. And I'm starting to get the feeling that this movie's not even going to be seen by anybody so I'm not really sure what I'm doing here."

"You have no faith in the project then," I said.

"Look, all I'm saying is... I don't even know what I'm saying. No, you're right. I don't have much faith in the project. It's a disaster! This is seriously, like I thought this was going to be a good opportunity, but this is seriously like a joke, this movie. A crew of three, a cast of two, and eight hundred rewrites."

"Don't exaggerate," I said. "There haven't been eight hundred rewrites."

"Well, there've been at least six."

"There have not."

"Actually," Chris said, "if we rewrite again, it will be the seventh."

"If you're going to have that kind of an attitude..." I told Jack.

"You know what? You know what, no! I, I gotta walk. This movie's gonna end up in production for three years, if it ever gets finished. I don't have the time or the patience. You don't know what you're doing. This movie's never going to be seen by anybody. The whole thing's a mess. And it's too stressful. I gotta walk. I'm done."

"You're quitting?"

"I'm quitting."

"Fine. We'll find someone else," I said.

He walked over, picked up his backpack from the kitchen, waved to Liz, said call me. And I thought, what an arrogant... But I couldn't think what an arrogant what, I don't know exactly, just, something arrogant.

He and Chris shook hands, and Jack said, "Well good luck to *you*, my friend."

"So, ah, I've got your headshot and resume, so maybe in the future," Chris said.

"Yeah, that'd be cool. Let's work on something together," Jack said. And then he left. Didn't slam the door on his way out like I expected, but he might as well have.

Scott hung up the phone, turned around, said, "So what are we doing?"

"Jack just quit," I said.

"Yeah, I gathered that."

"Umm," I said, "well, uh... Why don't we break for lunch, and, uh, we'll figure things out." I looked at Chris. "Man, you were right about having ego problems with him."

I expected Chris to say, "See I told you so." But he didn't. He just raised his eyebrows and said, "Yeah. Whatever."

"Where we eating today?" Scott asked.

♂ ♂ ♂

We went to this little deli in the basement of the Boston Building downtown, which was kind of out of the way, but Chris insisted that the food there was awesome and as it turned out he was right. I'd never heard of or seen this place before and I wondered why. The walls were covered with instruments and jazz memorabilia (the music, not the basketball team), but I'm not sure why, because they had rock music playing.

About halfway into the meal, Chris finally spoke up. No one had said a word about our situation this whole time.

"So I guess I get to play the lead then," he said.

Scott snickered.

I looked at Chris and for the briefest second I wondered if he'd orchestrated this whole thing, like paid Jack off to quit. But I really didn't think he'd actually do that. But he was right; I didn't have a lot of options here.

"I guess so," I said.

"Which means we have to reshoot the first two scenes, I'm guessing," said Scott.

"No, we're gonna keep the ones with Jack and confuse the hell out of anyone who watches this thing," Chris said.

"Okay, mister sarcastic," Scott said. "I'm just pointing out that we're going to have to do that."

"Shouldn't take too long," I said.

"As long as you don't insist on thirty more rewrites," Scott tossed out there.

"We could shoot them after lunch," Liz said.

"Seriously," Chris cut in, "we're done rewriting now."

"Maybe," I said.

"No. We're done. The script is fine just the way it is, and we can't keep going around like this. Jack was right, we'll never finish this if we keep rewriting, because we'll all get frustrated and give up."

"I won't," I said. "But what do you guys think?"

"I love the script," Liz said.

"I don't know," Scott said. "It's good, I guess. But I agree that I'll get frustrated and quit if you keep rewriting and re-shooting everything."

"Yeah, but if we can make it better..." I started.

"Constantly rewriting and getting frustrated is only gonna make it worse," Chris said.

"I don't know," I said. "I just think you're being kind of a hypocrite, after you went on and on about not using the first draft when that's what I wanted to do in the first place, and now you refuse to rewrite and polish."

"*I'm* a hypocrite?" he said.

"Do you know the lines? Could you shoot this afternoon?" I asked him.

"I should. I've written them a million times."

But we didn't shoot that afternoon. We actually all went home, except that me and Chris talked for a minute about revising the schedule, and he lectured me about sticking to it this time, like that was what I needed to hear right then. Then right before he left he was like, "Oh, one other thing. That thing about flying to Europe to get that coverage; I'm not going to be able to do that."

"Why not?"

"Umm, my wife doesn't exactly work for the airline anymore."

"What do you mean?"

"I mean," he said, "that she doesn't work for the airline anymore and so I can't get the tickets for cheap."

And let me tell you what I thought here. I thought, Yeah, right. She never even worked there, and he just made up the whole thing, but now he couldn't really follow through. Maybe he just wrote it in hoping I'd buy him a ticket to Europe.

"So what are we gonna do then?" I asked.

"I don't know. We'll have to figure something out. I just wanted to give you a heads-up."

CHAPTER 33

STAKEOUT

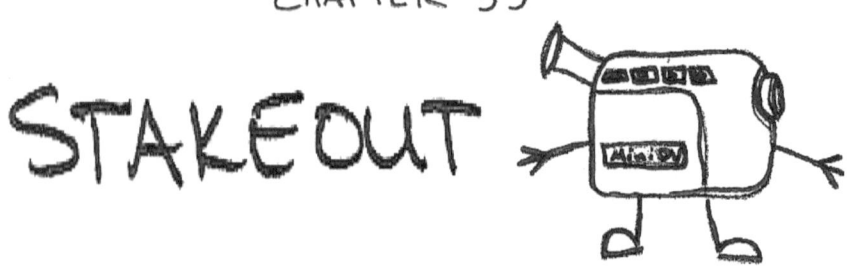

I turned the corner onto her street. Well, onto her parents' street anyways, because I assumed that since that's where she lived before that that was probably where she lived now because it was only a few days after the time when I knew she'd lived there for sure and also she was supposed to have moved in with her husband into the apartment right below mine, but since that obviously hadn't happened I just assumed that she probably didn't move anywhere. So it was likely that she still lived here.

And I'm pretty sure she did, because when I turned that corner and her parents' house was in sight there was something else in sight that pretty much told me that Allison still lived there. And it was not a pretty sight.

Parked on the street in front of the house was a white Subaru Outback. And I'm realizing right now as I tell you this that the fact that there was a white Subaru Outback parked in front of Allison's house doesn't mean anything to you. Because I told you about riding in her car, but I didn't tell you before what kind of car it was. But that meant that Sherry was inside, or at least that she was probably inside.

I couldn't believe that I hadn't thought of this before. That of course if Sherry was Allison's best friend before, then she would probably still be Allison's best friend now because it was only a few days after the time when I knew she was her best friend for sure and nothing had happened that should alter that friendship. Then of course I realized that Sherry was crazy and maybe they weren't best friends as much as just that Sherry thought they were best friends, just like she thought we were boyfriend and girlfriend and engaged or married or whatever.

But whatever they were, friends or not, it didn't change the fact that Sherry's car was parked outside the house. And when I got a little closer I saw the license plate frame that said, "Give me the chocolate and nobody gets hurt," or whatever it was, something retarded like that, and so I knew for sure that it was Sherry's car because her car had had the exact same license plate frame thing a few days before when I'd ridden in it.

And so she was probably inside, or else she and Allison had gone out for dinner or a movie or something in Allison's car and wouldn't be back for a while, which meant that Allison wasn't home anyways and also that when she was Sherry would be with her.

Now all of this thinking and analyzing and whatnot turned out to be pointless because just after I passed the house in my car, and I was a couple doors down, I pulled over to the side of the road and sat. I turned my headlights off, of course, because I didn't want to draw attention. I was thinking about what I could do. And I was thinking about the fact that because Sherry was Allison's best friend or at least her friend in any case or acquaintance or whatever, that if my destiny with Allison was fulfilled then I would indeed have to see Sherry again and that also she would know my real name and also that she would tell Allison all about me, which I then realized she had probably already done, just that Allison didn't know it was me (mostly because she didn't know who I was) and also thought that my name was Brett. Not mine exactly because we'd never met, but the me of the stories that Sherry would tell is named Brett, and Allison would probably hate Brett, but hopefully she'd get to know Warren first before she found out that Warren and Brett were the same person, even though really they're not.

But I was sitting there in my car thinking and also watching Allison's house through my rear view mirror, when Allison and Sherry both came out. Allison was walking Sherry to her car and Sherry was crying probably about what I'd done to her, or rather what Brett had done.

And I couldn't hear anything, but I'd seen enough movies to know that what Allison was saying to her was something along the lines of, "That rat bastard. I can't believe he'd do something like that to you. If I ever meet him I'll reach right down his throat and pull his still beating heart from his chest and stomp on it for you. Then I'll gouge his eyes out with my thumbs, and I'll cut off his..."

Well, you get the picture.

And suddenly then I realized that I was going to have to be very creative if I was going to pull this off, and I definitely couldn't just rush in there and introduce myself, even with two dozen roses, which I did incidentally happen to have sitting on the passenger seat of my car.

I either had to work my way covertly into Allison's life or Sherry would have to be eliminated.

⚇ ⚇ ⚇

I couldn't kill Sherry, so the idea was going to be to kind of just slide into Allison's life, but the main thing was that it had to be smooth and it also had to be when Sherry wasn't around.

This was easier said than done, because with Allison just having annulled her marriage and Sherry breaking up with her first "boyfriend," Sherry was convinced that they had a special bond and really needed each other all the time now.

I know this because like a week later I had followed Allison to this restaurant and I was about to make my move when Sherry came in the door to meet her and I ducked down behind like a planter thing with fake plants in it. Well, fake ivy anyways. And I overheard Sherry telling Allison that with what happened in both of their lives at the same time that they shared a special bond and really needed each other right now.

But that was like a week later, and we can't start there. We need to actually go back to the beginning, and by that I mean that we need to go back to just after that night when I'd seen Sherry and Allison come out of Allison's house.

And so my plan was to start with some recon work. I got a camera and I was going to follow Allison everywhere she went and figure out her routine, y'know?

So what I did was I sat in my car a couple doors down from her house, just like I'd done before, way early in the morning and got out my video camera. I didn't actually start taping anything yet, because I didn't want all the other neighbors who were all leaving for work to get suspicious and maybe call the police or whatever.

So I waited and waited until finally she came out of the house and got into her car, which was this little blue thing — not the same car she'd been driving when I followed her to the mall all those years before. I video-taped that walk to the car and all that.

And then she pulled away and drove off down the street in the opposite direction from the way I was facing, which meant I had to hurry and start my engine and flip a U-turn to follow her. And she'd turned right onto the main road and I was worried that I might lose her, but luckily she was caught by a stop light and I pulled up to the same light, just two cars behind her.

Obviously, I didn't know where she worked or I'd have staked out the place already and probably actually waited for her there. But that was what I was here to find out was where she worked, and I followed her across town until she pulled into the parking lot of kind of a shopping complex I guess. What I mean is that there was a clothing store (one of those trendy ones), there was a grocery store, a Pizza Hut, a video rental store, some fast food places, what looked like a DMV location, a dollar store, and also a bank.

The bank was where she worked I assumed, because that was the nearest building to the parking space she chose. As it turned out, she did work at the bank, and so she headed in there from her car. The thing was that when I'd done my scouting of all the banks, y'know, like years before, I'd checked this one and they said there was no Allison that worked here. So now I was kind of pissed.

Now, you'll hopefully remember that this was in the winter. Well, November, which is pretty close to winter in Utah, and pretty cold in any case. And if you don't remember, then I'm telling you right now. So I was wearing a pretty heavy coat, and it was pretty easy to tuck my little video camera down inside and covertly carry it into the bank, which I didn't know whether that was allowed, but I was pretty sure I'd draw attention to myself if I walked in there video-taping the whole bank, because they'd think that I was planning on robbing the place, and I was casing it, y'know.

So I went in there, recording for I'm not sure what purpose except to have as much recorded information as possible about this girl.

Now I want to step back from the story for a minute to explain something. Now I'm aware that some of the things I was doing here seem like stalker behaviors, but they're not. First of all, I had no intention of harming her in any way. And also this wasn't like a fetish where I'd go home every night and watch the video over and over. Except that I actually did watch the videos over and over, but only because I thought she was so beautiful. But it's not like I was stalking her, as much as I was just trying to plot the best strategy for inserting myself into her life. I was not dangerous in any way. And how can it be wrong to follow your destiny?

And looking back, I also recognize that some of the things I'd done in the past might have appeared stalkerish, but like this, they weren't at all.

I mean, haven't you ever been so... I don't want to say obsessed. But I mean we've all had these kinds of feelings, and I was no threat, so calling me a stalker is totally extreme, and I have to disagree.

I went into the bank, and it wasn't the bank I normally banked at, and also it was not part of the chain that I normally banked at either. I saw Allison taking off her coat and setting down her bag, but since the camera was hidden in my coat, I didn't really get the best angle. I looked around the place for a second, waiting for her to take her place at the desk. It kind of took a while because she had to get a cash drawer and stuff, and I had trouble trying to keep busy and look inconspicuous while I waited.

In the meantime I shut off the camera and slid it into an inside pocket of my coat. Then I picked up a little pamphlet about small business loans and I wondered if I could get one to finance my movie, which — if you're confused about the timeline — we didn't start shooting for eighteen months after this.

Some lady came over and said, "Can I help you?"

"No, I'm fine," I said.

"Well, if you have any questions..." she said and walked back to her desk.

If I have any questions, what?

I looked through a few more brochures until finally Allison was in place at the desk. I jumped in line behind some tall bearded guy, relatively thin, but with an atrocious beer-belly. I counted up the people in front of me and the tellers to make sure that I would get Allison. It looked good.

After a minute, the bearded guy was called over to some guy's station, where he pulled out a cashier's check or traveler's check or something.

"I'm supposed to sign this in front of you," he said as he picked up the pen.

"Yeah," the teller said with a smile. "Most people don't do that."

"Yeah, well I can actually read. I'm not from around here," the bearded guy said.

Wow, what an asshole saying that in a bank full of people who are from around here.

"Can I help who's next?" I heard a man's voice say and looked over to see that Allison was still helping some old lady. And I realized that I was who's next.

I didn't want to talk to that guy.

I wanted to talk to Allison.

I turned to the woman behind me, whose kid had been running around the bank the whole time she'd been in here and was also making obnoxious noises.

"Why don't you go ahead?" I said.

"No, you were here first," she said.

"Yeah, but I'm not in a hurry and your kid looks like he wants to get out of here."

"Are you sure?"

"Absolutely."

And she walked up to the teller.

Now I just had to hope that this old woman would hurry up and finish her business quickly, but she was digging through a gigantic purse and muttering, "I know it's in here somewhere."

Allison just smiled at her, this gorgeous, patient smile.

Luckily the bearded man was having problems too.

"I'm sorry," his teller said, "but I've never done one of these. Marjorie," or whatever her name was, he called, and some woman looked up. "What do I do with these?"

"What is it?" the woman asked and the bearded man snorted in disgust.

"A traveler's check," he snapped. Or cashier's check, whichever it was. And the woman walked over.

"I want a sucker," the little kid screamed and his mother sighed and handed him one from the desk. She had a stack of checks piled on the desk, probably for deposit, and her teller was working feverishly through them.

The old lady, I think, had found whatever she was looking for but it didn't mean she was done, because she'd also come across some pictures of her grandchildren and was now showing those to Allison.

Marjorie, if that was her name, had taken the bearded man's check and gone into some other room.

"So how's your day going?" the bearded man's teller asked.

"Fine, I guess," he said. "We need more snow though."

"You think so?" his teller said.

"I know so."

"They're very cute," Allison said. "How would you like that?"

"All ten-dollar bills," the old lady said. "It's all for birthdays and Christmas."

"That's a lot of grandchildren," Allison said.

"I've been blessed," the old lady responded.

Marjorie returned from the back room. "Just cash it like a normal check," she told the teller.

"I could have told you that," the bearded man said.

Allison dealt out ten-dollar bills with incredible speed and precision.

Done with all the check deposits, the teller asked the mother, "Is there anything else I can help you with?"

She shook her head.

"Here's your receipt," he said, handing it to her.

"I want another candy," her kid screamed and she looked at the teller, embarrassed.

"You have a nice day," the bearded man's teller said.

"We'll see," the bearded man said as he headed for the door.

The other teller handed the little kid another candy.

"Thank you for coming in," I heard Allison say.

All the customers walked away from the desk.

"I can help the next person over here," all three tellers said almost in unison.

So of course I walked up to Allison's station.

"Hi," I said.

"Hi, how can I help you?" she smiled at me.

"My name's Warren."

"Nice to meet you. I'm Allison."

"I was, uh..." I kind of stumbled. "I wanted to, umm, open a checking account."

"Oh, okay," she said, "what you need to do is go over there," she pointed, "and talk to Melissa," or whatever her name was. "She can get you all taken care of."

I walked over and talked to Melissa, or whatever, and I opened a checking account, and I left.

But I'd had a conversation with her, an actual conversation, and I was thrilled.

♀ ♀ ♀

That was all for that day.

I had enough I figured to start planning a strategy, but what strategy I didn't have the slightest idea. I knew where she lived, where she worked, and approximately what time she left for work every day. Also, I could guess when she got off work by adding eight hours to the start time and another half-hour for lunch. What I didn't know is when she went to lunch, but that's what I'd find out tomorrow.

I went home and hooked the camera up to the television. I watched the maybe two-minute video of Allison coming out of her house, brushing the snow off her windshield and getting in her car. Also, I'd put the camera on my dashboard as I followed her to work, so I watched that, but only once. I didn't even watch the footage of the bank, because like I said, you couldn't really see anything anyways.

But I watched her brushing the snow off her windshield probably like a dozen times, just because she looked so fantastic. You know how girls just look so much better, even if they're beautiful indoors, they just look so much better, y'know, outside in a winter coat when it's kind of chilly and the cold brings a little extra color to their face, and also I don't know there's just something about girls in winter.

I was re-watching the video when Ashleigh came home from work.

"What are you doing?" she said.

"Nothing," I said, but I didn't stop the tape because I didn't see anything wrong with what I was doing.

"Is that Allison?" she asked, moving in view of the television set.

"I shot this this morning," I said. "I waited in my car outside her house until she left for work."

"You did what?"

"I'm doing a little recon work, so I can plan my next move."

"Don't you think that's a little..." she trailed off.

"A little what?"

"Creepy, maybe. I don't know. Video-taping girls. Isn't that what stalkers do?"

"I'm not a stalker!" I said.

"No, I'm not saying..."

"And I thought you believed that she really was my destiny. What's your problem?"

"I do. I just..." she said, and paused for a minute. "I just think that maybe you're going about it the wrong way. This is a little..." Another long pause. "You know you could get arrested."

"Not if I'm careful," I said. "Which I am."

I was kind of upset that she'd suggest what she was suggesting. I stood up and ripped the A/V cable from the TV. I took my camera into my bedroom and slammed the door. I don't know why it made me so angry exactly, because she was totally wrong. I wasn't a stalker, and she was totally misunderstanding the whole situation.

♀ ♀ ♀

Even though I assumed that Allison probably worked Monday through Friday, with the occasional Saturday shift, since she did work at a bank, I didn't want to take any chances, so I assumed my position, parked just down the street from her house, and waited until she left for work.

Yeah, I realize now that I could have just waited at the bank, but I wasn't thinking like that I guess. But I did think far enough ahead that I didn't get there at like five in the morning like I had the day before. Instead, I showed up about a half-hour before the time she'd left yesterday.

I got out my video camera and waited.

At just about the same time as the day before, she came out her front door. It hadn't snowed the night before, so there was no windshield scraping to be done, so she was in her car and off a lot more quickly.

I also had had the presence of mind to park on the other side of the street so I didn't have to flip that U-turn like I had the first day.

And again today I put the camera on my dash, just in case she took a different route to the bank. Y'know, I guess just so I could kind of get into her head. Is she the type who likes new kinds of visual stimulation every day, like does she take a different route depending on her mood? But she took the exact same route as she had yesterday, and I followed.

Now you might be wondering how I had all this time when I had a job. But you might remember also that Ashleigh had told my boss at the copy center that I had strep, so I figured I had about ten days of sick leave and I could probably milk this for about a week and a half.

I figured it would be at least a couple of hours before she took her lunch break, so I went into the video store and rented a movie. It was a shorter one so I could make sure that I could get home, watch it, and be back before she took her break. It was times like this that I really wished I'd had one of those little portable DVD players.

When I got back, I returned the movie and got back in my car, where I waited, watching. It was still another hour or two before she finally came out of the bank, but I had my camera ready.

I started my car, ready to follow, my camera on the dash. But she didn't get into her car.

I grabbed my camera from the dashboard and held it to my side window while I pushed the car along slowly forward, following Allison as she walked from the bank to one of the fast food places across the parking lot.

I wasn't really paying attention to my driving like I should have been, because my eyes were glued to the viewfinder on the camera, trying to keep Allison in frame.

That's when I heard a thud.

"What are you doing, you moron?" some guy screamed from in front of my car.

I'd hit him.

I dropped the camera into my lap.

I looked at this guy, horrified.

I mean I was horrified, but he probably was too.

I hadn't been going very fast. I hoped I hadn't injured him.

I slammed my car into park and shut off the engine.

He was already at my door.

"What were you doing?" he shouted.

I rolled down the window, kind of wincing, because I thought he was going to punch me in the face. But he didn't.

"Does that girl know you're taping her?" he said.

"What?!" I screamed. "I wasn't... Who?"

"That girl. Should I go tell her?"

"No, I..." I stammered. "I'm sorry. I wasn't taping her. I was just... I'm sorry."

"Whatever you're up to, you shouldn't do it while you're driving," he said.

"Are you okay?"

"Yeah, but don't be stupid anymore. Okay?" he said, and then stared at me like he was waiting for a response.

"Okay," I finally said.

He nodded at me, then walked away.

"I'm sorry," I said.

Then he said, and this is for real, he said, "Hey, these things happen. I shouldn't have blown up like that. I've got anger management issues. Just pay closer attention when you're driving."

As I rolled up my window and drove over to the fast food restaurant I'd seen her go into I thought, Wow, that was really weird. If I had to run over someone, I'm glad it was that guy.

I went into the restaurant and got in line. Allison was up at the counter ordering.

After she got her food she passed me walking to the dining area. She kind of made eye contact, so I smiled and said, "Hi, there. Didn't we meet yesterday?"

When there was no immediate response I added, "At the bank, right? You work there?"

"Yeah," she said, but I could tell I hadn't made much of an impression, which crushed me to my very soul.

"What was your name again?" I asked, trying to play this exchange off casually and then immediately realizing that it was a stupid question because she was wearing a nametag, which she pointed to as she said:

"Allison. What was yours?"

"Warren. Yeah, I work around here, so I just came in to get something to eat. It's my lunch break. It's funny that we'd run into each other here."

"Why is that funny?"

"It's not. I guess," I said. "I mean, I guess you probably eat here a lot since you work next door. And it is lunchtime, so…"

"Well, good to see you again," she said, and walked away from me.

"You too," I said weakly, actually under my breath, and I doubt she heard it.

I didn't want to make this any more humiliating than it already was, so I ordered some food, and I got it to go, and on my way out the door…

"Have a seat," someone said to me.

I looked.

It was the guy I'd run over.

"Sit down," he almost commanded.

I did, only because I didn't know what else to do.

"You like that girl, don't you?" he said.

I nodded.

"Well that makes the video-taping kind of creepy, dude," he said.

I didn't say anything.

"You're kind of an awkward guy, aren't you?"

I just nibbled on some fries.

"Go ask her out."

My eyes went wide.

"Seriously," he said. "You want me to do it for you?"

"No!"

He didn't have any food, so I wondered what he was doing here.

"You're not eating anything?" I asked.

"I'm meeting a buddy here. I'm gonna wait to order. But seriously, dude, this is not going to end well for you if you just drive around following that girl with your video camera. If you like the girl, talk to her. But don't mention the video tapes, because that would really freak her out."

"Well I should go," I said and stood up.

"The meek may inherit the earth," he said, "but they will never get the girl."

♀ ♀ ♀

I came back to the bank a few hours later, before I guessed Allison's shift would end.

Her car was still there, so I waited.

I could guess that she was probably going home, but I was going to follow her, see if she went anywhere unexpected, what kinds of places she frequented.

She went straight home that day, and I figured it probably was stalkerish to hang around outside her house all night, so I went home.

♀♀♀

The next day was the same basic routine except she didn't eat fast food for lunch. Instead she walked over to the grocery store, and I hid in the produce section, watching her pick out fresh fruit.

♀♀♀

The next day after that was Friday, so I figured we should see something different, at least at night.

Lunch was the same, I mean she bought a salad at one of the restaurants, but the timing was the same. She also went straight home that night, but I had a feeling she'd probably go out again, so this time I waited outside in my car watching the house.

The fact that it was November, besides meaning it was cold and I had to keep the engine running, was good because it meant that it was already dark when she got home from work, so I wasn't sitting out there in the light of day where everyone in the neighborhood could see me and think I was a burglar or something.

It was about an hour before she came out again, and that was in response to a knock on the door, and that knock was from Sherry, who'd come to pick her up.

I followed that damn Subaru Outback to a movie theater, where they saw that movie where Edward Scissorhands writes the play about Peter Pan. I watched the movie too, from the back row, and was amazed that nothing had changed. Sherry still talked through the whole thing.

♀♀♀

Saturday and Sunday were a little different. I came early and watched the house, but because so many people in the neighborhood were home all day on Saturday and walking to church on Sunday, I couldn't stay long, because I didn't want to draw attention. So I kind of let those days slide.

Monday and Tuesday were pretty standard. Just like Wednesday and Thursday had been the week before.

But that Wednesday was when I'd finally worked up the courage to talk to Allison over lunch. I was going to ask if I could sit with her and all that stuff, and then hopefully ask her out. But this is the time I told you about, where she was meeting Sherry and I had to duck down behind a planter box.

⚬ ⚬ ⚬

That night I followed her home again and video-taped her walking from her car to her house. I don't know why exactly, but I just couldn't get enough footage of that.

She was opening the front door, and I had a great angle in my view-finder, when there was a deafening knock on my window.

My stomach jumped into my throat and I really thought I was going to puke.

I dropped the video camera into the back seat.

It took me what seemed like an hour to turn around and look into the face of the man standing outside my car.

He was middle-aged, wearing glasses, and pretty strong from what I could tell. I'd seen him before, just a couple of times. In fact, I think he was on one of my tapes.

He pounded on the glass again.

I slowly rolled down the window.

"Do I need to call the police?" he asked.

"I'm not doing anything illegal," I said.

"Oh, no?"

"No, I don't think so."

"You've been parked out here every night for the last week, and I just caught you video-taping my daughter."

What he said wasn't exactly fair, because it was only like one night where I parked out there for more than just a minute or so.

"I'm pretty sure I could have you arrested," he said. "Or at least get a restraining order. I hope that won't be necessary."

"It won't be necessary," I said. "I was just about to leave anyways." And I pulled on my seatbelt.

"Let's have the tape," he said, holding out his hand.

"The tape?" I asked. I really didn't want to surrender it.

"The video tape. Let's have it."

"I promise I'll erase it when I get home," I said.

"Forgive me if I don't believe you."

I reached back and pulled out the video camera and ejected the tape.

"Can I just destroy it?" I asked.

"I want to see you do it," he said.

I cracked the tape in two with my hands and pulled out enough of the ribbon to make a display of it. I threw it all on the floor of the passenger's seat.

"I don't ever want to see you around here again," he said.

I nodded but didn't say a word.

He took a step back from my car.

I rolled up the window and drove home, actually crying, scared half to death.

I arrived at two conclusions during my car ride back to my apartment.

The first: What I'd done was terribly inappropriate. I'm not a stalker, and I wouldn't classify my behavior as stalker-like, because stalkers are in a crazy obsessive mindset when they do what they do. But inappropriate and maybe a little weird, I'll admit to that. And I think it was more the video-taping and watching the footage over and over than it was the actual following her around. But both were inappropriate.

So I resolved to destroy the tapes as soon as I got home, but I didn't actually destroy them because tapes are not cheap. What I did was I erased them all, and what I mean by that is that I recorded black over all of them, and I stayed up half the night doing this, even though I had to go back to work the next morning.

The second thing I realized that night was the one that really destroyed me: I'd ruined everything.

It was no longer possible for Allison and I to ever really be together.

I'd destroyed the life of her best friend. Her father had caught me staked out outside her house and told me he never wanted to see me around there again. I'd made a fool of myself on two occasions, both at the bank and at the restaurant. If she didn't know that we were destined to be together then maybe I was wrong.

But I was so sure.

But look at what I'd done. The weird and terrible things I'd done. The crazy things I'd done.

And I'm not talking about just over that past week. Buying a ring for a girl I'd never officially met. Crashing her wedding. I'd rationalized it by saying I was just crazy in love, but maybe I was just crazy.

I remembered what that guy I'd hit with my car had said. And he was right, I was just too meek. I didn't know how to go about any of this. I was awkward and I was weird.

And it was over.

I'd destroyed my own destiny.

It devastated me to say it, but I knew it was true.

CHAPTER 34

L.A. STORY

Even though I thought my dad had done the right thing, I was still pretty pissed about the whole situation. Mainly, I think I was pissed about his whole attitude toward the family.

He didn't even care about my mother. He definitely didn't care about Ashleigh, and from what she told me it sounded like he wasn't even the least bit concerned about Kara running off on her own.

I hated that man anyways, and this just gave me one more thing to detest about him.

But at least Ashleigh wasn't across the Atlantic with him and this strange woman he was living with.

What did she see in him, this woman?

Why would anyone want to live with that guy?

The whole scenario boggled my mind, yet I was obsessed with the idea of a woman who could see my father, the way he was now, and actually be attracted to the man.

"Did he show you a picture?" I asked Ashleigh.

"Did who show me a picture of what?" she asked. And it was a fair question, because this was like three days later, and it wasn't like we were talking about my father at that moment. We were actually just sitting on the couch in front of the TV eating cereal.

"Did dad show you a picture of that woman he's living with?"

"No."

I wondered.

She was probably ugly, and also fat.

I wondered if she was German or if she was like some American woman that he'd met over here and taken to Europe with him.

I wondered if maybe he'd met her clear back when he was still living at home with my mother. And I wondered if she was the reason he left us.

That was a lot of years ago, and I wondered why, if this was the case, he hadn't married this woman yet. Then of course I realized that he could never do that. He couldn't commit. Or at least he couldn't honor a commitment.

At this moment I really kind of wished Brian was still around to track down this information, but the fact is none of this really mattered. I don't know why any of this bothered me so much or why I was so obsessed with it. Until he'd mentioned this to Ashleigh and she'd told it to me, I guess I'd just assumed that he was miserable, living all alone and suffering the way he'd made us suffer. Well, not me really; he hadn't made me suffer so much, but that's because I was older and I lived on my own anyways, and I was perfectly happy. His leaving hadn't really affected me at all. But I mean I guess I'd assumed that he was suffering the way he'd made the rest of my family suffer, especially my mother. And basically I think I could blame him wholly for what happened to Brian too.

Anyways, none of that really matters, and I'm not sure why I told you any of it. Because the thing is, there's no story that goes along with any of that.

♦ ♦ ♦

The car my mother drove, that we'd picked up from the impound in Nevada a year before, was a small, black SUV. And that's the car Ashleigh was now driving.

This is August, 2005 now.

I'd gotten Ashleigh a job working with me at the copy center. Actually, she'd been working at the copy center for almost a year already. Not because she needed the money, but because she wanted to y'know be responsible I guess. The checks from my dad were more than double what she needed to cover her expenses, so she now had quite the savings account for a seventeen year old.

I had opened the store one morning and her shift didn't start for another couple of hours, but she came in early waving this scrap of paper.

"I was cleaning my car out," she said.

"Why?" I interrupted.

"So it would be clean. And I found this."

"What is it?"

"I can't believe it took us this long to find it. It was tucked down in the back seat and when I was vacuuming it out..."

"What is it?" I asked again.

"Read it."

She thrust the piece of paper into my hands and I unfolded it.

"Well we never sit in the back seat is why we never found it," I said. Then I read the note. It was from Kara, to us.

She said basically what I'd already assumed, that she had to ditch the car, because she didn't want anyone to be able to track her, and that we shouldn't worry. She was okay, and she hadn't been raped or kidnapped or murdered or anything. Also, she wasn't alone. Apparently she'd had a boyfriend here in Utah who went with her. I didn't know she had a boyfriend, but then again I didn't know much about her at all. They were going to catch a bus in Reno and make their way to California. "I've gotta hide this note pretty good," she concluded the note, "so no one else will find it but you guys. I hope you find it someday." She signed it and in the P.S. she left a web address with no explanation.

We had internet back in the manager's office, and since I was the manager-in-charge today, because the real manager was on vacation, I didn't even have to be sneaky to get in there and use the computer. We logged on to the site Kara'd left for us, and obviously it was a blog.

The first entry was addressed to us, basically saying that she was sorry she'd just left us, and that if we were reading this then we'd obviously found the note. She said that no one else knew about this site, and she didn't want them to. The site's only purpose was to keep us from worrying about her.

The second entry apologized for not giving us any way of contacting her, but maybe in the future if she felt more comfortable with that, she'd post contact information. We quickly scanned all the entries for something like that, but there was none. I wasn't sure how I felt about that. I mean, an email address wouldn't give up her location. But then I sort of understood.

I won't go through every entry, but some were months old. The newest, however, was only posted about a week before.

I don't remember which information was in which posting specifically, but what she told us was that she was living in Southern California now with her boyfriend, and there was a picture of the two of them on the website, and she looked really happy, and this was painful to me. Not that she was happy, but that she was happy and I wasn't, because of what had happened to me since she'd left. But that's a story I've already told you.

The next part, addressed to me specifically, hurt me almost as deeply, but it really wasn't meant to at all. I was proud of her, but it was like this:

She was living my destiny.

She had her soul mate.

She'd gotten away from the family.

She'd left Utah.

She was making movies.

Not her specifically, and she wasn't exactly making them as much as she was painting the sets. Because that's exactly what she was doing was painting movie sets. She'd even designed one for some little independent movie down there. But she was painting sets for the movies.

Before I knew it, she was going to be famous.

Kara was living out *my* destiny.

"You wanna take a vacation?" I asked Ashleigh.

"They're not just gonna let you on to the sets," she said.

"I didn't say they would."

"It's a huge place. We're not going to find her. And even if we did, I'm not sure she'd be happy to see us."

"Yeah, but she's…" I stumbled. "We know sort of where she is. Shouldn't we at least try?"

"You want to go down, because you think that if we find her, she'll get you a job working on a movie set, which she won't. She'll just be pissed," Ashleigh went on. "But if you'll admit that that's why you want to go, then I'll agree to go with you."

"No, I just think…"

But Ashleigh just stared at me, arms folded over her chest, glaring.

"Fine," I said finally.

"Fine. But let's make it a vacation and have some fun while we're down there."

"Disneyland?" I suggested.

"Of course."

⚬ ⚬ ⚬

Along southbound I-15, St.George is the last city in Utah, and Mesquite is the first city in Nevada. In between, you drive through the ominous and winding corridor that is the Arizona canyon. Not the Grand Canyon, just the smaller one in the state's northwest corner.

The road swerves in every direction, and the speed limit goes up and down, and it's chaos with the mountains bearing down on you, their sheer rock faces pockmarked with tiny caves and sprouting hideous shrubs, like green pimples, in the most random places.

It was somewhere in here when Ashleigh turned to me from the passenger seat. "Did you know that mom has a brother?"

"No, she doesn't," I said.

"Yes, she does. She told me one time. He's a few years older and he's serving a life sentence in some state prison somewhere."

"I don't believe that," I said.

"That's what she said."

"Maybe she was having one of her drug-induced fantasies and made the whole thing up."

"Maybe," Ashleigh said. "But I don't think so. It sounded pretty sincere."

"Then how come she never said anything and how come we've never seen any pictures?"

"He's serving a life sentence," Ashleigh explained. "Must have done something pretty bad. I'm sure mom doesn't want anything to do with him."

"Why'd she bring it up with you?" I asked.

Ashleigh paused, looking out the window. "I don't remember."

"And even if mom didn't want anything to do with him, I can't imagine grandma and grandpa..."

And there I trailed off, because I didn't really have any words to complete that thought.

"Did you know them?" Ashleigh asked me.

"Why?"

She just shrugged.

"Yeah," I said. "Grandpa died when I was, I think, five or six, just before you were born." He died of liver failure, which you probably guessed and Ashleigh already knew, so there was no need to add that.

"And grandma was just a couple years later, right?" Ashleigh asked. "Mom said she died of loneliness."

"I guess, I don't know how she died," I said.

"But Grandma West. She died before you were born, right?"

"Just after, but I don't remember meeting her."

I wondered why she was suddenly so interested in our family. I'd never heard her ask any of these questions before, but probably she'd had this similar conversation with my mother at some point.

I've told you all there is to tell about my mom's dad. He was an alcoholic and a violent one and that's that. His wife was submissive as she would have to be and in spite of everything she stuck with him until the end, then she died, maybe of loneliness but probably of a stroke or something. And my mom also had a sister, which is where my cousins come from.

My dad's mom was actually a pretty sweet lady from what my mom told me, which is hard for me to believe considering she created my father. Now I told you already, my father always claimed to not know who his father was, and his mother was never married. He grew up pretty much in a house just him and my grandma, no brothers or sisters. I don't know much about his upbringing, because he never really said anything about it. Really, he never really said much of anything about anything.

But I do know, also from what my mother told me one time, that he was devastated when his mom died. I've never seen him really emotionally broken up about anything, so there really must have been some kind of relationship there.

"How did she die?" Ashleigh asked.

"I don't know."

She couldn't have been much more than fifty when she went, but I'm not sure of her exact age. No one ever said how she died, but I never got the impression they were keeping it a secret. And it wasn't something I really ever thought about, but now Ashleigh'd got me wondering.

"You think it has anything to do with mom's brother being in prison?" Ashleigh suggested, but I don't think she was serious.

"I doubt it," I said. "That wouldn't even make sense."

⚇ ⚇ ⚇

I was glad to leave that conversation behind the same way I was glad to leave Nevada behind.

Once into California, we stopped and took pictures at the giant thermometer in Baker and we stopped for lunch at the boxcar McDonald's in Barstow. Not so much because we like McDonald's but because it's a restaurant inside a bunch of old boxcars, and that to me is interesting.

And despite all the stopping, we still made it to the Los Angeles area in about eleven hours, which is good time.

The thing is we'd left Salt Lake at about seven in the morning which meant we hit L.A. right in the middle of rush hour, which sucked because it really makes me nervous to drive in that kind of traffic.

We spent three days at Disneyland, mostly because it was a much better deal if you spent three days there as opposed to one or two, y'know. And I was kind of annoyed, because the Pirates of the Caribbean was shut down that week for some reason. So we couldn't ride on that, which made me mad because that's *the* ride. That's the one that everyone remembers from being a kid, y'know.

But while we were there, it was the weirdest thing, kind of. I had this flash of memory from being there as a kid, before the twins were born so I must have been very young. But I remembered driving down there with my parents, and me and Brian in the back seat, and he was being an idiot as usual, like poking me or saying dumb things the whole time. And my mom kept talking about going to Disneyland with her family when she was a kid, and she was from Idaho, and she said they drove, and maybe she talked about sitting in the car with her brother bugging her the whole time, but maybe I was just remembering it that way because Ashleigh had just told me about him.

And both my parents were maybe still in diapers when Disneyland first opened for the first time. But my dad said he had been there once with a friend's family, because his mom could never afford to take him. And they both, my parents, kept talking about Pirates of the Caribbean and how much they were looking forward to riding it again. And also the Haunted Mansion they both really wanted to see and see if it was still as amazing as it had been so long ago.

And I can't remember if my mom was pregnant with the twins at the time or not, but I couldn't have been older than six anyways. And I remember going to the Haunted Mansion ride, and that thing at the beginning with all the pictures, and the guy hanging from the ceiling freaked the hell out of me so bad that I wouldn't ride the ride. And somehow I remember my dad saying that my mom could go ahead and ride with Brian, and he'd stay outside and wait with me, and he was so patient about it, and didn't even make me feel at all like he was upset about not getting to ride his ride or anything.

And when I remembered that, I thought I must be remembering it wrong, because that doesn't sound like my dad at all. Maybe it was my mom that stayed outside with me, or maybe the whole thing never happened.

But just in case, I did ride that ride, twice just to spite him. And I know that as long as he lived with us he never got back to Disneyland, and I could bet that he hadn't been back since, and probably hadn't made it out to EuroDisneyland. And so I got the ride and he didn't, and it's his own fault.

♀ ♀ ♀

After Disneyland, we made our way down to San Diego, which I already told you about, with Tijuana and all that, where I got some M-80's, and a butterfly knife, and also some blankets and a hammock. I didn't know what I was going to do with a hammock, or why I even bought it, but it was just such a good deal, so I had to have it.

And then also, while we were in Tijuana, we had some tacos at this little place, and because I'd heard things like "Don't Drink the Water" and stuff, I was kind of concerned about like getting a disease or something from the food, so I didn't get pork. But the food seemed all right, and it definitely tasted good, so I ate it, and I didn't get sick anyways, but who knows, I guess it's always possible that I do have a thirty-five foot tape-worm in my digestive tract that I don't even know about.

Also, we went to Sea World.

But let me tell you what I learned the next day after that.

I learned that if you just drive up to security on a studio lot and ask if Kara West works for this studio, they won't tell you. And also, if you try to follow that up by asking if there are any job openings (even if you explain that you worked at a movie theater for several years), they will only laugh at you.

Apparently there are a lot of people that want to work in the film industry.

So we had two days left and we were going to have to come up with some new strategy for finding Kara.

We went to lunch at some restaurant, I don't remember which, but I'll tell you that maybe fate or destiny was seeming like more of a probability. Because, by coincidence, our waiter just happened to be an actor. I don't remember how it came up, but I think maybe it was that I was telling Ashleigh about my movie idea, y'know the one I ended up directing, and maybe he was listening because when he brought the check, he also brought me a head shot and resume, which I thought was weird, but then I asked if he was an actor, and he said he was.

And I told him that I was looking for a set designer, and he said that he had a friend that was a set designer. And I noticed that he was wearing make-up, but that's beside the point. And I told him that I was looking for a particular set designer, Kara West. And he said he hadn't heard of her, but his roommate was also an actor who was on some set today and maybe he knew of her, and I could come talk to him if I wanted.

And I asked him when he got off work, and he said whenever was convenient for me. And I thought that was weird that he was so accom-modating, but I told him I was free all day and whenever his shift ended I'd drive him back to his apartment.

His apartment was ridiculous. It was like one room, plus a teeny-tiny bathroom. In the one room was a twin mattress lying on the floor, and a pulled-out sofa bed. Then there was this little kitchenette-type room of maybe thirty square feet jutting off to the side.

As soon as we walked through the door, this guy scurried all over the room picking stuff up and apologizing for the mess. He said his roommate should be home anytime and pulled out his cell phone to call while he folded up the sofa bed and put the cushions back on the couch.

"Troy," he said into the phone, "umm, call me when you get this. I have a movie director here looking for some set designer, named, uh, Kara West. If you know her..."

He finished the message, but I don't remember what else he said. I didn't remember telling him that I was a movie director, but I was flattered that he thought of me like that.

"So how long have you lived here?" I asked.

"I just moved out from Wisconsin about a month ago," he said.

I didn't realize he wasn't from around here. I had meant how long had he lived in the apartment.

"Can I get you anything to drink? I've pretty much just got water and lite beer," he said.

"I'm fine," I said.

"Have a seat," he said.

I sat down on the sofa. Ashleigh was looking at his DVD and video collection.

"You've probably heard of *Pippin*," he said to her.

She shook her head.

"I was the lead in my high school production. I have it on tape," he said. Then he asked her, "So what do you do?"

"I just make copies," she said.

"Well everyone's got to start somewhere," he said. "So tell me about your movie." He turned to me.

"My movie?"

"I'm sorry, I overheard you in the restaurant," he said as he flopped down Indian-style on the carpet like a little kid waiting to hear a Shel Silverstein poem.

Ashleigh looked at me wide-eyed and kind of smirked.

"Umm," I said and then just sat there for a minute.

I basically laid the plot out for him, and he thought the whole thing was brilliant and he told me so. It was really nice to hear.

"I would love to play the guy in that," he said.

I was surprised that he loved it so much. I mean, he was living in Los Angeles and could probably take his pick of any of those Hollywood features, but he wanted to be in mine.

"Really?" I said.

"Definitely," he said. "It sounds like a great project."

"The thing is," I said, "I don't know what kind of a budget I'm going to have yet."

"Hell, I'd do it for free."

There are actors willing to work for free?

"Really?"

"Really," he said.

"You like it that much?"

"It's brilliant."

"Wow," I said. "The thing is I'm probably going to shoot it in Salt Lake City, Utah. That's where I'm from."

"So you're going to take a trip back to your hometown kind of thing. That's cool."

"Yeah," I said.

Just then his roommate came home, and this guy was totally flaming. There's really no other word to describe him.

"I got your message," he said with a lisp. "I'm sorry. I don't know a Kara West. There is a Kara something that's working on that movie that Ty's doing, but she's not the set designer. I don't even actually know what she's doing over there, but I called him and he's not answering, the bitch. I left him a message, but I don't know if he'll call back. I think he's mad at me right now. Hi," he turned to me, "I'm Troy."

I shook his hand, though I was dizzy after all that which was spoken in about two seconds, like this guy'd just had two dozen pots of coffee and three Red Bulls.

"Warren," I said.

"And you're a director. What project are you working on right now?"

"He just told me all about it," our waiter cut in, "and it's fabulous. You would love it."

"Well let's hear it," said Troy.

"We have to go," Ashleigh said.

I looked at her.

"Really?" Troy gasped.

She looked at her watch. "He has an appointment with one of the executive producers."

I didn't know why she said it, but I was glad because these two guys were really starting to creep me out.

"Oh, I totally understand," Troy said.

"Can't miss that," said the waiter.

"That Kara that your friend Ty knows," Ashleigh said. "What studio's she at?"

"She doesn't work for a studio," Troy scoffed and flicked his wrist. "Ty would never sell out like that. The movie he's working on is an independent film."

He gave us the address of the producer's office, which turned out to be another crappy apartment, but that's another story.

"You have my number," the waiter said as we were heading out the door.

"We do?" I said.

"On my resume."

"Oh, right," I said, and we got ourselves the hell away from there.

♀ ♀ ♀

Remember when I told you that we'd gone to the producer's office that just turned out to be a crappy apartment but that was another story? Actually, I'm sure you remember it because it was like two seconds ago.

Well I shouldn't have said that because it's right here. It's just that at that point in the telling I thought in my head that it was going to go on longer than it did, but then I realized that it was over right then.

But anyways, we went the next morning to that address the gay guy had given us, and like I said it turned out to be just some crappy apartment. And we got there at like nine in the morning, but when we knocked there was no answer, so we waited a little bit then we knocked again, and then we heard some kind of shuffling around behind the door, so I knocked again, then finally some guy opened the door wearing nothing but a pair of boxer shorts, which I thought was completely inappropriate for Ashleigh to see. But then I realized that she was seventeen years old and she'd probably seen a lot worse, but I still thought of her as my little sister and just a kid.

The guy's hair was sticking up all over and he yawned as he cracked the door, but he didn't say anything like "hello" or "can I help you?" He just stood there and stared at us, I guess waiting for me to say something.

Finally, I did.

And he responded, "You want some coffee?"

"No thanks, I'm good," I said.

And he looked at Ashleigh.

And she just stood there, and it was kind of an awkward moment.

Then she must have realized that he was asking her if she wanted coffee and she shook her head.

"Well, I need some coffee," he said, and disappeared from the doorway. We just stood there and looked at each other.

I heard some banging from what I assumed was the kitchen. Then finally, "You can come in!" the guy shouted.

We walked into the apartment, which was a lot like the other one, only there was no sofa just a double bed with a topless girl lying in it. Only when I say topless, I couldn't see her boobs, because she was lying face down.

She turned her head toward us and smiled. "Hi."

I gave her an awkward wave.

"You sure you don't want any coffee?" the guy said from a similar kitchenette to the last one, only this apartment was a little bigger.

"I'm fine."

"I'll have a cup," said the girl as she stretched out. "When I get out of the shower," she added as she stood up, apparently not caring what I saw. I guess she wasn't ashamed, because she was tan and shapely, and...

Well that's beside the point.

Anyways, she walked past me into the bathroom.

"Anyways," I said. "As I was asking before, is this the office for..." Now I don't actually remember the name of the production company, so for now let's just call it Kelmer Films just for fun, so... "Kelmer Films?"

"Yep," the guy said as if this explained everything.

"And you're making a movie?" I asked.

"Yep."

He'd gotten the filter in the machine, but he was struggling with the bag of grounds.

"Are you..." I didn't know. "The producer?"

"And director," he said.

"Really?"

"That was Lily," or whatever. "She's the lead actress."

Then he gave me like this thumbs-up.

"So what can I do for ya?" he said, once he got everything in the machine and was pouring the water in. "You wanna invest or something?"

"I'm actually interested in your set designer, Kara."

See, I hadn't realized it, but Ashleigh was pretty on top of things and had explained to me that especially if Kara didn't want to be found she would probably be using a different name, but not necessarily a different first name. It was obvious once she said it. I just hadn't thought about it.

"She's not the set designer," the guy said. "She's like an assistant or something. I'd offer you a place to sit, but there's not really anything to sit on."

"I'm fine," I said.

He pushed a bunch of dishes off the counter, including this thing that looked like a big plastic test tube or something from a chemistry set anyways. I guess he was looking for a coffee mug, which he found and hardly rinsed with tap water. I was really glad I'd turned down the coffee.

"How come you're looking for her?" he asked.

"Nothing. No reason. Just..."

"Let me guess. You took her home one night, and after you fell asleep, she robbed you blind."

"What? No," I said.

"I only say that because you definitely have a type. I mean this one," he pointed to Ashleigh, "looks just like her. I mean I think. I didn't see her much or get a very good look at her. No offense babe, but when I can get that," and he pointed toward the bathroom without turning his sentence into a complete one.

"Do you know how I can get a hold of her?" I asked.

"No, actually we wrapped a couple of days ago, and she's probably off on some other thing. But I'll tell you what. You leave me your card and I'll have her call you."

"You don't have a number where we can reach her?" I asked.

He shook his head and poured himself a cup of coffee.

"Can you get it?" I asked.

He shook his head again.

I knew if I gave him my number, he'd probably never give it to her. Not that it mattered, because she already had our number, and she wasn't going to call it just because she got it from this weirdo.

"Well, thanks anyway," I said.

"No problem." He tipped his cup in my direction.

We made our way to the door just as the actress came out of the bathroom, all wet but wrapped in a towel this time.

"Nice to meet you," she said, even though we hadn't really met.

I nodded and we left.

♀ ♀ ♀

About the time we passed Cedar City on our way back home, Ashleigh turned to me from the driver's seat because I decided to let her drive for a while.

"So when are you going to make your movie?" she asked.

"Yeah, that'd be nice, wouldn't it?" I snorted.

"I'm serious. That guy loved it. I think it's a good idea."

"Yeah, but I don't really have any equipment. And I don't really know how to make a movie." I was admitting this for the first time ever, even to myself.

"Well what about that guy you said you were working with before. Why don't you call him?"

"Chris?" I almost laughed as I said it. "I haven't talked to him since, well, since we tried working on it before."

"So call him up." She said it like it was such an easy thing to do.

"I don't even have his number."

I just stared out the passenger window for a minute.

"Besides," I finally spat, "movies cost a lot of money."

"I've got money," she said.

I looked at her.

"That's nice of you, but..."

"But what?"

"But I can't take your money to make my film."

"Why not?"

"Because I can't."

"Let's call it an investment, and I own a percentage of what it makes," she offered.

"It probably won't make anything."

"Well I'm not going to invest if you have that kind of attitude," she said. "Seriously, I think you need to make your film. Call this Chris guy, and get it made, and I'll pay for whatever you need."

"I can't take your money," I said.

"You'll take my money." And this was a command.

Neither one of us said anything for a long minute.

"Only what I absolutely need," I said.

When we got home there was a new entry on Kara's blog. It said, "Don't come looking for me again."

CHAPTER 35

THE DEPARTED

I'm not going to tell you what was in the letter, because that's just for me.

But I will tell you some other things.

The obituary ran in the paper; the home had sent it over. They weren't going to hold a funeral because Marty didn't really have any friends or family still living, but they did schedule a viewing.

Since we were shooting when I got the news I asked Chris if he would come with me, mostly because I didn't want to go alone. He said if it were anything other than a funeral, because death just freaked him out. I told him it was just a viewing and he said there was no difference.

So I got Ashleigh to come with me.

Now you've probably been to a mortuary or a funeral parlor before; I had not.

We went in through a small foyer and into the room where the casket was sitting. We were a little early and I could see before we entered the room that the casket wasn't open yet. I'd just assumed it would be kept open until the end of the viewing, but that really doesn't have anything to do with anything.

When we walked into the room I was struck by the sheer emptiness of the place, looking at row after row of slatted folding chairs with no people in them. Then I saw one man sitting in the very back corner, his head bowed and his hands folded.

"What are you even doing here?" I said, then I walked right back out of the room. "We'll come back after he's gone," I told Ashleigh as I hurried through the foyer.

"Warren!" Steven called behind me.

I spun around ready to throw down.

He held up a manila envelope. "I need to talk to you," he said.

"I can't believe you'd even dare show up here, after what you did to him," I spat.

"What did I do to him?" he asked.

I saw Ashleigh watching from the doorway, but she hadn't followed me into the foyer, and she didn't now. She just took a seat in the viewing room.

Steven approached me and opened the envelope. From inside, he pulled another, smaller envelope with my name on it and held it out.

I didn't take it right away. Instead I just kind of stared at him. I kind of half-reached out my arm, but not really, not where I could reach the envelope anyways. And I guess maybe I kind of scowled at him.

"My father wanted you to have this," he said.

I took the envelope from him and unclamped the little fastener thing on it, y'know the kind with like the two prongs that stick up through the little hole and then clamp down on either side. And then I lifted the flap and looked inside.

Two more envelopes.

I wondered if this wasn't like one of those presents that comes in the gigantic box, that you open and there's another box, and another, and another, until the last box is really tiny and there's just a Junior Mint in it. Or like one of those Russian dolls.

But this was just a couple of envelopes, and there wasn't a lot smaller you could get.

"What is this?" I said.

"He wanted me to give it to you."

The one envelope wasn't really an envelope exactly, as much as it was just kind of a flap that didn't seal, and under the flap were two plane tickets, round-trip from Salt Lake City to Berlin.

"Those are vouchers. You can book the flights anytime, and they're not standby," Steven said.

"What, Marty bought these?" I asked.

"He asked me to get them for you. I don't know why you're going or who you're going with. He just said two round-trip tickets to Berlin."

Why would this guy do this favor for a father he hated without any explanation?

As if in response to that question I didn't ask out loud, he said, "I'm an executive for the airline, so they didn't cost me anything. If you have trouble booking it, just give them my name."

I think he just added that last part so I'd think he was someone important and be impressed.

But I wasn't.

The other envelope was a real letter envelope and sealed and also had my name on it, in Marty's handwriting but only barely legible. He'd obviously lost some of his fine motor skills by the time he got around to writing this.

I opened it and peeked inside to see yet another even smaller envelope and a typed letter, which I didn't read right then.

"Why'd you put him in the home?" I said.

"He couldn't take care of himself anymore."

"Why didn't you take care of him?"

"It's not as simple as that."

"How is it not as simple as that? What does that mean? He was your father. You had a responsibility."

"Yeah, well, we all have responsibilities," he said. "My father wasn't so good at honoring his; I didn't feel like I needed to fulfill mine."

"He told me everything," I said.

"He told you everything?"

I nodded.

"I'm pretty sure he didn't tell you everything."

I think we argued for a little bit, and you never can remember how these things escalate, but eventually he was yelling at me. I remember some of the things he said, things that didn't really make sense to me at the time but do now. But where it peaked was with him shouting this at me: "You're just like your father!"

Now you can imagine what this statement did to my insides. It's like if you were a bibliophile and someone came into your personal library, tied you up and glued your eyes open, then forced you to watch as they pulled every book off every shelf and tore out every page, one by one, dropping each into a shredder, but one of those cross-cut shredders that cuts the paper up diagonally in two directions so the page is virtually impossible to piece back together. Then they lit that pile of shreds on fire. That's how angry I was at that moment.

But it was my brain that was so engulfed in flames that it couldn't formulate anything to say to that. And I don't really remember any internal process for what happened. I just remember my arm suddenly swinging around, a tight fist screaming towards Steven's snot-nosed face.

But he leaned back, I don't know what the boxing term for that move would be, but the force of my swing carried me into a full three hundred and sixty degree spin. My legs wrapped around each other like a spinney mcbiscuit and suddenly I was on the floor.

"And he's just like my father," Steven added.

I was embarrassed and I was angry, but I was undaunted.

"I'm nothing like my father, and my father is nothing like Marty," I said.

"You're so naïve. You look at my father like he was some kind of saint. It's sickening."

"You're such an ungrateful..." I started but he cut me off.

"Didn't your father leave your family for some other woman? That's what I heard."

How did this guy know these things about me and my family?

"I don't see..." I started.

"I caught my father having an affair." He stated it with such nonchalance that I was sure he was making it up.

"I don't believe you," I said.

"You don't have to. But that doesn't change the fact that it happened."

"He loved Sarah," I said.

"Apparently that didn't mean a whole lot."

"I don't believe you," I said again.

"I told my mother about it. I tried to talk her into leaving him, but she wouldn't do it. She was just living with it. She said she knew and they were working through it. I couldn't believe what she was telling me. If it was a one-time thing, then..." and he trailed off like he couldn't find the words.

Then finally, "...but this had been going on for years and years. That's why I couldn't accept that my mother would stick by him."

"Well, you don't just abandon someone because they do one thing you don't agree with," I said.

"Clearly, you have no frame of reference," he said.

Clearly he didn't know anything about me or my frames of reference.

But he did.

"Catching him was just the capper, because I think I'd always known," he said. "Even though I was an only child, I always felt like his attention was divided."

"Marty always felt like you were jealous of his relationship with Sarah, like you needed more attention or something," I prodded. "Of course you'd make something like this up."

"What the hell are you talking about?"

"Even if he did have an affair, wouldn't your mother have had more right to be jealous of this other woman than you'd have?"

"That's not even what I'm talking about," he said.

I didn't understand what that meant.

"There were other things!" he shouted. "The affair was just the climax of it all. We never saw eye to eye on anything. I don't have to explain myself to you. It was *my* relationship with *my* father, and it's none of your business. If you want to hate me for hating him, then that's not really going to hurt me, is it? I know what I grew up with and I know the real man lying in that coffin. You only know the stories."

"But he was a good man," I said.

"He threw *me* out. He pushed *me* away."

"My father packed a suitcase and told me he wanted nothing to do with me anymore. That was the last thing I ever heard him say," I shouted.

"My father told me I could never see my mother again."

"My mother told me I could never see her again."

"My mother died, and he wouldn't let me say goodbye. I had to sneak in to her funeral."

I think we were competing, but for what I don't know.

"My father is a son of a bitch," I said.

"My father was an ass," he said.

"Yeah, but yours reached out to you. Yours wanted to fix things."

"Only at the end."

"At least he made an effort," I said. "At least he recognized..."

"Only when he knew he was about to die."

Then Steven paused.

"I don't need to have this conversation with you," he finally went on. "I don't need to explain myself to you. I don't need to justify..."

And he trailed off again.

Then I watched his temperature drop from fire to ice and his whole expression changed, and I don't know how else to explain except that it was like when you take an empty soda can and set it on the sidewalk and step on it and it crushes into this flat circle of aluminum. That was what happened to Steven, something crushed him into this flat circle of a person.

And then it was like he was compelled to keep talking.

"There were things I didn't know," he said. "There were things I was wrong about, but there were things I was right about. There were things... There were... Growing up was... But it doesn't change the fact that... You can't go back in time."

There was nothing to say to that.

"I'm saying this for you, so you don't go through what I went through. I don't know you. And what I know of you, I don't really like you, but I feel like I have to say this. It's hard to forgive people," he said.

"But Marty didn't deserve..." I started, but he cut me off with...

"Shut up! You stupid kid. You don't have to say everything that comes into your head. It doesn't make it any easier, the fact that he actually did deserve what he got."

Then he told me this: "As hard as it is to forgive someone, in the end it's harder not to forgive them."

I thought that was profound. And that's why I remember it so well.

Actually I wrote it down later.

He may not have said it so eloquently, but that's how I remembered it.

"I wish I'd known that yesterday or last week or four years ago," he added, then, "or when I was your age."

Then he walked away from me, and I didn't have anything else to say.

He walked over to the casket and lifted the lid. And he stared down at the waxen likeness of his father, and I wondered what was going through his head.

But since I couldn't read his mind, I sat back down next to Ashleigh, just kind of fingering my letter.

"What's that?" she asked.

"From Marty," I said.

"When did he write that?"

I shrugged, because I didn't know.

It turned out that he'd written it just after Steven put him in the home. And it didn't occur to me right away, but I wondered later how Marty had known to ask for plane tickets to Berlin, because I hadn't told him where my father was. In fact, at that time I didn't even know.

Steven didn't stay much longer, and he didn't go to the grave site to see the casket buried I don't think. But I don't know that for sure because I didn't go either. I couldn't stand to see what was left of Marty lowered into the ground.

After Steven left, Ashleigh reached over and touched my shoulder, then she stood up and walked out of the room without saying a word.

I walked over to the casket that Steven had left open and I looked down at Marty, lying there, gone completely now, and I wished I had an explanation for the way things were.

I didn't want to believe what Steven had said, and I kept telling myself that I didn't believe it, but I did, I mean, somehow deep down I knew it was true.

But it was like my whole belief system was brought down by that single conversation. And I don't even know what that belief system was except that it was that Marty loved his wife deeply and that men who do that don't cheat on their wives, and also that men like Marty are better people than most people and they're better fathers than my father.

And how could Steven feel about this man that I so admired the way I felt about my own father?

And I stood there staring at this man whose mind had gone long ago and whose body had finally caught up, and I held in my hand two plane tickets to Berlin and a letter that I wasn't sure I wanted to read.

I couldn't make sense of any of it.

Of people.

Of this life.

Of anything.

My eyes lost focus and I stared through the wall, seeing scenes from my own life playing out of sequence, jumbled and not always making sense, and fuzzy some of them.

I raised my hand and touched my hair...

Then my forehead...

And my face...

And I pushed my thumb up under my chin.

I don't know why.

Maybe to make sure I was real; I really don't know.

And I pulled out the letter.

I leaned my back against the wall then slid down 'til I was sitting on the floor, and I unfolded the papers.

CHAPTER 36

TWO WEEKS NOTICE

I was running really late and scrambling because I knew how mad Chris got when I didn't show up on time. And also because now that he was playing the lead role, he'd get there early and Scott would be there and if Liz showed up on time (which she did about two-thirds of the time) then he'd start blocking the scenes himself, and by the time I got there everyone would be settled on doing it his way, and if I argued one of the three would say something like "you should have been here on time then." And Chris would say something like, "We have a schedule and we're going to stick to it whether you like it or not."

All I remember exactly is that I was scrambling to get out the door with all the props and this t-shirt I'd found that I wanted Chris to wear in the scene, which he ended up not doing because, as he pointed out, he needed to be wearing the same thing he had worn in another scene that we'd already shot. And when I suggested that since it was not a very long scene we could maybe re-shoot the other one, Scott gave me about the dirtiest look ever.

On my way out the door, after I'd grabbed a popsicle or something for breakfast, the phone started ringing. And I'm talking about our land line, which we still had even though both me and Ashleigh had cell phones. I'd been meaning to have it disconnected but I kept forgetting, since the only people who called that number were telemarketers and such. I mean that's why I'd been meaning to get it disconnected, not why I kept forgetting. And since that was all that called that phone I almost didn't pick up, but then I decided to, because I find it very hard to resist a ringing phone. Like if I pass a pay phone on the street and it starts ringing, I'll always pick it up. Not that that happens very often. In fact over the past few years I don't think I've even passed a pay phone at all, let alone a ringing one. But the half dozen or so times that I have passed a ringing pay phone, I've answered it. But that's not really the point. The point is that I picked up the phone and said "Hello," which is always what I say when I answer the phone.

I didn't hear a response on the other end, so I said "Hello" again like anyone else would, and there was still no response. Then I heard the click of the other person hanging up. I said "Hello" again just in case that click was something other than the hanging up of the phone on the other end, but when there was no response I reset my receiver and hurried out the door.

☺ ☺ ☺

Oh, I forgot. Shoot, I wanted to start this chapter with me telling you that what I did was asked Chris if he wanted to go with me to Germany with those tickets Steven had given me a couple weeks before. Because then we would actually be able to get that footage of the European cathedrals and churches and whatever that we needed for the movie, since we still hadn't figured out precisely how we were going to shoot that.

And you were going to wonder why I would take Chris with me to see my father and not Ashleigh, and then I was going to take you back to explain all that.

Oh well. Let's pretend and do it now.

"You want me to use your free ticket?" he asked.

"Sure," I said.

"Where are we going exactly?"

"It's up to you."

"Can we go into Poland?"

"How far is that from Berlin?"

"A couple hours by car, but if we had a few days, then we could go far in and get a lot of great cathedrals and stuff."

"I can get off work for prob'ly like ten days," I said.

"Let's do ten days."

And you're asking, "So why couldn't Ashleigh go with you?"

And maybe you're only asking that because I mentioned it already, but prob'ly you'd ask it anyway, because I think if it were me hearing this story, that's what I'd be asking.

Well, the thing is this episode where I invited Chris to use my plane ticket took place a few days after that incident where I was rushing out the door that I told you about just a minute ago, and what's important to this whole story is what took place in between.

☺ ☺ ☺

So I rushed out the door and got to the location only about fifteen minutes late, and the other three were there waiting for me.

That day we were shooting this scene where the two characters were walking down this street, and we were shooting in downtown Salt Lake. And just like I said, they were already rehearsing and Chris had pretty much already blocked the scene.

So Chris immediately walked up to me and said, "So here's what we were thinking..."

And before he could finish his thought, I just blew up, because I don't know why exactly. He really liked to be in control of everything and he liked to tell people what to do. Actually, the thing is Chris was a control freak before, and I guess I'd thought that had changed. But really he'd just kept it under at first, y'know, but now it was coming back to the surface.

"I don't care what you were thinking," I yelled. "I'm the director, you're not!"

"Okay," he said very calmly, "but you weren't here on time."

"I'm fifteen minutes late, and you do this to me all the time."

"That's because you're late all the time," he said.

"That doesn't mean you just take over."

"We talked about this. We're going to stick to the schedule, and in order to do that we need to start on time with or without you."

"So if I like got in a terrible car accident and couldn't show up at all one day, then you'd just take over that whole day's shooting and that's that?" I asked.

"Probably, yes."

"Well I don't like that."

He just shrugged.

And I just stared.

Then finally, he said, "So here's what we were thinking..."

"You mean what *you* were thinking," I said.

He flicked his eyes back and forth, then said, "Yes, what we were thinking."

"I mean you personally, not them included, you mean what *you alone* decided we need to do today."

"Well we all talked about it, but okay I made the decisions."

"And that's my job, isn't it?"

"Okay, then never mind. What do you want to do?" he said.

"First of all," I said and pulled the shirt from my backpack, "I want you to wear this in this scene."

And this part I already told you.

I guess this is kind of jumbled, isn't it? But it's like my memory I guess, so it works. Anyways, I'm sure Chris will change it all when he edits the thing.

But then he asked what I wanted to do about the scene and I'd been so frazzled that I hadn't come up with any, y'know, concrete ideas about how to shoot it, and this really irked me because I felt like not saying something here was letting him win.

So I tried to think of something to say really quick with all three of them standing there staring at me.

But because I knew that Chris was going to battle whatever I said anyway, I just said, "Well show me what you guys were thinking and we'll see if it works."

And they did, and it worked, all except this little part. But in the interest of full disclosure, that little part that I told them didn't work actually worked just fine, but I just felt compelled to pick on something, because it was just that kind of day.

But anyways, we went ahead and shot the thing. And Chris kind of got on my nerves because he kept saying that the sunlight was changing the whole time and the light levels weren't going to match, and he got Scott to agree with him, and they were talking about how like shadows were going to be all different sizes from shot to shot, and all this other stuff. But seriously, no one notices that kind of thing, so I think he was just being picky. It was a control thing.

After shooting Scott had to run before we finished putting away all the equipment and stuff, and even though we had a couple more scenes to shoot at other places I was just going to man the camera myself.

So I was standing there coiling this cable around my hand and elbow like any normal person, but Chris kept insisting that I was doing it the wrong way. But who really cares? It's not like there's a right way and a wrong way to coil a cable, just because I do it differently than he does.

Anyways, I was wrapping this cable, I think it was for the microphone, over my hand and around my elbow, when I heard a terrible noise behind me. It was more of a screeching than a noise, but it wasn't so much the noise itself but what it came from.

"Brett?!" the cacophony beat upon my eardrum.

I froze.

Chris looked over at me. He had this weird look on his face that I knew meant, "Is someone calling you Brett?"

Then he looked past me, and I knew what he saw before I saw it, and he smirked and I knew that the little guy that lives down inside him was in hysterics, but at least Chris had the sense to stifle the little guy and not laugh out loud.

Liz turned and looked, saw what I didn't want to see then looked up at Chris. While she spoke too softly for me to hear, I could read her lips as she said, "Brett?"

Then there was this total eclipse of the sun and also a very powerful earthquake, and even though it was the middle of the summer it got very, very cold. So cold that my fingers went stiff and I could no longer wind the mic cable.

See, I think I'd known that this moment was eventually going to come, but if you've never faced it, I'll tell you that it's a moment that you really can't plan for. No matter how many scenarios you run through your head, none of them will ever match the real deal.

So what I did was I did what I knew I had to do, and when the sun came back out and the ground stopped shaking and I thawed out, I turned my head.

You know what I saw, so I don't have to tell you, but I will anyway. I saw Sherry, and she'd put some weight back on, and she was coming toward me. And I tried to read her face for any indication of what she was planning to do to me. After all, I needed to know if I had to duck or run or just brace myself for a stern talking to.

See, the first thing she did was she ran up to me when I turned around, I guess because she saw my face and knew it was me for sure, and threw her arms around my neck.

This was weird.

See, what you need to have calculated here is that this happened about twenty-one months after the last time I'd seen her, if I remember right.

Anyways, it had been a long time.

"I'm so sorry," she cried through her tears with her arms still wrapped around me and the wetness dripping down my neck and soaking my t-shirt.

"What do you have to be sorry for?" I asked, but I think only because it seemed like the polite thing.

She pulled back leaving her hands on either side of my face, like a concerned mother. And she smiled at me shaking her head.

Chris and Liz picked up some of the equipment and walked it back to his car, which was like two blocks away, which left me with some privacy that I wasn't sure I wanted.

"I'm sorry," Sherry said again.

I raised half my mouth and both my eyebrows in some kind of odd facial contortion that I guess I wanted to imply that no matter what she was sorry for it was okay and she could let go of my face now.

And now I don't know if I could really feel it then, but reliving the incident in my mind, I can feel just this little sliver of cold metal against my right cheek. And as she lowered her hands I saw the enormous diamond perched atop that sliver of metal. Then I looked at her head-to-toe again, a little more clear-headed than before, and I realized she hadn't put on weight. She was pregnant.

"Brett, I'm so sorry for the way I treated you," she said. "I was a little, no not a little, I was really, really crazy then. I don't know what it was, just, I was just maybe I guess I was lonely. Or I was hormonal, or, it doesn't matter, there's no excuse. I'm sorry."

"It's okay," I said. And I was still trying to process everything that was happening.

She smiled at me and I smiled back at her and neither of us said a word for like a full minute.

Finally, her smile started to fade.

"You have to admit though," she said, "what you did to me was pretty awful."

"Yes," I all but shouted. "Yes, and I'm so sorry about that. I was a little out of my mind at the time too."

"But it was all for the best," she said and fanned out the fingers on her left hand as if I hadn't already noticed the eight-hundred carat diamond.

"Congratulations," I said, just because it seemed like the thing to say.

"And..." she pointed to her stomach.

"Really?" I said, pretending to be surprised.

"Five months," she said, fanning out those same fingers and still with the back of her hand facing me. I figured it was probably really about six months, but she said five so she could flash that ring again. It was much bigger than the one I'd bought for Allison.

"So how are you?" she said.

"Good. You?"

"So good. So wonderful. My life is perfect. So what are you doing down here? What's all this stuff?"

She meant the camera equipment.

"Oh, I'm just…" I started and saw Chris and Liz coming back and waved them over. "We're just shooting a documentary," I said. I don't know why I lied.

"Really, what about?"

"This is Chris and Liz," I introduced them. "Sherry," I added.

"So what's your documentary about?" Sherry asked Chris this time.

And this is where he really shines. I have to hand it to him really. Chris is a fantastic liar. He can sit for an hour weaving this elaborate story that he alleges is true and for no reason whatsoever. He'll just start spilling out this tale about how when he was ten or whatever his family went on a trip to Canada or wherever and such and such a thing happened. And it's all a lie, and there's no reason why he should lie about something like that because it's not getting him anywhere, but that's what he does.

So I watched as he really sunk his teeth into this opportunity.

"Umm," he started like he didn't know where to begin, though I'm sure he'd already mentally macramé'd a plot and characters and synopsis in just those few seconds.

"Well the whole thing was Brett's idea really," he said. "See he was volunteering at the homeless shelter a few months ago. Well, let me go back. Brett actually got fired from his job back in December and was having trouble finding a new one for the longest time, until finally he had to take whatever he could get which meant a job at [some fast food restaurant]. I don't know if you've ever worked in fast food, but it doesn't really pay very well, so he couldn't make his rent and pay all his bills and whatnot, so he uh, in maybe a lapse of judgment, he took a little extra money from the till one shift when he was working the front counter. What he didn't know was that they were watching all the employees very closely and so he got caught… Well they not only fired him, but he actually got arrested. But since it was only what? Fifty bucks? A hundred?"

"Something like that," I said.

"Since it wasn't very much, they didn't make that big a deal out of it. He just had to pay it back which he'd already done right after they caught him and they made him do some community service. Which is why he started volunteering at the homeless shelter. But don't think he did it only because he was compelled to. Because he only had to do what? Twenty hours, was it?"

"Something like that."

"And after he was done, he kept going back. Because he said it gave him such a good feeling to help out like that, do his part. So he kept going back, and then he got this idea. Why not make a documentary profiling the day-to-day existences of these, what people so demeaningly refer to as 'bums.' 'But they're people too,' he insisted. And when he told me about the idea, I thought why not? I've done several documentaries myself, a couple of them even went to Sundance."

"Really?" Sherry said.

Liz stood there with her hand over her mouth, probably holding back laughter.

"Really," Chris said. "I even had one on the History Channel."

"What was it called?" Sherry asked.

"The one on the Discovery Channel?"

"I thought you said History Channel."

"I had one on each, but which one are you talking about?"

"The one on the History Channel," she said.

"It was about the early explorers of North America and how their constant fidgetiness, they're compulsion to explore, was actually the result of Restless Leg Syndrome. Have you heard of it?"

She shook her head.

"Well, it's a new theory anyway. The title wasn't so great, it was just called *The Legacy of the Vikings*. That was a producer decision, y'know."

"I'll have to watch for it," Sherry said.

"Sure," Chris said. "It was a couple years ago though, so I don't know if they'll be rerunning it anytime soon, but watch for it. You can tell all your friends that you met the guy who made it."

"Yeah," she said. "Well it sounds like a good thing you guys are doing. Hey listen, are you done here? Would you like to have lunch?"

"Umm," I said.

"Yeah, we're done," Chris jumped in. "You go, and me'n Liz'll get all this stuff." And he smirked at me where Sherry couldn't see.

"Are you seeing anyone right now?" she asked as she dragged me away.

"No, not at the moment," I said as if this was a rare reprieve from the many women I was typically juggling.

"I'm really glad to hear that, because I have this friend I'd like to set you up with."

Suddenly I was really glad I was going to lunch with Sherry.

"What's she like?" I asked.

"She's great. Don't you want to know about the guy who replaced you though?"

"Yeah, I meant to ask," I said, even though I didn't.

"He's a CPA," she said.

I shrugged. "I don't know what that is."

"An accountant. Only you can be an accountant without getting your CPA, but a real accountant...blah, blah, blah..."

She went on and on about her husband and some stuff about what he did for a living, but I wasn't paying much attention because I was thinking about being set up with her friend and just praying that that friend was Allison Shepard.

When finally it sounded like she was done talking about her husband I asked her, "So what about this friend you want to set me up with?"

"Oh, you'll love her. She's my best friend. The only thing is..."

And her cell phone rang.

"Hold on," she said.

You see this in movies all the time, where they'll get interrupted and leave you hanging, but this was honestly the first time I'd ever seen it happen in real life. I don't remember what she said, but when she hung up she had to leave right away.

"What about lunch?" I asked.

"We'll have to do it another time."

"When?"

But she was already on the move.

"I'd really like to catch up and hear about this friend of yours," I said.

"How about next week? A week from today. Same place, same time," she suggested.

I looked at the clock on my phone.

"One-thirty," I said.

"One-thirty," she said, and then she took off, but not until she'd given me a kiss on the cheek.

I just stood there on the sidewalk already dreaming about next week, when maybe destiny would bring Allison Shepard back into my life.

The shooting schedule had us doing the make-up shoot for the scenes we'd missed the next evening. I got there at about six o'clock, which was right on time, but Chris and Liz were already there.

I remember that the first thing Chris said to me was, "Do you think they'd really force you to do community service for taking money from a till that you immediately gave back when you were caught?"

I shrugged.

"Because I told that girl yesterday," he continued, "that that's what happened to you, but I don't know if they'd really do that."

"I don't think it really matters," I said.

"Yeah, but she might realize that I made the whole thing up."

"So what if she does," I said.

"Well I don't like getting caught."

"You'll prob'ly never see her again."

"That doesn't matter," he said.

Anyways, we moved on to the scenes at hand and got them all shot that evening, and I got home later that night, like around eleven o'clock, and Ashleigh wasn't there, which I thought was weird, because even though she did have friends and she did go out every once in a while, she usually left a note.

I tried not to worry about it and went to bed.

But the thing was I didn't worry about it at first. But as I laid there in bed I started to worry about it. It started with me just wondering what she was doing. And I thought about maybe that she had a boyfriend and they were out together. And that thought was okay. But then I started to worry that maybe she had been hit by a car. Maybe she was lying in the hospital. Or maybe she was dead. Or maybe worse. I had these horrible thoughts that she'd gone to the grocery store and had been abducted on her way through the parking lot and had been raped in an alley and then stabbed and was lying bleeding somewhere just barely clinging to life.

And around one in the morning, still awake with these awful scenarios dancing in my brain, I got out of bed and put my jeans back on and found a jacket.

I was going to get in my car and drive around looking for her, but I didn't know where I'd go or how I'd find her, but I couldn't just lie there.

It was then, before I'd actually left my bedroom, that I heard the front door open.

I listened to see if anyone was with her, but it sounded like she was alone.

Suddenly I was furious.

I was so angry that she'd made me worry like that.

"Where have you been, young lady?" I demanded as I burst into the living room. But that was just in my head, because I didn't really do that. I just kind of imagined myself doing it, and I also imagined the response I'd get if I did. And because of the response that I imagined, that's why I didn't do it in real life. I wasn't her father, and besides she was legally an adult and she had every right to be out doing whatever she wanted as late as she wanted. But that didn't mean I wasn't going to worry.

☿ ☿ ☿

The next morning I asked her, as nonchalantly as possible, where she'd been last night.

"Nowhere," she said.

"Well you didn't come home 'til one in the morning."

"What, were you waiting up for me?"

"No, not..." I stammered. "I just... I couldn't sleep and I heard you come in."

"Because you were worried about me?" she smiled.

"No. No, I just couldn't sleep."

"You were worried about me," she sort of laughed, but I think she was really touched.

"So where were you?"

"Doesn't matter."

"Really. Why won't you tell me?"

"Because I don't want to."

"Why not?"

"Because I don't."

"Were you out with a boy?" I asked. "Is that why you won't tell me?"

She laughed. "If I was out with a boy, I'd have no problem telling you. No. I just... I can't tell you right now. Later."

"Later when?"

She just shook her head.

"Don't you think it's weird living with your sister?" she asked after an awkward minute of silence.

"What do you mean?"

"I mean, we're both adults, shouldn't we..."

"You want to move out? So it is about a boy."

"No, it's not. And it's not that I want to move out. I mean, I like living with you. It's just…"

"Just what?" I said.

"Just, I don't know. It's weird. You should be dating girls and be able to bring them back to your apartment and not have to worry about me being here and being in the way."

"What girls am I going to date? And if it's because you want your own place where you can bring boys you can just say that."

"That's not what I'm implying," she said. "I'm just saying maybe it'd be better for both of us…"

"Just say that you want to move. Do you think you're going to hurt my feelings? Wherever you go, we'll still keep in touch. I lived by myself for a while and I'll be fine doing it again. And you should too."

"Well I'm not talking about living on my own…"

"So…"

"No, I'm not moving in with my boyfriend."

"So you have a boyfriend?"

"No," she said. "Look, we can't talk about this right now. I'm not moving in with a boy. I'm not even sure I'm moving out at all. I'm just rambling. Just… Don't worry about it. You're my brother, I love you, whatever we decide…"

And she walked out of the room without finishing that sentence.

That day at work I wondered why Ashleigh wanted to leave. I mean, I understood why she might want to get out on her own, but I wondered why suddenly now. And honestly, it made me kind of sad. And even though it hadn't happened yet, I suddenly felt very lonely.

That evening me and Chris were shooting a scene with just him in it and I asked him, or rather I told him that I thought Ashleigh wanted to move out.

"Hmm," he said. "That'd probably be good for both of you, don't you think?"

"Why do you say that?" I asked.

"I don't know, I just… You're both adults and it just seems kind of weird that you live with your sister. I don't know, maybe it's not. It just seems like… I mean, what if you had a girlfriend or if she had a boyfriend? Wouldn't that be awkward?"

"See, that's the thing," I said. "I'm thinking that maybe she's wanting to move in with her boyfriend."

"Is that a problem?"

I looked at him. "Well…"

"No, I gotcha. Yeah. I don't even like when my sisters talk about guys. We're despicable creatures. But she's gonna do what she's gonna do."

"It's not that so much. Honestly, I don't even know if she has a boy-friend. And she said she's not moving in with a boy, but…"

"Maybe she's not," he said.

I rolled my eyes. "What else would she be doing? I just don't know why she'd lie to me. And she's being all cryptic."

"Maybe she just anticipates having a boyfriend sometime in the future. I mean she probably will."

This didn't really help me at all, but at least I felt like I had someone to talk to.

♀ ♀ ♀

I don't know, maybe three days later or four, Ashleigh told me she was moving out. Also, she'd given two weeks notice at the copy center.

"Where you going?" I asked.

She curled her lips up to her teeth, pulling her mouth into a flat smile and softened her eyes.

"California," she finally said.

"What?"

"I'm moving to California."

"That's kind of...not very close to here."

"No. It's not too far though. I mean, you could still visit me every once in a while. Or you could move there too."

"With you?" I asked.

"Your own apartment. But why not? What's really tying you here? You wanna be a movie director, California's the place to do it."

"Yeah, but..."

"But what?" she said. "See, I know, and that's what Kara said."

"What do you mean that's what Kara said?"

"She was in town, but she didn't want me to tell you. I don't know why. But that's who I was with the other night. Keith left her for some actress. She's on her own, but she doesn't want to come back. She asked me if I wanted to move down there with her."

"Why can't I..."

"Because you're a boy."

"I'm your brother," I said. "I'm her brother too."

"After dad, and then Keith, and... Can you blame her? Really?"

I didn't understand.

"I don't understand."

"Of course you don't," Ashleigh said. "But that's not the point. The point is I'm going. She's already back down there. She has an apartment and a job for me for a little while until I find something."

"So you're basically abandoning me then," I said, and I realized how that sounded as soon as it came out of my mouth.

And Ashleigh realized that I realized how that sounded so she just gave me that look.

Then she said, "I asked her if you could come. She said she couldn't stop you from moving down there, but she said you'd never do it. She said you're too afraid to really do anything. I defended you, but she has a point, Warren."

"What do you mean?"

"I mean you never step outside your comfort zone."

"I'm not even that comfortable in my comfort zone," I said.

"That's kind of the point. But Warren, at any time, I would love for you to move down to California. I will help you find an apartment. I will help you find a job. I will help you with whatever you need help with."

"I don't know," I said. "I'd like to. I just…"

She shrugged and shook her head.

Neither one of us spoke but both of us were thinking the same thing.

Finally I asked her when she was planning to go.

"I gave my two weeks, so…two weeks."

"So are you not going to Berlin with me then? To see dad?" I asked.

"No. But please still go anyway."

The next morning, at least I think it was the next morning, I told Chris I had a plan to shoot the European cathedral stuff and I showed him the tickets.

We called that day to get tickets for October 29th, 2006, roundtrip from Salt Lake International to Berlin Tegel. Then I had to run to get to that restaurant where I had an appointment to meet Sherry for lunch. She was going to set me up with her best friend, the girl I was destined to spend the rest of eternity with.

I sat just inside the restaurant in the *Please Wait to Be Seated* area. I waited for fifteen minutes, then I got antsy. I worried that maybe I was in the wrong place. So I went back outside and paced in front of the restaurant. I would have called, except I hadn't thought to get her number.

I waited until four o'clock, but Sherry never showed up. I don't know if she planned it, but now I knew how she felt twenty-one months ago when I stole back my ring and snuck out while she was in the shower.

CHAPTER 37

A CHRISTMAS STORY

On the first day of Christmas, my true love gave to me a partridge in a pear tree.

What would I do with that? Who wants a partridge in a pear tree? Or even a partridge not in a pear tree?

That's what I was thinking anyways.

I hate that song.

But that's the song that was playing in the mall that day. And I'd tell you the date if I could remember it, but I can't exactly. I think it was the twenty-first or twenty-second of December.

I was in the ZCMI mall downtown, doing some shopping, not that I had a lot to do. Pretty much I was taking advantage of the sales to buy some things for myself, which I'd also done at five a.m. the day after Thanksgiving and was planning to do again the day after Christmas. Also, I was buying a couple of things for Ashleigh.

It's Macy's now, but I think it was Meier & Frank then. And before that it was ZCMI, which I think is where the mall got its name. But none of that matters. In any case, that's the store I was in, because I wanted one of those Magic Bullet food mixer/blender things.

So I was in the kitchenwares section of the store, and I guess I need to tell you about how the store is laid out. So there's like kitchen gadgets and whatnot there on the top floor, where there's also like relaxation fountains (y'know, the little ones for your desk or whatever, where the water trickles out of plastic candles or over rocks or down a series of fake metal leaves) and foot spas and those massaging pad things that you put on the back of your chair or your car seat, and all that.

The next floor down is full of like linens and things. I mean like towels and bed sheets and quilts and comforters and all the kinds of things you might buy for your bedroom or bathroom.

But back up on the top floor where I was they had a whole display set up with the Magic Bullets, kind of stuck in among the Cuisinarts and the four-slice Texas-wide toasters.

So I was looking and trying to decide whether eighty dollars was a good price for a Magic Bullet, which I think it was but it was also the regular price because the Magic Bullet was not on sale at that time. So even though I really wanted one I was trying to decide if I should wait until after Christmas to see if they went on sale.

So as I was thinking about it, I was kind of handling the different-colored plastic rings that screw on top of the blender-cups. And I was holding the red one, I remember specifically, while looking at the aerodynamic-looking container sitting on top of the motor. Then I was kind of looking through that container, because if you've never seen them, they're transparent. Actually even if you have seen them, they're still transparent. And through the cup, even though it was kind of distorted, I could see this female figure. Not close, but down one floor, in the linens.

I didn't give it a lot of thought right away, but if you're a guy then you know that when you spot anything with long hair and that curvy female form, it's compulsory that you give it at least a second look. So I leaned my head to the side, around the blender and looked directly down between the escalators.

I couldn't see her face, because from my angle actually her whole head was cut off by the floor of my floor which was her floor's ceiling. But I could pretty much see her from the neck down, and I could see the chestnut hair spilling down over her shoulders and down her back. And I recognized all those curves.

And I was frozen for a second, trying to figure what to do.

Two turtle doves, the overhead speakers hummed.

I remembered the last time, when her father'd pounded on my window. I thought maybe he'd forgotten about me, or at least forgotten what I looked like. I searched my brain for some kind of encouragement, and what I came up with was that maybe her father had suffered a heart attack and was dead or in a coma. This was a terrible thought I know, but I needed something. Then I decided that I'd cross that bridge, y'know, whenever.

Right now, I decided this was another of the universe's manifestations of destiny. She was here and that meant something. I don't know.

It suddenly didn't matter that I'd resigned myself to losing her, that rationally there was no way it could ever work. It was like seeing her here renewed my faith in...

...destiny, I guess.

It's like I'm told if you quit smoking for a long time, you give it up completely for say three years, then most of the time, though you might occasionally get a craving for a cigarette, it's usually pretty easy to stay away from tobacco. But if you were to, say, sit down next to someone who's smoking, then the desire becomes almost unbearable, and it's much more difficult not to take a puff.

It was like that for me now.

I thought this was over, but this was my addiction. I was addicted to Allison Shepard. And while usually it's best to fight your addictions, sometimes the best thing is to feed them. Sometimes you just have to give in.

So I took a chance and darted around the display table to the escalator.

"Hey!" someone shouted behind me, but I figured they weren't talking to me so I didn't turn around.

Three French hens. As I descended from kitchenwares to linens.

When I hit the floor, she wasn't where she had been.

She was somewhere else.

I scanned the floor and saw some towels that looked like good towels, but they were way too expensive.

Then I spotted her at the counter. She was signing a receipt and the lady was handing her back her credit card. I headed in her direction as she picked up a bag and walked to the escalators, but I'd gone around the other way and wasn't where I'd intercept her.

Four calling birds.

"Allison," I heard myself shout.

She turned a little and looked around, but then shook her head like she figured she'd just been hearing things and stepped onto the escalator.

I darted after and heard that familiar, "Hey!"

Then I was intercepted.

"You can't just take that."

I just stared at the guy.

"What are you talking about?" I said finally.

He pointed to my hand.

"Here," I shoved the red plastic ring into his palm, and took off toward the escalator, but he grabbed my arm.

"You know, shoplifting is a crime," he said.

"I didn't realize I was carrying it," I said. "I'm sorry."

"I'm supposed to believe that?"

"Believe what you want. I have to go."

"If I believe what I want, I'll have to prosecute you."

"I didn't take it outside of the store," I said and wrested my arm from his grip.

He didn't say anything else and I got on the escalator.

Down one floor to women's clothes, I looked around for Allison. There she was still descending on the next moving staircase. I ran to it and followed her down to the ground floor, men's clothes and perfume and handbags. She headed down between the jewelry counters, past...

Five golden rings.

I chased after her, but not at a running pace, because I didn't want to scare her. It was more of a brisk walk.

Another person intercepted me, some woman wearing way too much makeup. She had a bottle of perfume and asked if I was looking for a gift for my girlfriend.

"I don't have a girlfriend," I said.

"Well, we also have some nice colognes," she said.

I asked what she was implying, and she just thrust a couple samples into my hand.

As I squeezed out of the department store into the center court of the mall, I popped the cap from one of the samples and dabbed some of the stuff on my neck. If I caught her, I wanted to smell delicious.

Six geese a-laying.

They were playing this damn song throughout the whole mall, not just in the one store. Man, I hated this song.

I couldn't see her now. The mall was very crowded.

I looked right and left and everywhere, but she was gone.

I walked into the center of the mall for a better perspective. And I did try to avoid the long line of whining and screaming children waiting to sit on Santa's lap.

I backed up against the fountain...

Seven swans a-swimming.

...and spun around looking all over.

Then there she was.

I saw her through the glass.

She was on the elevator, going up.

I thought that was kind of weird, taking the escalators in the store all the way down to the ground floor, only to get on the elevator and go back up again. Maybe she thought the store she wanted was on the ground floor, but then when she came out of the store, she saw it or something.

I stepped back so I could see if she came out on the second floor, which she did. But instead of waiting for the elevator, I darted over to the stairs, which meant breaking through the line of snot-nosed kids, and I think I may have accidentally knocked one down. I really hope not, not that I can do anything about it now. Then I ran around to the staircase and got up to the second floor as fast as I could.

Eight maids a-milking.

She was going into the bookstore. And I followed, only I went in through the other entrance at my end of the mall.

I'd like to say that we saw each other across the bookstore, like in that one movie where the two characters see each other across the bookstore. But I'm pretty sure she didn't even notice me.

She was just browsing, I think, and I saw her pick up a book. I think is was that *Purpose-Driven Life* one, but I'm not sure. She was probably planning on buying it as a gift.

I made my way through the fiction section and past the classics, over to the inspirational books, which of course was where she was standing.

I was just one row behind and was trying to figure out what to say.

I didn't want to look conspicuous, so I picked up a copy of...

Nine ladies dancing.

...some book whose title I don't remember.

I put the book back after a second, then figuring out how to do this I stepped up next to her and picked up a copy of the same book she was holding.

What I was going to say was, "Have you read this?" Because then she'd either say yes or no, and I'd just go from there. But just as I opened my mouth Allison flipped open her cell phone and said "Hello" into it. I didn't hear it ring, so I guess it must have been on vibrate. I'll tell you what. Sometimes I really hate those damn things!

"No, I'm just…" she set the book back on the shelf. "No, I just wandered into the bookstore," she said into the phone.

I flipped the book over and pretended to read the back cover as Allison walked away.

"Really, where at?" I heard her say.

I put my copy back on the shelf and watched her walk out of the store.

Ten lords a-leaping. And I wondered what the hell that's even supposed to mean. I really hated this damn song.

I followed her out, but quite a ways behind, so I couldn't hear anything she was saying.

Once out of the bookstore I saw where she was going. You may have seen this coming, but I didn't even think about it until now. She was heading into the food court.

And you know how much I hate the food court.

But I steeled myself. And I followed.

I didn't know what I was going to do. I just wanted to talk to her. So I followed, and luckily she wasn't sitting down to eat anywhere. She was just passing through. She angled left and headed toward the west entrance to the mall.

Eleven pipers piping.

I followed her.

She got to the steps and that's when I saw her snap her phone shut and put it back in her pocket. She left the building.

When I emerged onto the sidewalk I had to zip up my coat, because it was really cold out.

There next to the planter was an older guy playing the saxophone with his case open for people to drop change in. I gave him whatever was in my pocket, which was probably like sixty-seven cents or something. But you'll never guess what he was playing.

Jingle Bell Rock, or something, I don't really remember. I just know it wasn't *Twelve Days of Christmas.*

I never had to hear about the "twelve drummers drumming," which at first I was glad of. But the thing is when you hear an annoying song but you don't hear the end, that annoying song gets stuck in your head and plays over and over and over again for days and days.

I spotted Allison up ahead at the crosswalk, and I jogged to catch up with her.

Then the problem.

She jumped onto a TRAX train heading south to Sandy.

I ran as fast as I could, but I'd maintained such a safe following distance that when I reached the platform the train doors had just closed. I watched her through the window as she found an empty seat, one facing me.

The thing is, here she did see me.

We did make eye contact as the train pulled away, and her head actually turned holding that connection for just those few seconds as the train slid down the tracks, carrying her away from me forever.

The universe could not have sent me a clearer signal than that. Whether I wanted to accept it or not, I knew that was the end. And the truth is I did accept it, y'know.

It was the last time I ever saw Allison Shepard.

This was 2005, and if you'd known that up front, then you'd've known that this is how it would all end.

And as I walked away from the platform, back into the mall, to the elevator that took me up to the parking lot, where I walked back to my car, to drive back to my apartment, without Allison or a Magic Bullet, that horrible song started over in my head again with a lousy partridge in a stupid pear tree.

CHAPTER 38

GHOST

Passport control was really easy, y'know. You just go up to the little glass booth and show the guy your passport. He looks at you like he's trying to read your brain then he stamps it and lets you go. I don't know why, but I thought it was going to be a much bigger deal than that.

At Tegel, passport control is the threshold to baggage claim, but since we had carried everything on we just passed through to the main corridor.

See Tegel is like a big hexagon, if I'm remembering right. Or maybe it's an octagon, but I think it's a hexagon, a polygon in any case, with the terminals kind of jutting out from the center. It's pretty easy to navigate anyways.

Chris had been here twice before so he pretty much knew how to get to the car rental place, which was around the way and outside, down an escalator and then like a block away over some sketchy sidewalks.

When we got up to the building Chris said, "I forgot to mention this before, but you told them we were taking the car out of the country, right?"

I hadn't told them that, no. "You didn't tell me I needed to."

"I hope that's not going to be a problem," he said. "I don't think it will be, because I forgot last time, but they had one for us anyway when we got here. It's just that only certain cars can be taken out. I'm not sure why. Shouldn't be a problem I don't think."

He was repeating himself there, which meant he was worried that it might be a problem.

"What do we do if they don't have a car for us?" I asked.

"Well there was no deposit, right? So we just cancel the reservation and go somewhere else. But I don't think it should be a problem. It shouldn't be. It'll be fine. Just make sure you tell them we plan to take the car into Poland when you get up to the counter."

When I got up to the counter, I asked the girl if she spoke English.

"Of course," she said like I'd just asked her if she had two arms and two legs, which she did have by the way.

"Umm, okay," I said. "I have a reservation for Warren West."

"Yes, I see it," she said.

"We need to take the car into Poland."

"You should say that when you are making the reservation."

"I know. I just didn't know then, and they didn't ask, so..."

"Well because we only have certain cars that you can take out of Germany," she explained. "I will have to be checking and see if we have one at the present time."

"Thank you," I said.

She did some typing on the computer while I watched. Then she said, "Sir," like she was trying to get my attention even though she already had it. And even though I was looking right at her, she didn't say anything else until I said, "Yes?"

"Sir, at the present time we do not have any automobiles that may be taken out of Germany."

"Really?" I said. It was October, not like the height of tourist season, so I really couldn't believe there were no vehicles available that I could drive into Poland.

"There is nothing," the girl said.

Chris heard the whole thing, then walked over to one of the other counters.

"I guess I need to cancel my reservation," I said.

She said she could call another airport whose name I don't remember. It might have been the Flughafen Airport or something. I seem to remember seeing that somewhere. But I told her no, because I figured Chris was getting us a car from the other company.

"Thank you anyway," I said.

Then Chris came back from the counter and told me that they didn't have any either.

There was a third company, and the result was the same with them.

"Here's the thing," Chris said. "We can go to the other airports and hope they have a car for us or we can just take a train into Poland. I know there are a couple that run in the afternoon, so that gives us a few hours."

"Could we just get a car and go into Poland anyway?"

"They check your rental contracts at the border."

"Well if we take a train, what about getting to my dad's office?"

"Take a cab. Overall, the cost'll be about the same I think, and actually we could take an overnight train back and cancel our hotel in Berlin. Save a little money there maybe."

"I guess let's take the train," I said.

"Then we also won't have to worry about parking."

We walked back outside and down that sketchy sidewalk, then up the escalator again. This was pretty much the area for ground transportation and there were cabs all lined up.

"Look, you wanna just meet me at the train station?" I said.

"You sure?"

"Yeah, you can go buy the tickets or something."

"You don't want me to come with you?"

"I'd rather you didn't," I said.

"Okay, I'm not gonna buy the tickets yet, cause...who knows how long you'll be, right?"

"How far's the train station?"

"I think it's like a ten-minute bus ride, so..."

"I'll meet you there at three."

"It's a big place," he said.

"I'll meet you by the ticket counter at three o'clock."

"All right," he said reluctantly. "It's the Bahnhof Zoo." And he wrote down the name for me on a three-by-five card that he pulled from his coat pocket.

Then he walked in through the gigantic revolving door to a kiosk and bought a bus ticket. As I was getting into a cab, he reemerged and stepped onto a bus.

"Do you speak English?" I asked the cab driver.

"Of course," he said.

I handed him the address of my dad's office and asked how much.

"Fifteen Euro," he replied.

That was like twenty bucks, which I thought was extreme but I didn't really have a lot of choice, so I told him to take me.

On the way over, I just sat there in the back seat thinking about what I was doing, and whether I even wanted to do it, whether this trip even made any sense at all, whether I shouldn't just have this guy head to the train station and get on the earliest train straight into Poland with Chris. But we'd already decided to meet at three, so I probably wouldn't be able to find him anyways.

Secretly I hoped my dad wouldn't even be there, that they'd sent him to Budapest or somewhere for a convention or something. Then I'd be off the hook.

Because what was I even going to say to him?

It's not like things had been so terrible. I mean, it's not like I was still a kid when he took off. If anyone should be angry it was Kara and Ashleigh. I was already out of high school when he left, so...

Maybe I'd tell him that, that he should be ashamed for leaving his two daughters.

But he already knew that.

Why was I even here?

I pulled out the card one more time and looked at the address, then I raised my other fist to my mouth and bit my first knuckle. I almost made it bleed, but not quite.

⚥ ⚥ ⚥

The building my father worked in was not that impressive really. Not like I'd pictured in my mind.

See, I'd pictured some grand architectural masterpiece. I don't know, maybe some glass and steel skyscraper with sharp edges and elegant curves and I don't know what else, but I figured since he was so well off financially so was his company. And the company may have been, but this was Berlin and so the building was basically a big cement block. The inside however was very nice but also kind of oddly designed. Almost like something from a Tim Burton movie or a Dr. Seuss book.

There was a security guard in a little room just inside the entrance, but he didn't stop me as I walked past looking for the elevator.

I found it and with some trepidation stepped inside and pressed the button for the fourth floor.

I'm not sure if the elevator really was the slowest elevator in the entire world or if it just felt that way, but it seemed like it took forever to rise up just four stories. And it was four stories because the first floor was actually the second floor, because the ground floor was like floor zero or something but not floor one. This, I discovered, was the way all the buildings were over here.

I stepped out of the elevator into an elegant reception area, where a very attractive woman smiled at me as I approached the desk. She said something in German that I didn't understand.

"Do you speak English?" I asked her.

"Yes," she said. "I'm an American."

I don't know why it was so exciting to see an American, because just twelve hours earlier I'd been in a country full of them.

"I'm here to see Martin West," I told her.

"Do you have an appointment?"

"I don't."

"What is it regarding?"

"I'm his son," I said, then thinking better I added, "but I'd rather you didn't tell him that."

"I see," she said. "Just a minute."

And she walked back through a glass door and I couldn't see where she went from there. A minute later she came back and said, "Your father's in a meeting right now, but you can wait in his office if you'd like."

"How long will he be? Because I have to meet someone at three."

"Should only be a few more minutes," the woman said as she escorted me through the glass door. We went down a darkish corridor and she motioned me into a rather large office.

"My name is Miranda, by the way."

I smiled and nodded at her.

"Are you Brian or Warren?"

"Warren." She'd heard about us.

"It's a pleasure to finally meet you, Warren. Can I get you anything?"

I shook my head.

"If you need anything..." she said and left me alone without telling me what to do if I needed anything.

Through the window of my dad's office I could see another big grey cement building covered in graffiti, and I could see a lot of apartment buildings. The view wasn't the greatest, but down below it was definitely a city, a bigger city than any in Utah, and there were about four thousand dogs being walked just within a four-block radius. And there were teenagers on skateboards, and really the whole thing wasn't so different from any large city in the U.S. except that things weren't as flashy and colorful.

My dad's office was a typical office except for one thing that caught my eye. It was made of cherry wood I think, and it was definitely hand-carved. Each pawn was different from the others just slightly, but each was precisely chiseled. The whole thing was exquisite and it wasn't so large as it was just the perfect size.

I didn't even know my father played.

I looked at every piece, admiring the craftsmanship, not that I was qualified in any way to judge that kind of thing. The board just looked beautiful.

"What are you doing all the way out here?"

I looked up from the chessboard to my father standing in the doorway. He closed the door behind him.

"I..."

I started, but at that moment I realized I didn't have a thing in the world to say to him.

"You've come a long way. You must want something."

I couldn't speak.

"If you've come to tell me what a terrible father I am, I can't argue with you. You're right." He sat down behind his desk. "But I don't know what you hope to accomplish by saying that. You know, you could have just called. Would have been a lot cheaper than flying all the way out here. Really, Warren. What are you doing here?"

I didn't know how to answer, because I didn't know what I was doing here.

"Have at it. Lay into me. Tell me what a terrible person I am," he said. "If you don't do it, you wasted your money."

"Marty bought me the tickets," I said.

"What are you talking about?"

"In his will, he left instructions for his son Steven to fly me here to see you, and he wrote me a letter..."

"In his will?"

And here my dad did something unexpected. He didn't cry. He didn't even tear up. But he swiveled his chair around so I couldn't see his face. But before he did he tightened his hand into a fist and bit his first knuckle.

I guess it wasn't so much what he did that was unexpected but what I could see was going on inside him. He was feeling something.

It was remarkable in a way.

I don't think I'd ever seen him care about anything.

"He finally passed?" he asked, his face still hidden from me. "How long ago?"

"Almost three months."

"How was the funeral?"

"Empty," I said. "Ashleigh went with me. And his son showed up."

"How'd Steven take it?"

"I think he was glad Marty was dead."

"Yeah, that's what I'd've expected. He was always an ungrateful little sonofabitch. Why'd he want you to come out here and see me? Did he say?"

I shook my head, then realizing that he couldn't see me, I said, "We never talked about it."

"I mean in the letter."

"Oh. Not in so many words."

"Well, what did he say?"

"That's for me only. It's private. But he had this one for you."

I pulled out the smaller envelope that had been enclosed in mine. It was addressed to my dad. He swiveled his chair back around and took the letter from my hands and set it on the desk and stared at it.

"Are you going to read it?" I asked.

I sat down in a chair next to the chessboard.

"Eventually," he said.

I just stared at him, and he just stared at the envelope.

I wondered if by "eventually" he meant after I'd gone, but I wasn't sure. I didn't want to say anything, or more accurately I didn't have anything to say. I was still just sitting there by the chessboard wondering why I was here.

And I wondered a little bit why Marty, who apparently had had my dad's address when he wrote all these letters, had instructed me to deliver my father's letter. I'm sure he left behind enough for postage, or at least Steven could have spared a dollar or whatever it costs to slip the thing in the mail. And then I sort of asked myself why I didn't just drop the thing off at the post office myself.

And I wondered a little bit more about why people leave things like this behind when they die, these letters that say all the things they couldn't say when they were alive. And I wondered why people can't say all these kinds of things when they're alive.

I mean, seriously.

As much as I admired Marty and as much as I respected him, I don't understand why he didn't just make the effort when he still had his faculties. I mean, he had the presence of mind to write it all down for everyone before his senses left him, so why couldn't he just say it instead of leaving all these almost voiceless letters behind for anyone who still remembered him.

After what seemed like an hour but was probably only about five minutes, my dad picked up the envelope from the desk and held it in his hands. I watched him, but kind of from the corner of my eye because I didn't want him to look up and make eye contact with me.

He held the envelope at one end and slapped the other against his palm a few times. I don't know what he was doing.

Finally, he opened his desk drawer and pulled out a letter opener.

The only people I've ever seen use letter openers are old people whose hands are too frail and also pompous people who do it because a letter opener seems like something a "successful" person should have. It's the same kind of people who sit in interviews or meetings and clip their fingernails, pretending to be disinterested, because they think it makes them look impressive or something.

He inserted the letter opener under the flap and sliced the envelope open. He leaned back and swiveled around again, his back to me, and I can only assume he took out the letter and read it since I couldn't see through his high-back leather chair. I don't know what else he could have done, though I suppose he could have just stared at the now penetrated envelope for a little while longer.

I gave him time, I don't know how much.

Ten minutes.

Maybe fifteen.

Then I had to do something. I'd traveled all this way, I still didn't know why, not really. But I couldn't fly across the ocean and just sit there in his office in agonizing silence then leave. That would be ridiculous.

But since I didn't want to talk to the bastard, I just stood up and walked over to his desk. I didn't make any effort to muffle the clap of my sneakers along the hardwood floors, so I'm sure he heard me coming and I'm sure that's why he turned around.

I held two closed fists out in front of his face.

He looked at them, then up at my face.

He was stoic.

Me, not so much. But I don't know what my feelings were exactly.

He tapped my left hand.

White. This time I'm sure.

He stood up and we took our places on opposite sides of the chess-board.

After his predictable open, I started with my signature move, the left flank pawn out two spaces.

He was surprised, I could tell. And I'm sure he wanted to tell me that that was no way to start a game of chess and that clearly I didn't know what I was doing.

But he held his tongue, and I appreciated that.

He leaned down near the board.

We weren't playing clocks, I'd never played clocks, so he had all the time he wanted to choose his next move, but I knew what it was going to be so I had pretty much my next three already mapped out.

And he did exactly what I expected. He slid his bishop all the way out to the edge of the board. Just like Marty, just like anyone.

So just like I'd always done I brought out my knight and hedged it behind my pawn.

He saw what I'd done and knew what it meant. Now he had to consider his next move. He pushed his fist up under his chin and hooked his fore-finger over his lips.

Then he made eye contact, and I think it made us both uncomfortable because he quickly looked away. But I think he could see that I was going to win this game. I had the confidence and I had the desire, and I knew how to play.

Now I can remember every single move made in this game, but you don't care about that. Listening to someone describe a chess game is probably worse than filling a bathtub using an eyedropper or counting the seeds on the skin of a strawberry. In other words, it's something only an obsessive-compulsive would enjoy. But the point is, without clocks, a chess game can go on for several hours, and this one did go on for a couple of them.

After my dad had collected three of my pawns and a rook, and I'd collected two of his pawns and both of his bishops, and about an hour of silence had passed, he said, "So what are you up to? You in school, or..."

He made sure to keep his eyes on the board as he said it and he fingered one of my captured pawns at the same time.

"No," I said. "I never went to college."

"That's a shame."

"I'm okay with it."

And I think that made him feel judgmental, and even if you are judgmental no one wants to feel that way, so he stopped talking.

It was another collective four pawns, one knight, a rook and a queen later that I finally spat, "I heard you were living with another woman," in an acidic tone that I didn't try to mask. I was surprised at myself that I could even broach the topic. Maybe it was the high of capturing his queen. I don't know.

"You met her," he said.

"When?"

"Miranda, the receptionist."

How cliché, I thought. Hooking up with the receptionist.

And as if reading my mind my father continued, "She wasn't the receptionist at the time. We started seeing each other back in the States before..."

And there he stopped.

"She actually got me this job," he went on after considerable pause as if trying to hide the adulterous elephant in the room under a two-by-two-foot cloth napkin with chewed meat spat in it. "Her father is from Hamburg, so she speaks German and lived here for several years. And so..."

"Do you speak German?" I interrupted.

"I'm learning. I speak a little."

"It's gotta be hard living in a country where you don't speak the language," I said. I didn't really want to acknowledge the pachyderm either.

"You get used to it. And it's Berlin. Everyone here speaks English anyway."

There was nothing to say to that. Not really.

So I made my next move in silence, and I must not have been paying very close attention because he took my queen, but I turned right around and captured a rook. I still had the advantage in pieces, but he had one of my knights and that's my strategy, sneak up with the knights. I also had to keep my eye on this one pawn that he had slowly creeping up to my edge of the board.

A couple speechless moves later, in which no pieces were taken, I leaned forward over the board.

I put my fingers around the head of my one remaining knight.

"So what's the deal?" I said. "Was Marty your father?"

I looked at his face.

The question didn't even faze him. Like he'd been expecting it.

Then I took my fingers off my knight and slid my bishop across the board to prevent my father's pawn from taking that final space.

CHAPTER 39
EVERYTHING IS ILLUMINATED

In order for me to tell it, I need to go way back to Preston, Idaho, which means going way back to the 1940's.

You'll remember that Marty and Sarah were running away to get married, because Sarah's father Abe forbade her from seeing Marty. And since you'll remember that, I don't have to tell it all to you again. But I'll remind you that Sarah's brother Hyrum helped them do it. I'll also remind you that Hyrum was going to Boise to see this new oven or something at some new bakery. I'm still not sure what kind of innovations they could have been adding to ovens back then that made them so revolutionary, but that's where Hyrum was going anyways.

Then I'll remind you of one more thing. Marty and Sarah settled in West Valley, Utah, and so a couple years later Hyrum made his way down to open a bakery in Kearns.

At the time, Kearns was pretty much a field. Hardly anything had been built there, and that includes houses and whatnot. And so Hyrum got in at a good time, where his bakery could almost be like the city's centerpiece. But that also meant that he would have to build it up from scratch. He couldn't just move into some rented space.

So Hyrum drew up all the plans for his bakery, he ordered the oven he'd seen that day in Boise, and he worked with the bank to get a business loan which at the time I guess required some heavy collateral, which meant investing everything he'd saved himself and then some.

Marty and Sarah agreed to let him live with them as long as he needed. It was the least they could do, and he assured them it would only be until his shop was up and running. Marty also got him set up with a temporary job at the local macaroni factory through a neighbor whose car Marty had worked on.

It's a funny thing about dreams. I mean, I personally don't see anything exciting in the least about opening up a bakery, but then again Hyrum probably wouldn't have seen anything at all interesting about directing a movie. But to every man his dream supplies limitless excitement, and that kind of excitement can be infectious, especially the excitement of a dream in the process of coming true.

See, Hyrum would go to work every day at the macaroni factory and while he would do the work required and do it well, he would talk non-stop about the bakery he was opening, and he would tell people about the oven, and he would tell them about his recipes, and he would even describe the flour as if it was somehow different from what they were using in the pasta. It might have been an alien flour for all Hyrum raved about it.

But people were interested. They wanted to know more, or at least they took interest because how could you not when someone speaks so passionately.

Also every night after work, Hyrum would walk the few blocks to the construction site and check the progress of his bakery. Every new cinder-block, every dollop of mortar was analyzed and approved. Everything had to be perfect. And even if he couldn't be there during the day when the builders were, he'd make sure to leave them instructions when something wasn't done properly, often making them do bits of the work over and over again. He was a bit of a perfectionist.

One evening, as Hyrum came out of the factory, probably turning up his lapel as I imagine it was cold that night, he found a woman waiting for him. I forget her name, because I only heard it the one time, but we can call her Mildred because that's just what comes to mind — or Millie for short. She worked in the factory but Hyrum had never spoken to her.

I don't doubt that she was attracted to him, because from what Marty said Hyrum was a handsome guy. And I'm sure he was charming, and I'm sure he sounded like a man who was going to be successful and by extension wealthy.

Now I'm not saying Millie was a gold digger, that you can judge for yourself. I'm just saying, I can understand why a woman who'd never spoken to Hyrum might be inclined to wait for him outside the factory at night and want to be noticed by him.

"Hi," she said.

"Hello," Hyrum replied.

"I'm Millie," she said but probably used her real name.

"Hyrum."

"I know," she smiled at him, and I'm sure he liked hearing that, because what guy wouldn't if a beautiful girl, and I'm sure she was beautiful, was waiting outside and virtually throwing herself at him in that understated way.

"You do?" he replied. "What else do you know?"

"I hear you talking all the time about your bakery."

"Oh, yeah?"

"I'd love to see it."

Why wouldn't he say okay and take her there? So that's what he did.

It was only a half-constructed building with no interior to speak of, and there was really nothing impressive about it. Yet Millie was impressed. She made it known, in whatever way, that she wanted to see Hyrum again. And he was not opposed.

They started dating, or courting or whatever they called it back then. They courted for a while even, several months I assume. In any case, it came to a point where Hyrum bought a ring, got down on one knee, asked Millie to marry him, and she said yes.

But here's the rub, because shortly after the engagement Hyrum was walking home from the bakery site — it was nearing completion — and just a couple blocks from Marty and Sarah's house he came upon another girl, with whom he was immediately enamored.

Despite his engagement, Hyrum passed by that house several times a day hoping to get another look at that girl. It came to a point where he was spending more time in front of this mystery-woman's home than he was spending at his prospective bakery.

Over time he learned her name was Elaine — of this name I am sure. He learned that she lived in that house with her father, who was very sick, with what the doctors did not know. She had lived alone with her father all her life, her mother having died in childbirth, something which I guess happened much more frequently back then.

One day he decided that he would throw to the wind whatever it is you throw to the wind and walked right up to the front door and rang the bell.

When she opened up, he said, "Hello. My name is Hyrum Coldwell. I've seen you here several times over the past weeks and I think you're very beautiful, and I don't know what else to say, except I think I'm in love with you."

When I heard this, I thought, Why didn't I think of that?

But he lived in a different time, and even then I don't know that all women would have been quite so flattered as Elaine was at that moment.

Well, the thing is, they started seeing each other, seeing a lot of each other. They'd sneak away and steal moments together under the stars. And the only problem was Hyrum forgot to tell Mildred that he'd fallen in love with someone else. And he didn't tell Elaine that he was engaged to be married to another woman. This is never a lie you can keep up for too long.

Fortunately, Hyrum figured that out sooner than later.

He came clean to Elaine, and she demanded that he make a choice as any rational woman would. He told her there was no choice to be made; he was not in love with Mildred, but he didn't know how to get out of the engagement. And Elaine actually helped him compose what he would say to Millie and how he would say it. She even set a day and time for him to do so. And he left with a resolve to resolve the situation.

It was two nights before his bakery was scheduled to be finished when he sat Millie down in the partially furnished building and broke the news to her. Every indication was that she understood. She was upset, but she understood. She even gave back the ring, leaving it there on the counter in Hyrum's new bakery.

Watching her go, Hyrum picked up the phone and dialed Elaine. She rushed over to the bakery to be with him, and also because there was a lot to be done and she had agreed to help with the final touches.

Alone together in the unfinished bakery late into the night, probably with the excitement of his dreams coming true mixed with the relief and thrill of Millie being out of the picture, one thing led to another.

In an effort to be discreet, and also because these are my grandparents we're talking about, let's just say that Hyrum's fancy new oven wasn't the only thing heating up the bakery.

They knew they shouldn't have done it. They'd both been raised to wait for marriage. But it had happened and they couldn't exactly take it back. So Hyrum resolved to make an honest woman of Elaine then and there. He took the ring from the counter and slipped it on her finger without saying a word. He didn't need to ask and she didn't need to say yes.

With the bakery so close to completion, Hyrum had quit the macaroni factory and was working full-time to prepare for the grand opening.

That's why he went in so early the next morning.

This next part was never proven, but it's what Marty believes, and my dad is sure of it, and so am I.

Hyrum was busy organizing the baking trays or whatever back in the kitchen area — performing all those tasks that you'd perform the day before opening your bakery — when Mildred came through the front door.

We're sure it was Mildred.

She walked back behind the counter into the kitchen, pulled a six-shot revolver from her purse and fired a bullet right into the back of Hyrum's head.

She had the presence of mind to open the cash register, and even though it was already empty the police would never know it. She was questioned, and she was the only suspect the police ever had. But she had a slick lawyer, whom she later married.

They never made an official arrest. So I can't say conclusively that it was her. But it was her.

The worst part, Hyrum never got to see his bakery open.

Of course no one realized that Elaine was pregnant right away. In fact, no one knew she was engaged either. And she didn't tell anyone.

I imagine that when she heard the news that Hyrum had been murdered she probably tucked her hands behind her back and slid the ring off her finger, creeping it into her pocket, or setting it discreetly on a corner curio table.

I don't know for sure why she never told anybody, but I can understand it. I mean, maybe she thought that if the police knew, they'd look at her as a suspect. Or maybe she was worried that people would think she was a tramp for stealing Hyrum's affection from the poor, grieving Mildred whom everyone now felt sorry for. Or maybe it was just too painful, that's what I think it was probably.

But everyone did feel sorry for Millie, because they didn't know that Hyrum'd broken off the engagement, and she told a story about a kind of premonition I guess you'd call it, where she lost the ring just the night before and she knew then that something terrible was about to happen.

And I wonder if maybe Elaine had produced that ring, if that might have sealed a case against Mildred, but then again perhaps she was smart not to, because Millie might have pointed at her as the "real" culprit.

There was only one living person (with the possible exception of Elaine's father) who knew that Hyrum and Elaine had been seeing each other, or courting or whatever. And that person was Marty. Not even Hyrum's own sister was aware of the couple's affair.

But Marty knew nothing of the engagement or that Hyrum had finally done the right thing and broken off his engagement to Millie. It wasn't until about four months later that Marty began to suspect something. Because you know what happens at about four months. In a pregnancy, I mean. If you don't know what happens at four months, that's when a woman starts to show, and by that I mean her belly starts to swell and you can tell she's pregnant.

Since Hyrum's death, Elaine and Sarah had become very good friends. The reason is not clear, but I'd imagine that it had to do with Elaine seeking some kind of connection with Hyrum through his living sister.

Or maybe it was destiny.

In any case, Marty and Sarah saw a lot of Elaine around their home, and they in turn spent a lot of time at Elaine's home helping her to care for her ailing father.

So four months later Marty noticed the swelling in Elaine's mid-section. When she had gone home for the night, he addressed the situation to his wife.

"I don't see how that's possible," Sarah said.

"You don't remember how it happens?" Marty asked sarcastically. "I mean, it wasn't that long ago that Steven was born."

"But who could the father be? And she doesn't seem like the type."

You'll remember that back then, especially in this area, having sex was not something people just did for recreation. Well, I mean, maybe they did, but not unmarried people regularly. Or if they did, they did it in secret, because it was taboo, and so there was a reputation that went along with getting unweddedly knocked up.

Marty figured it was time to tell his wife about the relationship between her brother and Elaine. Sarah wasn't surprised by their attraction, but she was surprised by the idea that they'd consummated it. In fact, she refused to believe it for some time. Another month, however, pretty much confirmed it. And it was then that she asked Elaine outright.

Elaine told her about their relationship and even that it was the night before he was killed that it had "happened." She did not, however, tell her that they'd been engaged. I don't know why.

☿ ☿ ☿

When Elaine was about eight months pregnant, things started to not go so well for her. I guess the pregnancy was kind of rough on her body — it was my dad, I'm sure it was rough, and I don't know if it was a doctor's call or if her body just forced her into it, but she was basically on her back for the remainder of the pregnancy.

Sarah and Marty did all they could to take care of her and her father, but this was when her father took a turn for the worse. I mean, I guess you could say that, if what you mean by a turn for the worse is that in the middle of the night he passed away, which is only a polite way of saying he died.

As sad as it was, and as heartbroken as Elaine was, it was better for her that he was gone. He didn't do much for her except require basically all her attention. And now she'd have a baby to do that.

Financially, he left her with enough for a while, and he left her a house — the house my father grew up in, and the house I grew up in, and a house that now belongs to a bank.

But after the expenses of childbirth with no insurance, she'd have to go back to work sooner than later.

And my father was no easy delivery; he had to be cut out by c-section. Then Elaine had to remain in the hospital for some time, I'm not sure how long. The whole thing, I can only imagine, probably ended up costing an arm and another arm.

Once home, she was able to spend a good six months with her new son, whom she named after his uncle who helped her with everything she needed throughout the pregnancy and afterwards. I don't doubt that had my father been a girl he would have been named Sarah, but he was a boy.

So he was named Martin. Martin West.

♀ ♀ ♀

About a year later is when things began to get a little sticky. This is when Steven started school, a thing that required a good deal of his parents' attention as he was not such a superb student in the beginning. In addition, Sarah accepted a part-time position at his school and discovered a love for teaching.

In any case, Sarah became very preoccupied with her son's education and the lessons for her school children, and she just didn't have as much time to help Elaine with her child.

By this time Marty was pretty senior at the auto shop, which, I don't know, may have meant he was like a manager or chief mechanic or something, so he was able to set his own hours. If he wanted to work some early mornings and some swing shifts and some evenings, he could. Hell, if he wanted to come in and work on an engine block in the middle of the night, he was welcome to it.

Mind you, it was at Sarah's request that Marty spent so much time with Elaine and her son. When she accepted the position at the school, she knew she wouldn't have time to help her friend, but she knew that as a single mother more or less ostracized from her own community, her friend needed help. So she asked her husband to do what he could and make sure that Elaine had everything she needed.

"After all," Sarah said, "she's family."

Maybe Sarah trusted her husband a little too much.

And you know what happened, and I don't have to go into details, because honestly I don't know them. What I will say is that apparently it went on for years and years. And in a way, Marty did become a father to my father. And Steven only had his mother, so in the end I can kind of understand his resentfulness.

When Sarah discovered the affair, I think she blamed herself.

And I think that's why she never left him. How could she? If it was her fault, as she believed it was? And Elaine was family and so was her son. And I'll bet the way Sarah saw it, Marty was as much husband and father to Elaine and Martin as he was to Sarah and Steven.

But it did hurt her deeply. And she confronted him, and as messed up as this sounds, she allowed the affair to continue. I'm sure, I'm positive, that she wanted it to stop. And really, I think Marty wanted it to stop. But sometimes we can't control ourselves. And maybe they were both torn over the right thing to do; I can't possibly explain the psychology of it.

It hurts me too, what Marty did, having that affair. But I'll tell you this. I used to think it was absolutely, unequivocally despicable that a man would cheat on his wife. And I'm not saying it's not. But what I am saying is that the more I learn about the world, the more impressed I am by the men who don't.

But we all want. And we all need. And sometimes things, including ourselves, are totally out of our control, or get totally out of our control. And the whole situation was totally out of control...

Until sometime around 1970, when Steven came home from college.

See, Steven caught Marty at Elaine's house. He naturally assumed he was having an affair with Elaine. And he was right. But not entirely, because he also believed that Marty was Martin's father. And why wouldn't he, I guess. I mean, since they had the same name, and Steven and my father had grown up playing together all their lives and their parents had been such good friends.

I thought it too.

And it was that night that he confronted his mother.

He begged her to leave him. How could she just sit there and let this go on? It had been going on for years. What did she mean, they were working through it? His father was leading a double life and had been their whole marriage.

As far as Steven was concerned, Marty was a con man and a bigot and a philanderer. It wasn't because his father forbade him from coming home that he never returned, it was because he hated his father so much for who he was. Marty could have opened his arms wide, and Steven would still have stayed as far away as he could.

I'm sure Sarah tried to explain everything to Steven. I'm sure she told him it was partly her fault, and I'm sure he didn't accept that.

I wouldn't have, had it been my mother telling me.

And so he severed all ties with his father and resented him until he died. But he resolved that he would never be like him. He resolved that he would never be unfaithful. And he never was. And I have to say that in that respect I am very impressed with Steven Page.

♀♀♀

After the fallout of banishing his biological son from his life, Marty observed firsthand the real impact his illicit relationship was having on himself and on his family, especially his wife.

He made the decision that it had to end, and he withdrew himself from the relationship with my grandmother, which meant in a way severing his relationship with my father, though he tried his best to remain a father-figure to the boy, who was now a teenager.

It didn't work out so well.

When she realized the real extent of the pain caused by their relationship, Elaine was horrified. Some things you just refuse to recognize until they're explicitly pointed out to you. She apologized profusely and begged Marty to allow them to remain friends, she and Marty and Sarah.

He knew this wasn't possible, and so it was over.

Before he left, and I don't know why and she probably doesn't either, Elaine retrieved her old engagement ring and placed it in Marty's palm.

"What's this?" he asked.

"He proposed to me. That night," she said. "The night we... Before he died. He'd just broken off the engagement to the woman that killed him."

"How do you know she killed him?" Marty asked.

But Elaine said nothing.

Marty knew. He'd known already somewhere inside him.

"What am I supposed to do with it?" he asked.

"Give it to Sarah as a peace offering, or an apology."

I don't understand why she thought that would repair anything. I think she was just a little crazy at that moment. You know, how when you get really upset or emotional and you just start spitting stuff out that makes no sense and is totally irrational and after you're done you look back and say to yourself, "Did I really just say and do all that stupid stuff?" and you're so unbelievably embarrassed. Because life's not like in the movie's where people deliver these impassioned speeches at the height of their anger, and it's all eloquent and meaningful and relays their feelings in a clear and powerful way.

No, when real people get emotional in real life they do stuff that makes absolutely no sense at all.

♀♀♀

When Elaine got sick with something the doctor's couldn't diagnose and my father returned home with his wife and two children, Marty made one last visit to the house. He kissed Elaine goodbye and it was not long before she passed.

My father seemed to understand better their relationship, and a bond was reformed between Marty and Martin, though he never said a word to any of us about who this man was or how he knew him.

Fourteen years after that, my father decided I should spend some time with Marty, that it would be good for me. Why me instead of Brian, I couldn't tell you. And why he never told me who Marty was, I also couldn't tell you. But I'm glad I got to sit there and listen to this old man tell me stories about life and love and hope and mostly love.

*   *   *

After breaking off the affair, Marty spent the remaining years of Sarah's life trying to repair the damage he'd done.

That was his only focus.

He found it ironic that she should die of heart disease, or at least I find it ironic. And I know Marty believed her death was his fault the same way Sarah believed Marty's affair was hers.

And after she died Marty was haunted by the memories of the ways he'd hurt her.

And I believe that's why the Alzheimer's struck him.

If a disease was ever a blessing, this one was.

His mind was protecting him from the memories of all the terrible things he'd done. Because the fact was when I'd seen him, especially on towards the end, the only memories he had left were of his beautiful bride and the happiness they shared.

All the bad times were gone forever.

CHAPTER 40

LIFE IS BEAUTIFUL

After my father told me that story — or most of that story anyways, parts of it I filled in with stuff Marty and Steven had said to me that suddenly made sense — there wasn't much else to say. We'd finished the game a while ago, and even though I do remember who won, that's beside the point. And it's not like suddenly everything was right between us and all the problems had been cleared up. Because just telling a story or having a game of chess doesn't really fix anything.

And when I left I didn't hug him, but we did shake hands. And I'll admit to this much, I did think at that moment that maybe I could see him again in a year or two for another game.

Funny thing though, that year or two became actually about two weeks, and that's because I ended up needing money, but that's later and we'll get to that.

So I walked out of his office and past the reception desk where Miranda said, "It was nice meeting you." To which I just nodded curtly. No, this woman I was not fond of in any way. She was a home wrecker, if our home had ever not been broken.

I had planned on taking another taxi to the train station, but I hadn't thought ahead to realize that I couldn't just walk out of the building and have a taxi parked right there in front. And I had no idea how to get a hold of a taxi in Berlin. In fact, I realized at that moment, I didn't really know how to get a hold of a taxi anywhere. They're not too common in Utah, and I'd never been in one before the one I'd brought here from the airport.

Anyways, I didn't want to go back in and ask my dad to call one for me, and I definitely didn't want to ask his slutty receptionist. So what I did was I just walked for a while. I picked a direction and went in it. I figured it wasn't even two o'clock yet, so I had some time and if I kept walking straight eventually I'd come to a public area where I'd find a cab.

I was right, only it was a long walk before I found one, and I was a little worried the whole time about getting robbed because with my huge backpack I clearly looked like a tourist.

But I didn't get robbed and I did find a taxi, and he did take me to the Bahnhof Zoo, and he did charge an exorbitant amount for the ride, but it's not like I had a choice.

In any case, we arrived at the Bahnhof Zoo, which was unlike anything I'd ever seen before. This had a lot to do probably with the fact that I'd never been at a train station before. But this thing was massive. And it sort of looked like an amusement park. Because there were these elevated tracks going in and out at both ends that you could see from the outside. And also under there were like some roads coming from all angles, where trams or what they call streetcars were also coming in and out, and there were bus lanes, and I'm trying to remember if there was actually a road going into the station or not, but it seems like there was, in my head anyways, but that doesn't make a lot of sense so maybe not. And also, it was called Bahnhof Zoo because it was right next to a big zoo, which I didn't really go in and I couldn't really see any animals, but you could see the foliage or at least some trees or something, down at the one end.

So I paid the cab driver, with no tip because the fee was already much too high, and I went into the station through what looked like the front entrance.

When I got in there, there were stairs running every which way and everything was written in German, and there were tons of people every-where, and I realized that it may have been a mistake to just say we'd meet up here, because I had no idea where I was or how to get around.

It was only two-thirty, so I had a half an hour to find him, and in order to do that I had to find the ticket counter.

I had no idea how to find the ticket counter.

Even though this wasn't that long ago, I couldn't tell you for the life of me how I found that ticket counter. I do remember somehow getting to what I imagine was the center of this place with little shops and kiosks all around and hallways going in all directions, a place that reminded me of a mall and kind of was in a way. I wandered some way from there, into a room that was long, but not in the direction you'd have expected it to be long in. It was long in the other direction. And in this room there were these tall stands, which I think they called kiosks also, that were like electronic ticket vendors I think. And after I passed through that room, I think it was immediately after, I was in this bigger room with a big line of ticket counters. And actually that line was not just a straight line, but halfway along it turned ninety degrees, so it was actually like an extended corner of ticket counters, and some of them said international and they all had information written in German and in English, so at least I knew I was in the right place. I just hoped that this was the only ticketing area in the station, because this place was so huge there could easily have been more than one and this would cause problems since I didn't know, first of all, if my cell phone got service here, and second of all, if Chris's did.

But that turned out not to matter so much, because I wandered around for a second, and just around the corner I found Chris sitting on a bench reading some book, I don't remember which.

"Hey," I said.

He looked up. "How'd it go?" he asked, and handed me this flimsy transparent little bag with a pastry, in another flimsy transparent little bag, and a yellowish-green Fanta in it.

"What's this?" I said.

"Pastry and soda," he said. "How'd it go?"

"Fine. As well as could be expected, I guess."

"Train doesn't leave for about an hour," he said. "So if you want to get something else to eat, we can, but I looked around. Most things'll be much cheaper in Poland."

"I'll eat this and we'll see," I said.

I sat down and pulled the soda out of my bag. It was a little different but not bad. Then I took out the pastry. It was some kind of Danish it looked like. I don't know. A cheese Danish I guess. It had some kind of cream cheese in the middle and the whole thing was frosted with this really wet frosting that almost dripped off the edges, and it stuck to the bag it was in, and to my fingers. For all that, I couldn't believe how bland it was. It was like they didn't put any sugar in it at all.

"You'll get used to it," Chris said, "the no sugar," like he knew exactly what I was thinking.

When I was done eating, we walked over to the platform, which if it was my job to tell you how to get there from the ticket area, I would be fired. But Chris seemed to know his way around, or at least he'd been in enough train stations to have a rough idea how to navigate them.

It was still a while, but we sat there watching the pigeons until the train finally pulled up.

I expected something with cabins, like I'd seen on all the trains in the movies and also all the other trains that were pulling up and leaving around us. But this one was laid out kind of like a bus, y'know, with the aisle down the middle and on each side row after row of double seats. Only above the seats there was a big rack, for luggage.

"How come there's no cabins?"

Chris shrugged, "Some of the trains are just like this. There's probably cabins in some of the other cars. But our seats are in this one. On most of the trains though you won't have assigned seats, but this one has reserved seating for some reason."

It's funny how when someone's been somewhere before or done something before that you haven't, they explain every little thing to you without you even asking. I don't know if it's to be helpful or to show off.

"So we'll get a cabin on our other trains?" I asked.

"Well, I mean, we'll share a cabin with other people. In most of the cabins there are eight seats and they're kind of close together. I mean, it's like a bench with room for four people, so it's scrunched. Except on like express trains which have six seats per cabin, and those're clearly separated. But on those, you also have reserved seating, so…"

By this time we'd located our seats, heaved our bags up on the luggage rack, and taken our places.

About a minute later, this elderly German couple approached us. Chris had the window and I had the aisle, so she spoke to me, only it was in

German and I had no idea what she was saying, so I nudged Chris with my elbow. He looked over and she repeated it to him.

"I'm sorry," he said. "I don't speak German."

The husband's eyes brightened. "English?"

"Yes," Chris said.

"You are Americans?"

We both nodded.

Say what you want about the rest of the world hating America, these people were so nice to us, and they seemed genuinely excited to talk to people from America, and the man was thrilled to have the opportunity to try his English out on us. And I'll tell you this too. For all the time I've now spent in Europe, the story is almost always the same. People have always been very nice to me, they ask about America, many of them want to move there, and they seem excited to talk to an American. Except actually in Athens, where everyone was extraordinarily rude, but everywhere else.

"Welcome to Germany," the man said.

"Thank you," Chris said, then added, "Danke," which if you didn't know is German for Thanks.

"Oh, I see you speak good German," the man said.

And Chris said something else, and the man and woman both chuckled, then Chris said, "That's about all I know."

"It is good," the man said. I got the impression that his wife didn't speak any English at all.

"We have problem," the man said. And he held out his tickets. "You see," and he pointed to his ticket. "Three," and then he pointed to the row number over our head. "And see." And he pointed to the letters on their tickets and over our heads. Apparently, we were in their seats.

But then Chris pulled out our tickets, and showed them that we also had those seat assignments.

"Oh, no," the man said. "It is mistake."

"It's okay," Chris said. "We'll move over there." And he pointed across the aisle.

We were lucky the train wasn't very full. There were plenty of empty seats. So we just moved to the other side, and the old couple took our seats, or their seats I guess.

Once we sat down, the old man leaned over to me, "You are going Poland?"

"Yes," I said. "You?"

"Yes, yes. Poland. Which city?"

I looked at Chris, because I couldn't remember the name. "Which city are we going to?"

"Wrocław," he said.

"Wrocław," I repeated.

"Yes, yes. We also, Wrocław," the man said. "You are from America. What for are you here?"

And I told him, and he asked several other questions, and we had a very pleasant conversation.

♀ ♀ ♀

I don't know, probably an hour later, we made a short stop at some little station that looked like it was in the middle of nowhere. I mean, I couldn't see a city around anywhere. And this kid, probably about my age, with glasses got on and wandered down the aisle, stopping at our row. He looked at the numbers and at his ticket.

Chris looked up at him and said something I didn't understand. The kid shook his head and said something else that sounded like mumbling then sat down in the row behind us.

"What did he say?" I asked.

"Now we're in his seat, but he said it's no problem, he'll just sit back there."

"Is he Polish?"

"I think so. He speaks Polish."

"Are we in Poland already?"

"I think we're still in Germany."

And then I tried to go to sleep as the train pulled away again.

I don't know if it was the next stop or a couple stops later, but this woman and her kid got on and walked past us to the row behind.

I heard her talking to the kid behind us, and I saw Chris laughing.

"What?" I said.

"He's in her seat now. And he's telling her that we're foreigners and we don't know how the tickets work, and we're sitting in his seat, so he sat in her seat. And she wants him to move, but he's saying the train is practically empty, so she can just find another seat."

And I saw her walk back a couple of rows and take a seat back there.

And now I'm not kidding you at all when I tell you that at one of the next stops this old lady got on with about five big plastic shopping bags, the kind with the reinforced handles, and walked back to the row with the lady and the kid. And they got into it.

And I watched while Chris explained what they were saying.

"The old lady is mad because that woman's in her seat, and the woman is saying that there are some stupid Americans up there who are in that guy's seat, so that guy is in her seat. And the old lady says that it's clearly printed on her ticket that that is her seat. And the other woman says that she doesn't want to have to move her child and that there are plenty of empty seats. And the old lady says, no, it clearly says on her ticket that she needs to sit in that seat. That's her seat."

And then I saw the woman get up and move her child to another seat, and the old woman sat down.

"Should we move to another seat?" I asked.

"It's just as likely we'll be in someone else's seat then," he said.

"Yeah, I guess you're right."

"We're pretty close now. I can't imagine this will happen again," he said, and it didn't.

We got to Wrocław without pissing anyone else off.

There's really not a lot to tell you about Wrocław. There were lots of churches there, and we got some good footage. Actually, there were *a lot* of churches, including this one place where you could stand in just one spot and within probably a block there were four huge, I don't know, cathedrals or something. And we wanted to go out at night and get some shots, and I'll tell you what. These buildings were kind of ominous in the dark, kind of creepy really.

And we walked around and saw some really pretty buildings, and it was weird to be in a country where I didn't speak the language, and it was cool to be in Europe where everything is so old. And I realized that I'd never really been anywhere.

Then I got kind of sad, because I started to realize that I'd never really done anything with my life. You know, how my life to that point had been all the same. Every day, or five days a week anyways, I'd get up and go to work at the copy center, then I'd go see a movie, whatever was playing, then I'd go home and maybe watch another movie or whatever. It was all so repetitive, all so the same.

And that was my life.

But this was different, and even though we didn't really do all that much that first day in Wrocław, it was still an adventure. It was somehow exciting just to be there.

The next day we spent most of the time on a train to Warsaw. It was something like a five or six hour ride, but at least this time we had a cabin, which I thought was awesome, just because I'd seen it in the movies, and it was just an experience. And we started off just the two of us in the cabin, which was good, because with jet lag we were pretty tired, even though I'd woken up at five-thirty and wasn't able to get back to sleep. But now at like nine I was able to fall right to sleep on the train.

That was for about the first hour or so, then as we made more and more stops, the train started filling up and so did our cabin, until prob'ly an hour out of Warsaw our cabin had the full capacity of eight passengers and it was totally squished, so I couldn't sleep anymore, even though I kept drifting off on the shoulder of the guy next to me.

Just before we got to the station the train went underground and a few miles later we rolled up to the platform. The first thing I saw when I stepped off the train was a homeless man with a thick, old brown sweater, lying under a bench with a big plastic shopping bag with a ladybug on it. I'm not sure he was alive, but I couldn't tell for sure. Also he had a big bottle that looked like it probably once contained wine, and I thought it was funny that the bottle actually said "Wino" on it. But not that funny.

We had to walk past him and it smelled terrible, worse than any homeless man I'd ever walked past in the United States.

This train station was different than the other two. Where the one in Berlin had sort of looked like an amusement park or a mall and the one in Wrocław looked like a castle from the outside and what I'd have imagined a train station to look like on the inside, the one in Warsaw was basically a giant cement box. All the platforms were down below ground level, so all the trains I guess ran underground. And echoing throughout the place every few seconds you'd hear a *bong* sound, then a woman speaking in Polish, followed by that same woman with a thick accent I assume repeating what she'd said before only in English this time saying things like, "The fast train to Kraków will be leaving from platform three in two minutes."

From the platform, you take an escalator up to this area where there's lots of shops and kiosks and stuff, little restaurants y'know, and we stopped at a newsstand where Chris bought some bus tickets. Then we climbed this long set of stairs up to another wide-open cement box room that felt very empty. Up ahead was a huge board listing cities and times for all the trains running in and out of this station, and below that was a wall of ticket windows.

We went to the right and left through some sliding glass doors.

Warsaw was a big city, and it kind of reminded me of New York in a lot of ways. Not so much that it looked like New York, because the buildings were not nearly as tall, just really that it was massive and busy and there were traffic and people going every which way very quickly. There were electric streetcars running over just about every surface and lots of buses everywhere, some just regular looking buses and some of those extra-long accordion-type ones. There were lots of drunks and homeless people and lots of pigeons, and everything looked really dirty with graffiti covering half the buildings. When you came to an intersection, you didn't just cross the street at like a crosswalk or anything. You'd actually go down a ramp into this big hallway that ran around in a circle with other ramps up to every corner. And down in that hallway were all these little shops. I think that's the thing I noticed most about Germany and Poland both is that there were little shops and newsstands and kiosks everywhere, in every place you could conceivably put them.

I'm realizing now that if I keep going on like this, you're probably going to get bored, because what I'm doing is trying to give you a feel for how I spent the ten days in Poland, but if I describe each day and each little thing we saw and did, you're probably going to stop reading this, even though you're very close to the end. So what I'll do is I'll tell you really quickly about the big and interesting things that we saw that you might want to see, just in case you're ever in Poland, which you should go I think, because there's not a lot of tourists and there's lots to see. Of course I was with someone who had lived there so I could get around really easily.

Anyways, we saw lots of churches, which was why we were here obviously, and some of them were pretty cool. We also saw a lot of castles, like the one in downtown Warsaw, and we went to this big one up north called, I think, Malbork, which was still completely intact, and that was worth seeing. And we went up to the coast, where all the buildings were kind of unique, I mean compared to the layouts of other cities. That's the

Baltic Sea coast if you didn't know. And we saw these castle ruins at I don't remember the name of the place. And we also went to this big salt mine where there were all these things inside made out of salt, like little statues of the seven dwarves from Snow White and all kinds of stuff like that. And our tour guide was this little guy with a mustache that spoke English all right, but he was kind of weird and he kept making jokes about how women love men with mustaches. And we went into the city of Lublin to this old concentration camp, whose name I also don't remember because it's not one of the real famous ones, but that was an experience. I'm not going to tell you too much about that, because it's not very uplifting, except to say that if you're ever near there you should go, because as depressing as it is, it gives you a better appreciation for...everything. And we also went to Auschwitz concentration camp and saw that big *Arbeit Macht Frei* gate, and that one was more of a memorial or a museum but still affecting in a lot of terrible ways that I don't really want to talk about.

But anyways, that was just outside of Kraków, and that's the part I do need to tell you about.

Quickly, I'll lay out the city for you so you can kind of get a visual. You've got the Old Town square which has this big castle-looking thing in the center that's full of all these little shops where they sell like hand-carved statues and chessboards and boxes, and amber jewelry, and souvenirs, and all kinds of things. Also in the square is a big statue and a huge church I think that's called St. Mary's Cathedral, and then a huge tower on the other corner of the square, and there are tons and tons of pigeons, and people selling art and stuff like that. And around the square is a little road where there are horse-drawn carriages that you can hire to take you around. And everything is kind of paved with cobblestone. Basically, this Old Town Square is exactly what you'd expect everything in Europe to look like if you've seen a lot of movies.

Going out from the square in I think eight directions, one at each corner and one at each side, are little streets that extend out into the city. About a block out is what they call the Planty or something like that, which is like a park that encircles the town square with a path and trees all over, and it's really nice. And also, lots of people make out there, even in the late fall.

Then the city kind of extends out from there in concentric circles with spokes.

But if you walk around the Planty, you'll come to a point where there's kind of a break in the circle or more like a growth or appendage to it, with a road that leads up to this huge palace called Wawel, and just outside it is this huge twisted metal sculpture of a dragon that blows fire every once in a while, which is pretty cool. And on the other side of the path from the castle runs the Vistula river.

Now down near the bank of the river there's this green metal statue of a crying dog with these two giant hands that look sort of like seaweed curving up around him. And I forget the dog's name, but Chris translated the story on the plaque for me, and basically it's about this dog whose owner died, and the dog got so depressed that he made his way to this bridge and threw himself into the river.

Anyways, it was when we were there along the Vistula that Chris told me some things. We had just bought some Fornetti, which are these tiny pastries, like croissants, stuffed with different flavors of cream or jam, like blueberry or strawberry or apricot or chocolate or cream cheese or whatever, and we were walking along the path through the Planty.

"When I lived here," Chris said, "that river flooded way up over the banks. It was bad. It was clear up to street level, here where we are now."

I looked down at where it normally ran. It looked like a good fifty-foot drop to me, but really logically it must have only been fifteen or twenty.

"All those streetlamps down there were completely submerged," he went on. "This river runs through the whole country, and it flooded pretty much everywhere. A lot of people's homes were ruined. I remember walking out here when the rain was pouring down buckets. And it would rain all day long. I've never seen rain like that."

We stopped to watch the dragon spit fire, while all the little kids were climbing all over him, parents with cameras snapping pictures.

"You know," he started talking again, "I was living in this city on September 11, 2001. We were teaching an English class when we found out what happened. It was what? Nine o'clock in the morning when the planes flew into the towers? Over there. So it was about three in the afternoon here, and our class started around four I think. The students started drifting in and telling us that there had been this huge attack in New York City. Sounded unreal. The first report we heard was that missiles had been fired into the Empire State Building. Then more accurate information. People had flown planes into buildings. No one knew who'd done it, but the assumption was Saddam Hussein, even over here. Then we heard the Pentagon had been attacked. This was absurd. With that, there was no way any of this was true. I mean, an attack on the Pentagon? Someone else said the White House had been hit. But there were so many different versions of the story. With everyone talking, it became pretty clear that something had happened, but what exactly we didn't know. The initial numbers from our students, two million people were dead. That's a pretty significant percentage of New York City's population. Two million? No way. One of the teacher's ran downstairs to an internet café two floors beneath us to dig up as much information as he could. The next couple of days were spent in the bookstore picking up issues of *Time* and *Newsweek* and searching the internet to find out what had happened and why. We speculated about the possibility of a third world war. Would we be called back to the U.S. and be drafted into the army?

"Everyone, I mean all the people here, they were all so sympathetic for a long time afterwards. We were Americans and so we were victims. Even street punks would approach us in broken English saying, 'Hey Americans, we are so sorry for your country.' It wore off though, this feeling of vulnerability, comparatively pretty quickly. For us, we'd forgotten about it after a couple of months. When I went back to the States nine months later, I was surprised that people were still talking about it. I didn't understand how it affected them and why it was still affecting them, because to me it happened so long ago. People referred to a post-9/11 world and the government was still planning retaliatory action.

"I'm not saying people were wrong to feel the way they felt. I mean, they even got me to jump on the invade Iraq bandwagon at first, because going after Saddam Hussein put a face with this amorphous enemy. But I didn't understand how the country had changed really, because I wasn't there. I think that's what Americans forget, that while it was a huge and devastating tragedy, the rest of the world has a different frame of reference for it. They don't look at it through the same eyes. So why should we always expect them...

"I mean, shoot, you remember the London train bombing?"

"Sure." I sort of shrugged.

"But you don't have any idea when it happened, do you? You don't remember because it wasn't personal. It was the same terrorists, for the same purpose, but..."

"Y'know, that's my problem with religion," I cut him off, kind of angry, because he was now getting into territory that really crawled under my skin. Not that *he* was making me angry, just what came into my head after he said what he said. "I think people do more terrible things in the name of God than they do good. Like flying planes into buildings and bombing subway trains."

"That's people though. That's not religion."

"I just... If God's real, how does he let things happen, like nine-eleven for instance?"

"You think God was responsible for that?"

"He let it happen," I said.

"You think He should have stopped it?"

"Absolutely."

"You think if He came down and made everything happen the way it *should* happen all the time, according to you, you'd be happier and better off?"

"I think so."

"You're either giving God too much credit or not enough. You just don't want to have to ever take responsibility." He was up on his box of Irish Spring now.

"So like you think it was those people's destiny to fly those planes into those buildings, and it was the destiny of those people to die jumping from those windows?" I asked, almost accused.

"Destiny? No. It's just what happened."

"You don't believe in destiny?"

"What do you mean? Like do I believe that there's some cosmic force orchestrating everything that happens and that everything's part of a plan, and all these things are meant to happen and therefore will?"

"Yeah," I said.

"No. No, no, absolutely not. No. I think we have more control over our lives than that. I think we have more responsibility for what happens to us than we want to admit. I think for the most part what you will to happen will happen. And it's actually scary, kind of. You know. The idea that we are responsible for our own destinies. If that's the case then we have to accept the fact that when things don't work out in our favor it's probably because we didn't do enough. It's up to us to make things happen. I think too much you hear people say it wasn't meant to be or it was in God's hands and this wasn't what He had in mind for me, and I think that's more of a way of shifting blame than anything."

"I'm just... I don't think I agree with you about destiny, but anyways..." I was lost for a second as I tried to weave the conversation back into a direction where I wanted it to go. Then I said, thinking about my dad, then Marty, then Allison, and loss, and love, and loss of love, "I've been thinking a lot, because of things, about the meaning of life."

"Oh, that's a hell of a thing. You don't want to spend too much time doing that."

"I mean, look around right here, what you've just been telling me, and you have your theories. That's great. But everyone else has theories too and none of them mesh. I mean, I don't even think I agree with you about half the things you're saying."

"Frankly," he said, "half the time I don't even agree with half the things I'm saying."

"But you've got dogs jumping off of bridges, floods, people herded into camps where they were gassed and turned into soaps and hairbrushes, planes flying into buildings, wars, and the only thing to take any pleasure from is the damned fire-breathing dragon over there."

"You're on a two-week free trip to Europe," he said. "If the damned fire-breathing dragon is the only thing you're enjoying, you're focusing on the wrong things in life."

"The dragon is pretty cool though."

"Yeah, it is pretty cool."

"But tell me this," I said. "How do you not focus on all the horrible things going on around you?"

"Tell you the truth?" he said. "I do focus on it, too much. And I get so damn depressed I just want to lie in bed for days and days, but there are a few things. The first, this Fornetti is delicious. That alone is worth getting up for. Second, I have things I love to do and when I'm doing those things I don't think about wars and injustice."

"Like what?"

"Like I love just building furniture. I mean sort of. I just like to go out and buy some ready-to-assemble set of shelves or a desk or something. I just love putting that stuff together. Or also, I like crossword puzzles."

"But shouldn't we be thinking about like the war? Isn't paying attention to that important? Shouldn't we be doing something?"

"I don't know. But what are you going to do about the war? And if Osama bin Laden and George Bush spent more time building bookshelves..."

"What else?" I asked, jumping away from war politics, which never lead to a pleasant discussion, no matter who you're talking to.

"What else what?"

"I don't like building shelves, so what else?"

"I'm sure there's something you love doing, like keep making your movies."

I didn't say anything, so he just went on like I knew he was going to.

"Also," he said after a pause, because I could tell saying what he was about to say made him a little uncomfortable because it was so personal and he's not the type to really talk about feelings.

"I have a wife," he said finally. "I'm not saying you should get married, necessarily. I'm just saying that having someone, another person around who really wants you to be happy even if work sucks and your fifth screenplay didn't even make the quarterfinals of that stupid competition you entered. Someone who will convince you that it just got to the wrong judge, one that doesn't have a sense of humor, and if you could just somehow get it in front of Vince Vaughn then it'd get produced and be a surefire hit and you'd become rich and famous..."

Then he paused for a second.

"...and being even partly responsible for another person's happiness," he said, "and she for yours, opens you up to what's good in the world, and that's the people and the relationships with them. Love's good, however childish that sounds. And recognizing that and being around people you love and who love you, family, friends, it's so much harder to dwell on the bad things."

"How'd you and your wife meet?" I asked.

"We had a class together in school. It wasn't some big cosmic thing, like your destiny."

"You really don't believe in destiny at all? You don't believe that you and your wife were meant to be together?"

"I don't believe in meant-to-be's. I do believe in ought-to-be's."

"Like how so? What does that mean?"

"Like okay, for instance," and he stepped away from the personal stuff with, "maybe you ought to be a filmmaker, and it's up to you to figure that out, and then it's not just going to come to you. You work at it. But..."

"What's the difference then between what you want and what you ought?"

"Not a lot."

Then it was my turn to get personal, so I took a long pause just like he had, because two guys by a river having sharing time, that's not really a comfortable space unless you're very secure.

"Well there is this girl..." I said.

"You made me write an entire screenplay about it," he said.

"Well that wasn't exactly... Well, anyways, she's my destiny. At least I thought she was. I don't care if you don't believe in it. You have your own... But I do, I believe in it, and... But I know we're supposed to be together. Or at least I *knew* it, but..."

And I trailed off, because I didn't know how to say what I was thinking.

"But what?" he said after a pause.

"But I don't know," I said.

"But you didn't do enough. You thought she was your destiny and therefore it would just happen without any effort on your part? See, that's why..."

"No!" I cut him off, then with a second to think about it, I added, "Not exactly..."

"How not exactly? That's exactly right. You didn't do anything."

"But I did. You don't know."

"Tell me what happened then."

"I don't want to go into the whole thing right now. It would take too long, but..."

"Well, then I think there are three possibilities," he said. "First, you're wrong that you *ought* to be together; but if you want it, I doubt that's the case. Then again, if she doesn't 'know it,' as you say, then maybe you are wrong, and there's someone else."

"No," I said, but I'll admit I wondered.

"Anyway, second, you've been given plenty of opportunities and you didn't take proper advantage, and it's over for you. Or third, she'll present herself again. But if it's the third, you had damned well better do whatever you have to to make it happen, because you only get so many chances."

It wasn't like there was anything to say after that. I mean, the conversation didn't just stop, but it did kind of drift away somewhere over the Vistula.

I thought about everything he'd said, and I disregarded some. But I thought about relationships being what gets you through all the crap in the world, like he said, and about having someone to share your life with and, though he didn't say it, how that's kind of the meaning of life if there is one.

I told him I wanted to stay here by myself for a bit, and I thought about what he said about his own life and his own experiences as he walked away down the cobblestone path toward the castle, but then I remembered how he told Sherry he'd made an award-winning documentary about Vikings. And I wondered if he'd just made up every word he'd said to me.

♀ ♀ ♀

That night was when we had to catch our sleeper train back to Berlin. We got to the station and Chris went to buy tickets, but he came back empty-handed.

"I don't understand," he said. "She said we can't buy tickets. We have to get them on the train, but it's all reserved, so I'm confused."

"We're not going to miss the train, are we?"

"I don't know. We just have to wait and see, I think. I couldn't understand her completely, because it's been a long time since I've spoken, but I think she said it's all sold out but if someone doesn't show up, then we can get beds, or something like that. I don't know."

"Well I hope we can get on the train," I said.

"Not me. I hope we get stuck here and miss our flight and I get fired for not showing up to work on Wednesday."

"So what do we do?" I asked.

"We just go to the platform and try to buy tickets when the train gets here."

Which is what we did, and when the train pulled up, we walked down the platform looking for the conductor. It turned out to be this woman standing there, and this was the good part: she was Ukrainian, and she didn't speak a word of Polish or English.

Chris tried to talk to her anyway.

In Polish.

About halfway through the conversation when it looked to me like nothing was getting accomplished, I asked what was going on.

"She doesn't speak Polish."

"Well, what does she speak?" I asked.

"Ukrainian."

"Ukrainian? Why Ukrainian?"

"Because this train is coming from Kiev."

"So what do we do?"

"Well, I'm working on that," he snapped. "There are a few common words here."

Then he turned back to her, and I heard him say "Berlin." Then a bunch of other jabbering, and I could tell they were both frustrated.

Finally, she pulled out a pad of paper and wrote a number on it.

Chris pulled out his little passport and money pouch that was hanging around his neck under his shirt and pulled out all the money he had.

"No, no," the woman said. And Chris looked at her.

She drew a little symbol and said, "Euro."

We had been trying to pay with Polish Zlotys.

Chris's hands went right up over his face. "Oh, this is going to cost a lot of money," he said. "How many Euros do you have?"

I pulled out everything I had, and he did the same and we pooled it. It wasn't enough, but he handed it to her and said something.

She replied and I think I heard "Frankfurt."

He scratched his head then pulled out a credit card and said something like "Karta?"

She responded.

Then he said something else.

Then she replied.

Then she handed us two little receipts which I guess were tickets and led us onto the train, down the corridor to this little room with two little bunk beds along one wall and a closet and small countertop on the other side.

She demonstrated the lock for us, like we didn't know how to use a dead bolt, then handed each of us a little plastic bag with a towel in it and a little bar of soap and a bottle of water and a chocolate-filled croissant. Then she left.

"What's going on?" I asked.

"We only had enough money to get to Frankfurt," he said. "Which is just over the border."

"So what do we do?"

"If I understood her correctly, which I'm not sure I did, she said that when we get to the German border there will be a new conductor who can sell us a ticket into Berlin, and he might take a credit card."

"Will he speak English or Polish?"

Chris threw his hands up in the air, "Probably not. Probably just German. I don't know, we might get stuck in Frankfurt."

"Why didn't they get a new conductor at the Ukraine-Poland border who spoke Polish?"

"Good question. I couldn't tell you."

"So what if we get stuck in Frankfurt?" I asked. "And what if they don't take a credit card?"

"Then we'll need some money," Chris said. "I don't know. We'll just worry about it when it happens. For now, I'm just going to try to get some sleep."

And he climbed into the top bunk, which was the one I wanted, but whatever.

CHAPTER 41

AS GOOD AS IT GETS

After telling you about concentration camps and floods and dogs committing suicide and September Eleventh, I want to finish this off by telling you why this life is still worth living, because I finally figured it out after more than twenty-five years on this planet.

So this is it, maybe the meaning of life.

Or whatever.

I'll just tell the story and you decide.

*　*　*

I couldn't sleep.

That is, I had slept a little, only a couple of hours. It had been hard to get to sleep at first, but after some tossing I finally drifted off. Then it was about two-thirty when I woke up. It was one of those moments where you're up suddenly awake and you feel like it's for a reason, but you don't know what that reason is exactly. But fight it all you want, you can't fall back asleep.

So I sat up in the bunk, or rather I sort of sat up. The bunk above hung so low that I was really just kind of wedged with my head poking out and my calves dropping down, my knees folded up to my chin. I reached over to the counter for my water bottle and took a swig. Then I rubbed my face. I sat there for another second then decided I'd go out in the corridor and stretch my legs.

Chris was still asleep on that upper bunk, his mouth hanging open like a flytrap. I clicked open the lock, and the sound echoed through the whole compartment.

"What the crap?"

I looked. Chris was only half-awake, if that. His sub-conscious or semi-conscious or unconscious or whatever must have been jarred into expletive mode by the clacking of the lock. He rolled onto his side, and I could tell that not much was going on up there, then his mouth dropped back wide and his head lolled around for a second, then no more movement.

I snatched up my chocolate-filled croissant from the shelf, along with my complimentary towel-and-soap bag the Ukrainian lady had given me. I don't know, I thought maybe I might give my face a wash or something. Then I crept out of the compartment.

Outside in the hallway, I eased the door closed as quietly as I could, and I thought I heard swearing from inside when it latched, but I may have just been imagining things.

I turned around and watch▸the trees and fields and occasional little rock houses pass by through the window. It was probably a minute or so before I even realized there was someone else in the corridor, watching out the window a little ways down.

It was dark, so I couldn't see much, but it looked like a girl.

She wasn't looking in my direction, so I didn't say anything right away. But I did keep looking, so when she turned I could give her one of those hello nods, which I did.

She nodded back.

I stuffed the plastic bag, the one with the towel and soap, into my pocket where it bulged awkwardly. I started walking towards her and she seemed to stiffen, bracing herself in case I was dangerous. I saw her pull her big backpack a little closer to her body.

"Hi," I said.

Then she relaxed a little bit.

"Are you an American?" she asked.

It hadn't even occurred to me that she might not speak English.

"Yeah, you?" I said as I got a little closer.

"Yes," she said. "Where are you from?"

I was close enough to see her a little better now, and I smiled. I couldn't help it. In the moonlight I could see her long, dark hair spilling down her shoulders and back. Chestnut, I decided, was the proper name for the color, at least in this light.

"Salt Lake City," I said. "In Utah."

"Seriously?" she said. "Me too. Boy, that's weird. Actually, I'm not from Salt Lake exactly."

"Me neither."

"I live in West Valley."

I didn't want to say me too, because that might seem like I was trying too hard, so I didn't say anything.

"So what are you doing out here?" she asked.

"I'm just here with this guy," I said. "But not in like a gay way or anything. I'm not gay."

"No," she said. "I wouldn't have…"

"Not that there's anything wrong with that," I blurted.

"No, of course not."

"I mean, I'm just here with a friend of mine. We've been… We were just… We've just been traveling around Poland seeing stuff."

"Just for fun?"

"Well, yeah, I mean…"

It sounded so juvenile when I thought to say we were shooting a movie. I was almost ashamed. But then I decided to hell with it. Why shouldn't I be honest?

"We were shooting some footage for a movie," I said.

"That's really cool."

"Yeah?"

"Yeah. What's it about, your movie?"

"Actually," I said. "Actually it's about these two people, a guy and a girl, and the path their relationship takes. A romance sort of thing."

"Definitely something everyone can relate to," she said.

"Yeah, there's actually a scene, which is based on a dream I had, where they're standing in a corridor on a train, just like..." and there I paused realizing what I was saying. "Not that I..."

"No, it's... Don't worry about it. I know what you mean."

Then we stood there at adjacent windows, both of us staring out at the dark, rushing landscape.

"Listen," she said and turned to me. "Listen, do I know you? I feel like I know you from somewhere."

I smiled at this, still staring out the window, where actually, to tell you the truth, I could see her reflection, but I don't think she knew it.

She was beautiful.

"Yeah?" I said. "I don't know."

"I don't know either," she said.

Then another short silence.

"So what are you doing out here?" I asked.

"You know, I don't know."

I looked at her directly. As she talked she pulled her long hair back on her head and ran it through one of those things. Is that called a scrunchie?[9]

Or just an elastic.

"I just had to go," she said. "I guess I'm just kind of backpacking across Europe. I'm a couple days in. I started in Kiev, I've got family from there so I'd seen pictures, and now I'm just going."

"By yourself?" I asked.

"Yeah."

"You're not scared to be out here alone?"

"Why, because I'm a girl?"

"No. I mean, I think I'd be scared if I was traveling through all these foreign countries all by myself." And I really meant that.

"I don't know. I just, after all the things in my life lately, I just needed to get away."

"Like what things?" I asked.

"No, nothing."

I wasn't going to pry.

"I don't know why I picked this," she said. "Except, I think, I had a friend in high school, and we always used to talk about backpacking across Europe after graduation. But things happen. You know how it is. Life takes over. Before I knew it I was engaged, which didn't really work out for me. Now she's married and pregnant. And there were all these other problems. My parents got divorced after more than thirty years of marriage. My brother's in Iraq, fighting a war with no end in sight. I'm sorry if you're a..."

---

[9]"It's just an elastic." I hear a different voice on the tape.

"No," I shook my head.

"Anyway, he's doing some good, you know. At least he believes he's doing good, but sometimes I don't know. And then my little sister, she's moved in with her boyfriend, which I'm not judging her, and he may not hit her, but there are plenty of different kinds of abuse. You know? But she just... I'm sorry, I don't even know you and I'm dumping all this..."

"No, it's fine," I said. "Dump away."

"Are you sure we don't know each other?" she asked.

I just shook my head without saying a word.

"Anyway, I'm sorry," she said.

"Really. It's okay."

"So anyway, I just had to get away from all that. So I'm out here, by myself."

"Did you stop in Kraków?" I asked.

"No."

"It's really great. I loved it there. So you didn't see Auschwitz either then?"

"Yeah, that's the last thing I need right now is a concentration camp. No, I didn't stop there. I don't think I could take it."

Then we just stood there. I wanted to talk some more, but I couldn't think what to say. Finally here's what came out of my mouth: "Hungry?"

I'm such a wordsmith.

"Starving," she said and kind of laughed. Then she looked at me with those eyes. And if you've seen those eyes then you know the ones I'm talking about. They're the eyes that make you forget about everything else in the world. I could barely form a sentence, but finally I did emit one, a simple one but with both a subject and a predicate.

"I have this croissant." And I held it out to her. "Would you like some? Or the whole thing? Or just take whatever you want, I'm not that, I don't know, I don't need any..."

I was babbling, and I realized it so I stopped.

"Thank you," she said and took it from my hand. She tore open the package and pulled out the pastry. She broke it in half and handed me one of the pieces. And there we stood in the dark corridor nibbling on half each of a chocolate-filled croissant that didn't have as much sugar as it should have had and wasn't really that good.

But the company was perfect, so the croissant was inconsequential.

"You know," I said finally. "You remind me of this girl I met at a party, probably about eight years ago, a birthday party I think. I mean, I didn't actually meet her as much as I just kind of saw her. But there's some similarity."

"It's possible it was me, I guess," she said. "Maybe that's why I feel like we've met."

"Wouldn't that be crazy?" I said.

"I don't know. Could be destiny," she said. "You know, the universe brings two people together. Some things I think are just meant to be."

"What are you saying?"

"Oh no," she looked shocked realizing what she'd just implied. "I'm not saying... I just..."

I waved my hand, indicating that it was okay.

"Do you believe in that kind of thing?" she asked me.

"I absolutely, one-hundred percent do now," I replied.

"I didn't ask you, what's your name?"

"Warren West."

I realize the proper thing would be to ask her for her name, but I didn't. I just didn't. And she didn't offer.

"Warren, do you sometimes feel like you blew an opportunity?"

"Like how do you mean?" I asked.

"I mean, okay, for instance, one time I was sitting on a bus I think it was. And this guy runs up to the bus stop just as the doors are closing. I don't think I'd ever seen him before, but somehow our eyes locked and the bus started to pull away and I couldn't break that eye contact. And I had this feeling like I should get off at the next stop and go back and find him, but I didn't do it. And since then, I've always wondered what if."

"I definitely know the feeling," I said. "Where was that?"

"Oh, I don't even remember. It wasn't recently. And actually I may have dreamed the whole thing. It's entirely possible it never happened."

I couldn't stop smiling the whole time. This was the most perfect moment of my entire life. And I think she noticed.

"What are you smiling about?"

"I don't know," I said. "I just... I really like you, y'know? I don't know, I guess I feel kind of like you do, like we've known each other for a long time. And even if we just met, I feel this connection. It's like moments like this are what life's all about."

I stopped for a second, but when she didn't say anything I went on.

"I just, I live at a distance, I think. I like to be alone, I avoid people. I think sometimes I even push people away. Most people don't know I exist, and sometimes I'm not even sure myself. Y'know?"

"I think you just summed up my whole life," she said.

"But this," I said. "This is good."

"This is good."

And we didn't need to say anything for several minutes, and I can't speak for her, but I felt like everything was as it should be.

"Can I come with you?" I said finally.

"Where?"

"Wherever you're going."

"What?"

"What you're doing sounds pretty good. I spend my life doing the same thing day after day after day. I get up. I go to work. I go home. I could use something like this. Is this creepy?"

"No, it's not creepy," she said. "Not exactly. It's just..."

"This is a good moment," I interjected, "and I'd like to have more of these. I'd like to have a lifetime full of these."

"But I don't even know where I'm going."

"Well where are you headed right now?"

"Dresden," she said. "I'm getting off here at the next stop in Poznań, then catching a train to Wrocław," only she pronounced it Roh-klah, which was cute but wrong, "then catching a train to Dresden. I know it doesn't make a lot of sense, seems like the long way around, but I looked on the internet and the routes really kind of seemed like sixes, only this one got me in there a little earlier."

"You don't have to explain yourself."

"I have this book *1,000 Places to See Before You Die*. I'm not hitting all of them, but there are like three in Dresden."

"I wouldn't mind seeing Dresden. And I know a great place to eat in Wrocław," only I pronounced it correctly, "if you want to stick around there for a while. My treat."

"Why do you want to follow me?"

"Why wouldn't I?"

"You can afford this?"

"If you don't mind heading to Berlin for a little bit, I can probably get us all the money we could possibly need."

"Berlin's on my maybe list. You know someone there?" she asked.

"Someone who owes me."

She looked at me for a long time, just staring deep into my face and I looked deep into hers.

"Okay," she said. "Maybe I'm being stupid or crazy, but I guess I couldn't stop you anyway."

"Really?"

"I'll tell you, I wanted to get out here on my own, but after only a couple of days I really wouldn't mind the company." Then she looked at her watch. "You got a bag? We'll probably be pulling into Poznań any minute."

"Yeah, don't ditch me," I said and dashed back to my compartment.

I threw open the door and it smacked against the bunks.

"What in the hell? Holy..." and Chris drifted right back to sleep.

I grabbed my bag and scribbled a note:

> Met someone on the train. Got off in Poznań. I'll
> be in touch. Thanks for all your help.
> —Warren West

I set it on his bag and on my way out I stole his croissant.

When I came out into the corridor, she was waiting for me, smiling. And I was smiling too; I couldn't help it. And we made our way down the corridor toward the exit. And it wasn't too much longer before the train screeched to a halt at the Poznań station.

As I pushed open the door, which wasn't an easy thing, she put her hand on my forearm and that moment Chris would have referred to as awesome, but this time it really was, as awesome as any moment in my entire life. I don't know why she did it, but I didn't care why.

It was cold on the platform and you could see your breath. I mean, after all, it was like three in the morning in November in Poland. But the cold didn't matter, and as cliché as it sounds I was warm inside. And I'll say it, because the way I was feeling clichés didn't matter at all.

And she stepped onto the platform with me, and I could see her breath too, and that's how I knew this was all real.

And that's how the story ends, except that I'll tell you that as I'm recording this we're still making our way around Europe. What we do is we'll go to an internet café or look at a map or open her little book and we'll pick a place and we'll go, even if it means zig-zagging across the continent.

It doesn't matter.

And at least a couple of times we've found ourselves on a train in the rain. I don't care how cliché it is. Chris doesn't have to write it; it's not his story.

We've been going for about six months now.

And one more thing.

Because she's out of the room right now, I'll tell you this. I still have the ring. Of course I brought it with me. Not that I thought I'd need it, just...

I don't know.

But I have it.

And when the time's right, I don't know...

But shoot, she's coming back now, so...

So anyways, I told her this story, the one I've just told you. And it was her idea that I record it on these little tapes and send them to someone who could write it out for me. And so I'm doing most of this while rushing along on trains from Madrid to Brussels to Rome to wherever else. Right now to Copenhagen.

And the last thing you're wondering is whether I lied to you before, even though I said I wouldn't, when I told you that that day downtown, when Allison got on the train, was really the last time I ever saw her.

You're skeptical that it could really be her all the way out in Europe and coincidentally we should run into each other, if there really is such a thing as coincidence. So what you're really asking is, "Was that Allison you got off the train with in Poznań?"

And I'll answer that question by asking you this one, because I think the answers are the same:

"Do you believe in destiny?"

AFTERWORD
by Chris Henderson

I can't confirm the truthfulness of that last chapter, but he did ditch me in the middle of the night and he did steal my chocolate-filled croissant. And the postmark on the package with all the little cassette tapes was from Denmark. So draw your own conclusions.

And if you're curious, when I got to Frankfurt the new conductor did not speak a word of English or a word of Polish, but he did accept credit cards. The only problem, and I'm not kidding you here, was that for some reason his reader wouldn't accept mine.

So they threw me off the train in Frankfurt.

I was furious.

I wandered around the train station until I found an ATM and withdrew enough money to get to Berlin, but by that time the train had gone. So I had to wait a couple more hours for the next one, which of course meant I'd missed my flight and had to wait for the one the next day and hope that there were empty seats on it.

Fortunately, I did find a nice little bakery near the station in Frankfurt, since Warren had stolen my breakfast. And I got to see the Brandenburg Gate and a few other sites during my extra day in Berlin, while as it turns out Warren was cavorting with a beautiful woman two hours away in Dresden. And they did bump me up to business class on the flight from Berlin to New York, which is something you just can't beat.

Unfortunately, all the flights from New York to Salt Lake were full, and I had to stay the night in the Big Apple, and I had to pay for it. The next day all the flights to Salt Lake were full again, so I had to fly from New York to Atlanta, from Atlanta to Cincinatti, from Cincinatti to Albuquerque, then finally from Albuquerque to Salt Lake.

Boy, those were good times.

So if this book does get published, I'm keeping the entire advance to pay for my hotels and my time and just the work I've done in transcribing the whole thing, which was no small task.